THE

C O N V I C T :

A   R O M A N C E.

BY THE AUTHOR OF

"KATHLEEN," "HEBREW MAIDEN," &c. &c.

LONDON.

PUBLISHED BY E. LLOYD, 12, SALISBURY-SQUARE, FLEET-STREET;

1846.

PREFACE.

MANY of the incidents to be found in this work are founded on fact, though of course the greater part of the story is pure invention. For obvious reasons the name of Guy Harrowby is a fictitious one, but no doubt many of our readers remember the original, whose death—though not in the manner we have described it—occurred in a country town about twelve years since. The author has frequently seen him, and it is from the stories at that time in circulation that he has woven together the narrative which forms the subject of the following pages. Had any part of the convict's family been alive at the present time, the work would never have been published; but as no feelings could be wounded, the writer willingly set himself about his task, believing that the example of Guy Harrowby will not be without a good effect upon those young persons into whose hands the work will fall.

It is true there are some people who loudly protest against making heroes of highwaymen and other notorious characters; but then it may with as much fairness be contended that the examples brought forward are intended to deter the mind from vice, not to encourage it. In the present work our object has been to show the misery that is certain to succeed when once a man steps aside from the path of rectitude; and in detailing the endless misfortunes that pursued the convict throughout his career, it has been our endeavour to make his example useful to others. At any rate we have been gratified, as upon former occasions, by receiving a large share of the public patronage, which fact goes far to prove that our design has been appreciated.

In conclusion, we may be permitted to observe that the pictorial embellishments of this work have been got up in a style as novel as it is beautiful; all of them are admirable—some are perfect gems.

September, 1846.

CHAPTER I.

A WELL-KNOWN LOCALITY—THE RETURN— OLD COMPANIONS.

BILLINGSGATE was in all the bustle of a market morning. Five o'clock had scarcely struck, yet hundreds were congregated there, some bargaining at the stalls of the wholesale dealers, some urging their way with difficulty through the dense mass of human beings, and some amusing themselves by giving utterance to the peculiar slang for which the place has obtained so unenviable a notoriety. A few persons of a different class might be seen mingling in the motley group: these were men who had been spending the night in dissipation, and had repaired to this spot, partly to recover themselves from the effects of their intemperance, and partly to witness a scene that has no parallel, even in the vast metropolis.

At the quay were lying a number of fishing-smacks, some of which had discharged their cargo, whilst in others that process was still going on in full activity. From one of these latter vessels, a man of rather peculiar aspect emerged from the cabin, and, having reached the deck, cast around him a glance expressive of the most intense apprehension and alarm. A large cloak completely enveloped his person, and his hat was worn with a slouching air that nearly concealed his countenance. The look he cast around, however, seemed to have satisfied him that he was in no immediate fear of being recognised; and, gaining a little more courage, he followed the porters that were assisting in unloading the vessel, and, in a minute or two afterwards, reached *terra firma* in safety.

Arrived here, he paused for a minute or two, directed another look around him, and then, as if again satisfied that he had nothing to fear, forced his way through the crowd till he reached a dark, narrow lane, that runs into Thames-street. Here, the throng being less dense, he was able to quicken his speed; and, quitting that scene of bustle, he proceeded towards the Tower, and from thence to Wapping, where he entered an obscure public-house, that, from its appearance, had not been closed all night. The stranger, however, seemed to know the place well, for, passing by the bar, he made his way to a small room at the rear of the premises, where four or five men were engaged smoking and playing at cards. On his entrance the men looked up as if wondering who it was that had entered their *sanctum sanctorum*, and then one of them, starting suddenly from his seat, shook the hand of the stranger, as he recognised him for an old familiar friend.

"What! Guy Harrowby!" he exclaimed with astonishment; "why, who the devil would ever have expected to see that precious mug of yours again?"

"Hush!" returned the other, eyeing the other persons with a look of suspicion; "you have betrayed my secret, and I may be lost, after all the trouble and dangers I've gone through to escape from the cursed place they sent me to."

"Oh, you needn't be afraid of anybody here," answered the other, "for they're all chaps of the right sort; and here's two of 'em that you've seen often enough before, though you seem to have forgot 'em. Dick Fordham and Mike Rowley," he added, calling to a couple of fellows that he had been playing cards with—"won't you come and welcome an old friend back to England?"

The men advanced, and having recognised their former acquaintance, expressed the most unbounded joy at seeing him again. In the fulness of their delight, glasses of grog were ordered in; and, as the rest of the company departed shortly afterwards, those who remained were most urgent in their demands to know by what piece of good fortune their friend had contrived to make his escape from the place to which he had been transported. Guy Harrowby would rather have deferred his narrative to a future occasion; but, finding that they were determined to have it at once, he said:—

"I've neither time nor inclination to enter into all the adventures that I've met with in the last few months. As you may suppose, I didn't find the life of a transport a very comfortable one; so, from the time they landed us in New South Wales, I was constantly thinking how I might give 'em the slip."

"And I suppose you thought long enough before they gave you a chance of cutting?"

"You are right there, Mike Rowley," answered the convict; "for morning, noon, and night I was watched, as if my task masters knew what was passing in my thoughts. For the slightest offence, too, I was punished with the lash, and that made me more hardened than ever; so that at last I began to think death would be better than the slavery I suffered, and I determined to commit a crime that should either give me a chance of escape, or send me to the gallows."

"What did you do, then?"

"What did I do, Dick?" exclaimed the fugitive; "why, murdered my keeper, and then, taking from him the key of my cell, escaped in the darkness of night, and took to the bush. I made friends with some of the natives, and lived with 'em, till I found an opportunity of getting away from the place."

"Was no search made for you?" asked Sam Snatch.

"I dare say there was," answered Harrowby; "but what was the use of looking after a man that had found a home in the bush? My new friends bore a deadly hatred to the settlers, and, if any of 'em had come after me, they would have met with the fate of my keeper."

"And how long did you remain with 'em?" asked Mike.

"Nearly six months," replied Guy Harrowby. "I was like one of 'em—went out on their hunting parties—fought with 'em when they made war on a neighbouring tribe—and became almost as savage as they were."

"Yet," observed Richard Fordham, "you didn't feel so happy in their company, but you were glad to leave 'em."

"That's because I couldn't forget old England, and the wife I left behind me," answered Guy Harrowby. "Poor Jane! many an hour of bitterness and sorrow has the thought of her cost me, for she was fond and faithful, and I knew my conduct must almost have broken her heart."

"Why, the poor thing did take on terribly," exclaimed Dick Fordham; "but she found a kind friend in the mistress she lived with before she married you, and she never knew what it was to be in want of a meal."

"It's some consolation to hear that," cried Guy Harrowby, "and yet she must have suffered dreadfully in her mind, for she was a fond and faithful wife, though I never deserved half the affection she bore me. I remember the last time I saw her, on the morning I was sent from prison to the convict ship, and, as they bore her fainting from my arms, I believed her suffering soul would have taken its flight for ever. She was soon to become a mother, too—tell me, does the child yet live?"

"I believe so," answered Mike Rowley; "at any rate, it was alive when she left London, and a rare fine fellow he was, too."

"Where did she go?" demanded Guy.

"That's more than I can tell you," answered the other; "but perhaps you can guess, when I say that it's about thirty miles off, and that she lives in a small cottage that came to her when her mother died."

"I know the place then," exclaimed Guy Harrowby; "and this day will I walk down, to gladden her heart by my presence."

"You must be mad to think of such a thing," exclaimed Sam Snatch. "Why, you would be seen by some infernal prying eyes or other, and then, for the murder you have told us of, they'd hang you, as sure as you've got a neck."

"I'll run the risk of that," answered Guy; "it was to see her that I made my escape, and I'll hazard even the fate you speak of, rather than deprive myself of the happiness of once more seeing her."

"Well," exclaimed Mike Rowley, "if you're determined to throw yourself in the way of danger, it would be useless for us to say anything more about it. But I should have thought it would be better for you to stay in London, and one of us might have gone down and brought her up to you."

"Where can I find concealment in London, more than in any other place?" demanded Guy.

"Why, in my house, if you like it," replied the other; "it'll do for a little while, at any rate; and, if there should be any danger of a discovery, you can go somewhere till you are hunted out again."

"I shall be more safe in the country than anywhere else," replied Guy Harrowby. "I know the place well where my wife lives; 'tis a quiet, retired place, and no one will be likely to see me while I remain there."

"As you please," exclaimed Rowley; "but it would be a d——d hard thing to be taken, after all the trouble it seems you've had to escape. And, by-the-bye, you may as well tell us how you managed to get away from your friends—the natives."

"I told you we were on good terms together," replied Guy Harrowby, "and though at first they didn't like the idea of my going away, they consented to it in time; and then about a dozen of 'em set to work to make a large canoe that would carry me safely through the wide waters that lay between me and the nearest land. At length, when it was finished, they stored it well with provisions and water, and, with a supply of fishing tackle to help out my stores, I set sail, not a little sorry to part from my kind friends."

"They seem to have been a jolly, good set of fellows, at any rate," exclaimed Sam Snatch.

"I found more kindness among them than I had met with since I was torn away from my wife," answered Harrowby. "They gave me a home when I needed one, and would have fought till they died, had my pursuers followed me."

"And how did you fare on your voyage?" asked Rowley.

"Badly enough," replied Guy Harrowby; "for, having no compass to steer by, I sailed completely by guess, and my reckoning was all wrong, as you may suppose. Then, after being four or five days at sea, a terrible storm came on, and, for a long time, I thought every moment would be my last. But at length the tempest wore itself out, and, as well as I can judge, I must have been driven at least thirty leagues out of my proper course. By that time my provisions began to run low, and I had then the horrors before me of a lingering death by starvation. To avoid that, I several times thought of throwing myself into the sea; but, somehow or another, I still clung to life till the provisions and water were entirely gone. Then, after two or three hours of the most dreadful suspense, a vessel hove in sight, but she was too far off for me to hope that there was any chance of being saved by her. Fortune, however, stood my friend; she sailed direct towards me; and, after three hours of fearful suspense, I was taken on board."

"Where was she bound to?" asked Richard Fordham.

"To Holland," answered the convict.

"How did you manage to understand the outlandish lingo of her crew?" asked Rowley.

"Why, as good luck would have it, there was an English sailor on board, and he acted as interpreter between us. But, to cut short my story, they landed me, about six months afterwards, at Rotterdam, where I got employment in a merchant's warehouse, and earned money enough to bring me over to England. About a couple of hours ago I landed at Billingsgate, from a fishing-smack, and made my way here, thinking it the most likely place where I might meet with some of my old companions."

"Well," exclaimed Sam Snatch, "you've had trouble enough to escape, at any rate; so I hope you won't be foolish enough to throw yourself in the way of people that would send you back to your old quarters."

"I'll do the best I can to keep out of harm's way, you may depend on it," answered Guy Harrowby; "but even the certainty of being taken should not prevent my going to see my suffering wife."

"Are you going to walk the thirty miles?"

"Ay," he replied; "how else am I to get to the end of my journey, with only a few shillings in my pocket?"

" Why, we'll lend you some, to be sure, till you can pay us," answered Mike Rowley.

" Thank'ee for the offer," returned the other; " but I'll not borrow whilst I've got the use of my hands."

" Psha!" exclaimed Dick Fordham; " why, you're not going to work again for your living, as was the case before we got acquainted?"

" Yes, but I am though, if I can get it to do."

" Oh! that's well put in," returned Snatch; " for it won't be quite so easy to get work as you seem to fancy. Who'd take a man into his employ who has been transported, and returned before his time's up?"

" I shall try whether I can't get something to do in the country again," answered Guy Harrowby. " Nobody knows me in the place where my wife is living, and, as I've been used to farming work, it's likely enough I shall soon be taken on by some one."

" Ay," replied Fordham; " and it's still more likely that you'll take up to your old trade of poaching. It ain't likely that you can help it, Guy, for I've often heard you say that partridges and hares, and the like of them things, were sent as much for the poor man as the rich."

" And as I still say," exclaimed Harrowby; " and, what's more than that, the rich man can't make out his claim to the wild birds and beasts that are on his land one day, and on somebody else's the next. There's no mark to know 'em by; yet a poor devil is punished if he happens to knock down a hare or a rabbit in the high way, that's open to everybody. I've always thought I had as much right to 'em as anybody; but they put me in prison for it three or four times, and at last, when they found there was no other way to stop me, they pressed for the heaviest sentence, and I was ordered to be transported for fourteen years! And what has been the consequence? Why, I committed a murder to get away from that cursed place, and may be hanged for it, if it should be known that I'm come back to England!"

" That's about as true a word as ever was uttered," said Dick Fordham. " They'd have no mercy; yet you're fool hardy enough to think of walking down to your wife, when it's almost certain you'd be seen by somebody that would go and inform against you."

" I must take my chance about that," exclaimed Guy Harrowby. " So far I've escaped dangers that almost make my hair stand on end when I think of 'em, and now I think but little of those I may have to meet with on my journey into the country."

" But you've got to go through some of the most crowded parts of London," observed Mike Rowley; " and I'm thinking you won't be able to pass through many streets before you'll meet with some one or another that will do you a bad turn."

" Then I'll tell what we'd better do," said Fordham. " Let's call the landlord in, and ask his advice about it; he knows Guy Harrowby well, and won't desert an old friend in his difficulties."

" I saw Doublechalk in the bar just now, as I came by," exclaimed Guy Harrowby; " but though he looked hard in my face, he didn't seem to know me."

" How the devil should he, when you're about the last person he would have expected to see?" asked Fordham. " Besides, he's too wide awake a fellow to betray a chap that has spent many a pound in his house, and may spend many more, if he has the good luck to keep out of harm's way."

" He's to be trusted, at any rate," said Sam Snatch, " so we'll call him in; and I'll be bound he'll think of some scheme to get Guy clear out of London, if he's determined to leave us, instead of keeping himself snug till a better chance offers itself."

The bell was now rung, and, on the pot-boy making his appearance, he was desired to tell his master that he was wanted for a few minutes. The boy vanished, and shortly afterwards Doublechalk entered, and, recognising Guy Harrowby, shook him heartily by the hand.

" Why, who, in the name of all that's wonderful, would ever have expected to see you?" he exclaimed. " I thought, when I saw you pass by just now in such a hurry, that I remembered your face; but, if anybody had told me you were in England, I should have ——"

" Never mind that just now," interrupted Harrowby; " I'm here, safe and sound as you are, and these chaps will tell you how I came back when you've answered the question I've got to ask. The long and the short of it is—no one must know I'm in England; and I now want your advice as to the best way of getting out of London without being discovered."

" If you ask my advice," said Doublechalk, " it is that you stop where you are for the present. There's plenty of places where you may hide, and you've got friends that will take care to keep you snug enough, till we see how matters are likely to go."

" The truth of it is," interposed Rowley, " he's determined to go in search of his wife; and all we can say won't put him off from it. So, if he chooses to run the risk, we must do the best we can to get him clear off."

" Which way is he going on this wild goose chase?" demanded the burley host.

" About thirty miles down in Surrey, I believe."

" Then I know a plan that'll just suit him," exclaimed Doublechalk; " that is, he may have a good lift out of London, if he don't mind going a little out of his way."

" I care for nothing, so that I can only make sure of reaching the place I'm going to," said Guy Harrowby. " For the matter of that, I wouldn't mind riding in a dung cart, so that I can only make sure of being safe."

"And safe you will be, if you'll do as I'd have you," said the landlord. "There's a barge, loaded with straw, moored just at the back of my house; and, when the tide turns, she's going up the river as far as Battersea, and if you like I'll ask the bargemen to take you with 'em, which they'll be glad to do for a pot of beer."

"Are they to be depended on?"

"To be sure they are," replied Doublechalk; "they've both been in trouble themselves, and are not very likely to betray a poor devil that has had the good luck to make his escape from Botany Bay."

"And how long will it be before the tide serves?"

"Why, it will begin to flow in less than half an hour," replied the landlord; "so I suppose you'll be ready for 'em when they're going to start?"

"I'm ready now," exclaimed Guy Harrowby; "and as for the men, here's half a crown for them; it's nearly all the money I've got, but it will be well bestowed if they land me safely at the place you've spoken of. It happens to be pretty nearly in the direction I want to go; and as there won't be much fear of my falling in the way of anybody that knows me, I begin to hope there's a fair chance of my reaching home without interruption."

"And when you get there, don't be showing yourself to any one in the neighbourhood," said Mike Rowley. "There's no telling who might see you, and a word or two would send you to Newgate."

"My stay there may not be for long," answered Guy. "A week will be enough, I dare say, and then I'll come back to London, and perhaps bring Jane with me."

"Perhaps!" exclaimed Dick Fordham; "why, if the woman likes you half as well as you seem to fancy, she'll follow you to any place you choose to fix on."

"But why should I insist upon removing her from a home where she is perhaps happy?" asked Harrowby. "She may have set her mind upon remaining there for life, and if so, I shall do as I said just now—seek for employment upon a farm, and try what I can do to make her forget past troubles."

"Eh!" exclaimed Doublechalk; "are you going to turn honest?"

"If people will let me alone, I'll try what may be done that way," answered Guy Harrowby. "I've had suffering and punishment enough to make me tired of the sort of life I led before they sent me away, and now I should like to see whether my mind wouldn't be all the happier for taking the good advice that has so often been given by my wife."

"Psha!" exclaimed Rowley; "don't put yourself in leading strings like a child. If you didn't remain honest it was no fault of yours, but the blame falls upon those that hunted you out like a thief, when you had done nothing more than take a hare that belonged to you as much as it did to anybody else."

"But I can't forget what I've suffered for it though," answered Guy, "and the remembrance will last as long as I've life. And what are my own sufferings, great as they have been, compared with those of the faithful wife who has been left to mourn for the errors that I have committed? I can well imagine her grief; and surely it is now time that I try to make amends for the many pangs I have caused her."

"And you are going home," sneered Dick Fordham, "to promise you'll be a better boy in future?"

"I want none of your taunts," exclaimed Guy; "and, if you are a man, you'll not insult a poor devil that's anxious to do what's right. If people will only let me alone, I mean to act very differently to what I did before I left England; but if they won't give me a chance, why, then I must do as I have done before, and I know pretty well what the end of it will be."

"Ah!" cried Mike Rowley, "it's all very well for you to make good resolutions now; but it's as plain as a pike-staff, that we shall have you among us again before long. Why, it ain't likely that you can be in England long before somebody or other finds it out, and then you'll be glad enough, I'll warrant, to come and find a hiding-place among some of us."

"I must be driven to the last before I do that," answered Guy Harrowby.

"And you'll find, before many days are over, that you are driven pretty closely," exclaimed Doublechalk. "Not that I want to say anything, either one way or the other; but it seems rather unlikely that you can stop any time in one place without the officers of justice nosing you out."

"In that case," said Harrowby, "I must rush into any path they drive me to. My own wish is to make a change for the better; but, if I am still to be hunted out like a wild beast, they that drive me to crime will have to answer for it."

"That's a very fine thing to console yourself with," exclaimed Fordham; "but, when you find yourself within view of the gallows, you'll wish you had taken our advice, instead of following your own foolish notions."

"Why, they surely wouldn't hang him for returning from transportation?" cried the landlord

"They've hung men for it before now," replied the other. "However, that's got nothing to do with what we're talking about now; for Guy Harrowby has told us of something he did before he got away from t'other side the water, and he knows as well as I do, that if they try him for it, and find him guilty, he's as sure to be hung for it as that I now tell him so."

Doublechalk was very inquisitive to learn what all this was in allusion to, but the others put him off with the promise that they would tell him after Guy was gone, and he left the room to make the necessary arrangements with the bargemen. His absence did not last many minutes, and, when he returned, it was to announce that the men were willing to take him, and, as the tide now served, they were just going to get under way. Once more, then, the fugitive wrapped himself in his cloak, and, bidding his friends good bye, left the house, and crossing the back premises, entered the barge just as it was about to leave the moorings. Here he felt himself safe enough from observation, and, maintaining a strict silence, he was safely landed at Battersea, within two hours afterwards.

CHAPTER II.

THE BROTHERS—A BRAWL AT THE GAMING-TABLE—DISINTERESTED FRIENDSHIP.

LEAVING the fugitive for a brief period, we beg the reader to accompany us to the neighbourhood in which stood the humble cottage of Jane Harrowby. Here she had dwelt during nearly the whole period of her husband's absence, and, under the circumstances in which she was placed, her life might have passed in tolerable comfort, but for the persecuting addresses of a young man, who, presuming upon her defenceless situation, annoyed her with attentions that she could find no way of avoiding. Go where she would, Charles Heathingdon followed her like a shadow, and neither her entreaties nor remonstrances had the effect of prevailing upon him to desist from importunities that filled her soul with consternation and scorn.

At this period of our history, Colonel Heathingdon resolved upon taking Charles with him to London, leaving behind him, at Farley Park, his younger son Edward, whose education had not yet been completed, and whom he entrusted to the care of his friend, Major Corfield, a man upon whose honour and integrity he could fully rely. Charles, however, for reasons of his own, entreated that he might be allowed to follow in two or three days, and, under a promise to that effect, Colonel Heathingdon set out alone on his journey to the metropolis. As may easily be guessed, the motive that actuated Charles was, that he might take the opportunity of his father's absence, to carry into effect the designs he had formed against Jane Harrowby. Of that, however, we shall have occasion to speak hereafter.

If Edward Heathingdon had been gratified at the confidence reposed in him by his father, when they bade adieu to each other, he had also felt some bitter apprehensions lest he might not acquit himself to his entire satisfaction. This diffidence in his own resolution induced him to solicit the society of Major Corfield, till the return of his father, and the request was no sooner made than readily acceded to.

The major, from his first introduction to Edward, had been pleased with his ingenuous, gay, and confiding disposition. He had observed the most anxious endeavours of a fellow-officer—Captain Melton—to ingratiate himself in the favourable opinion of the young man, and though he did not consider himself armed with sufficient authority to put Edward Heathingdon on his guard against the evil example of the captain, he deemed him by no means a proper associate for him during the absence of his father. The major, therefore, the more willingly fixed his residence at Farley Park; and while the avowed ignorance and quick conception of his young companion rendered Captain Melton daily more and more pleased with him, the easy good nature, and occasionally the boyish levity of the major attached Edward still more to him, and won so completely on the frankness of his nature, that the thoughts and wishes of his heart were gradually laid open to him.

The desire of following the military profession was pre-eminent in the heart of the young man. The major, also, was too much attached to the same honourable pursuit to be surprised at, or to condemn, the same feeling in another. He admired the spirit, and undertook to instruct him in the use of the broad and small sword, and the pupil, aspiring as he did to attain perfection, soon proved himself to be, in every respect, worthy of his master.

The hours passed in the study and practice of this science, in shooting at the target, and in accompanying the major to the parade in the neighbouring town, left him but little time on his hands, beyond what he thought necessary to dedicate to visits to the friends and acquaintances of his father, who lived in that neighbourhood.

The praises of Edward Heathingdon were so frequently repeated, that all were anxious to cultivate his acquaintance. Among other pressing invitations that he received, was one to dine as often as he pleased with the officers, and the consequence was, that the young man frequently became their guest, and sometimes went there without being accompanied by his friend, Major Corfield. On one of these occasions, when Captain Melton had not joined the mess, Edward was listening to a narrative of some great battle, recounted by one of the officers, when the major, to whom it had not the attraction of novelty, after reminding him of a visit they had to pay, hurried away, expecting him soon to follow; but the attractive narrative was succeeded by others of no less captivating a description, and more than an hour had elapsed before Edward thought of quitting the pleasant society in which he found himself.

At length he was leaving to follow Major Corfield, when, in passing the door of a lower apartmen', the voice of Captain Melton, in loud terms of argument, met his ear. The subject was terminated by a wager, at the moment Edward joined him, and a party of the junior officers, and others who were assembled with him.

"Here is Mr. Heathingdon," exclaimed one of them; "he is totally uninterested in the affair, and shall be our umpire, to see fair play between us."

"What is the subject of your debate?" inquired the young man, rather puzzled at the words with which he had been saluted.

"Oh, it's a mere trial of skill, that's all," answered Captain Melton; "I have wagered ten pounds with Deverel, that at a game at billiards I pocket twelve balls before he pockets half that number."

"You could not have made a worse selection for an umpire," answered Edward, good humouredly, "for I am totally ignorant of the game, and therefore am unable to decide upon the merits of either of the players."

"There is no necessity for any knowledge of the game," exclaimed Captain Melton. "All that is required of you is to watch that the game is fairly played, and if you will oblige us in this instance, we shall not detain you more than a quarter of an hour."

Edward Heathingdon, to whom the proposition presented a novelty, was soon induced to accompany them to the house of a friend, as Captain Melton chose to denominate it, at no great distance off, where a billiard-table, with its appurtenances, was found, not only ready lighted up, but already surrounded by several persons, whose respectable appearance precluded from the mind of the young man every idea that he was in the society of persons that he might afterwards see reason to be ashamed of.

After the delay of some little time, the game was played, and decided in favour of Deverel, who was immediately afterwards challenged to a trial of his skill in a regular game, by a man, apparently a perfect stranger in the room, and once more Deverel was the victorious player.

After this a fresh set was proposed. One game followed another, and numerous bets were laid on the skill of the contesting parties; till Edward, who thought Deverel far superior to the others, led by the example of those around him, and the apparent indifference with which considerable sums were lost and won, was induced to bet against the play of Captain Melton.

As the game proceeded, the bet was doubled, and even trebled, when, by an apparently unfortunate hit of Deverel's, which gave the concluding advantage to his adversary, Edward found himself indebted to Captain Melton upwards of fifty pounds, besides several minor sums to others of the bystanders. It then first occurred to him, that he had not sufficient money about him to discharge these heavy calls upon his purse; and he experienced no little mortification in being compelled to acknowledge that he had been betting beyond his means.

"It seems," said Captain Melton, with apparent good nature, "that our young friend Heathingdon came unprepared for this kind of business. I can, however, assure you, gentlemen, his promissory note will be as good as if you had his money already in your hands."

The name, together with the reported wealth of his father, were too well known to admit of any one hesitating to accept of his note of hand; and Edward Heathingdon—the dupe of designing villains—soon found himself the self-acknowledged debtor to a set of men, who had no sort of acquaintance with honour or principle.

Captain Melton would now have resumed the cue, but, perceiving Edward impatient to be gone, he thought it advisable to quit his pursuit, and attend him at least part of his way homewards.

"I hope you feel no annoyance at the trifle you have lost, Mr. Heathingdon," he exclaimed, taking the arm of the young man as he entered the street.

"Not at all," answered the other, thoughtfully.

"I am glad of that," resumed the captain; "but had you ventured another wager, you would most probably have recovered all your former losses. I wondered, indeed, at your betting on such a man as Deverel, and am sorry that you happen to have lost your money to me. In truth, my dear fellow, I would rather myself have been a loser, than see my friend suffer in pocket. It must, however, be confessed, that I admire your spirit; for the game of billiards, when properly played, is one of the most gentlemanly, though, as I think you told us, you do not at present understand much about it."

"Scarcely anything," replied Edward; "nor, indeed, have I practised any other game, with the exception of chess."

"Humph!" ejaculated Captain Melton; "that is a pity, too, my dear fellow, for recreation is necessary in every station of life, from the very highest to the lowest. I do not pretend to be a first-rate player, but I shall be most happy to give you an insight into such as is generally resorted to by persons of your station, for amusement. In short, with tolerable quickness, a very little practice will render you an adept in whatever you please to attempt."

Edward Heathingdon listened with apparent attention to all that was said, but remained silent.

"I see," continued Captain Melton, "that you have been rendered nervous and timid by the bad luck which has attended your first attempt at this sort of thing. But take good heart, my dear fellow! A single cast of the dice may serve to re-establish you in a better opinion of your own skill and judgment."

"Believe me, Captain Melton," exclaimed the young man, "I have no reason to regret the money I have lost, for my father, I doubt not, will readily enable me to pay that, or a much larger debt, if necessary for the preservation of my honour. But who, pray, are the men to whom I have lost a portion of the money?"

"They are gentlemen," replied Captain Melton; "as, indeed, their appearance is sufficient to prove."

"It may be so," replied Edward; "but I have no recollection of ever having seen any of them as visitors at my father's house, though at some of his parties he has invited everybody of good name and respectability."

"Upon my word, Mr. Heathingdon, I can scarcely help smiling at your perfect simplicity! Are you, then, such a perfect novice in life, as to suppose that there are no gentlemen except those who are invited to partake your father's hospitality?"

"Certainly not," answered the young man; "and yet it seems rather singular that I have never met with any of them at the houses which we are in the habit of visiting."

"Not at all strange, my dear young fellow," exclaimed the captain. "Every man has his particular circle of acquaintance, of which he himself forms the focus. Colonel Heathingdon, from his naturally reserved habits, though a most liberal and excellent man, happens to possess a smaller circle of what are termed visiting acquaintances than any other person that I know."

The latter assertion Edward was unable to contradict, and having by this time arrived at the door of the house where the officers messed, he turned in, accompanied by Captain Melton, without remembering anything of his purposed visit to the family where Major Corfield had gone before him. They entered the lower room, where three or four of the officers were yet standing round the fire, and who eagerly inquired of Captain Melton if he had won his wager.

"No," he replied, with a careless laugh; "Deverel proved himself a more skilful player than I took him to be. I have, however, won a trifle of Mr. Heathingdon, for which I am sorry, because it is discouraging to a young beginner. But never mind, my dear fellow, I will now make you a fair offer, as I have no wish to pocket your money without giving you a chance of getting it back. What say you? shall it be double or quits?"

Whilst speaking, he produced a box and dice from a drawer, and shaking them, threw them upon the table; on perceiving that he had thrown a four and a five, he burst into a loud laugh, in which he was accompanied by the others, as he exclaimed:—

"Confound it! I have lost without a chance of your having any merit in beating me."

He placed the box in the hand of Edward Heathingdon, who, imposed upon by his apparent disinterestedness, and the easy way of discharging the debt, agreed to the suggestion that had been thrown out. But fortune still frowned upon him, and the exclamation of disappointment that burst from the lips of the by-standers, was followed by the repeated cry of:—"Try again, my dear fellow! Have another throw, and you will win."

Edward now became really anxious to cancel the debt, and conceiving that the chance of the dice must vary, was induced to repeat the attempt, till he found himself indebted to Captain Melton in a sum very little short of a thousand pounds! Maddened by his losses, he was again taking the dice in his hands, when he was startled by a deep groan behind him, and turning round, perceived the senior officer of the regiment standing behind him.

"Forbear, young man!" he exclaimed, in a solemn tone of warning; "you have already lost more than I, with honesty, have been able to accumulate during a long life of hardship and danger. Half the sum you have this evening squandered away by this idle and destructive game, might have secured comparative happiness to many a worthy man and his family. Your father, Mr. Heathingdon, was never guilty of indulging in this wild and ruinous propensity!"

"All has been conducted in a perfectly fair manner," answered Captain Melton. "Examine the dice yourself, sir, if my word is to be doubted, and you will easily detect if they are loaded."

"It is but too probable that a loaded pistol may terminate your own career!" answered the veteran officer, in a tone of reproach. "It is the gamester's fate, I believe, when fortune begins to frown upon him."

"Mr. Heathingdon entered the lists against me of his own free will," retorted Captain Melton, sullenly. "I produced the dice, it is true, but I did not ask him to venture any of his money against me."

"Perhaps not," observed the officer; "but it also appears that you did not think proper to warn him against the fearful consequences of gaming."

"You are my senior in years, as well as my superior officer," exclaimed Captain Melton, warmly, "and as such I am restrained from saying what I otherwise should do. But recollect, sir, this is no business in which you have any right to interfere. If I have done wrong, I am ready to answer for it to those who may arraign my conduct."

"At least," returned the other, "I may claim the privilege of saving a young man from destruction."

"But not to call my character in question," retorted Captain Melton. "From motives of the purest friendship towards Mr. Heathingdon, I have given him an opportunity of retrieving his loss; but, if fortune is against him, that surely can have been no fault of mine."

"But, in giving him a chance as you call it," said the veteran, "you have plunged him still further into debt."

"That's a misfortune that I regret, though there's no help for it," returned Captain Melton, hypocritically. "However, if there is any doubt upon the subject, it happens luckily that here are sufficient witnesses present to prove that all has been honourable and straightforward between us."

"*Honourable!*" repeated the other, with sarcastic emphasis. "If honour had no better champion than yourself, Captain Melton, its cause would, I fear, be lost for ever!"

"What do you mean by that insinuation, sir?" demanded Captain Melton, fiercely, and grasping the hilt of his sword. "Dare you to breathe a suspicion against my honour? If so, I can only retort that both that and my courage have been well tried, when duty called me to fight against the enemies of my country."

"Many other professed gamesters may, I am sorry to say, make the same boast," answered the elder officer. "These can refer, with satisfaction, to former deeds, yet the assertion has not the slightest effect towards giving them the enviable characters of honest, upright men."

An ensign, who was the son of the elder officer, and who had been one of the by-standers, apprehensive that his father might be drawn into a quarrel of a serious nature, with some difficulty now succeeded in withdrawing him from the scene of contention. Captain Melton was about to follow him, when Edward, who had stood confounded at the words of the veteran officer, and at the sharp conversation which had ensued, recovering at length from his bewilderment, exclaimed with firmness :—

"Stay, Captain Melton—stay, sir! After what has just now passed, I must insist upon having an explanation of this business before we part !"

"What explanation can you possibly require?" demanded the captain, with assumed composure, which he was, however, unable to sustain. "You have, as these gentlemen can testify, lost a sum of money to me, which, by the laws of honour, you are bound to pay ; and, in return, I am ready to give you your revenge, whenever you may think proper to make the demand."

"If any revenge is necessary," answered Edward Heathingdon, "there is no occasion to defer it for a moment."

He had misconceived the meaning of Captain Melton's words, and now, for the first time, began to entertain a suspicion that he had been cheated at play. The exact import of the words was, however, immediately explained to him, when he declined having any further recourse to the dice, acknowledging, at the same time, his inability to pay the large sum of money he had lost, till he could procure it after an explanation with his father had taken place.

"I should imagine there can be no occasion for that," answered Captain Melton ; "for if you apply to his steward, he will, of course, supply you with the sum of money necessary for the discharge of this debt of honour. You can, doubtless, command more than is necessary for the liquidation of this matter, and, if you are apprehensive of reproof, there is no need to mention the peculiar circumstances which have led to your requiring so heavy an amount."

"I shall apply to no one but my father," answered Edward, in a tone of determination. "I am aware of the folly I have been guilty of, and will risk the anger which my confession will draw from him."

"As you think proper, my dear fellow," exclaimed Captain Melton, shrugging his shoulders. "You are quite a novice, I see, in life, or you would have learnt, ere now, that affairs of honour, like those of love, are not always to be divulged, even to those who are nearest and dearest to us. Now your brother, Charles, I'll dare venture to say, has never been foolish enough to hint a word to his father about his passion for the convict's wife—Jane Harrowby."

"I am not to be guided by what my brother does," answered the young man ; "nor do I quite understand what you mean, by saying that we are not to confess our errors when we have been thoughtless enough to commit them."

"Well, then, to be frank with you," answered Captain Melton, "I thought you were more of a gentleman, than to seek to create an unpleasant feeling between me and my colonel."

"Really, sir," exclaimed Edward, "I do not think that practising a deceit towards my father is a necessary step towards establishing my reputation as a gentleman. In short, to be as plain with you as you have been with me, I must observe, that if the means you have used to render me thus your debtor are honourable ones, you need not be scrupulous about avowing them to him, or even of applying yourself to my father for the money I have this night lost in thoughtlessness."

"I see," retorted Captain Melton, "that you are but an inexperienced boy, and more fit for school, than to be admitted into the society of men."

"Be that as it may," exclaimed Edward, with spirit, "I am man enough to assert my principles, and to maintain them, even against your insolent sneers. Nay, to be plain with you, Captain Melton, I both can and will chastise a scoundrel, wherever or whenever I may happen to meet him."

The blow which was aimed at Edward Heathingdon, as he concluded these words, was prevented by one of the officers standing near; and the cry of "shame! shame!—Melton !" burst from nearly every lip.

The momentary confusion occasioned by what had just passed, was interrupted by the entrance of Sergeant Daly, who loudly demanded if Mr. Heathingdon was there, and then, on perceiving him, hastily advanced towards Edward, exclaiming :—

"Your presence, sir, is immediately required at home. Something of consequence—I know not what—has happened, and I was sent here to request that you will return with as little delay as possible."

"Has anything happened to my brother or my father ?" demanded Edward, eagerly ; his ideas and feelings instantly hurrying his thoughts into a fresh channel.

"I know nothing beyond the message I have delivered to you, sir," replied the sergeant; "and have only to repeat my request, that you will hasten home without delay. The major——"

"Aye," interrupted Melton, with a sneer ;—"return to your nurse, young man, for it is clear you are not fit to be trusted out alone."

"Captain Melton," exclaimed the young man, firmly, "the name of a friend has been pronounced, and I think anything in which he is concerned of much more consequence than staying here, to resent your insolence. You have, I begin strongly to suspect, led me into a grievous error, from which, however, I shall take such measures to extricate myself as my own judgment dictates. At the same time, I deem it necessary to tell you that, ignorant of the world as I am, and *boy* as you are pleased to term me, I shall feel neither fear nor scruple in calling you to an account for your conduct, if I find it has been inconsistent with that honour which you profess."

He was then leaving the room with Sergeant Daly, when Melton exclaimed insolently :—

"You imagine, then, that I am to be bullied out of the money which I have so fairly won?"

"No, sir," answered Edward, with the same coolness that he had maintained throughout, and returning three or four paces towards his antagonist; "bullying, I trust, will never form any portion of my character. The money I have lost to you shall be paid. Give me pen, ink, and paper." They were instantly placed before him, and, having written a memorandum, he added :—"There, sir, is an acknowledgment of the sum that I am indebted to you."

He threw it with an air of disdain towards Melton, and then, accompanied by Sergeant Daly, left the room.

It was not till they had passed through the town, and were just entering Farley Park, that vexation permitted Edward Heathingdon to renew his question about what had occurred to render his immediate return home of so much importance.

"Has any accident occurred to Major Corfield?" he demanded, anxiously, "or has he been taken suddenly ill? or ——"

"No, sir," answered the sergeant, shaking his head, "neither one thing nor t'other has happened, that I know of."

Then Edward, recalling to mind the ignorance professed before by the sergeant, hurried on with a quicker step till he reached the house. Here his first demand was for the major, and, on being informed that he had not yet returned, he regarded the sergeant with a look of inquiry and doubt. Daly, however, followed him in silence into the parlour, when, shutting the door, he, after some little hesitation, said :—

"Forgive me, sir, for the trick I've played to draw you from a danger that I trembled to think of. I happen to know the character and temper of Captain Melton well; he is artful, treacherous, and insinuating, when he has a point to gain in his own favour. But, if found out in any of his schemes, he becomes ferocious and dangerous. Such, sir, you would have found him, had you remained with him perhaps only a few minutes longer."

"What is it you mean by all this?" demanded Edward, with impatience. "Have you then only used an artifice to induce me to return home at an earlier hour than I had intended?"

"That's just it, sir," answered Daly; "you've guessed the truth, and if I've done wrong, I hope your honour will consider I did it all for the best."

"How dare you, sirrah, take so great a liberty?" exclaimed Edward, angrily. "Think you, then, I am such an errant coward as to be afraid of Captain Melton; or so absolutely helpless as to need either your protection or advice in an affair of this kind?"

"Pardon me, sir," returned Sergeant Daly. "I know the stock you've sprung from too well to believe, even for a moment, that you would be afraid of Captain Melton; but, though I've a high opinion of your courage, young gentleman, I confess I'm rather afraid of your skill, and mere valour is too unequal a defence to be placed against such a man as Captain Melton."

"This is insolence beyond all endurance!" exclaimed Edward Heathingdon; "nor are you authorised to take such a liberty with me, or with any of my concerns."

"Call it affection rather than insolence," returned the sergeant, respectfully bowing to the young man; "call it regard for your safety, and you will give it the right name. Many a time, Mr. Heathingdon, have I carried you in my arms; many a time have you fondled and slept in my bosom; and many a hardship have I faced on your account; nor is there perhaps a man living who has a more devoted affection for you, except, it may be, your own father."

"You amaze me!" exclaimed Edward; "what knowledge could you have of me before my arrival in England?"

"My knowledge of you commenced before you left England," answered the sergeant. "Since that time I have fought under the command—nay, at the side of your father. I have been wounded in his defence, as this scar upon my forehead can testify; and think you, with all these ties to attach me to him and you, I could with indifference stand by and see you victimised by a man that I know to be one of the greatest scoundrels in the world; or subject your father to the horror of finding you a mangled corpse on his return, when he expects to meet your welcome and embrace?"

The heart of Edward Heathingdon was of too kindly a nature to be proof against these professions of attachment and regard in the sergeant.

"I have no doubt, my good fellow, that your intentions are well meant," he exclaimed, after a pause; "but do you reflect to what an imputation you may subject me by it. Captain Melton has grossly insulted me in the presence of other persons, and will it not be said that I am the coward he deems me, and that I merit the scornful treatment I have just now received from him?"

"I can't go so far as to say that," replied the sergeant, eagerly. "Captain Melton has succeeded in his present purpose; he has stripped you of a large sum of money, and the hope of plundering you of a great deal more, will rather incline him to excuse himself under the plea of intoxication, in order that he may enrich himself at your expense as much as possible. But be on your guard against him, sir, or he may lead you into many a vice that at the present moment you little think of."

" If such is the character of the man," exclaimed Edward Heathingdon, " why does my father suffer him to remain in his regiment?"

" Because the colonel has no power to deprive him of his commission," answered the sergeant ; " nor can he interfere with him beyond his duties as a soldier and an officer. I belong to his company, and have seen more of his character than most others have done. Of course I needn't tell you, sir, that it is the interest of Captain Melton to keep his views a secret from his superior in rank."

Edward, grateful for the service that had been done him, would now have rewarded the sergeant for the zealous kindness that had actuated him. But Daly obstinately refused all offers of a pecuniary nature, and, satisfied that the young gentleman would not, for that night, at least, seek Captain Melton, he took a respectful leave, and directed his steps towards the town, to watch the return of the major, to whom he thought it advisable to impart at least a portion of the evening's adventure, only stating his own interference as accidental, and resulting from the impulse of the moment.

The major, though too agreeably engaged for some time to bestow a thought on the delay of Edward, at length became surprised at his non-arrival, and, at an earlier than was customary with him, he quitted the society of his friends, to go in search of Edward Heathingdon. He was soon joined by the sergeant, and, with considerable anxiety and concern, listened to his narrative of the events that had taken place within the last three or four hours. After expressing his approbation of the conduct of Sergeant Daly, they separated, and the major pursued his way to the park, vexed, yet wondering that Edward had so immediately and so deeply been ensnared by Captain Melton ; yet ultimately taking all the blame upon himself, for having left him in the society of men, who, he well knew, would practice upon the inexperience of all that came in their way. He had, in the fullest extent of the word, constituted himself guardian to the young man during the absence of his father, and he now bitterly reproached himself with having neglected the serious duties with which he was charged.

On his arrival at Farley Park, he found that Edward had retired for the night, and as, from the spirit of his replies, he drew the conclusion that he would be led to seek Captain Melton, he arose at an early hour on the following morning, and, leaving a request that he would wait at home for him till his return, hurried away to the lodging of Captain Melton.

The latter appeared to be surprised at this unexpected visit, and his astonishment was still further increased, when the major demanded to know what amount of money Edward Heathingdon had become indebted to him the preceding evening.

" It's a trifle of no consequence whatever, Major Corfield," answered the other, with hesitation. " Mr. Heathingdon can settle it with me when it suits his convenience."

" I understand he has given you a note of hand," returned the major, " and if such is the case, I request that you will favour me with a sight of it."

The tone in which this was uttered implied a demand rather than a request, which the captain strove to evade, under the plea of delicacy in exposing the note of honour of any one. Major Corfield, however, now informed him that he had come to discharge the debt, upon which assurance he at length produced it.

" Nine hundred and fifty pounds !" exclaimed the major, with astonishment ; " is this the sum, Captain Melton, that you called a mere trifle ?"

" To a man of Colonel Heathingdon's fortune it can be of very little consequence," answered the other.

" But to one of yours," retorted Major Corfield, " I should think it must seem immense ! You are, however, I presume, aware that Mr. Edward Heathingdon is a minor, and as such this acknowledgment of his is of no legal value."

" But by all the rules of honour it must be paid," exclaimed Captain Melton, excited by the last observation. " He has acknowledged the debt before several witnesses, and if he suffers his honour to be sullied before he comes of age, he may find some difficulty in retrieving it at a future period of his life."

" You speak from experience, I presume, Captain Melton?" said the major, with marked emphasis.

" I speak from my experience of mankind generally," answered Melton, stung by the sarcasm conveyed by these words. " And for Mr. Heathingdon, I can only say, that if he dares to insinuate that I have acted otherwise than honourably by him, I will chastise him as his insolence and ungentlemanly conduct deserve."

" Utter such a threat again," exclaimed the major, wrathfully, " and I will make you ask pardon of him at the head of the regiment itself, for the disgrace you have brought upon it by last night's transaction."

" He is, I repeat, no gentleman, if he refuses to pay his debts of honour," replied Melton. " Nor does he show himself to be one in deputing you to negotiate for him in this affair, when he must be perfectly aware of the authority you hold over me by the superiority of your rank in the army."

" You mistake, sir," replied the major. " Mr. Heathingdon has not deputed me to be his representative in this affair, though you shall find that I take the task upon myself. I have neither seen nor heard from him. I was informed of this shameful business last night, and came to see if you had sufficient regard for your own honour to give up the note of hand."

"Not till he redeems it," exclaimed Melton; "and if it be not redeemed, I will expose the transaction to the whole world. If such boys choose to take upon themselves the character of men, let them be made to pay for their presumption."

Major Corfield, who was well aware that a stigma of any nature fixed on a young man's name, was not easily removed or forgotten, finding Captain Melton so determined, took out his pocket-book, and laying bank notes to the amount of the debt on the table, demanded the acknowledgement, which now Melton delivered up; and judging that both Edward and the major were apprehensive of the circumstance reaching the ears of Colonel Heathingdon, he assumed still more upon it; and, as he pocketed the money, threatened, that if Edward misrepresented, as he termed it, the affair to his father, to seek such satisfaction as his sword and the laws of honour afforded him.

"I advise you to let this subject drop, and to be exceedingly cautious how you act," said the major. 'Your character is in more danger of suffering than Mr. Heathingdon's. But if you choose to come to action you shall commence with me; and, though Edward may not be a match for you, I think I can, without boasting, take on me to say, I am as good a swordsman, and as steady a shot as yourself."

The tone in which these words were uttered, informed Captain Melton that the major was really in earnest; and as he was conscious he should stand as bad a chance with his superior officer as Edward would with him, he began to think the most prudent course would be to adopt the major's advice. But the circumstance had already reached the ears of other of the officers, and two of the captains, whose esteem for the colonel had been extended to the son, attended by the senior lieutenant, made a point of waiting on Melton, to advise him, if he valued his own reputation, to have so much consideration for the inexperience of the young man as to return his note of hand, and even to offer such a moderate apology as they should dictate.

Understanding, however, that the major was already in private conference with him, they seated themselves in an outer apartment, where they unavoidably overheard the greater part of the conversation; and, when the sentiments expressed by Captain Melton so little accorded with the advice they proposed giving, and that he had already accepted the money, they joined the major on his departure without condescending to speak to Melton.

The frown left on the brow of the major, more than his words, implied his dissatisfaction at the result of his interview, and gave a licence to the more openly expressed disapprobation of the officers, by whom his behaviour was freely reported to their associates, and whilst Edward was readily exempted from blame, for his youth and unsuspecting nature, Melton rendered himself so unpopular by the action he had been guilty of, that when he attended the muster he found every eye turned away from him, or, to use a significant term, the captain was sent to Coventry.

On parting from the officers in the morning, the major returned to Farley Park, where he found Edward, as had been requested, waiting for him. He appeared embarrassed and oppressed, and on his friend asking him if he had been indisposed on the previous evening, he entered into a candid explanation of what had occurred, and concluded with requesting his advice respecting the line of conduct he ought to adopt towards Melton.

"I feel excessively irritated against him," he added; "but have been taught to doubt my own judgment when under the influence of passion."

"My advice is, that you treat him with the contempt he deserves," replied the major.

"He attempted to strike me," exclaimed Edward, "and has insulted me in every way he could think of."

"For which he deserves to be severely punished," said the major. "However, he has so far forfeited the respectable portion of his character, that I think him utterly beneath your notice."

"Or, perhaps," returned the young man, "like Sergeant Daly, you do not think me competent to match myself against so experienced an adversary?"

"I cannot say I do," replied Major Corfield. "Not that you can be held in disesteem for that, for you have had but a few days' practice with your weapons, and he has been an experienced soldier for some years past. However, my young friend, you have learned a useful lesson, though, it must be confessed, it has been dearly bought. You perceive, I dare say, that he who has any intercourse with sharpers must expect to meet both shame and degradation?"

"I knew him not as a sharper," answered Edward; "and though I will not shrink from my father's reproof, I hope, in this instance, he will not judge me with too much severity. I knew not that I was acting wrong till Melton advised me to conceal the circumstance from the knowledge of my father."

By his perfect ingenuousness, Edward Heathingdon effectually prevented the good-natured major from reading him the lecture on his imprudence that he had intended. He now produced the note of hand, and, presenting it to him, said,—

"You shall not, then, meet your father's reproof. Let the embarrassment in which you have been placed, put you in future on your guard against such characters as Melton proves to be. Tell me the amount of the rest of the money you have lost to his associates of the gaming table, and then let the transaction be for ever buried in oblivion."

"You have been, then, already informed of this affair?" exclaimed Edward, with surprise.

"I knew of it last night," replied the major. "There were too many witnesses present for it to be kept any long time from my knowledge."

"It must be confessed that I have acted like a fool!" exclaimed the young man; "and of course I shall become a laughing-stock to all who hear of the folly I have been guilty of."

"Your youth and inexperience will most likely find you more persons to excuse than to condemn what has taken place," answered Major Corfield. "It has been an error of judgment on your part, and if it should happily prove the only one of the kind you fall into, you may have reason to rejoice that you have paid for the lesson."

The opinion of Major Corfield was justified in the reception given by the officers to Edward, on his appearing with them on the parade. The spirited nature of his retorts the preceding evening, they thought, gave the promise of a gallantry of character answerable to that of his father, and the extended hand and cordial salutation soon conduced to prove that he was not despised. This was a source of no less gratification to the major than it was to Edward himself; and they returned home, after the military duties of the day were over, highly pleased with the kindness that had been manifested by those whose good opinion it was worth preserving.

From that time, however, Edward Heathingdon did not mix in the society of the officers as he had done on previous occasions. He applied himself to his studies more closely than he had previously done, and associated chiefly with Major Corfield, whose kindness and friendship had been tested, and whose example was well worthy of being followed.

From his father, who was still in London, he heard frequently, but no hint was thrown out of his return, as he was still detained there on business of considerable importance, and his presence was required up to the moment when the affair would be brought to a close. Charles, however, it was at length stated, would return home immediately; and, in a letter addressed to the major, a request was conveyed that he would keep a close watch upon the eldest son, as fears were still entertained that his misdirected attachment to Jane Harrowby was now as powerful as ever. This was a matter in which Major Corfield foresaw more trouble than he would be likely to get over; for Charles was wilful and headstrong in his disposition, and, scorning all control, would pursue his object with more determination than ever. But the duty that had been entrusted to him he was determined to perform as far as possible, and three days afterwards Charles Heathingdon returned home.

CHAPTER III.

THE LIBERTINE REPROVED.—ATTEMPTED ABDUCTION.—AN UNLOOKED-FOR ARRIVAL.

It was late in the evening when the young man reached Farley Park, and the few hours that intervened between then and bedtime were occupied in conversation of a general nature. The next morning, however, as soon as Edward had left the room, Major Corfield introduced the subject he had so much at heart; and, having intimated that he had no desire to interfere unnecessarily, ventured to express a hope that Charles would cease his visits to the cottage of Jane Harrowby, in deference to the wishes of his father.

"Not but what her character is, I believe, irreproachable," he continued; "but Colonel Heathingdon is naturally anxious to prevent the misery that he sees will be the consequence of persisting in a guilty passion."

"Guilty passion!" repeated Charles; "and, pray, major, what great guilt can there be in paying a little attention to a pretty woman?"

"At least," answered the other, "there is guilt in coveting the wife of another man."

"But her husband has been transported," answered Charles; "and she is now free to do as she pleases."

"Indeed, my young friend, you are much mistaken there," exclaimed the major. "She is as much the wife of Guy Harrowby as ever she was; and her love for him must be slight indeed if she can forget him, under the affliction that has fallen upon him."

"A romantic notion that, major," answered the young man; "Guy Harrowby deserves all the affliction he may meet with, and his wife has little reason to regard his memory with kindness, seeing that all she suffers has been brought on by his own vicious course of life."

"Still he is her husband; and I'll be bound, if the truth was known, she would be the last person in the world to think harshly of his past errors. Besides, all that you have been advancing does not, in the slightest degree, warrant you in persecuting her with your lawless addresses."

"Can I help feeling admiration for a pretty woman?"

"Admiration may be excited, certainly," answered the major; "but you, my young friend, have suffered yourself to be hurried from admiration into love. The woman bears an excellent character in this neighbourhood; and, I dare say, if the truth was known, your attentions are a source of much sorrow and uneasiness."

"Why should she be either grieved or uneasy at having won my regard?" demanded the young man. "She is poor, and to convince her that my love is not a mere empty assertion, I have offered money to her many a time when I knew she was in the greatest distress."

"Did she accept your offer?"

"No; it has been invariably declined."

"A proof then has been given that she is too virtuous to become the easy victim you expected," replied Major Corfield. "I have been told that she is in constant grief at the cause which led to her separation from her husband; and surely you ought to place some sort of restraint upon yourself when you see that your attentions serve only to aggravate the sorrows of an almost broken heart."

"Really, Major Corfield," exclaimed the young man, angrily, "I know not by what right you have taken it upon yourself to tutor me upon this subject."

"The right has been conferred upon me by your father," answered the other. "He feels uneasy, and has requested me to speak to you upon the subject."

"It would have been better had he kept the authority to himself, instead of delegating it to others," exclaimed Charles, haughtily. "To *his* advice I am always inclined to listen with becoming respect; but I neither can, nor will, recognize the right *you* have assumed to yourself."

"You have heard your father's wishes from my lips," returned the major; "and if the professions you have just uttered are really meant, you will at once yield to them without any further hesitation."

"I can make no promise of that kind, Major Corfield," answered the young man. "Jane Harrowby has gained an influence over me that it is beyond my power to resist, and if I gave the pledge that is required, it is but too likely that I should break it before long.".

"You will, at least, forbear to see her till after the return of your father?"

"On the contrary," answered Charles; "I shall not delay the visit I intend paying her for a single moment. It is now some time since I saw Jane Harrowby, and I am not without hopes that she may prove less unkind than when I last parted from her."

"Do you think, then, that in so short a time she has forgotten the husband whose forced absence she has so bitterly mourned?"

"That is a question that remains to be solved," answered the young man. "Guy Harrowby's term of transportation has yet some years to run, and it is more likely than not, that he will never see England again."

"At all events there is no certainty of that, since good conduct may obtain for him a remission of his sentence," exclaimed Major Corfield. "It is far from being unlikely that he will come back sooner than is expected; and should that be the case, he would scarcely fail to revenge himself upon the libertine who has sought to undermine the virtue of his wife."

"Upon my word, sir," cried Charles, "you make use of harsher expressions than I am inclined tamely to put up with. If it is upon the authority of my father that you act thus, I must at once declare that I shall pay no heed to any advice that is given with any other than his own lips."

"In that respect you must do as you please, young man," answered the major; "but it would be well for you to examine your own heart rigidly upon this subject before you commit yourself too far. Colonel Heathingdon is most anxious that you should obey him in this instance, and I need not remind you of the grief your disobedience will occasion him."

"In most things I have always shown a willing readiness to follow his wishes," answered Charles; "but, in this instance, I find more difficulty than I have ever had to encounter before."

"You cannot marry the woman, seeing that her husband is alive, and likely to return home."

"I never thought of marrying her."

"So much the worse," replied Major Corfield; "for hitherto she has borne an unspotted reputation, which you would destroy, for the gratification of your own criminal passion."

"Major Corfield," exclaimed the young man, in a tone of defiance, "I have endured much of this language; but my patience will not bear me out any longer, and I shall therefore bring to a close a conversation that can only cause an ill-feeling between us, without leading to any satisfactory result."

Charles Heathingdon rose from his seat as he said this, and putting on his hat, as he passed through the hall, left the house, to wander he scarcely knew whither. The subject which had just been discussed, however, occupied all his thoughts; for the impediments which had been thrown in his way only served to make him the more resolute to overcome them, and from that moment he determined to possess himself of Jane Harrowby, even though he might have to use violence to effect his object. This notion once thought of, he commenced laying out his plans, and as his father's return might be immediately expected, to carry her off that very night, and to convey her to some place where she would not be easily found. His next design was to confer with his valet upon the subject; for Roberts possessed one of those pliant consciences that are easily to be gained over, even in a bad cause, and, in the present instance, he was found to be all that could be desired. He not only agreed to give his assistance, but to secure the service of the coachman; and all other matters having been planned, it was arranged that the carriage should be at an appointed spot near the house at twilight, that evening, and that they should then proceed to the cottage of Jane Harrowby, who, either by force or entreaty, was to be conveyed to a distant part of England.

Little suspecting the perfidy that was intended, Jane sat at her window that evening, watching the declining sun, and thinking of her absent husband, whose punishment fell with even greater weight upon herself than it did upon him. Some years she knew must elapse before his term of banishment expired; and long and weary did the time seem to one who believed him less guilty than he was, and who never could see half the faults that were so evident to other people. She believed, too, that return when he might, he would present himself before her a wiser and a better man, and her heart eagerly panted for the moment when he would be restored to her. These and similar thoughts occupied the mind of Jane Harrowby, and she was almost lost in unconsciousness when a carriage was seen to stop at the gate, and, in another moment, Charles Heathingdon sprang out, and advanced towards the door. Unprepared as she was for this visit, Jane had not time to flee, and scarcely had she risen from her chair than he stood before her.

" Jane," he exclaimed, " my presence here seems to have surprised you ; and yet how can you wonder at it, when you know the ardour and intensity of my passion !"

" Leave me, sir !" exclaimed Jane, in a tone of command ; " leave me, I say, for you have already heard me declare that I can never listen to your terms without shuddering at the infamy that has prompted you to avow a passion for one whom misfortune has deprived of the protection of her husband."

" These heroics may be all very fine," answered the libertine ; " but I have heard them so often repeated, that I have grown weary of the reproach they are intended to convey. In one word, I have resolved to be trifled with no longer, and if you refuse to go with me upon fair entreaties, I must use force to convey you to a place far enough from this neighbourhood."

A feeling of dread crept through her heart as she listened to these words ; but, remembering that all her fortitude was required at a moment like this, she recovered herself with an effort, and again commanded him to be gone, if he would avoid the exposure which would follow any alarm that she might raise."

" I am not much afraid of that," he replied ; " for the loneliness of this place is my best security against danger, and even if any fool should be rash enough to interfere, I have people waiting without who would soon overmaster the difficulty."

"Then I appeal to your honour, as a gentleman."

" Honour must be forgotten when love like mine beckons me on," he replied, with calm indifference. " I have given you a fair chance of going with me without having recourse to violence, and, knowing my determination, it now only remains for you to decide how this affair is to terminate."

" I have already told you," answered Jane, " that no inducement you can urge shall ever prevail on me to forget the duty I owe to him whose unfortunate absence has given you the advantage you are base enough to take."

" These reproaches, at any rate, will not serve to turn me from my purpose," exclaimed the libertine. " I was prepared for them, and can hear all you have to say without feeling either surprise or anger."

" If you have no pity upon me," cried Jane, despairingly, " you may, at least, have mercy on the helpless child, whom, by this act, you would render motherless."

" The child shall be well taken care of," replied Charles ; " so you need feel neither apprehension nor alarm on his account. I have given directions for him to be conveyed to a widowed tenant of a cottage hard by, and under her fostering protection, the boy will scarcely know the loss of his parents."

" All has been prepared before hand for this villanous affair," exclaimed Jane ; " but Heaven will not desert me in the hour of need, and I warn you to desist from the unholy plot in which you have engaged."

" Your warning has little effect upon one whose mind is already made up," answered Charles Heathingdon. " If I suffer this night to pass away without accomplishing my plan, it is, indeed, probable that I might be disappointed ; but I have made up my mind to seize upon the present, and all your threats and entreaties combined will not deter me from the purpose I have in view."

" Will nothing warn you," exclaimed Jane, " of the shame and foul dishonour that this act of treacherous violence will bring upon you ?"

" You are mistaken in supposing that such will be the consequence," replied the libertine. " Some straight-laced people, indeed, may deem the act a scandalous one, but the majority of people will not trouble their heads about it, and there are others who will regard it as a spirited act that is hardly to be censured."

" Depraved, then, must be the hearts of those who could think so lightly of such an act of villany !" exclaimed Jane Harrowby. " I have never given you the slightest encouragement, Mr. Heathingdon, but have avoided you on all occasions when I could do so ; and yet, knowing the deep hatred this violence of yours must give rise to, you are still unmoved by my prayers for mercy."

" I come not here to listen to your complaints or remonstrances," answered the libertine ; " and, having now heard my proposition, it only remains for you to say whether I am to expect resistance or resignation."

" You have heard my determination, and nothing shall ever move me from it," she replied. " Force alone shall secure your triumph over me, and though you may, perhaps, accomplish your base purpose by violence, you may dread the vengeance of my husband when he returns—as one day he will—to England !"

" Ay, but it will be some years first," retorted Charles Heathingdon ; " and, whenever the time comes—if ever it does—I shall be prepared to defend myself against any puny efforts he may make to do me an injury. Besides, I have heard a rumour that Guy Harrowby murdered the

guard set over him, and afterwards escaped into the bush. There may be truth in the report, and, if so, your husband will be most assuredly captured, and hanged."

." This," exclaimed Jane, "is only a falsehood, invented to deceive me in aid of your own base purposes. Guy Harrowby fell into veil company, and was sent abroad for a crime that he had committed; but I know him too well to believe that any tyranny he may have had to bear, would have urged him to shed the blood of a fellow-creature."

" 'Tis as well that you should think so," answered Charles Heathingdon, coolly; "but, for my own part, I am not quite so hard of belief, when there is probability for the groundwork of such a report. He may have been averse to murder at one period of his life, but a man's nature gets hardened when he finds himself among the hardened criminals that he must needs associate with upon his getting over to the land of his banishment."

"It needs but the confirmation of that rumour to seal my earthly misery!" cried Jane, despondingly. "And yet why should I give credit to such a tale as that you have told me, when I know the cowardly motive that has urged you to utter this foul and odious falsehood?"

"Psha!" exclaimed the libertine; "what motive can I have for telling you so, when I have already got you in my power?"

"I scorn your power," she replied; "and dare you to put your threats into execution."

"All this bravado will not serve your purpose," answered Charles Heathingdon, "for I have arranged my plans, and there is not the slightest chance that you will be able to thwart me. I would spare myself the pain of resorting to violence, and it will depend upon yourself to save me from an act that I would avoid."

"Rather save yourself the shame of making a cowardly attack upon a helpless woman!" exclaimed Jane, collecting all her courage to resist the violence she had but too much reason to expect. "I have told you, Mr. Heathingdon, that willingly I will never accompany you from this cottage, and, if you persist in forcing me from it, the consequences must fall upon yourself."

"No consequences shall deter me from the object that brought me here," retorted Charles; and, making a signal to his servants to open the carriage-door in readiness, he advanced to seize upon the retreating form of his intended victim. Jane, however, was resolute to defend herself to the last; but as, with a loud scream of terror, she was rushing towards the door, the powerful arm of the libertine detained her, and all hope of escape seemed at an end. With an exclamation of triumph, Charles then raised her in his arms, and was rushing with her from the cottage, when a man sprang forward, and, with a heavy blow, struck him to the earth. Jane also would have fallen, but the arm of her deliverer sustained her, and, with a thrilling exclamation of joy, she sank, half fainting, upon the bosom of her husband!

Charles Heathingdon, though struck down, soon recovered his feet, and from the few words that had been uttered by Jane, he knew that her deliverer was no other than the convict, Guy Harrowby. His first impulse then, was, to call in his servants, and arrest the man who had thwarted his purpose, and who, he had reason to believe, perpetrated a murder, in order to escape from the place of his banishment. Guy, however, seemed aware of what was passing through his mind, and releasing himself from the convulsive grasp of his wife, he took down, from over the chimney-piece, a gun that he had often used in days gone by, when he was engaged in the illegal occupation of poaching. Charles Heathingdon shrunk back as if to escape from death, but Guy lowered the weapon, and said to him in a firm, deep tone,—

"You needn't be afraid of my harming you, young man, if you leave this place without raising my fury by remaining in my presence. You have been base enough to insult a woman that you thought was defenceless; but you will find in future that there is one to watch over her, who will sacrifice his life, if need be, in her defence."

"This vain boasting of yours will soon be turned to sorrow and repentance," answered Charles, bursting with fury at the unexpected defeat he had sustained. "I know you are the husband of Jane Harrowby, and, unless reports prove false, you will, ere long, be in the county gaol on a charge of murder, committed by you abroad."

"Who dares accuse me of murder?" demanded Guy Harrowby, somewhat startled at discovering that the report had reached England before him.

"It matters not who will be your accuser," replied the other; "the crime I have named has been charged against you, and it will be for you hereafter to prove your innocence. And even if you are guiltless of that crime, you have left your place of banishment before the expiration of the allotted period, and for that a heavy punishment will be your doom."

"Your evil wishes will be foiled," exclaimed Jane, recovering as these latter words were pronounced. "The sentence passed upon my husband has, no doubt, been remitted, and he will remain here to protect me from the lawless violence of one who has set all honour at defiance."

"If the term of his transportation has been remitted, as you say," returned the defeated libertine, "let him produce the pardon, and I shall be spared the trouble of providing him with a lodging in prison."

"You, at least, have no right to demand its production," exclaimed Guy, scarcely knowing how to avoid a discovery that, if once made, must prove fatal to him.

"Your hesitation proves that my surmise is right," answered Charles Heathingdon. "You are a returned convict, having no pardon to allege as an excuse, and, therefore, liable to be sent abroad for the remainder of your life. The murder I am not quite so sure of; but I shall make diligent inquiry into the report, and, if it should prove true, my efforts shall not be wanting to send you to the gallows."

"And this vindictive feeling," cried Jane, bitterly, "is for no other reason than that my husband has thwarted you in the cowardly attack you made upon me."

"It matters not what the cause may arise from," answered Charles; "I have been struck to the earth by the hands of your ruffian husband, and the blow shall be avenged before I cease from my endeavours to bring him to punishment!"

"Beware how you urge me beyond my patience while I have this weapon in my hand!" exclaimed Guy. "I have no wish to harm you, though there don't seem to be the same feeling on your part towards me; but, if you threaten to turn informer against me, I may be urged to do that which would make me guilty of the crime you choose to charge me with."

"You forget, then," retorted the libertine, "that I have people close at hand who would secure you on the instant that you committed the crime."

"But it would be too late to save your worthless life from my vengeance," answered Guy Harrowby. "However, I have no wish to harm you beyond the slight punishment I have already inflicted; so, depart in peace, and never again cross my path till you have proved, by your conduct, that you repent the violence you would have been guilty of towards a helpless female."

"What have I to repent?" demanded the other, haughtily. "Is it a crime, then, in your opinion, that I have fallen in love with a pretty face."

"Had I encouraged you, there might have been some excuse for the conduct you have pursued towards me," replied Jane; "but I have always sought to avoid your presence, and, even when that was impossible, I have treated your words with scorn and contempt. Still you persecuted me with your hateful addresses, and, but for the unlooked-for arrival of my husband, you would this night have carried me by force from the humble home in which I in vain hoped to find the solitude I desired."

"You have little reason to congratulate yourself upon the presence of your husband," replied Charles; "for it is likely to lead him into a worse situation than he was in before."

"Surely," cried Jane, wildly, "you will not seek to injure him for interfering to prevent the violence you attempted?"

"He has neither mercy nor favour to expect at my hands," exclaimed the other, gloomily; "for he has done that to-night which time can never efface from my memory."

"Nay," cried Jane, imploringly; "in mercy do not seek to bring further misery upon me by an act that is unworthy of an honourable man!"

"Come, come, Jane, I'll have no pleading to him in my behalf," exclaimed Guy Harrowby. "His revenge has been excited because I thwarted him in his plans; but he will think twice before he puts his threats into execution; and, if he won't consider his own safety as depending upon the course he pursues, he must expect to meet such a punishment as I shall prepare for him."

"You will see, by-and-bye, how little effect your threats have upon me," answered Charles Heathingdon, as, with some reluctance, he prepared to depart. "I have told you, Guy Harrowby, what you have got to expect from me, and, though I shall not myself surrender you into the hands of justice, I will quickly send those who are not to be intimidated by your threats of assassination."

Mortified at the defeat he had sustained, the libertine now quitted the cottage, and, entering the coach, ordered the coachman to drive homewards with all possible speed. During the way the mind of Charles Heathingdon was occupied with a rapid succession of thoughts, each of which served more and more to inflame him against the man whose unlooked-for arrival had thwarted a plan that, at the moment, seemed certain of success. The opportunity he had so anxiously sought had been lost; but there was yet revenge for him in store, and that revenge he determined to carry out to its fullest extent. Not wishing to have any questions asked him, as to where he had been, he left the vehicle at the park gates, and then, calling Roberts, his valet, on one side, he desired him to hasten to the town and send the officers of justice in quest of Guy Harrowby, the returned convict.

CHAPTER IV.

HOME.—EXPLANATIONS.—THE SEARCH.

BEING left to themselves, Guy related to his wife the narrative of his escape, though omitting all mention of the murder, lest she, also, should share in the general feeling against him, for the act he had committed. As he proceeded, Jane became more and more uneasy lest he should be again torn from her; and, leading him to the bed-side of their sleeping boy, she besought him, for the sake of herself and her child, that he would seek some place of concealment without delay, and remain there till the search after him had ceased. To this suggestion, however, he would not listen, assuring her that the danger was not so great as her fears made her imagine, and that he would be at all times prepared against his enemies in case of any sudden emergency.

"Besides," he continued, "I can hardly believe that the young fellow will execute his threats; for he has heard mine in reply, and, judging from what I have already seen of him, I have a notion that he is too great a coward to risk his own life, merely to satisfy a feeling of revenge that will vanish when he comes to think seriously over the matter."

"But he accuses you of a murder!" cried Jane, shuddering as the word escaped her lips.

"That's true," answered her husband; "yet it will puzzle him, I rather think, to make out his charge from the little he can know about the affair."

"You admit, then, that there is truth in it?" cried Jane, gasping with apprehension and alarm.

"Why," replied Guy Harrowby, "there's no denying that a man lost his life, but the fault was as much his as mine. He wanted to prevent my escape; a struggle took place, and I was nearly overpowered, when I took the only alternative that remained for me. In short, the man perished and I escaped from my bondage, and fled into the bush for safety and concealment. I have already told you how I found more friendship from the savages than I had experienced for many a long day before, and I believe I should have remained with them till this time, but that I could never forget my home, and her that I had left there to mourn the absence of her husband."

"Alas! alas!" cried Jane, "my grief has indeed been heavy; yet I have been supported through all my trials by the one reflection, that the day would come when my peace of mind would be restored by your return. Years have passed by in heaviness of spirit, yet was there one bright ray in the future that bade me hope—and that hope, dear Guy, was the support and mainspring of my existence."

"What a villain have I been," he exclaimed, despondingly, "to bring misery and despair upon her whose love has never failed through all the trials she has gone through! But let us hope, Jane, there are better days in store for us; and, if that wish is but granted, I will yet prove that your unshaken confidence in me has not been unworthily bestowed."

"If you would live in security," answered Jane, "it must be in some other land than this; for here you have many foes, and it would be in vain to contend against the evil they would do you."

"Where else can we hope to live, if not in England?" demanded her husband. "Besides, I have a love for the land of my birth that even the persecutions I have suffered cannot destroy. It was that love of my country which tempted me to risk a perilous voyage, alone, and without even the assistance of a compass, across a rough and tempestuous ocean, when thousands of miles were between me and the object I was in search of. All those perils I have escaped, Jane, and it is not the trifles that at present threaten me, that will make me believe I am destined to fall again into the power of those who seek my destruction."

"This over-confidence will lead to certain ruin," she exclaimed, in despair. "Charles Heathingdon is enraged at the defeat he has this night met with; his deadly wrath has been excited by the blow you struck him, and never will he rest satisfied till he has had his revenge."

"Let him try his worst," returned Guy; "and he will find, when too late, that he has one to deal with who can overmatch him in spite of all the cunning he may bring to his aid."

"This confidence will, I fear, end in your destruction," cried Jane, anxiously. "Your enemy will have the assistance of many besides himself, and how can you hope to escape when every care will be taken to prevent the flight of him they have resolved to capture?"

"If the worst should happen," replied Guy, "it will then be time enough for me to think of seeking safety in flight. There is, however, reason to believe that young Heathingdon—as I think you call him—will not take any very active steps against me when he gives himself time for reflection, for he will then see that it will bring about an explanation of the course he has taken against you, and that alone will be sufficient to prevent the malicious designs he has promised to carry out against me."

"Charles Heathingdon has no such feelings of shame as you imagine," replied Jane Harrowby. "I myself reminded him of the disgrace that would fall upon him if the conduct towards me should be made public; but he treated my warning with contempt, and assured me that, though some few might condemn his conduct, there would be plenty of others who would rather applaud than utter one word in the way of reproach."

"Be that as it may," exclaimed her husband, "there is less to apprehend in this affair than you appear to imagine. Luckily, I am not without arms here, and, if too closely driven, I may turn them against those who are determined to keep up their persecution."

"Would you shed more blood?" cried Jane, shuddering.

"Not while it can be avoided," he replied; "but those who would follow me to my home us beware of the tiger that they place at bay. The gun, Jane, I suppose is loaded?"

"It is," she replied; "I have always kept it so, lest, in this lonely cottage, I should be attacked by thieves."

"'Tis well," exclaimed her husband, again taking it into his hands and examining the priming. "It is ready for use I see, and, woe to those that would come here to lay hands upon me."

"Give me that gun, Guy Harrowby," cried the wife, roused almost to madness by the deep and determined tone in which these words were uttered. "Give it me, I say, or from this moment I flee your presence for ever!"

"Why are you so alarmed, Jane, when I have only prepared myself against any attack that might be made upon me?" demanded her husband, with assumed calmness. "I have warned that young libertine of what the consequence will be if he again enters my doors; and the laws, rigid as they are, allow a man to guard his own house and person from attack."

"But not in such a case as this," answered Jane. "He accuses you of having returned to England before your term of transportation has expired, and that, I fear, will give him a right to come and apprehend you."

"The right shall be sternly disputed, though," exclaimed Guy. "Think you I would have plunged into the perils of that long and fearful voyage, but that I had resolved not to lose my liberty again without a struggle."

"Perhaps not," she sighed; "and yet I could have wished that you had remained till the term of your banishment was at an end. Then, Guy, you might have returned home in safety, and, by changing your course of life, we should have passed the remainder of our life in peace and happiness."

"And, if they leave me alone, I intend as it is to amend my course of life," replied her husband. "Let these busybodies only give me a chance, and I will labour night and day to wipe away the remembrance of the past."

"Alas!" groaned the unhappy wife, "how can that be when you have the blood of a fellow creature to answer for?"

"The man sought his own death, and it was no fault of mine that he perished," exclaimed Guy. "Methinks I now feel the grasp of the fellow's fingers, as he clutched me by the throat till I was nearly strangled. It was a moment, Jane, when any other man, as well as myself, would have put forth all his strength to preserve his own life. One of us I found must perish, and, collecting all my strength, I at length gained a slight advantage over him. All that time he had been calling loudly for assistance, but no one happened to be near, and we were left to continue our death struggle till one or the other could overmaster his opponent. At length, as we rolled fiercely together upon the ground, I succeeded in getting him under me, and then his cries for help were redoubled, and I was every moment in danger of being captured by those who might come to his assistance. At such a time as that, Jane, was it likely that I should think of crime, or the consequences that might follow it? I become more and more maddened, and, to prevent his cries, placed my hand upon his throat, even as he had done by me when the advantage was on his side. At first he breathed thickly, and with a gurgling noise; a few moments more, and his frame became convulsed, so that I could scarcely keep my hold; but at length a stillness succeeded, and, when I looked upon the blackened face of the man, I saw that he was dead!"

"Horrible!" cried Jane, trembling, as she heard the fearful narrative of her husband's crime.

"What I felt at that moment I cannot describe to you," exclaimed Guy Harrowby. "The crime, however, had been forced upon me, and it then only remained for me to escape from the punishment that would surely follow my crime. Fortunately no one stood in my way, or I might have had another life to answer for. Chance directed my way across fields and plantations, swimming rivers, and suffering no obstacles to stand in my way. At length I reached the beach, and, when there, soon fell in with the friendly natives that I have told you of. Of the perils I endured afterwards, when leagues and leagues away from land on a tempestuous ocean, I must give you a narrative some other time."

"You have thrilled my soul with horror, Guy!" she replied; "and yet, armed as you now are, I fear more blood will be spilt, should he, who left us just now, return to put his threat into execution."

"How am I to avoid it?" exclaimed Guy Harrowby. "With arms in my hand I should be a craven indeed to surrender myself quietly into their hands."

"Follow the advice I give, and there will be no fear of the danger you expect."

"If you counsel flight," answered her husband, "I tell you at once that it would be in vain, since it is most likely I should throw myself among the very people I would avoid."

"That is what I myself feared," exclaimed Jane; "and, therefore, I would have you remain in the house till those who come in search of you have taken their departure."

"Where in this place can I hope to find concealment?" demanded Guy, looking round him.

"There is a loft above this room where they will never think of looking for you," replied Jane. "The only entrance to it is from the back of the house, and, when you are once there, I'll remove the ladder to some place where it will not be seen, and I will myself answer all questions that these people may put to me."

"Can you tell a falsehood for me without flinching?" demanded her husband. "They will watch your countenance narrowly, Jane, and the slightest look of alarm will be enough to convince them that you are trying to deceive them for my sake."

"Fear not," she replied, "for my courage will rise in proportion to the danger you are threatened with. So now give me the gun, for you will not need it in the place where you are about to hide yourself."

"If it must be so, there it is," exclaimed her husband, returning it to the place from whence he had taken it. "Your words have prevailed over me, Jane, though I would rather have been armed in case they should happen to find out my lurking-place."

"Rely upon my words," answered Jane, "and you will find that your confidence in me has not been given in vain."

"But," exclaimed Guy, "suppose young Squire Heathingdon was to make another attempt to carry you off? Do you think, if I heard your cries for help, that I could remain sneaking up yonder, when my presence might save you from their violence?"

"There's no fear of that, now that he has another object in view," returned Jane. "He will not, as I believe, come himself; and, if he does, he will not dare to harm me in the presence of those he will bring with him. So now, Guy, hasten to the place I told you of, for we know not how soon the people we expect may be here."

Guy Harrowby offered no opposition to this, and, after Jane had looked out at the door to see that no one was lurking near the cottage, he followed her into the garden, where they found the ladder leading to the loft where he was to seek a temporary concealment. After taking a hasty farewell, he ascended, and, the ladder having been immediately conveyed away, he was left to endure all the suspense that the novelty of his situation occasioned. On the other hand, Jane, who could distinctly hear voices at no great distance off, hurried into the house, and, having secured the door, waited with intense anxiety the result of a visit that she had so many reasons to dread. Ten weary minutes passed away, and she could hear people passing round the house, as if they were resolved to examine the exterior first. A whispering at the front door was soon afterwards heard, and this was succeeded by a loud knocking, which was scarcely finished when a hoarse voice demanded immediate admittance in the name of the law. Hitherto Jane Harrowby had maintained a tolerable degree of calmness, but her spirits now flagged, and, when she attempted to rise from her seat, she sank back in a state of complete helplessness. Three or four times the knocking was repeated, on each occasion with greater impatience, till at length the persons without pushed violently, and, the slight fastening yielding to the pressure, the door flew back, and five men rushed tumultously into the room. Roused by the act of violence, Jane raised her head, expecting to see Charles Heathingdon, but, to her no small relief, he was not among those who had paid this unseasonable visit at her cottage.

"Now, young woman, where's your husband?" exclaimed the foremost of the men, flourishing a truncheon, to show that he bore the high dignity of parish constable. "Where is he, I say? for we are here to apprehend him, so it's no use for you to be hiding him from our sight."

"He is not here, as you may see," answered Jane, gathering all her fortitude for the trial she had to go through.

"So you'd like to make us believe," said one of the men; "but we happen to know that he is here, and, if you resist the officers of the law, you'll be guilty of ——"

"Psha," interrupted Rumble, the constable; "we don't want any of your long orations when there's business to be done. The young woman knows we don't come here without authority, and, if she don't tell us where her husband is, she'll be taken up for aiding and abetting a criminal."

"I have told you he is not here," said Jane.

"But we happen to know he is," exclaimed Rumble, "and, what's more, we won't go away till we've found him."

"What charge have you against him?"

"Charge enough," answered the constable. "In the first place, he's accused of murdering his guard over t'other side of the water; and, moreover than that, he has returned to England before the time of his transportation was up."

"These are heavy charges, indeed," said Jane; "but I have already told you he is not here."

"Humph! and perhaps you'll tell us he never has been here?" exclaimed Rumble, pompously.

"If I was inclined to tell so great a falsehood," said Jane, "there is one person who would gladly come forward to contradict the assertion. My husband was seen by Mr. Charles Heathingdon, to whose revengeful spirit I am indebted for this untimely visit."

"He certainly sent us here," replied Rumble; "but he was bound to give the information when he knew that a felon was at liberty when he ought to be in gaol. However, that's nothing to do with the present business, for we've come to search after one Guy Harrowby, and we'll not stir from the place till we've searched every hole and corner that it's likely he may have crept into."

The constable now turned to the men that had accompanied him, and, after a brief consultation among themselves, they commenced an active search, looking through every part of the two rooms the cottage contained, and turning over every article under which it was likely the fugitive might have concealed himself. All, however, proving of no avail, three of the men went out of doors to continue their search round about the premises. Rumble was one of those who remained in the cottage, and, addressing himself to Jane Harrowby, he demanded whether she still persisted in saying that her husband had left the place.

"You hardly need ask that question of me now," she said, "for you and your men have looked through every part of the house, and, had he been here, you must surely have found him."

"But it strikes me he is somewhere outside."

"A very short time will serve to satisfy you whether he is or not," replied Jane. "Your companions are well fitted, I dare say, for their bloodhound business, and, if my husband has not made good use of his time, he will fall into the hands of his merciless pursuers."

"You take this matter very coolly, Mrs. Harrowby," said the constable; "but, if your husband is not found before we go away to-night, you'll be very likely to find yourself in an awkward dilemma to-morrow."

"For what?"

"Why, for concealing a criminal, to be sure."

"But that criminal is my husband," answered Jane; "and I know not of any law that there is to compel me to surrender him up to the revengeful feelings of the heartless libertine, who but a short time since left this house."

"If you mean what you say, I'd have you take care how you slander the character of a respectable gentleman like Mr. Charles Heathingdon," exclaimed the constable. "Remember, his father is a justice of the peace, and he'll not allow those sort of things to be said without teaching you to have more respect for a gentleman."

"Mr. Charles Heathingdon has not proved any claim to the character you give him," answered Jane. "Had he been either a gentleman or a man of honour, he would not have sought to undermine the virtue of a wife during the absence of her husband."

"Psha!" exclaimed the official; "the world never troubles its head about such matters as that. Affairs of gallantry are never heeded, because, you see, Mrs. Harrowby, people have other matters of more consequence to think of."

"It is yet to be proved whether Mr. Charles Heathingdon will not have reason to repent the villanous schemes he plotted against me," answered Jane. " I have heard honourable mention of his father, and to him will I make my complaints of the son's infamous conduct."

" And what good do you expect to get from that ?" demanded the constable. " Colonel Heathingdon is, as you say, a good sort of man enough ; but Mr. Charles is too old to be taken to task about things of this kind, and, depend upon it, he'll play you such a trick afterwards that you won't be likely to forget in a hurry."

" Of his revengeful feeling I have a proof before me at this very moment," exclaimed Jane ; " my husband struck him to the earth for the insult he offered me, and his first act of vengeance was to send you and your people after him. But luckily I suspected the mischief in good time, and my husband is now safe from the treachery that was intended him."

" Ah ! so you'd like to make us think, Mrs. Harrowby ; but I don't believe a word of it," said the constable.

" The long absence of your people proves that they have been unable to find him."

" Well," exclaimed Rumble, " he may have managed to get away to be sure ; but his liberty won't last any very long time, for to-morrow there'll be handbills abroad, offering a reward for his discovery, and, if that don't put him safely under lock and key, I don't know what will."

Jane Harrowby felt sick at heart as she heard this, but the return of the men prevented her making any further observation. The constable looked anxiously round to see if the fugitive had been secured, and, observing that they had returned without him, his countenance assumed a marked expression of disappointment.

" What !" he exclaimed, testily ; " do you mean to say you have not found your man ?"

" We've looked everywhere," said Larkins ; " and now it's quite certain the woman told us the truth when she said he was gone away before we came."

" Are you sure you haven't left any place unsearched ?" demanded the constable.

" I'm quite sure of that," answered the other ; " for there isn't a hedge nor a ditch, nor anything of the sort, about the place but what we've examined "

" Have you any room or loft above this ?" demanded Rumble, looking up to the ceiling.

Jane was staggered by this question ; but the fate of her husband depended upon her reply, and, in a tolerably firm tone, she declared that there was nothing but the roof above the room in which they were standing.

" There don't seem to be a trap-door or staircase," said the constable, placing upon the table the candle with which he had been examining every part of the room. " The chap," he added, " seems to have been too cunning for us at present ; but he won't have his liberty long, unless he should have the good fortune to get out of England."

" And that is what I hope he may be able to do," exclaimed Jane, with a faint hope of misleading them as to the intentions of her husband.

" Has he got money then to pay the expenses of a journey ?" demanded the constable.

" He has a friend who will advance it to him," replied Jane Harrowby.

" What ! without the chance of being paid again ?"

" I myself will take care that it is repaid," answered the wife. " Luckily, I am not without friends to supply me with work, and from my savings I may be able to restore that which is lent for so kind a purpose."

" Well, upon my life, you're a strange sort of woman," exclaimed Rumble ; " but I suppose you think it's only right to help your husband out of the scrape ; though, to tell you my mind, I rather think you'll hear something more about this business than you seem to fancy."

" What I have done," answered Jane, " has been in defiance of all danger to myself, and in a firm conviction that it was nothing more than a duty to assist in the escape of my husband. For myself, I am in no fear of punishment, unless they should part me from my child."

" Ah ! ma'am, that's a matter I know nothing at all about," replied Rumble ; " though, I dare say, if they put you into prison, they won't think proper to suffer a brat to go along with you. However, that's no business of mine ; so, for the present, we'll leave you, Mrs. Harrowby, and, perhaps, to-morrow we shall have to pay you another visit."

Glad to be rid of them, Jane watched them by the moonlight, as they passed along the lane ; but she would not venture to open the door again till there seemed to be every probability that they would not return. And even then she stood in the garden, listening, to convince herself, as far as possible, that there was no further danger to be apprehended. She, then, after waiting a few minutes longer, proceeded to the rear of the cottage, and, in a low tone, pronounced the name of her husband. In an instant Guy appeared at the opening, and leaped down before she had time to get the ladder. Then, casting a hurried glance around to see if anybody was watching them, he followed her into the cottage, and secured the door to prevent the too sudden appearance of an enemy.

" This escape, Jane, is almost miraculous," he exclaimed. " The fellows were at one time within a few feet of the place where I was concealed ; and, just when I had given myself up for lost, something turned their attention another way, and I was saved."

" And I," said Jane, " had enough to do to make them believe that you were not hiding somewhere about the premises."

" I heard all that passed," replied her husband ; " and, when one of them asked if there was not a room or loft above, I thought all chance of escape was over. But I am safe, and now a few hours more will serve to convey me to London, where I may hide safely enough till the pursuit after me is at an end."

"I fear there is yet much danger for you," exclaimed Jane Harrowby; "for, since you overheard all that was said, you must be aware that printed bills are to be circulated offering a reward for your apprehension."

"I know all that," replied her husband; "but there's not much fear of my being taken, for I shall be with those that I can trust, and there's not one that would give up a friend for the sake of a paltry reward."

"But are they to be depended on if the reward offered should be a very large one?"

"Ay; my life on it they would not play me false," exclaimed Guy Harrowby. "Why, they themselves are sometimes obliged to depend upon the honour of their comrades, and there would be no security for any of us if a man was to be tempted to betray a friend for the sake of a reward."

"But shall I know your hiding-place?"

"Not for some time, I should think," he replied; "for it is most likely any letters sent to you would be opened, and then the secret would be out at once."

"True; I had forgotten that," exclaimed Jane; "every artifice will, I dare say, be tried to discover where you are, and I must, therefore, be satisfied to remain in uncertainty and doubt till the arrival of better times. But there is one thing, Guy, that I have not yet asked—you will need money, and, I suppose, have but little to support yourself with in London?"

"You are right enough there," answered Guy Harrowby; "for, after giving half-a-crown to the bargemen that gave me a cast to Battersea, I had but two shillings left to bring me the other thirty miles."

"Here is a small sum," said Jane, opening a drawer, and taking out a purse; "it is the savings of the last four or five months, and was laid by in case I should be ill and unable to work. It is yours, Guy, and may do something towards your support till you can escape to some place where you may live in safety, and where I can hereafter join you."

"Here is three pounds sixteen," exclaimed Guy Harrowby, as he finished counting the money, which he had thrown before him on the table. "It is more than I shall want, Jane; so do you keep two pounds of it, and, with the rest, I shall be able to rub on till a better time comes."

It was in vain that she urged him to take it all. Guy was resolute in his determination, and, ultimately, it was divided in the manner he wished. But Jane was still uneasy lest he should fall into the hands of his pursuers, and, in spite of his wish to the contrary, she urged him to take his departure without loss of time.

"I am afraid," she said, "that when those men take back the news to young Heathingdon, he will return with them to convince himself that they have not given him a false report. He is most inveterate against you, Guy, and, should you again come face to face, I fear lest his violence may urge you to take his life."

"No, no; he will be safe enough for me at present," said her husband. "I would take no man's life, unless driven to it by desperation; but he must beware how he again insults you with his infamous proposals, for, should it come to my ears, I would come down to have my vengeance, even if I was sure that it would lead me to the gallows."

"For my sake, Guy,—for the sake of your child,—let no rashness bring you near this place again."

"That will depend on the young squire's conduct."

"I do not believe he will ever attempt to annoy me again," replied Jane Harrowby. "A report of what has already passed cannot fail to be spread abroad, and he will hesitate ere he again exposes himself to the derision and scorn of all the neighbourhood. Nay, should he ever come here again, I will see Colonel Heathingdon, and claim his protection against the infamous designs of his son."

"I know nothing about what sort of a man Colonel Heathingdon may be," said Guy; "but, if he has any spice of the son about him, I should say your dependence on him would be slight, indeed."

"Colonel Heathingdon bears the character of being a kind and generous-hearted soldier," answered Jane. "Besides, he belongs to an honourable profession, and surely it is not to be supposed that he would encourage his son to pursue a course that, in his own mind, he must know to be unworthy the station he fills."

"Well," exclaimed Guy Harrowby, "if the colonel is the sort of man you say he is, I can leave you with more confidence than I thought for. And yet what need is there for the colonel's interference, when I myself ought to be your protector?"

"But you cannot," answered Jane; "for your return here would most certainly end in your own destruction."

"Better that than leave you to be insulted by a dastardly young libertine like him," exclaimed Guy; "I've no mind to throw away my life foolishly, but hang me if I can rest quiet after the news that he has been at any of his dirty tricks again."

"Let us speak no more upon a subject that angers you so," cried Jane, imploringly; "indeed, Guy, every moment that you remain here lessens your chance of escape; go—leave me at once, and my prayers shall be offered up to Heaven for your deliverance from danger."

"Prayers for me, Jane!" he exclaimed, with a wild laugh; "do you think Heaven would listen to your supplications when they are made in behalf of a man that has taken away the life of a fellow-

creature. But I see this affects you, Jane; so, kiss me, girl, and I will then away to seek my destiny once more in the wide unfriendly world."

"Will you not say farewell to our little one?" asked Jane, leading him towards the bed on which the child slept. "Kiss him, Guy; but do not wake him, for he is young, and might say something in proof of your having been here after those men left the cottage."

Guy Harrowby stood gazing upon the unconscious boy, and a tear started to his eye as he reflected that he must be a wanderer from those he loved. But the weakness—if such it may be termed—was instantaneous, and, wiping the moisture from his eye, he pressed Jane convulsively to his heart, as he was about to leave her, perhaps for ever. The sorrowing wife supported herself as best she could, but her heart was too full for utterance, and, as he rushed frantically from the door, the unhappy woman sank, despondingly, and almost without consciousness, into a chair.

Leaving this scene of sorrow and desolation, we must now return to Charles Heathingdon, who gave way to the most furious threats and exclamations when the men brought him back the news that they had been unsuccessful in their search after Guy

Harrowby. As for Rumble, the constable, he stood in a state of stupified surprise as the young squire gave utterance to the fullness of his wrath. At length, on recovering himself a little, he said,—

"Upon my life, sir, I don't know what more we could have done than search the cottage and neighbourhood in every part where a mouse might have hid itself. But it's always the case where people do their best, for ——"

"Silence, prating fool!" exclaimed Charles; "or, if you must speak, let it be to tell me, if you can, which way the scoundrel went."

"Can't say a word about that, sir," said the constable, shaking his head sagaciously.

"What! did you make no inquiry, then?"

"It would have been of very little use if I had," exclaimed Rumble, "for the woman was determined not to give us any information about her husband."

"Did you hear nothing that might afford me even the slightest clue?" inquired the young man.

"Why, I think she said something about his finding a hiding-place in London," replied the constable. "She certainly did throw out a hint of that kind, your honour; but who can place any confidence in what she says, when she may have done it only to set us all on the wrong scent?"

"I am not quite so sure of that," exclaimed Charles Heathingdon. "London is the most likely place he would go to for concealment, and thither I'll follow him."

"What! to-night?"

"No, in the morning. I'll have daylight to assist me, and, if I meet with the scoundrel, I'll never lose sight of him till I leave him bound hand and foot in the county gaol!"

He then dismissed the man, and afterwards desiring the groom to be sent him, ordered that a horse should be ready saddled for him by daylight next morning. He then retired to bed without hinting his plan either to his brother or Major Corfield.

CHAPTER V.

THE FLIGHT.—THE ROADSIDE INN.—THE ENCOUNTER.

It was a long time before Guy Harrowby could rouse himself from the melancholy feeling occasioned by his parting from Jane. He had, however, almost instinctively taken the road leading to London, and had proceeded five or six miles on his way, when the quick step of horses behind filled him with dread, lest a pursuit had already commenced. But the moon was shining brightly, so that he would have a good chance of seeing who the persons were, and darting behind a hedge on the roadside, he threw himself on the ground near a small gap, where he might see the passers by without much fear of being discovered himself. Presently the horses approached at a walking pace, for there was a steep bit of hill just at that spot, and he could hear the voices of two men, farmers by their appearance, who were returning home from the neighbouring market town.

"The fellow can't be very far off, at any rate," said one of them, "for I was in the public-house when the constables came back; and, from what they say about the matter, he couldn't have left the house very long before they went to search it."

"I'll be bound he was somewhere about the place, though the precious fool couldn't see him," returned the other farmer. "The chap seems to be used to making his escape, and, if he could outwit the knowing ones over the water, he would not have much trouble to get away from Rumble and the fellows he took with him."

"At any rate, he won't be able to escape for any long time," exclaimed the other, "for I've promised to mention the subject at all the public-houses as I go along, so that by to-morrow morning the news will reach pretty near up to London. The chap knows nothing about that, so, wherever he happens to be seen, he'll be nabbed as nice as ninepence."

Guy Harrowby could gather no more, for at this point of their conversation they had reached the top of the hill, and, putting spurs to their horses, they moved forward at a more rapid rate. The fugitive, however, had heard quite enough to convince him that his route to London was not so free from danger as he had imagined, and, rising from the ground, he began to debate within himself as to what would be the best course to pursue. Return he could not, for that way he was certain to involve himself in trouble; and, as for crossing the country to find some other road, there was a chance of losing his way and exciting attention by making inquiries to put himself right. After some anxious attention had been given to this subject, he determined to pursue the course he had originally decided, and, if any awkward adventure should befall him, to get out of it in the best way he could.

Returning, therefore, once more to the road, he walked on about a dozen miles further, without meeting any one who might be likely to give information in the event of there being any pursuers after him. His object was to reach London before daylight if possible; but he had walked many weary miles ere he reached home, and having partaken of but little refreshment in the course of his journey, he now felt that to proceed further without rest would be impossible. On arriving, therefore, at some corn-stacks that stood near the roadside, he crossed over the stile, and, throwing himself upon some loose straw that was scattered upon the ground, soon sank into as sound a slumber as if neither care nor anxiety were weighing upon his mind. When he awoke, the sun had been up at least two hours before him, and leaving the place where he had found his night's repose, he again took the road, and proceeded onwards, intending to stop at the first place he came to, where the refreshment he needed might be procured. Another mile served to bring him to a house of that description, and having entered the parlour, he called for bread and cheese, and beer, which were brought to him by a diminutive pot-boy, who, he thought, stared at him in rather an unaccountable manner. Guy affected to take but little notice of that, but presently afterwards the door was opened a little way, and the head of a very dirty-faced and dirty-capped girl was seen curiously peering in, as if to assure herself of some fact that had been related to her by the diminutive pot-boy. This somewhat provoked Guy Harrowby, and he was just rising to ring the bell to inquire why he was subjected to such impertinence, when the landlord, a round, burly-looking fellow, came rolling into the room. He also looked hard at his customer, and having satisfied his curiosity, was about to retire as the others had done, when Guy, calling him back, inquired if there was anything very remarkable in his appearance, that himself and his household should look at him with so much wonder.

"Why, as for that," replied the host, " I don't know that there's anything very remarkable; but the truth is, a couple of farmers called here last night on their way home, and told us about a chap— a returned convict they called him—that was supposed to be on his way to London."

" Well," asked Guy, " have you seen anything of the man?"

" No," replied the landlord; " but to tell you the truth, I and my servants were thinking whether you mightn't be the very chap they're making such a fuss about."

" Your suspicion is not very complimentary to a customer, at any rate," exclaimed Guy, tartly. " But, I suppose, if anybody else had come into your house, he would have been liable to the same suspicion?"

" Very likely he might," replied the other. " In a house of this kind, we can't tell who comes in, nor who goes out, and when we hear that queer folks are rambling in the neighbourhood, we're apt to look at 'em all with suspicion, unless we happen to know who they are."

" But without having good ground for your suspicion, you might, I think, spare your customers the insult of taking them for escaped criminals."

" I didn't mean to insult you, sir," answered the host, who now began to think he had made a mistake; " but when we hear that rogues are abroad, it's the duty of every man to lend a hand towards sending 'em off to prison."

" Perhaps," said Guy, who saw that his best chance of escape was to carry the affair off with a high hand, " you think it your duty to give me such a lodging as you have mentioned."

" Not I," answered the other; " I've a right to take your word for it that you're not the man; so, if you like, we'll have a glass at my expense, just to show that we shall not part bad friends."

" I shall take nothing more than I've got before me," said Guy Harrowby; " but, if you really believe I'm not the man you took me for, you will do well not to speak of the affair to any one. If you do, the news will fly, and I shall be subjected to the same sort of conduct at every house I call on my way to London."

"Oh, you *are* going to London, then?"

" Yes—is there anything very surprising in that?"

" Nothing particular," replied the landlord; " but the farmers happened to say the man they spoke of was supposed to be on his way to London."

" And so all persons journeying that way must be suspected as the man that has filled your mind with this most unaccountable notion."

" I tell you, sir, I don't think you are the runaway, now," replied the host. " At first, to be sure, I had a notion of it, because my pot-boy and maid-servant came and told me they were sure you was the person the two men were speaking about last night."

" Let me advise you to caution your pot-boy and maid-servant not to make quite so free with your customers," exclaimed Guy. " I saw both of 'em staring at me as if they thought I had dropped from the clouds; but I had no notion that they would make mischief of it that might have placed me in a very awkward dilemma."

" Depend upon it I'll tell 'em what you say, sir," answered the host; " but you can't keep quiet the tongues of folks like them, and I dare say all I tell 'em won't alter their opinion a single jot."

" At any rate you must insist upon their not saying anything about my having been here."

" Why would you be afraid of that if you are not the person I at first took you for?" asked the landlord, peering with a peculiar look of inquisitiveness at his customer.

" Because I do not choose to be put to the annoyance and inconvenience of being taken for an escaped convict," answered Guy Harrowby. " There is nothing very unreasonable, I should imagine, in wishing to avoid being placed, though for ever so short a time, in an unpleasant situation."

" Why, that's true enough," said the other; " but I should think a very few minutes would serve to convince people that you are not the person they take you for. However, as you don't seem to be the chap, I wonder what the devil has become of 'em, for we had no one here, either last night or this morning, but people that we knew."

" He's got to London long before this, I'll be bound," replied Guy Harrowby. " Of course, he was well aware that there was a hue-and-cry after him, and, if he wished to escape being taken, the only place where he might consider himself safe would be in town, where there's thousands of places to hide in that would never be thought of by people that were looking after him."

"Well, I've heard there's some queer hiding-places in London for rogues that want to cheat the gallows," exclaimed the landlord. "But you, I suppose, sir, like myself, only knows of such matters by hearing?"

"That's all," replied the other; and, drinking the remainder of his beer, he paid the host for what he had had, and immediately afterwards took his departure. As for the host, he was completely deceived by the apparent frankness of his late guest, and happening to meet the pot-boy as he was returning to the bar, he thought proper to lecture him upon the impropriety of his conduct.

"I'll tell you what it is, young shaver," he exclaimed, giving the hopeful youth a smart box on the ear, "if ever I catch you talking against my customers again, you and I shall have a word or two of a sort together, I can tell you."

"I never said nothing agen the gen'l'man," blubbered the boy.

"Well, if you didn't say anything, you went and looked hard at him, and he didn't seem to like it."

"I only looked at him because I thought he might be the chap they were talking about last night."

"And so, I'm to lose my customers because you think proper to have all sorts of queer notions about 'em," exclaimed his master. "But I've warned you not to do the like again, for if you do, we shall burn the writings, as sure as your name's Bill Spriggs."

The boy almost shrank into his leather highlows as this threat was uttered, and most grateful was he at the appearance of his fellow-servant, for the wrath of his master was now turned upon the offending housemaid.

"And you, too, Mary," he said, "must do all you can to offend your master's customers and send them where they can be treated with more civility."

"Me, sir!" cried the girl—"me offend your customers! Well, I like that, for I should thank anybody to tell me who I've been offending!"

"Why, the person that was just now in the parlour."

"He was a nice sort of a person to be offended, I'm sure!" exclaimed the wench. "I know'd him from the first that he was the very chap they was a looking after, and if there's any mistake about it, I'll eat the kitchen-bellows."

"Don't take your oath of that, Mary," said her master, "for you'll find 'em werry hard of digestion, and windy to boot. However, the gentleman, I can tell you, didn't like to be stared at, and it was as much as ever I could do to get him into a good temper before he went away."

"I'll be bound," exclaimed Mary, "it won't matter to you much, whether he went away in a good or a bad temper, for, depend on it, he'll never show his face in this house again."

"Very likely not, after the insolence he has received from my servants," exclaimed the landlord.

"I see how it is, sir," retorted the wench; "you've got tired of me and want somebody else to do your dirty work, so you may take a month's warning, for I'll not stay in a place where I'm to be abused because I happened to look a customer in the face."

"I didn't say a quarter as much as that to master," said the diminutive pot-boy, "and he gave me a precious punch of the head!"

"And you'll have another in about a minute, if you don't vanish, you young scoundrel!" exclaimed his master; and he was just preparing to make a spring at the boy, when a horse came clattering up to the door, and the rider, throwing himself from the saddle, came bustling into the house. The landlord's ire immediately evaporated, and he stood smirking and rubbing his hands, till the stranger, who was no other than Charles Heathingdon, ordered a glass of sherry, which was immediately supplied to him.

"I am on rather an unpleasant business to-day, landlord," he said. "In short, I am in pursuit of an escaped criminal, who, there is good reason to believe, has taken this road on his way to London. Have you seen any person that you should think likely to be the man I want to overtake?"

"No," replied the host, thinking of his late visitor, but afraid of committing himself by speaking of him.

"I'm sure you have," said the maid of all work, determined to be as provoking as she possibly could. "There was a chap in the parlour just now," she added, speaking to Charles Heathingdon, "and I thought, when I saw him, it must be the man that had run away from Bottomless Bay."

"You have heard, then, of the circumstance of such a person having been in the neighbourhood?"

"Oh, yes, sir; we heard of it last night," exclaimed the host, looking daggers at his female domestic, to stop her tongue if he could. "We had a couple of men here last night on their way home from market, and they told us that there was a rare to-do in the town they had come from about some chap that had returned from transportation before his time, and was supposed to be on his way to London."

"What sort of a man was it that your servant says went away from here a short time ago?" demanded Charles Heathingdon, eagerly.

" Humph ! a trifle bigger than yourself ; but a strong framed fellow, that I should say would be a devil of a chap in a fight, if he hadn't odds against him."

" Did you happen to learn where he was going to ?"

" Oh, yes," replied the landlord ; " I asked him that question, and he told me he was on his way to London."

" It must be the very man I am in pursuit of," exclaimed Charles, striking his fist upon the counter.

" Begging your pardon, sir," exclaimed the innkeeper ; " but, upon my life, I don't think it was the chap."

" And why don't you think it was, may I ask ?"

" Because I put the question to him point blank," returned the host, " and he was mightily offended at it, and declared that he was not an escaped convict."

" Why, you don't suppose he would have admitted the fact, even if he was the person I am after ?" said Charles Heathingdon. " However, it's unfortunate, too, that you did not contrive to detain him here a little longer ; for I intend to give fifty guineas to the person who may be the means of surrendering the criminal up to justice."

" Fifty guineas !" exclaimed the maid of all work, throwing up her hands and eyes with astonishment. " To think, now, that I shouldn't have locked him in the parlour, and set John the ostler to watch at the window, armed with a pitchfork. Well, I never was so near being rich in all my life before !"

" You say, I think," said Charles Heathingdon to the landlord, " that he took the road to London ?"

" Yes, sir, that's the way he went," answered the other ; " and, as you've a horse, I should think you could overtake him about two or three miles further on the road."

" At any rate, I'll satisfy myself," exclaimed Charles. " If there is any mistake, I shall at least be satisfied ; but, should it prove to be the man I am in search of, the trouble I have taken will be more than repaid."

" I think, sir, you had better give your horse a little time to rest," said the landlord, who always had a shrewd eye to business. " You seem to have rode him very hard this morning, and, even if you give the person you are after another half hour, you'll overtake him long before he gets to London."

" I'll wait a few minutes, at all events," said Charles, " for the scoundrel is now within my reach, and he cannot very easily escape my clutches."

" Not if you are a match for him in strength," said the worthy vintner, eyeing his customer from top to toe. " He's as strong as a lion, I'll be bound, and, judging from the looks of you, sir, I should say there's very little chance of your taking him, if he likes to offer any resistance."

" I have pistols," exclaimed Charles Heathingdon, " and, if need be, I will use them, rather than he should escape."

" You must bear him rather an ill feeling ?"

" And not without reason," answered Charles. " However, there is no occasion to enter into any explanation upon that matter, for I have now a clue to him, and, even if I have to follow all the way to town, I'll never give up the search till he is safely handed over to the custody of the police."

" Now don't you think it would be better to turn back, instead of pursuing him all the way to London ?" inquired the master of the house. " I've been told there's some queer dens there, and you may happen to get drawn into a trap that you'll never be able to get out of alive."

" I'll take my chance about that," exclaimed the young man. " Before setting out, I knew well enough that there was a good deal of danger to run ; so, as I told you before, I took care to arm myself, in case there should be a desperate resistance."

" But if he is armed, too, I'm afraid the odds would be a great deal against you, sir."

" I shall see how that's likely to be," said Charles ; " and, if there seems to be a likelihood of my being overmatched, I'll apply for the assistance of the police, and then there will not be much fear of his getting the best of me."

" You'd better take 'em whether or not," observed the landlord ; " for there's nothing like being on the safe side, and, somehow, I've a notion that this matter won't turn out quite so easy as you seem to expect."

Charles did not think proper to make any reply to this, and, throwing down the money on the counter, he left the house, mounted his horse, and rode off in pursuit of the fugitive.

" There'll some mischief come of this, or I'm a Dutchman," exclaimed the landlord, after he had watched his late customer as far as he could see him. " He seems to be a hair-brained fellow, and t'other one is not the sort of chap, I think, to knock under without making a desperate resistance."

" Perhaps," said the maid of all work, " you won't think me so very much out, when I give an opinion about people ? I knew well enough that the first chap was a bad 'un, but you wouldn't believe a word of it till t'other one came in and told you he was the man that was running away."

" Keep your tongue quiet, hussy, will you ?" exclaimed her master. " We don't know that the young gentleman was right ; and, it is my opinion, after all, that when he overtakes the man, he'll find out his mistake."

" But I don't think anything of the sort," answered the girl ; " for the man that came in first

was offended at our looking at him; and, if that ain't a proof of his being no better than he ought to be, I don't know what is."

"Well, we shall know all about it by-and-bye, I suppose," said the host, "for it's most likely the young gentleman will make a stop here as he goes back, and then we shall hear what happened when he overtook the person that he's taken it into his head is an escaped convict."

"As for the first chap, I shouldn't mind what happens to him," exclaimed the girl; "but t'other one seems to be a real gentleman, and I should be sorry if any harm should befal him when they meet."

"He must take his chance about that," said her master; "and, if he should get the worst of it, it will be his own fault, because it's my notion he ought to have left the pursuit for those that are paid for thief-taking. But I can see how it is; there's a bit of private revenge in the matter, and he's a mind to run a risk that he'll be sorry for afterwards."

"Maybe he has good reason for wanting to be revenged."

"And pray what business have you to give any opinion about the matter?" demanded her master. "You forget your place, girl, and chatter about things you know nothing about; so now go and attend to your own household drudgery, for I expect the gentleman won't be very long before he's back, and I don't choose to have your impertinent observations when I'm talking to my customers."

The girl eyed him as if she didn't mind him much, and then went away muttering and grumbling to herself.

We must now turn our attention to Guy Harrowby, who, on leaving the house, pursued his way, reflecting how he should act in the event of any one following him. At all events, a stout resistance he was determined to make, and having no other weapon in his possesion, he plucked a heavy stake out of the hedge, and using it as a walking-stick, he proceeded on his way pretty confident that he had now nothing to fear, unless he should happen to be overpowered by superior numbers. Three miles he walked, and nine more would bring him to London, which he intended to enter after nightfall, so that he might avoid, as far as possible, all chance of being recognised by those he had most reason to dread. But, in the midst of this fancied security, he was startled by hearing the quick trampling of a horse behind him, and instinctively he foresaw that some peril was about to befal him. Turning his head, he saw a horseman approaching him at full gallop, and that glance, brief as it was, convinced him that the person in pursuit was no other than Charles Heathingdon. And now a desperate resolution seized him to defend himself till the last; but as the road was no place for a conflict of that sort, he leaped over a stile hard by, and placing his back against a tree, poised the heavy stick in his hand so as to be ready, should the other venture to make an attack upon him. In another minute Charles Heathingdon, who had observed him, came riding furiously up to the stile, and, having fastened the bridle, he then advanced towards the fugitive, his countenance expressing the most furious rage.

"Villain!" he exclaimed, "I have at length overtaken you, and we will not part till I have surrendered you into the hands of justice."

"We shall see about that," answered Guy, flourishing his stick; "I have my life to defend, and I will do so whilst I have strength in my arm."

"But I am armed," said Charles, taking out his pistols; "and, if need be, they shall be used to rid the world of a murderer!"

"Have a care how you provoke me too far," exclaimed Guy Harrowby. "Your weapons give you a fancied advantage over me, but the instant you raise them against my life, I will prove to you that, with this good stick, I am more than your equal."

A loud laugh of derision was the only answer Charles Heathingdon made to this warning.

"You laugh at me," exclaimed Guy, resolutely, "but you have yet to see what a desperate man can and will do, when he has his own life to defend. I warn you again not to interfere with me, so that whatever harm may befal you, after this caution, will be through your own fault."

Charles Heathingdon made no reply to this, but advanced to within six paces of his antagonist. He then cocked both the pistols, and was about to present one of them at the head of the fugitive, when Guy, raising his stick ready for action, and preparing himself to make a sudden rush forward, exclaimed,—

"I see you are determined to force me to do what I would gladly have avoided, but again I warn you to quit this place without bringing on a conflict."

"You may well warn me when I have the advantage all on my own side," exclaimed Charles, scornfully. "But it is in vain that you offer any further resistance; for, if you surrender not after I have held up my pistol one minute, you will be a dead man. Now, Guy Harrowby, you understand me, so I have given you all you can expect."

He raised his arm as he spoke, and the pistol was pointed towards his adversary. But Guy was equally upon the alert, and fixing his eyes upon the object before him, he made a sudden bound forward, and, with one blow of his stick, sent the pistol whirling through the air. Petrified by the suddenness of this attack, Charles Heathingdon stood as if entirely unnerved; and, before he could recover himself, Guy had closed with him, and then ensued a fierce struggle for the possession of the remaining pistol. And now the superior strength of the fugitive became manifest; for, after a short time, the pistol, being in his hand, was discharged in the air, and in another moment Charles was extended upon the turf, his adversary kneeling heavily upon his chest.

"Now," exclaimed the latter, "you are convinced, I suppose, that it would have been better to have followed the advice I gave you. You have brought this upon yourself, Mr. Heathingdon, and it could be little wondered at if I were to leave you here a breathless corpse."

"Villain!" muttered Charles, "would you add another murder to the crimes you have already committed?"

"Your life is safe, as far as I am concerned," answered Guy Harrowby. "You shall be free to depart as soon as you please, but I must just have a promise that you will not pursue me any further."

"I will give no promise of the sort," exclaimed Charles. "I have sworn to give you up to justice, and it is not your threats that will prevent me."

"Then I have no way left but to take care of myself," replied Guy Harrowby, and, fumbling in his pocket with one hand, whilst he still retained his hold of the prostrate man with the other, he produced a piece of cord, with which, though not without considerable resistance, he succeeded in tying together the hands of his adversary. This done, he raised him from the ground, and, with another piece of cord, bound him fast to the trunk of a tree.

"Now," said Guy Harrowby, "you have discovered, I should think, that my boast was not a vain one. Your pistols were nothing against my good stout cudgel, and, through your own mad folly, you have placed yourself in a situation that you cannot escape from till some kind friend comes to release you."

"Your triumph will not last long," exclaimed Charles Heathingdon; "for some passer-by will presently set me at liberty, and I will then recommence my pursuit after you with more determination than ever."

"Take care you don't meet with something worse than you have on the present occasion," answered the fugitive. "You seem determined to tempt your fate, Mr. Heathingdon; but, remember, the next time we meet, I may not happen to be in so merciful a humour as you have found me now."

"In future I shall know how to deal with you," exclaimed Charles. "Hitherto I have placed too much confidence in myself, but I shall now apply for the assistance of the police, and hide where you may in London, your place of concealment will soon be discovered."

"And if you happen to be among those that come to take me, your life will not be worth a moment's purchase," answered Guy. "I shall always be prepared for your reception, you may depend upon it, and even the chance of having to die for it on the gibbet won't prevent me from having my revenge upon a villain that would first have destroyed the happiness of a virtuous wife, and then sought to bring ruin upon her husband. However, we understand each other perfectly well by this time, Mr. Heathingdon, so I shall take my leave, and you will have to remain in this awkward situation till some chance passenger or another comes this way to release you from bondage."

"Which will not be long first," answered Charles, almost choking with rage. "Rely upon it I shall soon be at liberty, and that I shall recommence my pursuit with a determination not to give it up till I have accomplished the purpose for which I left home."

"You may as well spare yourself the trouble, then," exclaimed Guy Harrowby; "for I now remember all this part of the country well, and it is my intention to take a route that you will not be able to follow on horseback. So get back to your father's house as fast as you can, for any further pursuit will only get you into a scrape that you may not find it very easy to get out of."

The quick eye of the fugitive now observed a man approaching at some distance off, and, having picked up the pistols, and put them into his pocket, to prevent their being made any use of against himself, he plunged into an adjacent thicket, and made his way through the tangled branches of trees till he reached the other side of the copse. A slight pause for consideration served to remind him of the direction he had to take; and, after crossing three or four fields, he found himself in another road, that of late years had been but little frequented. He now felt himself tolerably safe from pursuit, and laying himself down under a shed, he determined to rest himself there till towards evening, and then to enter London, when he was least likely to be recognized.

As for Charles Heathingdon, he was soon aware that a stranger was passing along the road, and as soon as the man came nearer, he bawled lustily to him, entreating that he would hasten to deliver him from the bondage in which he was left. The man hesitated for a moment, as if afraid lest some trick was about to be played him; but, when he saw the helpless situation of the person who craved his assistance, he quickly leaped over the stile, and, with his knife, cut the cords with which the captive had been bound. Delighted at being once more at liberty, Charles gave his deliverer all the silver he had in his pocket, and was hastening to mount his horse, when the man, who followed close behind, inquired if he could render any further assistance.

"No, my good fellow," he replied; "what remains to be done I can do myself; but there is not a moment to be lost, or the scoundrel will escape me after all."

"Were you bound to the tree by a robber, then?" demanded the man, inquisitively.

"Ay," answered the other, with impatience.

"It don't seem that he took *all* your money though," observed the other, looking at the silver he had just received.

"Robbery was not his object on the present occasion," returned Charles Heathingdon. "I was in pursuit of him, and overtook him at this place, when a struggle ensued between us that ended to my own disadvantage."

"And he has escaped, I suppose?"

"He has," replied the young man; "but it will not be long, if my exertions are not made in vain. His place of destination is London, which, though a large place to look in for a criminal, shall not long hide this ruffian from my vengeance."

"Do you know that he has taken this road, sir?"

"I am not quite certain about it," replied Charles; "but, at any rate, I shall be in London before him, and will have officers looking out for him in every direction, so that he will have very little chance of escaping when he enters town."

So saying he rode off at a rapid pace, and the man stared after him till he was lost in the turning of the road.

CHAPTER VI.

OLD QUARTERS.—THE CELLAR.—ATTACK BY THE POLICE.

It was about an hour after the darkness of night had set in, that Guy Harrowby, after threading the narrowest and least frequented streets of Wapping, entered the public-house that we have previously spoken of. Passing by the bar, he gave a nod of recognition at the landlord, and then entered the little back parlour, which, on the present occasion, did not contain so much as a single customer. In a minute, however, he was followed by Doublechalk, who, having closed the door, ask him how it was that he had come back from the country so soon after he had left to visit his home.

"Why, the truth of it is, I found that part of the country too hot to hold me," answered Guy; "so I cut away again, and, after all, had very nearly got into a scrape."

"Did they know you, then?" asked the landlord.

"Yes," he replied; "they knew that the husband of Jane Harrowby had been transported, and I hadn't been in the house half an hour, when my return was known to a man that I have reason to believe will stick to me like a leech."

"Who is he?" asked Doublechalk.

"A young squire in the neighbourhood," answered Guy Harrowby, "who has been villain enough to seek the ruin of my wife, because he believed her to be defenceless."

"How was it you didn't take the life of such an infernal scoundrel?" demanded the landlord.

"You shall know more particulars by-and-by," answered Guy. "At present it will sufficient for me to tell you that I have good reason to believe he has followed me to London, and of course I must find some place where I may hide till it will be safe to show myself out of doors again."

"That will never be, I'm thinking, Guy Harrowby," observed the landlord; "for I needn't tell you, I dare say, that a returned convict can never be safe from the prying eyes of people that are paid to look after folks that have done wrong."

"Has Dick Fordham been here to-day?"

"No, nor either of the other chaps."

"That's unfortunate," exclaimed Guy Harrowby, "for they all of them promised to give me shelter till we could find out how the land lies."

"To tell you the truth, I think you're better without their help, as far as that goes," exclaimed Doublechalk. "Their offer may be all very well meant, but, between you and I, there'd be very little chance of being safe at any of their places, for chaps like them are apt to have police-officers calling in upon 'em every now and then, and if you happened to be seen, the game would be pretty soon up."

"True," answered Guy; "but perhaps you may have a room in this house that I could have for a short time?"

"That would be quite as bad," answered Doublechalk, "for this house is known to be the resort of gentlemen of doubtful character, and very often, when least expected, the officers of justice take it into their heads to search the premises from top to bottom. As for refusing to let 'em do as they please about it, that you know is out of the question, for I should have my license taken away, and then what would my customers do for a place to meet in?"

"Do you know of any person that will let me have the accomodation I ask for?"

"Humph! have you any money?"

"A little," answered Guy Harrowby; "enough, perhaps, to last me, with care, for a fortnight or three weeks."

"In that case," said Doublechalk, "I think you may get a lodging close by here as long as your money lasts. The place belongs to an old hag of a woman, to be sure; but she has a son that has been transported, so, perhaps, she may feel some little pity for you."

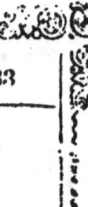

See p. 44.

"Do you think she may be depended on?"

"I shouldn't recommend you to be with her," answered the landlord, "if I thought there was any doubt about that. She's as poor as Job, so I think as long as she gets your money, she'll keep her tongue quiet, and bring in whatever provisions you may happen to want."

"And she lives close by, you say?"

"Oh, yes; quite handy," replied Double-chalk; "just at the corner of the court, about a stone's throw from here."

"But what sort of a place has she got?" asked the other.

"Why, it may not be the most comfortable in the world," answered the landlord; "but any port in a storm, you know, and old Betty Donovan's cellar may be as safe a hiding-place as any other that you could find."

"Is it a cellar she occupies?"

"Ay; you have to go down six or seven steps to it," replied Doublechalk. "She has a couple of underground rooms, such as they are ; and the hard crust she earns is got by selling a few vegetables, that are exposed for sale at the top of the cellar."

"Can I see the woman ?" asked Guy.

"To be sure you can," said the other ; "for I left her at the bar just now, drinking her half-pint of porter. Shall I call her into this room ?"

Guy Harrowby nodded assent, and the landlord went out to perform his commission. In a few seconds afterwards he returned, introducing a most extraordinary-looking personage ; but, whether male or female, it was hard to decide, for the garments belonged partly to one sex, and partly to the other. A torn-crowned hat, partly deprived of its brim, covered the head, and a coat of huge proportions gave warmth and shelter to the rest of her person. From beneath the hat protruded the borders of a regular Irish-looking cap, and under the coat might be seen the garments—though woefully tattered—usually worn by females. She was smoking a dudeen, or short pipe, and rolled forth volumes of smoke as she stood curtseying, and wondering what the deuce they could be wanting with her. At length the landlord took upon himself the task of enlightening her upon the subject.

"Mrs. Donovan," he said, handing her a small drop of gin which he had brought into the parlour with him, "can you keep a secret safe, when you happen to know one ?"

"Can I keep a secret !" she exclaimed, after swallowing the dram. "D'ye think I cannot hould my tongue, then, when a jontleman axes me to be aisy and quiet ?"

"I told this person he might depend upon you," said Doublechalk ; "so he's willing to take a lodging at your place, and to pay you well for it, provided you don't go chattering and talking about it among your neighbours."

"Is the jontleman in throuble, then ?"

"Yes, rather so," answered the host ; "but he is here to speak for himself, so you can make whatever bargain you like with him."

"Does he know that my apartments is underground ?" asked the old woman.

"I understand all that," replied Guy Harrowby ; "and, in my present situation, I am not inclined to stand very particular as to where or how I may be lodged. You have two rooms, I believe, such as they are, and one of them you'll be able to spare for a short time ?"

"Yes, honey, as long as iver you like," answered Betty Donovan ; "but may I make so bould as to ax, sir, what ye want to be burying yourself underground for, instead of showing yourself abroad in the blessed daylight, like an honest man ?"

"What's that to you, you old inquisitive hag ?" demanded the landlord. "This chap's a friend of mine, and, supposing he chooses to keep himself snug for a little while, is it for the like of you to be prying into his affairs ?"

"Axing your pardon, sir," exclaimed Betty, curtseying almost to the ground ; "but I thought if you tould me all about it, I should be the more likely not to say anything that might get him into a botheration."

"Well, then, the truth is, he wants to keep himself snug for a little time from the police," replied Doublechalk.

"Ah ! been taking summat as didn't belong to him ?"

"There's no charge of that kind against me at present," exclaimed Guy Harrowby.

"Humph ! then you haven't much to be afeard on."

"Yes, but he has, though," exclaimed the landlord ; "and as you ain't likely to split upon him for an affair of that kind, I don't mind telling you that he has come home from transportation before his time was up, and if he happens to be caught, they'd send him back again for life, if they didn't do something even worse than that."

"Divil a bit will I harm the poor fellow," returned Betty Donovan ; "for I've a son of my own,—the darlint !—that I should like to see back again ; and bad luck to them as would say a word agin him, if he should iver take it into his head to come back, and see his poor ould mother before she dies."

"That's just what I thought you'd say about it," exclaimed Doublechalk. "I told my friend he might depend upon your doing your best to keep him safe ; and, if matters should all go off right and quiet, he'll not forget to make you a handsome present for it by-and-bye."

"I want nothing more than to be paid for my time and throuble," answered Betty. "If I can keep him safe from the divils that's looking after him, I shall be glad, because it will only be doing as I should wish anybody else to do by my own dear boy."

"Well, all you've got to do, is to let him sit in the back cellar all day," said Doublechalk ; "and at night, after you've shut up shop, he can sit down with you and talk over past grievances. He's got rare adventures to relate to you, old woman, I can tell you ; and, perhaps, he can give you some little notion of the sort of life your son is passing t'other side the water."

"That, I rather think, would be best left alone," exclaimed Guy Harrowby ; "for the sufferings of a convict are worse than people here have any notion about. If they had not been so great I should have stayed till my time was up, and then what troubles and dangers I should have avoided."

"Do they use the lash to 'em ?" asked Betty Donovan.

"Ay ; and most unmercifully too," answered Guy. "A parcel of petty tyrants there have the power of doing almost as they like, and, as they can call anything an offence, a man may be punished when he has had no thought of giving displeasure to those that are put over him. If a man sings, in order to forget his troubles for awhile, he is immediately punished as if he had been guilty of some most dreadful crime."

"The spalpeens!" exclaimed the old woman; "I'd sing, though, if I'd a mind to it, in spite of 'em."

"You'd soon get tired of it, though," answered Guy Harrowby; "for after you have once felt the lash, or even heard the cries of those that are under it, you would feel very little inclination to bring down the vengeance of the tyrants you are made to dread. However, we won't talk any more of that now, for it makes me sick to look back upon the past, and I never do so but when somebody else forces the matter upon my mind."

"Well, then," said Doublechalk, "as the matter has been arranged between you and the old woman, perhaps you would like to go and take possession of your new lodging?"

This suggestion was at once acceded to by Guy Harrowby, and, after the old woman had taken a thimbleful of the "cratur," as she called it, she stepped out of doors, followed by her new lodger, and, after traversing a distance of about fifty yards, they both of them descended a small flight of steps, which led into Betty Donovan's front parlour, as she was most facetiously pleased to denominate it.

"This is the place for your lodgin', an plaze ye, sir," she said, on lighting a very consumptive-looking candle. "You see it ain't quite so nicely furnished as a lord or a duke might want to have it; but it's good enough for an ould Irishwoman, and I've eat my praties here with as good an appetite as some people swallow their venison and their turtle, and other fine things o' that sort."

"What's good enough for you will do equally well for me," answered Guy Harrowby. "Your doors, I suppose, are strong and sound, in case we should have unfriendly visitors, when they are least expected?"

"There's only one door," she replied, "and that's safe enough, barrin' they don't push too hard. It's got a touch o' the dry rot, so I prop it up with the broom handle, and that's as good as a lock, anyhow."

Guy Harrowby was not quite so satisfied about that, and, on examining the door, he found that it was barely sufficient to resist even a moderate puff of wind. He therefore drew a heavy, lumbering table, which he placed against it, and, having made all as secure as he possibly could, he sat himself down by the embers of an almost expiring fire, whilst the old woman busied herself in placing, upon another and a smaller table, the few things that were necessary for the only meal she had it in her power to give him.

"Ye haven't taken tay, honey, I'll be bound," she said, while raking up the embers to make the kettle boil.

"I've had no time to think of taking any meal to-day," he replied; "nor was I wanting anything, till you put me in mind of it by what you've been doing."

"It'll do you a deal of good," exclaimed the old woman, "though it ain't in my power to give it you in tip-top style. But here's a quarther of an ounce of tay to put into the pot all at wunst, and if that don't put fresh life into you, I don't know what will at all, at all. And maybe ye can do without shuggar, for it's too dear an article for the likes o' me; and, as for milk, it spiles the taste of the tay, so I never use it for myself, nor my friends neyther."

"It will do very well, Mrs. Donovan," replied the other. "A cup of tea, as you observe, will refresh me, and, with a slice or two of bread and butter, I shall ——"

"Bother!" interrupted the old woman, "are ye so dainty that ye can't ate your bread without daubing it all over wid greasy butther? By the powers, then, I'm afraid you and I won't keep together long, for them grand sort o' things never find their way down into my cellar."

"Oh," laughed Guy, "never fear that we shall quarrel about that, for I've seen quite hardships enough in life to do without luxuries."

"Oh, but ye'll be wanting meat, maybe, and I never have anything better than praties."

"If we have any while I am here, it shall be at my expense," said the fugitive. "My chief object is to remain in concealment till the pursuit after me grows cool, and then it will be for me to find some other place where they will be still less likely to find me than here."

"Then they're looking after you all this while?"

"I've every reason to believe that by this time my return to England is known at every station-house in London," replied Guy Harrowby.

"You've got some good-natured friend, I dare say, that owes you a grudge."

"I have."

"Then tell us all about it," exclaimed the old woman. "Let's know all about your throubles and misfortins, and then you'll find that an ould Irishwoman will be your friend when everybody else turns a could shoulder on you."

As briefly as possible Guy Harrowby related all that the reader is already acquainted with, and the old woman proved a most attentive listener, never interrupting him once from the commencement to the end of his narrative. At length, when he had brought it to a conclusion, she inquired if he thought young Squire Heathingdon would follow him to town on being released from his bonds.

"I have every reason to feel certain that he will do so," replied Guy Harrowby. "He has sworn to revenge himself for the blow I struck him in my own cottage; and knowing as he does, that I have returned home from transportation, he will get the assistance of the police to hunt me out."

" And maybe they'll be coming here afther you," exclaimed the old woman, with alarm.

" I think that very likely," he replied ; " and it was for that reason I have blocked up your door. It will give 'em some trouble, at any rate, to get in, and while they are doing that, I must make my escape by the back way."

" But there's no back way to escape from," exclaimed Betty Donovan. " There's neither door nor window ; so, if the chaps should happen to come, you'll have to fight your way through 'em as well as you can. Or stay, honey," she added, as a thought suddenly struck her, " there's one way to cheat the divils if you don't mind trying it."

" What's that?" asked Guy, anxious to be prepared, in case of the worst happening.

" Why you must dress yourself up like me, honey."

" What, disguise myself as a woman?"

" That's jist what ye must do," she replied ; and dragging out a large bundle from behind a heap of other lumber, she took from it the articles that would be necessary to complete the disguise. " There's my best gown," she said, " that I've only worn on Sundays for the last seven years ; and there's the cap that belonged to my poor sister Biddy, that's dead and gone, rest her soul ! and there's the ould hat that belonged to Patrick, my son, afore they sent him abroad ; and—and—here's a dudeen to stick in your jaws ; and when you've got all them complete, they'll not be afther knowing you from an ould Irish basketwoman.

" That is to say, if I'm not obliged to betray myself by speaking," observed Guy.

" Och, murther ! ye mustn't be afther speaking at all, at all," exclaimed the old woman.

" What must I do, then ?" asked Guy Harrowby.

" Do !" she exclaimed, " why smoke yer pipe, and roll yourself about as if you'd got a tooth-ache. Leave it all to me, honey, and I'll find a way to get you out of the mess."

" Your plan strikes me as being rather a strange one," said Guy ; " but you mean it all well, I believe ; and if there should be any occasion for it, I'll follow the directions you have given. And yet, if they should come here at all, it will be upon information they have received, and it will not be so easy to deceive 'em as you fancy."

" Only trust to me, and I'll tell 'em a story that should deceive the very divil himself," exclaimed Betty Donovan. Drat the fellows, I hate the very name of 'em ever since they dragged my poor boy away to prison. It was a sorrowful sight for me, I can tell you ; and they never let me see him but three times between then and the time when he was sent over the seas."

" What was the crime he committed ?" asked Guy.

" I never believed that he committed any crime," replied the old woman ; " but there were witnesses that swore hard and fast he was one of a gang of housebreakers, and the judge and jury took their words for it, though they wouldn't believe them that went to give him a good character. The judge as much as told the twelve men, that were sitting there, that they must find him guilty ; so they just put their heads together for a few moments, and when they turned round to say what their verdict was, my senses forsook me all on a sudden, and I fell down almost at the feet of my poor boy."

" Of course," said Guy, " from what you've said, the jury found your son guilty."

" Yes," she replied ; " but, when they told me of it, I was in the yard outside the court-house, and by that time the poor fellow was taken back to his cell. I asked to see him, but they only laughed at me, and I was told that now he was found guilty, I could only see him by an order. And throuble enough I had to get the order, and when I did get it, I could only see the boy when there was another person to hear every word that passed between us."

" Didn't you try to get up a petition for him ?" asked Guy.

" Yes," she replied ; " there was some good souls that stirred themselves, and got a paper signed praying for his pardon. But the great man that it was sent to, took no notice of it, and so he was sent away from me without a chance of my ould eyes ever seeing him again."

" How long was he sent away for ?" asked Harrowby.

" Ten years."

" And how long has he been gone ?"

" Only two ; so it'll be eight more before he come back, and by that time I shall have been laid in the churchyard."

" He may come back, as I have done."

" Ay, and be hunted about for it as you are now," replied the old woman. " It's hard enough to have had him taken away from me for ever, but even that's better than to know that he's skulking about like a thief, and afraid to show himself in the daylight, for fear of being seen."

" Thank'e for the compliment you've been paying me," exclaimed Guy Harrowby. " I know it's a sneaking sort of life that I'm leading just now ; but it's only for a little time I hope, and when once it's safe to venture out of doors again, I'll find some place or other where I may live without fear, and perhaps I may be able to support myself and those belonging to me, by honest labour."

" Oh ! botheration," cried Betty Donovan ; " whoever heard of a man doing well, after he had once been shut up inside of a prison ? People won't give him work, honey, and he's obliged to go and steal, or else starve."

A silence ensued, but it was soon broken by the sound of descending footsteps, and then a loud knocking was heard at the door. No doubt could be entertained that the visit so much dreaded was about to be paid them, and on a sign being given by the old woman, Guy Harrowby slipped on the gown over his other clothes, and then putting on the other articles of female wearing apparel, he lighted the pipe, and, according to Betty's instructions, commenced rolling himself about, as if suffering the excruciating agonies of a raging toothache. Whilst he was thus preparing himself, the old woman was holding a sort of parley with the persons without.

"Och! bad luck to ye!" she bawled out; "what is it you're wanting here with a poor lone widdy woman just when she's goin' to bed."

"Open the door, and we'll let you know what it is we want with you," answered a gruff voice.

"Open the door is it you want me to do?" cried the old woman. "But I can't open it, I tell you, for I've blocked it up to keep out the thieves."

"Then we'll save you the trouble by breaking it open," exclaimed the man.

"Gentlemen, for dear mercy's sake, don't go to do such a thing," implored Betty Donovan. "My poor sister here's got a raging toothache, and you'll be the death of her if ye come hammering and flying about the place in this way."

"D—n your sister and her toothache, too," blustered the other. "We don't want to trouble ourselves about any women, but I rather think we shall find somebody else here that we are looking after."

"There's no one here but myself and my sister, I tell you," answered Betty Donovan.

"Open the door, that we may see," returned the man; "open, I say, or we'll force an entrance without further ceremony."

The old woman now saw that Guy Harrowby had completed his toilet, and as it was vain to hope that the people would be kept waiting any longer, she began slowly to remove the table, muttering all the time she did it, and declaring that she would punish the intruders for daring to come and disturb her just when she was going to bed. At length, however, the barricade was removed, and the door being opened, three policemen entered, and glancing round the room to see if the person they wanted was there, they advanced towards the seat where Guy Harrowby was puffing forth huge volumes of smoke, and rolling about as if suffering the most intense pain.

"Is this the woman that's got the toothache?" demanded the sergeant, looking steadily in the face of the fugitive.

"Yes," replied Betty Donovan; "you see the pain she's in, so don't trouble her to speak, for the poor thing's almost mad with the pain she suffers."

"But she must speak, though," exclaimed the man, "for when we've a duty like this to perform, we're obliged to make everybody give an account of themselves." Then addressing himself to Guy, he said, "Do you always live in this place with your sister?"

A shake of the head was the only reply given to this question.

"What's the use of making these pantomimic signs when you're asked a question?" exclaimed the sergeant; "I must have a plain answer, or you must go to the station-house with us."

"You can't expect her to answer when she's in such pain," interposed Betty Donovan. "Besides, you're looking after some man, it seems, and yet you want to bother a poor female into speaking, though she's been obliged to hold her jaw, as you now see her, for the last three or four hours."

"Well," exclaimed the man, "if she can't answer, you must do it for her, that's all I've got to say about it. We're after a man that has returned from transportation before his time, and we've been told that a person answering his description came in with you not very long ago."

"I don't deny that there was a man," said Betty; "but I don't know who or what he was."

"What did he come for?"

"To buy some praties for his supper to-night," she replied, as soon as she could recollect herself.

"And where is he now?"

"That's more than I can tell you, honey," answered Betty Donovan. "He went his ways as soon as I'd served him, and it warn't likely that I should follow to see which way he went. But he seemed to be a decent sort of chap, and not like one that had ever been transported."

"It's pretty certain you've been deceived though," exclaimed the sergeant, "for there's no doubt of his being the man we are wanting, and if you had only kept him here a little while, there'd have been a handsome reward for you."

"I don't think he's very far off, sergeant," observed one of the men, who had been minutely observing Guy Harrowby, "for, if I'm not very much mistaken, this is no more a woman than I am."

"What mare's nest have you found out now, Bill?" exclaimed the sergeant, turning himself round.

"Why, I never saw a woman with whiskers before," answered the policeman, "and this one has got as fine a pair as ever I saw, underneath the cap."

"Hang me if you ain't right there," exclaimed the sergeant, snatching off the hat and cap as he spoke, and discovering the masculine features of Guy Harrowby. Then, seizing the gown, he with one pull dragged it from his back, and at the same moment, the fugitive threw himself into an attitude of defence.

"You have hunted me out," he exclaimed, "and I have the odds of three to one against me. But I know what my fate will be if you once get me in your power, and rather than yield, you shall carry me out of this place a breathless corpse. And mind, it may be the fate of one or two of you to meet the same fate, if you won't be advised to let me leave this place without further hindrance."

"I say, lads," cried the sergeant, addressing himself to the men under his command, "we mustn't be blustered out of doing our duty by a chap like this. Recollect, there's something for us all, if we lock him up safely; and, if we don't take him now that he's within our reach, we shall all of us be discharged as unfit to be policemen any longer."

"Och hone! what shall I do?" moaned poor Betty Donovan, as the probable consequences of her good nature suddenly flashed upon her mind. "I've been desaved, jontlemen, like yourselves, and thought it was a woman, though ——"

"You thought nothing of the kind, mother Donovan," exclaimed the sergeant, "for you told us it was a sister of yours, and, after all, it turns out to be a man that has escaped from Botany Bay. So it's likely you'll hear something more about this, for the law's precious strict against people that harbour and conceal criminals in their houses."

"Who is there here that knows me to be the person you have said?" demanded Guy Harrowby.

"Why, the description given is enough for us," replied the sergeant. "A gentleman from the country rode up on horseback, and left all the particulars at the chief office, so the news was sent round directly to all the stations, and orders were given to make a strict search for you everywhere."

"But I'll not be taken quite so easily as you expect," exclaimed Guy, collecting all his energies, and making a desperate rush to break his way through the impediments that stood in the way of his defence. The men, however, were determined not to be foiled, and drawing their cutlasses, they were just in the act of pursuing the fugitive, when, on a sudden, the only light in the place was extinguished, and they were left to finish their work in total darkness. But the sergeant was still provided with his lantern, and, having turned this on so as to produce a strong glare, he was again about to commence the pursuit, when a violent blow from a stick laid him prostrate on the ground, and once more all was confusion, uncertainty, and disorder. During this period, brief as it was, old Betty Donovan had been busily employed in securing the retreat of Harrowby, and those who had come to his assistance; and, having effected that purpose to her entire satisfaction, she crawled under the bed, and lay there snugly ensconced, whilst the policemen, after having assisted their sergeant to rise, groped about the place in a vain effort to lay hold of the man who had so narrowly escaped from their clutches. At length, however, she was dragged forth from her place of confinement, and questioned as to the share she had had in the escape; but she solemnly asserted that she had had no hand in putting out the light, and declared that she had seen three men rush down the steps just before they had been left in darkness, one of whom blew out the candle, while the others withdrew Guy Harrowby to the further corner of the cellar.

This story was but a lame one for the policemen to carry back; but, as it was plain the prisoner had escaped, they had no alternative but to make the best of it they could. After a brief consultation among themselves, it was agreed to leave the old woman behind, as she might happen to blab things that would not be to their own advantage.

CHAPTER VII.

HIDE AND SEEK.—THE PATROL.—THE DESERTED MANSION.

ASSISTED by Betty Donovan, as we have before observed, Guy Harrowby and his companions escaped from the cellar whilst the police were in all the confusion and uncertainty which had been produced by the sudden darkness. The old woman went with them no further than the bottom of the steps, on reaching the summit of which they found a crowd of persons collected, not one of whom, however, had the courage to venture down, nor to meddle with those who had risen from the darksome retreat, though some were clamorous in their inquiries to learn the cause of the uproar which had excited so large a share of their curiosity. But the men, of whom they would have asked these questions, moved away without making any reply; and, as the noise below soon afterwards ceased, the crowd gradually dispersed, till not one of them remained to satisfy the curiosity which but a short time before had been so strongly excited.

In the meantime, Mike Rowley and his companions—for they were the persons who had afforded such seasonable assistance—hurried Guy along all sorts of bye-places, till they reached a solitary and deserted-looking spot, known as the Isle of Dogs. Here they paused to take counsel as to their future proceedings, and for the first time Guy heard the voices of his deliverers since they had left the scene of strife and contention.

"I'll tell you what it is, Master Harrowby," exclaimed Mike, "you had almost got yourself into a pretty scrape in that cellar, for, if we hadn't released you as we did, there'd have been nothing less than the gallows for you."

"Why, as far as numbers went, I certainly had but a queer chance of it," answered Guy. "I had, however, made up my mind to struggle till the very last moment, and it's likely enough that they'd have carried me out a stiff 'un, and then there'd have been an end of all my troubles at once."

"Luckily we saved 'em the trouble of doing that," said Sam Snatch; "and, if you can only manage to get on board a ship, you may land at some place or another, and laugh at those that are so anxious to hunt you back to your old quarters."

"Where are we now?" asked Guy, looking around him.

"In the Isle of Dogs," answered Mike Rowley. "It's a place where you may walk about a long time without meeting any body; and yonder lies Blackwall, where you may find a ship ready to sail, and a life at sea for two or three years will be better than stopping on land, with a chance of getting scragged for that affair over the water."

"There's no occasion to remind me of that now," exclaimed the fugitive; "for it's quite enough for a man to have one trouble upon his mind, without being told he can hardly move or step but what he's in danger."

"Why, it's all for your own good that I do it," returned Rowley. "There's no disguising the truth, because you happen to know it as well as I do myself; but you seem to linger about England as if there was no other place for you to live in, and I want you to understand that there's plenty of other homes to be found, if you only like to make up your mind to go and choose one of 'em for yourself."

"What did I return home for, but that I loved this country better than any other?" demanded Guy Harrowby.

"And a great deal of reason there is to love it, now that you see the sort of reception that is given you," exclaimed Richard Fordham. "You've had two narrow escapes already, and perhaps the third time you may not be quite so fortunate in getting clear out of harm's way."

"You have not yet told me how it was that you happened to come just in time to serve me, when I thought it was pretty well over with me," said Guy.

"Oh, it was a lucky chance, that's all," returned Fordham. "We went into old Doublechalk's just after you had left, and as a couple of policemen came in and peered about the place as if looking for some one, I took it into my head that they were after you. So I watched 'em a bit, and finding that my notion was pretty correct, I left the house and set myself the task of watching about the cellar to be ready for 'em, in case our assistance should be wanted. Well, I hadn't been there many minutes when three or four of the chaps came in sight, and I hid myself in a corner where I could see all that was going on, without their being aware that anybody had got an eye on 'em. They talked together for some little time, but in so low a tone, that I could not understand a word they said, though I knew well enough all the time that they were talking about you. At last they crept down the steps, and they knocked at the door, demanding admittance; and knowing by that what was to be expected next, I hurried back to my comrades, and we agreed among ourselves to get you out of the scrape, even though we might risk the getting ourselves into one."

"What did you do when you saw them enter the place?" asked Guy Harrowby.

"Why, we crept down and listened to all that was passing," announced Mike Rowley.

"And did you guess the scheme that was going on when the old woman spoke of me as being a sister of hers?"

"We were quite sure that you had disguised yourself," replied Rowley, "and for some time we thought you would not be found out. The toothache seemed to be a capital thought, only you, perhaps, a little overacted the part, as it drew more of their attention towards you, and I've the notion it was the cause of their making the discovery just when everything seemed to be going on so smoothly."

"It was all fate, depend upon it," said Guy. "The part I played might, perhaps, have been a little overdone; but if they hadn't found me out then, my persecutor would have taken care I should not be suffered to rest for any long time together."

"Ah!" exclaimed Mike Rowley, "I supposed it was all through him that the police have been set to hunt you from one place to another?"

"The man acknowledged as much as that," replied Guy; "and it has given me one more reason to hate him as the bitterest foe I have."

"Yet, from what Doublechalk tells us, you had it in your power, not very long ago, to have served him in a way that would have prevented all chance of his ever doing you a mischief afterwards."

"He was bound by my own hands, and utterly in my power," returned Guy Harrowby. "Nay, the very weapons that he had armed himself with against my life, were in my possession; yet I forbore from shedding his blood in the vain hope that he might give up the deadly revenge he has formed against me."

"All I can say is, that your good feeling was thrown away," exclaimed Sam Snatch, "for a fellow like that don't deserve mercy when he happens to be thrown into the power of the man he's trying to injure. I know, if I had been in your place, he would have had a bullet through his heart, just by way of paying off some of the old scores."

"And what would have been the consequence if I had done so?" demanded Guy Harrowby. "Already there are charges enough against me, and had I committed such an act as you speak of, the whole country would have been up in arms against me."

"And then you would have done as you'll be obliged to do now," returned Mike Rowley. "You could have gone abroad, to some place where they would not have given you up, even though your enemies might have happened to trace out the exact place where you were living."

"It's all very easy to preach about what might, or what might not have been done," exclaimed Harrowby. "The truth of it is, I'm placed in a very awkward situation, and to get out of it will require more trouble than I at first thought for."

"That's because you want to turn honest when people won't let you," said Mike. "If you'd keep clear of those chaps, join your old comrades again, and they'll take care not to let you fall into the way of the land sharks. You've seen what was done for you to-night; and that's nothing compared with what they'd do if they could only reckon you as being one of themselves."

"I know all about that," answered Guy Harrowby; "but my object in returning to England was to see my wife, and, if possible, make some amends for the years of sorrow and anxiety that I have caused her. She has heard my plans and approves of them, and whilst a chance is given me of doing something to make up for my past faults, I will not advance another step into guilt. At present, indeed, there ain't much hope for me; but who knows what lucky turn may take place to restore me to the love of those that I have always held most in my esteem?"

"Don't bother him upon this subject now," exclaimed Fordham, "and I'll be bound we shall have him among us again before long. The chap that has followed him all the way up to London is doing the business for us, for by-and-bye Harrowby will find himself in a pretty mess, and then he'll be glad to join us, rather than run the risk of being provided with a lodging in Newgate."

"If I am forced into doing so," answered the other, "the fault will be with those that would not leave me alone when I was inclined to do better things."

"What will it matter whose fault it is if you get hanged?" demanded Mike Rowley. "You know, as well as we can tell you, that nothing will ever take away the liability of being punished for the death of your keeper; and, as I dare say the proof is pretty clear against you, there's only one chance, and that is, that you will have to take your leave of the world on the gallows."

"And pray," asked Guy, "did you assist me to escape just now only to persuade me to pursue a course that I have determined to abandon?"

"It was partly for that," answered Fordham; "and partly out of old friendship. We didn't like to see an old pal in trouble; and to lend you a helping hand out of it, we run a chance of getting into trouble ourselves."

"For which I thank you," said Guy; "but, if you would make the favour greater, you will let me follow my own notions till I find myself obliged to fall into yours. You said just now that there are ships lying hereabouts ready to sail away from England; take me to one of 'em, and I'll offer my services to go a voyage, and, perhaps, by the time I return, there may not be quite such a malicious feeling against me as that which now drives me out of England almost as soon as I had put my foot upon her shores."

"You'd find very little difference as to that, if you were away for twenty years," exclaimed Fordham. "There's blood to be answered for, and the law will never be satisfied till yours has been shed in return for it. However, don't let me persuade you either one way or the other; for it can't matter to us where you go, only we'd rather have had you among us, than see you lost for the want of a little friendly advice, such as we've been giving."

They had by this time reached about midway of the Isle of Dogs, when a horse was heard approaching them at a walking pace, and in a second or two afterwards they were accosted by one of the mounted patrol, who, in a gruff voice, demanded who went there.

"There's four of us," answered Fordham, boldly; for he knew that the least symptoms of hesitation would have subjected them to the suspicion of the man who had questioned them.

"What do you do here at this time of the night?" was the next inquiry put to them.

"Business of our own has brought us here," exclaimed Sam Snatch, rather testily.

"Business! humph! you are up to some robbery, I suppose?"

"Now that's what I call a d—d cruel suspicion of yours," exclaimed Rowley, with apparent simplicity. "We're four chaps just going to join our ship, and you must take us for so many thieves, because we don't happen to be quite so well dressed as some of the folks you meet."

"What makes you out so late?" demanded the patrol. "This is not the time when men generally go to join their ships, and I dare say you've no more fancy for being sailors than I have. What's the name of the vessel you're going to enter in?"

"The Cormorant," answered Rowley, who happened to know that a vessel of that name was lying in the East India Docks.

"Humph! where's she bound to?"

"Bombay, direct."

"What's the name of her skipper?"

"Don't know that," answered Rowley; "for though I heard it when we signed articles, I've quite forgot it now."

"You're a pretty fellow to forget the name of your captain," exclaimed the patrol, turning his lantern so as to direct the light successively towards each of their faces. "You've been telling me just what story you like about yourselves, and if I let you pass on without further questions,

See p. 36.

it ain't because I'm satisfied with the account given of yourselves, but that I've no comrade very near at hand to help me take you all into custody."

"You'll find that's all right, though," said Fordham; "we've told you nothing but the truth, and if you still doubt our words, you've only to go on board the Cormorant to-morrow, and you'll see all four of us among the crew."

This was said as the patrol was again slowly pursuing his way; and glad enough at having got over an adventure that threatened them with so much danger, they hurried on, but took care to diverge from the road at the first turning they came to, lest further suspicions should cause a subsequent pursuit to be made after them.

"What made you tell the man that lie about our going to serve on board the Cormorant?" asked Guy Harrowby, as soon as they had slackened their speed.

"I don't know what put it into my head," answered Rowley; "but I happened to know there was such a ship, and if we hadn't given the patrol a clear, straightforward answer, he might have sprung that confounded rattle of his, and then we should have been all four taken up as suspicious characters."

"And that wouldn't have been quite the thing," observed Sam Snatch; "for it might have led to inquiries into our characters, and then there's no telling where the mischief would have ended."

"Especially as far as you are concerned, Guy Harrowby," exclaimed Fordham. "You must keep out of such scrapes as those, or there'll be a terrible explosion before long."

"At any rate," said Guy, "this will put an end to my scheme of going to sea at present, for this meeting will be talked of among the police, and if any inquiries should happen to be made on board the Cormorant, it will at once prove that we have given a false account of ourselves, and then all sorts of suspicions and evil rumours will be raised against us."

"That's true enough," returned Mike Rowley; "the only way will be to think of some other plan for hiding yourself for the present."

"It's easier to talk about than to do," exclaimed Guy. "Twice already I've been hunted, and driven out from places where I thought myself safe; and now, I don't know of a hole or corner to creep into without the certainty of that infernal villain finding me."

"If he comes near where I am, he'll be likely to have something that will spoil his mischief-making for ever afterwards," exclaimed Mike Rowley. "However, if you want a hiding-place for a short time, Guy, I think I know of a crib, close by, where you may be safe, if you'll only keep yourself in-doors till we find out some place that will suit you better."

"Where is it?" asked Harrowby.

"A little further a-head," replied the other. "It aint very inviting to look at; but I've thought several times, that if a man wanted to hide himself, that would be just the place where he would be most secure."

They walked on in silence about five minutes longer, and then arrived at an old dilapidated building, standing quite by itself, and seeming, from its desolate appearance, as if it had been deserted from some superstitious feeling or another. They entered a sort of courtyard, through a gate that had fallen from one of its hinges, and passing round to the rear of the building, Mike Rowley opened a window that belonged to a small room which seemed once to have been used as a pantry, and having made his own way through, he desired his companions to follow him without fear of meeting with any one.

"Where the devil have you brought us now?" exclaimed Fordham, as he tried to penetrate the darkness with which they were surrounded.

"I don't know much more than you do about the place," answered Rowley; "but I've heard that the estate has been some years in Chancery, and the house has been suffered to fall into decay till it's almost ready to tumble down of its own accord."

"Don't anybody live in it?" demanded Sam Snatch.

"A pretty place it is to live in, to be sure," returned Rowley. "Why, there aint a room but what has nearly all the windows broken; and, I believe, even the rats and mice have made themselves scarce, because they found there was nothing to be got to eat, unless they could turn cannibals, and feed upon each other."

"Then how do you suppose I am to live in such a miserable place?" asked Guy Harrowby.

"Because beggars mustn't be choosers," answered the other; "and, I think, you may manage to stay here till we can look out for something a little more comfortable. At any rate, you can do as you like about stopping here, for if you like to run the risk of it, you may stay at my lodgings for a few days."

"This place shall do for me to-night, at all events," replied Guy Harrowby; "and, perhaps, when I see my lodgings by daylight I may form a better opinion of them than I have at present."

"Why, there's one thing to be said," observed Sam Snatch; "it aint very cold; and even if some of the windows happen to let in the wind, it aint so bad as sleeping all night under a hedge. For my own part, I shouldn't mind staying here, if it wasn't for the thought that it may be haunted by evil spirits."

"People about this neighbourhood say it is haunted," replied Mike Rowley; "but, for my own part, though I slept in it one night, when I happened to be in want of a lodging, I neither saw nor heard anything that a man need be afeard of."

"I myself shall have no fear of ghosts or hobgoblins," said Guy; "and as for the report in the neighbourhood of the place being haunted, it's all the better for me, since, I dare say, no one ever ventures to come within a respectful distance of it."

"I never saw any one near it," exclaimed Rowley; "but even if you should happen to be disturbed, you'll only have to act the part of a ghost, and they won't stop long to trouble you with their company."

"But how am I to get food here, since it won't be safe for me to show myself out of doors?"

"That's the worst part of the business," said Rowley, "because there'd be a consternation in the neighbourhood if anybody should be seen entering a house that everybody shuns. So I shouldn't be able to bring you anything to eat till to-morrow night, and that's rather too long a time for a hungry man to wait."

"Oh, I'll manage to come in the morning without any one seeing me," exclaimed Sam

Snatch. "I'll be here a little after daylight, and stay till it gets dark, so you'll have company some part of the time, and I shall not run any risk of being seen by any of the people in the neighbourhood."

"That'll do," said Mike Rowley; "so, now, follow me, and I'll take you to a room where I slept, and where, I'll be bound, we shall find the heap of straw that I laid in, just as I left it."

Following the sound of his footsteps, they now moved forward till they reached the stairs, which he recommended them to mount very cautiously, as they were so much decayed as to afford a very uncertain footing. They, however, succeeded in reaching the landing-place, from whence Mike led them into a room, through the broken windows of which the wind blew in chilly gusts. They could not, however, see much of the chamber itself, and Rowley, having found the straw he had spoken of, said,—

"This is the only bed you are likely to have to-night, Guy Harrowby, so you must make the best of it, till we provide you with a more comfortable lodging. In the morning Sam Snatch will come, as he has promised, and, perhaps, by that time we shall have thought of something that will suit you better."

As it was now late, Mike Rowley and his companions took their leave, and Guy was left in all the solitude of that dismal mansion. From the window he watched the departure of his associates, as their dark forms passed through the gate which had given them entrance; and, as the last sound of their footsteps died away, he threw himself upon the heap of damp and mouldering straw, in the hope of forgetting his troubles and anxieties, in sleep.

During that time Charles Heathingdon had not, for a single moment, relaxed the efforts he was making to hunt his victim to destruction. He it was that had given information at the chief police-office, that Guy Harrowby was in London, and no sooner did the intelligence reach him that the officers had obtained a clue to the fugitive's retreat, than he hurried away to witness the capture of the man whom he had vowed to sacrifice to his feelings of revenge. When he reached Wapping, however, he had the mortification to learn that Guy had escaped when within the clutches of the police, and that there was little chance of his being immediately discovered. He then set himself to the task of making inquiries, and, from the few particulars gathered, he felt certain that he had obtained a clue, and having previously provided himself other pistols, he forthwith commenced a pursuit, taking the very same route that had been pursued a short time before by Guy Harrowby and his companions. Even the cheerless place in which he very soon found himself did not deter him from the object he had in view, and he proceeded onwards till met by the same mounted patrol whom we have before mentioned. The man stopped his horse, and demanded who he was, and whither he was going.

"My name, I take it, you have no right to ask," returned Charles, haughtily; "but if you must know my business, it is to pursue a scoundrel who has just managed to escape from some of the police."

"Was there only one man?" asked the patrol.

"It is only one man that I want taken," replied Charles; "but, from what I have heard, there is reason to believe that some of his associates are with him."

"Are you sure they came this way?"

"I am pretty certain of it," replied Charles Heathingdon; "or it is not likely I should have chosen so dreary a road on such a cheerless night as this."

"I asked you the question," replied the patrol, "because I happened, about half an hour ago, to meet four men that I thought were not the best of characters."

"Did you speak to them?"

"It's my duty to stop people in this out of the way place, after dark," replied the man; "but all the questions you can put won't get the truth out of 'em, if they've a mind to keep their evil doings a secret."

"What questions did you ask these men?"

"Why, I wanted to know what caper they were up to, and they told me they were sailors going to join their ship; but a greater set of land lubbers I never happened to see. To be sure they might be going their first voyage, and as a good many chaps go this way to the docks, I let 'em pass on, because there didn't happen to be anything that I could take 'em into custody for."

"Did you take any particular notice of them?"

"As far as the light of my lantern would let me, I did," answered the patrol; "but I don't remember ever having seen any of 'em in trouble."

"The man I want to find," said Charles Heathingdon, "is about my own height, though stouter, and perhaps six or seven years older. When I saw him last he had remarkably thick whiskers; but he may have had them shaved off, to prevent a discovery taking place."

"One of the men I saw had very thick whiskers."

"Did he speak in a harsh voice?"

"He didn't speak at all, sir," replied the patrol; "for one of his companions took it upon himself to answer pretty well all the questions I asked."

"Yet for all that," exclaimed Charles, "I feel certain the man I am in search of was among those you met. Did you happen to ask what ship they were going on board?"

"Yes; and they told me it was the Cormorant, bound to Bombay."

" Is there such a ship going to India?"

" I've heard there is, sir, and that was one reason why I let the men go on their way."

" At any rate I'll satisfy myself as to the truth of their story," exclaimed Charles Heathingdon.
" What is the nearest place to the docks that I can get a bed at?"

" Poplar."

" And, I suppose, in the morning there'll be no difficulty in getting on board the Cormorant?"

" Not the least," replied the patrol; " but you must not let any of the sailors know what you are
going about, or they may find means to give you a ducking in the water."

" I suppose I can see the captain?"

" I don't think it very likely the skipper will be on board," answered the man; " because he has
very little to do with the lading of the vessel, and he seldom takes charge of her till she gets down to
Gravesend. If you want to see him particularly, sir, I think you'll have the best chance of meeting
with him there."

" It will scarcely be worth my while to do that," said Charles; " because there will be some one
on board that will be able to answer the few questions I have to put. Besides, I shall have an opportunity of looking about me; and if I should see the man I am in search of, the object that takes
me there will have been accomplished."

" Is the chap a thief, sir?"

" He is a returned convict."

" The devil! and I let him pass on when it was my duty to have made him my prisoner."

" To effect his escape from abroad," exclaimed Charles Heathingdon, " he murdered the unfortunate man that was set to guard him, and a large reward has by this time been offered by government for his apprehension. You have, therefore, lost an opportunity that would have put a handsome
sum of money in your pocket."

" I'll see about him as soon as I'm off duty to-night," exclaimed the patrol; " and if he don't
come under my clutches before many hours are over it will be no fault of mine."

Charles Heathingdon then passed on, all the better satisfied that he had secured the co-operation
of another in the task he had voluntarily taken upon himself. The rest of the way was cheerless and
desolate in the extreme, for the road was dark, and not a person crossed his path till he entered
Poplar. Here it was some time before he could find an inn to suit him, but at length he went to bed,
and dreamed of the revenge he was so anxious to secure.

———

CHAPTER VIII.

THE CHEERLESS MANSION.

WE left Guy Harrowby just when he had thrown himself upon his comfortless bed to obtain, if he
could, a brief respite from the harassing thoughts that afflicted him. But his mind was too full of
uneasy reflections for sleep to visit his aching eye-lids, and for more than an hour did he toss himself restlessly, from side to side, invoking the god of sleep, but invoking in vain. At length he fell
into a feverish slumber, in which dreams visited him that were worse even than his waking thoughts.
Home and wife were present to his imagination, and the dread came over him that Jane was again
in the power of the libertine. Two or three times he awoke, and could scarcely convince himself that
all which had just passed was not real; but again he fell asleep to be harassed with the same visions,
and just when he fancied himself rushing forward to grasp the seducer by the throat, he awoke and
was startled by hearing a sound as of some person pacing to and fro in the apartment beneath him.
He listened, and each moment served to convince him more and more that his ears had not deceived
him. Some one was certainly there, and the question now was, whether the officers had not traced
him, and were searching the place for the object of their pursuit. As he became more collected,
however, he felt convinced that there was not more than one person, and that being the case, he
supposed that some homeless person like himself had sought in that cheerless mansion, a shelter
from the rain that he could hear drifting through the broken window of his chamber. Gaining confidence from this latter suggestion, he would have risen to satisfy himself upon the subject, but as
he was about to do so, a light gleamed in at the open door, and then steps, slow, and apparently
feeble, were heard ascending the stairs, and the light which had at first been feeble, became every
moment more and more strong. It was a period of deep suspense to Guy Harrowby; and, as he
watched with staring eye-balls, he beheld the form of a venerable man slowly advancing along the
passage which led to his room. He was dressed in a loose flowing gown or gabardine, and his beard,
which was of silvery whiteness, descended in an ample mass upon his bosom. Altogether his appearance was ghostlike, and the glaring of his eyes added not a little to his supernatural appearance. In
his hand he held a candle, but he seemed not to be aware of a stranger's presence till he stood within
two or three paces of him, and then a marked and ominous change spread itself over his countenance.

" Who art thou," he exclaimed, in the feeble accents of age, " who hast dared to seek an asylum
within these walls? But I see, murder and all other crimes are written on thy brow, and thou
wouldst here find a shelter from those who pursue thee."

There was so much truth in these words that Guy Harrowby became alarmed lest he had fallen in
with some foe who would betray him. But the wildness with which the words had been uttered,

and the restless wandering of his eyes almost convinced him that the person before him was some maniac who had recently broken from his place of concealment. There was a brief pause, and then the mysterious being addressed him with more impatience than before.

"Why dost thou not answer me?" he exclaimed; "have my words reached thy conscience, or wouldst thou deny that I have uttered truth about thee?"

"I would first know," exclaimed Guy Harrowby, "who it is that questions me, and by what authority those questions are put?"

"My name thou wilt not know," returned the old man, "but that I am mortal like thyself, I believe thou art already inclined to believe. Some would have deemed me the inhabitant of another world, but I see thou art not without courage, and in thy sight I only appear that which I really am. Now, stranger, answer me; why hast thou intruded thyself in this house?"

"It was not of my own accord," replied Guy; "but through the advice of one who knew the place, though by me it had never been heard of before. He had himself found a shelter beneath this roof and brought me hither because I had no other house to go to."

"Nor money to provide a lodging?"

"I have money, it is true," answered Guy; "but all the coin in the world would not procure me the safety that I might have expected to find in this house."

"Then I was not wrong in saying that thou wert hiding thyself from thy pursuers?"

"How know you that?" demanded Guy, eagerly.

"Because none but such would seek for shelter in a place that is reported to be haunted," answered the old man.

"And you, I suppose, are the cause of all the fears that have alarmed the neighbourhood?"

"Yes," he replied; "people have seen lights glancing from window to window at all hours of the night, and their fears have prevented them from visiting the house, in order to satisfy themselves whether there is any real cause for the rumours that have been spread abroad. And 'tis well for me that it has been so, for I hate all mankind, and the presence of a crowd of gaping fools would have driven me from the only place in which I care to pass the miserable days and nights allotted to my existence."

"Then, if I understand your words," exclaimed Guy Harrowby, "my presence here has given occasion for your displeasure?"

"I am not quite sure of that," replied the old man; "for, like myself, you have little cause to be on friendly terms with the world, and for that reason I may, perhaps, hail you as a brother in misfortunes."

"But you just now accused me of having been guilty of murder, and other heinous offences."

"I did," replied the old man; "but what have I to do with that? half the crimes that are committed, are through the cruelty and oppression of one man against another. Evil blood is thus created—revenge fills the heart, and some fearful crime is committed, that never would have been thought of, but for the wrong that was inflicted in the first instance."

"Such, at any rate, has been my case," exclaimed Guy. "My first offence was the killing of a hare, which, being a wild animal, I fancied belonged as much to me as it did to the lord of the manor. But for that I was taken before the magistrate, and fined a larger sum of money than a poor man was likely to have in his possession. Of course the money was not paid, and I was sent to prison to learn vice and profanity from men that had been sent there for crimes far greater than my own."

"And you came out a finished scholar?"

"I came out with a name blasted, and a character that took from me all chance of getting employment from any farmer in the neighbourhood," answered Guy. "I wanted work, but there was no one would give it me, and rather than go like a beggar to ask relief at the parish poor-house, I killed another hare to keep me and my wife from starvation. I was caught in the act—again convicted, and then my imprisonment was just as long again as I had suffered before. When I came out of gaol, all good men shunned me because I had a stain upon my character, that even a wish to be honest and do right, could never remove. Bad men there were enough to flock round me, and driven as I was to desperation, I a third time committed the heinous crime of killing for my own support, that which is as free to us all as the air we breathe. For that third offence I was tried as a felon, and sentenced to be transported from the land of my birth. Ay, sir, they tore me from the only one who had ever loved me; and if, as you say, I have been guilty of shedding the blood of a fellow-creature, who, I ask, drove me to that crime, but the wealthy, hard-hearted man, that first punished me for that which was, in reality, no crime?"

The old man listened to him with rapt attention, and when he had concluded, a silence of some few moments intervened. At length, however, the mysterious visitor again spoke.

"Why," he demanded, "are you seeking concealment, when you have suffered the extreme punishment that the law awards to your offence?"

"Because," answered Guy Harrowby, "I ventured to return before the full period of my banishment had expired. I thought of my wife, and the land where I had passed a happy childhood, and every day the wish to return grew stronger and stronger. I could not acknowledge either, that the offence deserved so heavy a sentence, and at length I determined, even at the risk of my life, to see England and my wife once more. I'll not tell you all that happened to me, nor how I managed to make my escape. It is enough to say that I returned to my native land not many hours since; yet, in that short time I have been hunted and pursued, till I sought a brief shelter in this place. I believed it to be unoccupied, or I would not have entered unbidden the house of one that seems to have seen as much sorrow—though I hope less crime—as I have myself."

"Well," exclaimed the old man, "the place is large enough for us both, though it is fast falling into ruin and decay. You may remain here, because your story has touched my heart, that for years past has felt no sympathy for the miseries and misfortunes of my fellow-creatures."

"I have been plain and even with you," said Guy; "and, if it may be done without offence, I would ask if it is crime or misfortune that has made you hide yourself in this place from the world?"

"I have been sinned against," he replied; "but never wilfully did aught that could in any way injure another. This house, and other large estates became mine on the death of a relative, whose heir I was always considered to be. For five years I was suffered to remain in undisturbed possession, but at length a rival claim was made, and I found myself put to heavy expenses, in order to show a right that no one but my opponent and his lawyers had ever doubted. There was no will in my favour, and the title-deeds had all been either lost or mislaid. This the other party ascertained, and when no other chance remained of speedily settling the differences between us, he threw the affair into chancery, well knowing that I should be obliged to give up possession till a decision was come to. All that I had ever possessed of my own was swallowed up in law expenses, and then, after having lived a life of luxury and ease, I suddenly found myself reduced to the verge of beggary. In the sunshine of my prosperity I was surrounded by fawning, sycophant friends, whose professions had made me believe that they would have sacrificed fortune, or even life itself for me, if it had been needed. But when the darkening shadows of adversity fell upon me, those friends fled from my presence, and never more were to be seen. It was in vain that I applied to them for assistance—they turned a deaf ear to all that was urged in my behalf, and from that moment I took that bitter hatred against the world that never since has left me."

"And did you never see any of those false friends afterwards?" demanded Guy Harrowby.

"I would not have done, even if they had given me the opportunity," replied the old man. "As it was, however, I determined to collect together what little wreck of my former wealth remained, and when that was done, I took a small place in the north of England, where I might live retired from the haunts of my ungrateful fellow-creatures. For nearly twenty years I passed the life of a recluse, and then, all of a sudden, a strong desire came over me to visit once more the scene in which I had passed the only happy portion of my life. I chose the night time for my journey, because I would come in contact as little as possible with the worldly-minded wretches that I had learned to hate, and I preferred performing the whole distance on foot, because I could the better choose my own resting-places, which were generally in barns or other outhouses that happened to be near the road side. Thus I saw men only so far as might be necessary to supply my new wants, and, after about a week's travel, I found myself at length standing before the house, which had once been the scene of all my earthly happiness."

"You are speaking, I suppose," said Guy Harrowby, "of the place we are now in?"

"I am," he replied; "but, oh! how changed was it since I had last beheld it. The suit, which had been commenced in chancery twenty years before, was still pending, and the old mansion was suffered to fall into decay. It seemed to be almost falling, yet, as I gazed upon its tottering walls, a thought came across me that nowhere else could I find a home so welcome to my feelings as that which had witnessed the happier portion of my career. In the neighbourhood I seemed to have been entirely forgotten, for neither young nor old recognised me, and I wandered about, regarded by all people as some madman, harmless and unoffending, but who had escaped the watchfulness of his friends. Such thoughts I was not inclined to disturb, and having heard rumours that the old manor-house was supposed to be haunted, I determined to take up my residence there, and, in order to keep off the idle or over curious, I resolved to practise upon their credulity, and for that purpose, wandered about at midnight with a light in my hand, that I took care should be seen flitting from window to window. In this scheme my success was complete; and, during the fifteen years that I have dwelt here, I have never till this night been disturbed by a visiter."

"Once you have," said Guy Harrowby; "at least, a person told me that he one night had slept in this very room, and from the fact of the straw being here, as he had said was the case before we came into the room, I am inclined to believe it was no vain boast."

"I remember the circumstance, now you allude to it," answered the old man. "I heard a stranger enter late at night, but was too ill to rise and terrify him out of the place by my almost supernatural appearance. He, therefore, remained undisturbed till the morning, when he took his departure, and from that day to the present I have never seen him."

"He was here to-night," said Guy; "indeed it was he who brought me here, and who advised me that I should seek a shelter in the house, as being a more likely place than any other to afford me the concealment that I stand so much in need of."

"And it will be your own fault, if you do not remain here till the search after you is at an end," exclaimed the old man. "We are brothers in misfortune, though under different circumstances; and, since the world chooses to persecute you, I will at least afford you the little accommodation you require."

"Indeed, sir," cried Guy Harrowby. "I cannot give utterance to my thanks, nor ——"

"Give me no thanks!" interrupted the other, impatiently; "for what I do is more from a feeling of revenge against my fellow men than from any real regard for yourself. It is enough for me to know that people desire to ensure your destruction, for it will afford me all the gratification I desire to know that I am foiling the deep-laid schemes of those who aim at heaping ruin upon their fellow man. When I came hither to-night, it was in the hope that my almost supernatural appearance would scare you from the place. You are, however, above those idle fears, and now, having heard your history, I am inclined to give you that slight degree of support that is necessary to prevent the evil machinations of your enemies from being carried into effect."

"I accept your offer," said Guy; "but I ought, perhaps, at the same time to tell you that I expect a friend here in the morning to bring me food for my support."

"Let it be borne in mind then," exclaimed the old man, "that nothing must be said to him to remove the impression which has gone abroad that this place is haunted. Rather increase the notion, if possible, and when he asks, as most likely he will, if you have seen anything of the goblin, you may describe me to him, according to your own impressions, when first I met your sight."

"I will take care to do as you have said," answered Guy; "but there is one other question that I would ask, if you have no objection to answer it; how do you manage to obtain provisions for your support, when it seems that for fifteen years you have never left this house?"

"I do it," replied the old man, "by means of a youth who is faithful, and has ever kept my secret, though questions are constantly being put to him why he pays such frequent visits to the old ruined manor-house. Blanco, as he is called, is twenty years of age, but he is a dwarf in stature, and the crookedness of his body has imparted some of its qualities to his mind. But he is faithful to me, and the natural ascerbity of his temper is a good warranty that he will not be tempted to gratify the curiosity of the world by talking either of me or the reason that brings him here so often."

"But may I depend upon his being equally faithful in keeping *my* secret, when he knows that I am here?" demanded Guy Harrowby.

"I have only to caution him, and he will faithfully obey my wish," answered the recluse. "You must, however, continue to have provisions brought by your own friend, or suspicion will be excited in his mind that in no very long time will end in a discovery of your not being alone in the house."

"Perhaps," exclaimed Guy Harrowby, "it may be so contrived that your dwarfish attendant will not know of my having sought refuge here."

"It may be so contrived, certainly," answered the old man, "for we shall occupy different parts of the house during the time you remain here. Society I would avoid, for though your story has interested me so far as to offer you an asylum, I would still remain in solitude, except at night, when I may occasionally visit you as I have now done."

"May I inquire," said Guy Harrowby, "what part of the house you occupy?"

"A small room on the ground floor," answered the misanthrope; "which I have contrived to make habitable, though it has not one of the comforts which my age and infirmities require. When people approach, and I have reason to believe they mean to enter the house, I retreat into a vault-like cellar, beneath the building, and there I remain till the well-known footstep of Blanco assures me that I may ascend in safety."

"And will nothing tempt you to return to the world where you may obtain those necessaries which your solitary life deprives you of?"

"No," he replied; "here I have fixed my resting place, and here I will remain till death releases me from a world that I have learned to execrate and despise. But enough of this; I will now leave you to take the rest that I have broken, and, perhaps, to-morrow I may return with news for you; for Blanco will hear if there is any rumour of your having sought refuge here, and from him I shall be able to gather information that will serve as a guide to your future actions."

The old man now took up the light, which he had placed upon the floor, and without the formality of a farewell benediction, slowly left the room, and descended the stairs leading to his own room. The mind of Guy Harrowby was too much occupied with his singular adventure to permit him to sleep for some time, but at length he was overpowered with weariness, and he slept soundly, though his dreams led him back to the scene in which he had lately played so conspicuous a part.

When he awoke in the morning, the sun had been up some time; and, rising from his uncomfortable resting place, his first thought was to look from the window, to see if Sam Snatch was coming according to the promise he had made on the preceding evening. The view he obtained, however, was of very limited range, for a high wall surrounded the premises, and beyond that he could only see the tops of distant buildings. Beneath him lay what had once been the garden; but now instead of being gaily decked with flowers and shrubs, the place was choked up with rank and noisome weeds, some climbing the trunks of neglected trees, and others creeping on the ground, and hiding every trace of the gravelled walks which had once meandered through the garden. Altogether the place presented a picture of desolation such as is seldom witnessed in England, where order and neatness are regarded as of such paramount importance.

Leaving the window, Guy Harrowby listened to hear if he could distinguish any sound as proceeding from his strange visitor of the preceding night. All, however, in the place was hushed and still; and though he continued to listen for some time, not a sound was heard that might lead him to imagine the place was occupied by any other person than himself. In about half-an-hour afterwards, however, footsteps were heard, but as he could trace them to a room in the lower part of the house, he imagined that they proceeded from the dwarf, who chose that early hour in the morning, in order to avoid the observations of the neighbours. After some time the person, whoever he might be, left the place, and running to the window, Guy Harrowby could see a deformed youth, of diminutive stature, pursuing his way towards the gate, which formed the only place of access to the house. Having nothing else to occupy himself with, the fugitive remained looking out, till at length he saw his expected comrade cautiously approaching. Sam looked up, and seeing him at the window, quickened his pace, and in a minute or two more entered the room.

"Well," he exclaimed, "you've not been carried away by the ghost, I see; but you look confoundedly pale, though, so I suppose you've seen something to frighten you?"

"I've certainly not passed a very comfortable night," answered Guy Harrowby; "but it's anxiety more than alarm that has made me look pale."

"What! you've been afraid, I suppose, lest people should happen to find out that [you took up your lodgings in this queer old crib."

"There's reason enough for alarm," answered Guy; "for I know there's one that won't leave a stone unturned till he has found out where I'm hiding myself. If I could only be sure that he is gone back into the country, I should begin to think there might be some little chance for me. But I know him too well to believe that, and, I suppose, after all, I shall be doomed to fall by the man who has sworn eternal hatred to me."

"Then you shouldn't have spared his life while he was in your power," exclaimed Sam. "I know if I had been in your place he should never have had a chance of doing me any further mischief."

"I would avoid bloodshed," answered Guy, gloomily. "There's crime enough of that kind already to be atoned for, and even at a risk to myself I will never take the life of Charles Heathingdon, unless we should come to a mortal struggle, and there should be no other way to rescue myself from his infernal malice."

"You know best about that, of course," said Sam Snatch; "so I shall offer no further opinion upon the subject. But you acknowledge having seen an apparition, or something of that kind, and I'm all eagerness to hear what sort of an adventure you met with."

"Be it ghost or mortal," said Guy Harrowby, "the being that visited me last night, came in the shape of a venerable man, with a snow-white flowing beard that reached nearly to his chest."

"Wasn't you terribly frightened?"

"Why, it's no use telling a lie about it," answered Guy, "for I was alarmed when the strange-looking visitor first made his appearance; but, after a time, I plucked up courage, and felt no more alarm in his presence than I do in yours."

"Humph! he was pretty civil then?"

"Tolerably so," replied Harrowby; "though it seems my taking up my lodging here had given him offence, and I thought at first he seemed inclined to insist upon my immediately leaving the place. However, for a ghost, I found him tolerably reasonable, and, after hearing my explanation, he told me I might remain here as long as I may think proper."

"Depend upon it, Harrowby, it's no ghost at all," exclaimed the other, chuckling at the thought of having made a discovery."

"Then what do you think it was?"

"I cannot tell much about that," answered Sam; "but it's likely enough to have been some chap in disguise, that wanted to frighten you; or perhaps it may be somebody that's hiding himself here, as you want to do, and so he thought to get rid of you by making it appear as if the house is haunted."

"If such was his notion, he soon found out his mistake," answered Guy Harrowby.

"May be so; but are you sure he's not some chap that may go and give information about your being here?"

"I believe there's not much reason to be afraid of that," returned Guy Harrowby. "Indeed, be he ghost or mortal, I have faith enough in him to feel pretty certain that I have nothing to fear while I remain in this house."

"How long do you think of staying?"

"That must depend entirely on circumstances," replied Guy Harrowby. "Of course I shall take care to keep a good watch in case of surprise, and if there should be any reason to believe any danger is at hand, I shall be off without giving much notice of my intention."

"You don't happen to recollect then that you've got some cunning devils to deal with?"

"I know all about that, and have prepared myself against their evil designs as well as I can," replied Harrowby. "It will be some time, I dare say, before my enemy finds out where I'm

hiding myself; but, if the worst should happen, I'll rather die in my own defence than be taken to be made a spectacle of on a public scaffold."

"If that's what you'd do," exclaimed the other, "I should recommend you to change your lodgings as often as possible. They'll nose you out else, and then all your boasted valour will prove of very little moment."

"I may not be able to cope against numbers," answered Guy; "but even if the worst should happen, they shall not have the satisfaction of taking me alive."

"What would you do then?"

"Shoot myself with one of my own pistols, to be sure," exclaimed the fugitive. "Charles Heathingdon has, it seems, determined to hunt me out. He may, and no doubt will, succeed in the long run; but never shall he have the satisfaction of sending me to the gallows."

"If you wanted to hinder that," returned Sam Snatch, "you should have sent a bullet through his head when you had him so nicely in your power. However, your conscience wouldn't let you do it, so it now only remains for you to get out of this mess as well as you can."

"He may think better of this when he reflects upon the danger he's running himself into," unswered Harrowby; "twice, already, he has found that I am his superior in strength, and the lesson may not have been thrown away upon him."

"Trust to that, and you'll find yourself woefully deceived," returned the other. "The chap has taken the trouble to follow you all the way up to London, and if he only gets scent of his prey, it's my opinion, he won't give up the pursuit till he has sent you to the gibbet. But I suppose you don't thank me for speaking my mind plainly, so let's drop the subject, and, by way of relief, suppose you eat and drink some of the good things I've brought for you."

While he was saying this, Sam Smatch emptied the contents of his basket upon the floor, and, if the viands he had brought were not of the most delicate description, they were at least most welcome to one who had been many hours without food, and Guy, seating himself upon the floor, afforded pretty decisive evidence of the satisfaction he derived from his meal. A bottle of potent ale was afterwards discussed by himself and his visitor, the latter of whom took his departure, after remaining three or four hours to while away some of the time that would otherwise have hung so heavily on hand.

Being left to his own ruminations, Guy Harrowby began to see clearly enough that his present place of abode would not do for any lengthened residence. The visits of his companions must necessarily give rise to suspicions in the neighbourhood, if they should be seen prowling about, and even if that should be avoided there was danger to be apprehended from the old man who had mysteriously appeared before him on the night previous. It, therefore, seemed to him absolutely necessary that a change of quarters should speedily take place, and it only remained for him to decide whether to go immediately, or remain where he was till he had again seen and consulted his companions. The latter alternative, however, seemed to be the most prudent, and it was finally decided that he should continue in his lurking-place till the return of Sam Smatch on the following morning.

CHAPTER IX.

THE EAST INDIAMAN.—FRUITLESS INQUIRIES.—THE VOLUNTARY WITNESS.

CHARLES HEATHINGDON, whom we left in active pursuit of his victim, commenced his inquiries next day about as soon as he was out of bed, and taking his way towards the docks, he was shown the vessel on board which he hoped to find the man he was in search of. Engaging a waterman, he soon reached the vessel, and having requested an interview with the officer in command, he was taken to the cuddy, where he found the chief mate busily occupied in looking over the written instructions that were to guide him till the command was taken by the captain. Mr. John Bostock was a plain straight-forward sailor, and having desired his visitor to be seated, he finished the perusal of his papers, and then, throwing them upon the table, inquired the business that had occasioned this unexpected visit.

"My errand here, sir, is soon explained," answered Charles Heathingdon, taking from his pocket-book a memorandum which he handed to the officer. "You will perceive that I am in pursuit of a criminal, and the paper I have given you will serve to inform you whether a person answering it has, within the last few hours, entered himself as a sailor on board your vessel."

"I don't know of any such person on board," returned the mate. "Some men, I believe, joined the ship yesterday, and it's likely enough the man you want may be among them."

"Will you allow me to see them?"

"Why, you can do that if you choose," exclaimed the other; "but I don't see much good you'll do by it, because we want all the hands we've got, and I shall not suffer any of my men to be taken away unless upon sufficient cause being first shown."

"Is it not sufficient," demanded Charles Heathingdon, "that I tell you the man I am in search of is a returned convict, and that all who harbour or conceal him will be guilty of an offence that could be punished by a very long imprisonment?"

"How am I to know that what you have been telling me about the man is true?" demanded the mate. "You have brought no warrant with you, I suppose?"

"A warrant is not necessary in a case like this," replied Charles. "He has already been convicted, and if he is on board this vessel, I shall insist upon your aiding me to place him in the custody of the police."

"Insist!" exclaimed the other; "and pray, sir, who may it be that uses so much freedom with a person that he never saw in his life before?"

"My name is Heathingdon."

"Then I must remind you, Mr. Heathingdon," exclaimed the other, "that civil words will best become you when speaking to a person who conceives himself to be at least your equal. We are strangers, and as this interview was not sought by me, I must request that you bring it to a termination as soon as possible."

"You refuse, then, to answer my questions respecting the person I am in search of?"

"The man, I have every reason to believe, is not on board this ship," replied the mate; "nor in short can I see any reason why you should imagine he is here."

"The information I received from one of the patrols has led me to that belief," answered Charles Heathingdon. "He saw and conversed with the fugitive, and from what passed it seems quite certain that he was on his way to offer his services on board this vessel. I have told you that he is an escaped convict, and of course you know enough of the law to be aware that any person harbouring him, renders himself liable to a very severe punishment."

"Your threats, sir, will be little heeded by one who knows the law as well as you do yourself," exclaimed the mate, glancing scornfully towards his unwelcome visitor. "In short, I have no wish to screen any criminal from justice, though I may think proper to question the motives that have made you take so much pains to have this man apprehended."

"It is the duty of every one to assist in a case of such serious consequence as this," answered Heathingdon. "I have good grounds for the course I have taken, and if the fugitive has indeed placed himself under your command, I will not take my departure from the ship till he has been given to the proper authorities."

"Upon my life, sir," cried the other, "this is language that you have no right to use towards one who boasts that his honour is hitherto untarnished. I can assert that no person such as you describe has entered himself on board this vessel, and, even if he had, I should not suffer him to be taken away except by persons properly authorised to act as thief takers. You, I presume, are a sort of amateur in that capacity?"

"Your insults will, upon the present occasion, pass unheeded," exclaimed Charles Heathingdon, almost bursting with rage. "You may conceive that this conduct is honourable to you, but the world will think differently, when it comes to be known that you have aided in the escape of a notorious felon."

"And what think you I care for the world's opinion, when I know that I have done nothing to deserve its censure?" demanded the mate. "Besides, let people say what they may, I shall be far enough off by the time they make themselves busy with an affair that concerns them not; and by the time I return from India, the business will have been forgotten."

"You will hear more of it than may be pleasant, if I live to witness your return," exclaimed Heathingdon.

"In other words, you will take care to revive the subject when I come back to England?"

"I will."

"Then let me caution you to be careful how you excite my resentment," returned the other. "I am rough and ready, like most others that follow my profession, and, in the long run, you will see good cause to repent your interference with a person who is anxious rather to avoid than claim the honour of your acquaintance. Nay, more, I happen to possess a temper not very remarkable for its placidity, and if your stay here is prolonged, it is extremely probable that I may turn you over to the tender mercies of some of the crew, and if that should be the case, you will hardly be likely to reach the shore without a ducking in the water."

"You would deter me, then, from an act of duty, by threatening me with violence?"

"Why, nonsense, man!" exclaimed the mate; "the threat you speak of has been provoked by your own wilful obstinacy. You chose to seek me here, and I have acted with sufficient courtesy till you threw out a pretty broad hint that your revenge would last till my return home. Had the captain himself been on board, you would have had still more reason to complain of the want of courtesy that has been shown you, for he would have ordered your departure from the ship without listening either to your threats or persuasions."

"I am to understand, then, that criminals are to be protected from the moment that they enter on board a vessel?"

"Knowingly, we never accept the services of men of bad character," answered the mate. "You, however, come here on a wild-goose chase, and it therefore is not too much if I refuse to further the object you have in view. In fact, your words prove that there is much private malice in what you are doing, and any discourtesy that you may have to complain of, has been provoked by your own eagerness to secure your revenge."

"I grant that there are reasons for the course I have adopted," exclaimed Charles Heathingdon; "but, were those reasons thoroughly explained, you would admit that I have ample ground for pursuing this ruffian, even though it might be to the utmost limits of the world. The villain struck me to the earth, and never shall I know rest till he has met the death he so richly deserves."

"But, I suppose you gave him cause for the violence you complain of?" observed the other.

"The offence was a mere trivial one," answered Charles. "In short, I became enamoured of his pretty wife, who had no reason to believe that her husband would ever return from the place of his banishment."

"And did the woman encourage your unlawful advances?" inquired the mate.

"On the contrary, she treated me with contempt," answered Charles Heathingdon. "She still retained a lingering affection for the worthless ruffian she had, in an evil hour, pledged her faith to, and I was avoided as if I had been a serpent in her path. But love is not to be so easily conquered, and I resolved to obtain the prize I sought for."

"For which you deserve the scorn and contempt of every right thinking man."

"In the station of life to which I belong," exclaimed Charles Heathingdon, "such trifles are not thought of in the light you imagine. There is something glorious in laying siege to the heart of a pretty woman, and carrying the point you aim at."

"What! if she is already married?"

"Marriage forms no obstacle in matters of that kind," answered the libertine, with cool indifference.

"Then all I can say about it is, that we sailors claim a superiority over you landsmen," exclaimed the other.

"Ay, that's because you are seldom thrown into the society of females," returned Charles Heathingdon. "We have an advantage over you in that respect; and, for my own part, I love the sex so ardently, that I. shall never throw away an opportunity whenever one happens to come in my way."

"Then you will stand a pretty good chance of being either shot, or run through the body, by some jealous husband."

"The chance is one that I am quite ready to risk," exclaimed Charles. "I am no coward, and whenever I may be called upon to meet an adversary, it will be seen that I have no sort of inclination to avoid his anger."

"But will that serve to place you any higher in the estimation of your fellow men?"

"Their estimation I shall never seek."

"Possibly that may be the case," answered the seaman; "yet I should think no one would willingly bring upon himself the scorn and contempt of the world."

"It is a matter of so much indifference to me, that I never bestow a thought upon it," exclaimed Charles Heathingdon. "Even my own father has no control over me, when the conquest of some beauty is in view."

"Then your father can have little reason to congratulate himself upon possessing such a son," exclaimed the other.

"Your opinion is not very flattering to myself," returned Charles, sneeringly; "yet I can listen to it without anger, since the person who uttered it is quite indifferent to me. I shall continue my devotion to the fair sex, and, no doubt, in the long run, I shall add Jane Harrowby to the long list of my other conquests."

"And she, I suppose, is the wife of the unfortunate man you have come to seek here?"

"She is."

"Then I now perceive your motive for hunting him out, and the notion I formed of you is fully confirmed. I have, therefore, only to repeat that he is not on board this vessel, and having given that answer, you will oblige me by leaving with as little delay as possible."

"Beware how you tamper with me," exclaimed Charles Heathingdon, "for I am resolved to capture the fugitive at all risks to myself, and though I may be forced from hence by violence, it will only be to return with officers, whose authority you dare not oppose yourself against."

Against this threat the temper of the mate was not proof, and starting from his seat, he seized his opponent by the collar, and dragged him towards the door. But the other was possessed of no inconsiderable share of strength and courage, and recovering himself from the surprise into which he had been thrown, he grappled stoutly with his antagonist, so that for some few moments it might be doubted on which side victory would declare itself. At length, however, Charles struck his foot against the table, and losing his balance, he fell heavily to the floor. In another instant the sailor was kneeling upon him, and seizing his fallen enemy by the throat, he would have sacrificed him to his fury, had not three or four sailors at that moment entered the cabin, and by main force parted the combatants.

"What's the matter, sir?" exclaimed one of the men to Mr. Bostock, who stood glaring upon his foe as if only waiting for an opportunity to made a sudden rush upon him; "do you want this land lubber thrown overboard, or shall we carry him ashore to learn better manners from his own people?"

"He may give what directions he pleases about me," said Charles Heathingdon, with affected indifference; "but I warn him of the consequences of any violence that may be committed upon me."

"Will you tell me," said the mate, "by what right you have dared come on board this vessel?"

"My purpose you are already acquainted with," replied Charles Heathingdon; "and the object being a lawful one, you shall learn the submission that is due to persons armed with legal authority."

"Your threats may as well be spared," exclaimed the mate; "for, though no great lawyer, I know quite enough to feel satisfied with what I have done." Then turning to the men, he added, "This gentleman, as he calls himself, has come here in search of a person that I am well assured is not on board the ship. You know, as well as I do, what fresh hands have entered; and, upon hearing the name of the person, you can inform him whether he is among our shipmates."

"His name is Guy Harrowby," said the libertine, on observing that the men were looking towards him for information upon the subject.

"There's no such a person here," said the sailor, who had taken upon himself the part of spokesman.

"He may have tendered himself under some other name?" exclaimed Charles Heathingdon.

"We've none here but decent chaps," returned the sailor; "and the word of our chief mate ought to be quite enough, without calling upon us to be witnesses of the truth of what he has said."

"I believe he has wilfully falsified himself to screen a malefactor from justice," exclaimed Charles, in a tone of sullenness and defiance.

"Then here ends all further parley between us," returned the mate. "I have been inclined to let you quit this vessel without having recourse to violence, but you would degrade me in the eyes of these men, and it is now time that I should rid myself of further impertinence. You will, therefore, accompany these persons, and they will convey you to shore in a boat; and, if afterwards you should have any complaint to make against me, I shall be ready to answer it when and where you please."

As he said this he turned away, and Charles, finding that all further resistance would be of no avail, left the cuddy, and was conveyed to the boat which was still waiting for him at the place where he had left it. In a few minutes afterwards he was again on shore, and having paid the waterman, proceeded, in no very good humour, to the tavern where he had slept on the previous night. On arriving there, he ordered wine to be brought; and, whilst moodily pondering over the unprofitable labour he had been employed in, was interrupted by the entrance of a bustling little personage, who advanced smirkingly towards him, and inquired if he was the person who was asking about a man that had returned from transportation before his time. These words instantly recalled Charles Heathingdon to his recollection; and, looking inquisitively towards the intruder, he asked if he had any information to give upon the subject.

"Why, for the matter of that," replied the other, "I rather think I can tell you where he is to be found."

"Where is it?"

"In an old house that has not been inhabited for years," answered the man. "The place is said to be haunted, but, as I happened this morning to see a fellow sneaking towards the place with a basket on his arm, I followed at a little distance off, and saw him enter the house."

"And what has that to do with the object I have in view?" demanded Charles Heathingdon.

"Why, it proves that some one must be concealed in the place," replied the other; "and, as ghosts don't want provisions to be taken to 'em, I feel pretty certain that the man you want is in the house."

"How far is it from here?" demanded Charles, who now began to think his chance was not quite so hopeless as it had appeared a short time before.

"Not quite half a mile, I should think."

"Will you act as my guide to it?"

"Yes, provided you pay me well for my time, and the risk I shall have to run."

"You shall have a sovereign for your services," answered Charles; "but it must be on condition that you perform your task with zeal and caution."

"Why, as for that," exclaimed the man, scratching his ear, "I should not have taken the trouble to come after you, unless I had had a pretty good notion that my time would not be thrown away, so you may suppose I'm a chap that may be depended on, even though we happen to be strangers."

"At all events, I feel inclined to trust you," returned Charles; "and we may, therefore, speak to each other with some little familiarity. You told me, I think, that you had seen a man going towards the house, which is reported to be haunted with evil spirits?"

"I saw him as plainly as I see you at this present moment," exclaimed the other; "and, what is more, I rather think he knew some one was watching him, for he stopped several times to look about him, and it seemed to me as if he sometimes fancied all wasn't right, for he hesitated as if half inclined to turn back, and if I hadn't concealed myself, the affair would have come to an end without my finding out as much as I have."

"Upon my life I see very little that you have found out," observed Charles Heathingdon. "A man may surely walk with a basket on his arm without having such a purpose in view as you have imagined."

"True, sir," replied the little man; "but then the person I saw happened to be going towards a house that is shunned by every one in the neighbourhood."

"That may be because he was not aware of the ridiculous reports that have been raised of its being haunted."

"Ridiculous as you may call the reports, there's plenty of people hereabouts that believe 'em," replied the man. "I myself have lived more than twenty years in the neighbourhood, and, as long as I can remember, no man has ever ventured inside the house, though plenty have found courage enough to prowl round the place in the day time."

"There are few places without these reputed haunted houses," returned Charles Heathingdon; "but it has always happened that, upon inquiry, people have discovered the folly of yielding to popular delusions. Be that as it may, however, I am resolved to sift the matter to the very bottom, and if it should lead to the discovery of the man I am in pursuit of, you shall have no reason to complain of the liberality of a stranger. But I have forgotten to ask if the person you speak of has been seen conveying provisions there before this morning?"

"I have never seen nor heard of him before," answered the other; "and it was by a mere chance that I met with him to-day."

"And how did it happen that you knew of a person being in quest of a fugitive?"

"Why, that happened naturally enough," returned the other; "for, you must know, I am a barber by profession, and this morning a man happened to speak in my shop of some one being in this

neighbourhood looking for some chap that had escaped from transportation. So, thinks I to myself, there's something to be made out of this, and as soon as my morning customers had been turned out decent, I put on my hat, and walked towards the haunted house, because I had a notion that was the very place a man would choose if he wanted to hide himself."

"The thought was a good one," observed Charles, "and it may so happen that it will turn out considerably to your own advantage. Of course, you will have no objection to accompany me when I go to ascertain if the man I want to find has secreted himself there?"

"Objection I have none," exclaimed the other, "if you will only warrant me from getting into trouble."

"That is more than I can undertake to do," answered Charles Heathingdon; "but I'll not run you into any unnecessary risk; and, if it should happen that your information leads to any satisfactory result, I'll take care that you shall have no reason to complain of the reward."

"All that sounds mighty fine," exclaimed the other; "yet I can see no use of a reward, if it should happen that I get a bullet through my heart."

"Psha!" returned Charles, impatiently; "if you are afraid of that, I'll leave you at some distance off, whilst I go alone to see if the fugitive has sought an asylum in the place. But remember, the more assistance you render me, the greater will be your reward when we come to a settlement of our accounts."

"You won't want me to go into the house, I hope?"

"Not I, if you are too great a coward to accompany me there voluntarily," exclaimed Charles Heathingdon. "I am myself armed, and having sufficient courage of my own to urge me on, I'll enter the place unaccompanied, rather than take with me a man who is likely to desert me in the hour of danger."

"But I don't mean to desert you."

"So you may think when there is no immediate danger to be apprehended," exclaimed Charles. "At present you can vaunt, without fear of contradiction, of your valour, but when the moment of trial arrives, it is by no means unlikely that you will desert me."

"You think I'm a coward, then?"

"At all events," said Charles Heathingdon, "I shall take care to guard myself against such a disadvantage. You may have the courage of a lion, but I may be excused for doubting such to be the case, when I hear you acknowledge your belief in these idle rumours of the house you speak of being haunted."

"I have only told you of what other people say."

"Then, in future, be guided a little more by your own reason and judgment," exclaimed Charles. "The house, I suppose, has been closed for a number of years, from some cause or another, and, as is always the case under such circumstances, weak-minded people have spread abroad the rumours which have since obtained such general credit. However, I have nothing to do with that at present, since my object will be fully carried out if you act as my guide to the place we have been speaking of."

"That I'll do, on condition that you pay me for the service," answered the man.

"I have told you that I shall not be mercenary, if you perform your office faithfully."

"Very good; and now, sir, when should you like to place yourself under my direction?"

"The sooner the better," answered Charles Heathingdon; "and yet, upon consideration, I rather think my wisest plan would be to wait patiently where I am, till I am favoured with the darkness of night."

"Night!" exclaimed the man, with alarm; "why, you surely would not visit the haunted house when it is said the spirit walks about?"

"I have no belief in such ideal phantoms," answered Charles Heathingdon; "and, my mind being made up, I shall not change my resolution of going there at the time I have mentioned. You, however, can do as you please; for, by making my inquiries in the neighbourhood, there is no doubt I shall find out the house I am in quest of."

"Excuse the alarm I felt, sir," exclaimed the barber; "but make yourself quite easy about my going with you at any time, be it day or night, that you may need my services. I live just over the way, sir, and you have only to send for me, and I'll be with you in a brace of shakes."

"My sending for you," said Charles Heathingdon, "might only give rise to suspicions that I am most anxious to avoid. You will, therefore, come to me at eleven o'clock to-night, and we will then set out on the errand I have in view."

"Eleven o'clock!" groaned the barber; "why, that will just take us there at the hour when the ghost is said to walk!"

"Then leave me to prosecute this adventure alone," answered Charles; "for, in spite of all the ghosts that ever walked, I will visit the old house at the time I have said."

The fellow would have again remonstrated, but, at an impatient gesture from Charles Heathingdon, he bolted out of the room.

CHAPTER X.

DOUBT AND UNCERTAINTY.—THE RECLUSE.—THE FLIGHT.

NEVER did time seem to pass so long and heavily to Guy Harrowby as when left in the silent solitude of the gloomy house in which he had sought concealment. Nor did he feel quite satisfied that his presence there would not be discovered, for it was probable that the motions of those who came to visit him would be watched, and there was also a chance that the dwarf might find out his secret, and betray him, for the sake of obtaining a reward for his services. Of the old man he felt but little apprehension, for he had ceased to feel any interest in the world or its concerns, and the words he uttered during their conversation on the preceding night, served to assure him that no danger was to be expected from that quarter.

Yet for all that the fugitive was far from feeling satisfied that he was safe from the inquiries that would be made after him. Charles Heathingdon was an enemy not to be appeased, except by the full accomplishment of his revenge ; he had resolved upon the destruction of the man who had thwarted him in his evil designs, and no obstacles would ever induce him to forego the deadly object he had in view. Against him, therefore, it was necessary to be most guarded, and as it was likely that he might succeed in tracing him to his lurking place, it became necessary that he should quit his present cheerless abode, and find some other place where he might remain till an opportunity offered itself for going abroad. This, however, could not be done without consulting his colleagues, and he therefore resolved to remain where he was till the arrival of some of them, and to seek some other abode where he might have more frequent and easy communication with those upon whose assistance he would have to depend.

During the greater part of the day he stood looking from the window, in the hope that some of his friends might be lurking near the spot. But hour after hour passed away without any of them making their appearance, and at length, when the darkness of evening began to set in, he turned reluctantly away, and pacing up and down the room, gave way to the melancholy thoughts that passed in rapid succession through his mind. At last the full moon shone forth in all her splendour, and again the hapless fugitive placed himself at the window to gaze almost unconsciously on the scene of wildness and desolation that lay before him. In this manner more than half an hour elapsed, when his notice was attracted by something moving about the garden, and immediately afterwards a man darted forward, and presented himself beneath the window. It was Mike Rowley, who, having assured himself that the bird had flown, hurried round the house to a door which he had seen during a hasty examination of the premises. In two or three minutes afterwards he entered the room, and having shaken hands with Harrowby, expressed his satisfaction at finding him safe from the danger he had anticipated.

"So far all's right enough, my boy," he exclaimed ; "but this is no place for you to remain in much longer, for your enemy, Mr. Heathingdon, is not far off, and he thinks to surprise you to-night when you are asleep."

"Does he know of my being here then ?"

"He does," answered the other ; "and what's more, he's not half a mile away from you at this moment."

"D—n him !" muttered the fugitive ; "he hunts me with all the certainty and deadliness of purpose of a blood-hound. And yet, when I come to think of it, Rowley, I think you must be mistaken about his being so near."

"How can I be mistaken when I've seen him ?" demanded the other. "I was standing near the dock gates when he entered, and judging there was mischief in the wind, I followed at no great distance off, and saw him go on board a vessel that's just about sailing for the East Indies."

"What could he have gone there for, I wonder ?"

"Why, to look after you, to be sure," replied Mike Rowley. "He received information from the patrol that three or four men had passed him who were going to enter themselves as seamen, and, believing you to be one of them, he went this morning, expecting to have the pleasure of giving you into custody."

"'Twas well for him that he didn't find me there," exclaimed Guy Harrowby ; "for I would have had his life in revenge for the misery he has dragged me into."

"And serve him right, too," answered Rowley ; "the scoundrel deserves to have a knife in his heart, though the worst of it is, a chap can't kill him without running his own neck into danger."

"My neck is already in danger," returned Guy ; "so the fellow must beware how he again trusts himself within my reach. For my own part, I shall never willingly throw myself in his way ; but, if he will hunt me out, the consequences of his folly must fall upon himself."

"Do you mean to wait here then till he comes ?"

"That depends upon circumstances," replied Guy Harrowby. "If he is coming alone, there can be no reason why I should fly from him like a coward ; and, even if he should bring assistance, there's places enough in this old house where I may find concealment till they are tired of looking for me. But I've not yet been told how you happened to hear of his intended visit here ?"

"Why, that happened curiously enough," answered Mike Rowley; "though I believe there can be no doubt of the truth of what I heard. When this Mr. Heathingdon went on board the vessel, I remained on shore, watching for his return. He stayed there a long time, and I was not very well pleased with the reception he had met with."

"Did you speak to him?"

"Not I," replied Mike; "for though he don't know me from Adam, I had no wish to give a chance away. So I followed him till he went into a tavern, and from one of the waiters I found the young gentleman was going to stop there to-night."

"And was the waiter able to tell you also that he was coming to look for me here?"

"No; I got that out of another chap."

"Who was he?"

"A barber, that lives opposite the tavern."

"How did you manage to make acquaintance with him?"

"Easily enough," replied Mike; "for I had only to go in for a shave, and the fellow answered all my questions as readily as possible."

"What reason had you for supposing that he could give you any information?"

"Why, you must know, that while I was waiting near the tavern, I saw the barber go over from his shop, and, as he went into the room where the gentleman was, I began to think he must have some information to give against you. So I waited till he came out, and then went into his shop to worm out as much of the secret as I could."

"And he told you that Charles Heathingdon is coming here to-night to capture me?"

"Yes."

"Does he come alone?"

"No; the barber is to be his guide; but I rather think he would gladly be out of the business, if it wasn't for the reward he's to receive for his trouble."

"At any rate, I've not much to be afraid of if there's only two of 'em," exclaimed Guy Harrowby. "You, I suppose, won't mind staying with me to-night, and it will be strange if we can't teach these people the folly of meddling with affairs that don't concern 'em."

"Why, I don't mind staying here," answered Mike; "but it seems to me that it would be much better to let 'em come here and find an empty house."

"And where am I to go for shelter when I leave this place?" demanded Guy Harrowby.

"Oh! there's plenty of other queer cribs that will serve you on a pinch," answered the other. "Dick Fordham and I can take you to a score or two of 'em; only it won't do to stay long in any of the places, because this Mr. Heathingdon seems to have a great spite against you, and, if he should happen to get scent, he'll take care that you shall not get out of his clutches very easily."

"Let him have a care how he drives me too closely into a corner," exclaimed Guy Harrowby. "So far, I have been anxious to avoid shedding his blood; but now that I see his determination to revenge the blow that I struck him in my wife's defence, I feel that it will be impossible to meet him without his blood being upon my hand. I will, however, avoid him as long as possible, so that it shall be no fault of mine if he happens to meet with the fate he deserves."

"D—n it!" cried Mike Rowley, "why stand haggling so long about it, when the job must be done after all? The chap deserves his fate, come when it may, and when once you've served him out, I and the rest of your friends will do what we can to get you safe out of England."

"What! and desert my wife, for whose sake it was that I returned home from abroad?"

"She can follow you if that's all," replied the other.

"True; but when she does follow me, it will be to become an exile, as well as myself."

"What of that?" demanded Mike; "none of you have much reason to be very fond of England, and there's plenty of other places in the world where you may find a happy home for yourselves."

"A home we may find, but not a very happy one," answered Guy Harrowby. "Go where I may, people will soon find out that I am a returned convict, and, though their laws may not be able to reach me, there will be but little respect for the man that goes to live among them with a character as blasted as mine is."

"Why, then, they'll drive you to thieving," exclaimed the other; "and then you can do very well without the respect of the world. You have broken the laws pretty often, I dare say, before now, and, as a returned convict, there's no other way of getting a living but by helping yourself to the goods and chattels of other people."

"And so run the risk of being sent abroad, to spend the rest of my days away from my wife."

"Psha!" retorted the other; "what's the use of making your mind uneasy about what can't be helped? Your wife's a good sort of creature, I dare say; but she knows you must go if they choose to send you off, and so the best thing she can do will be, to make up her mind for the worst. At all events, if she cries her eyes out, it won't make matters a bit the better."

"True; but it will be so much the more added to my punishment, if I know she is suffering through the love she still has for me."

"Why," exclaimed Mike, "as for love, that's an affair that I know very little about. For my own part, I never turned my mind towards marriage, and a precious good thing too, for, happen what may to me, I shall not leave any body behind to grieve after me."

"But, as I happen to be differently situated," returned the fugitive, "my feelings, in such a

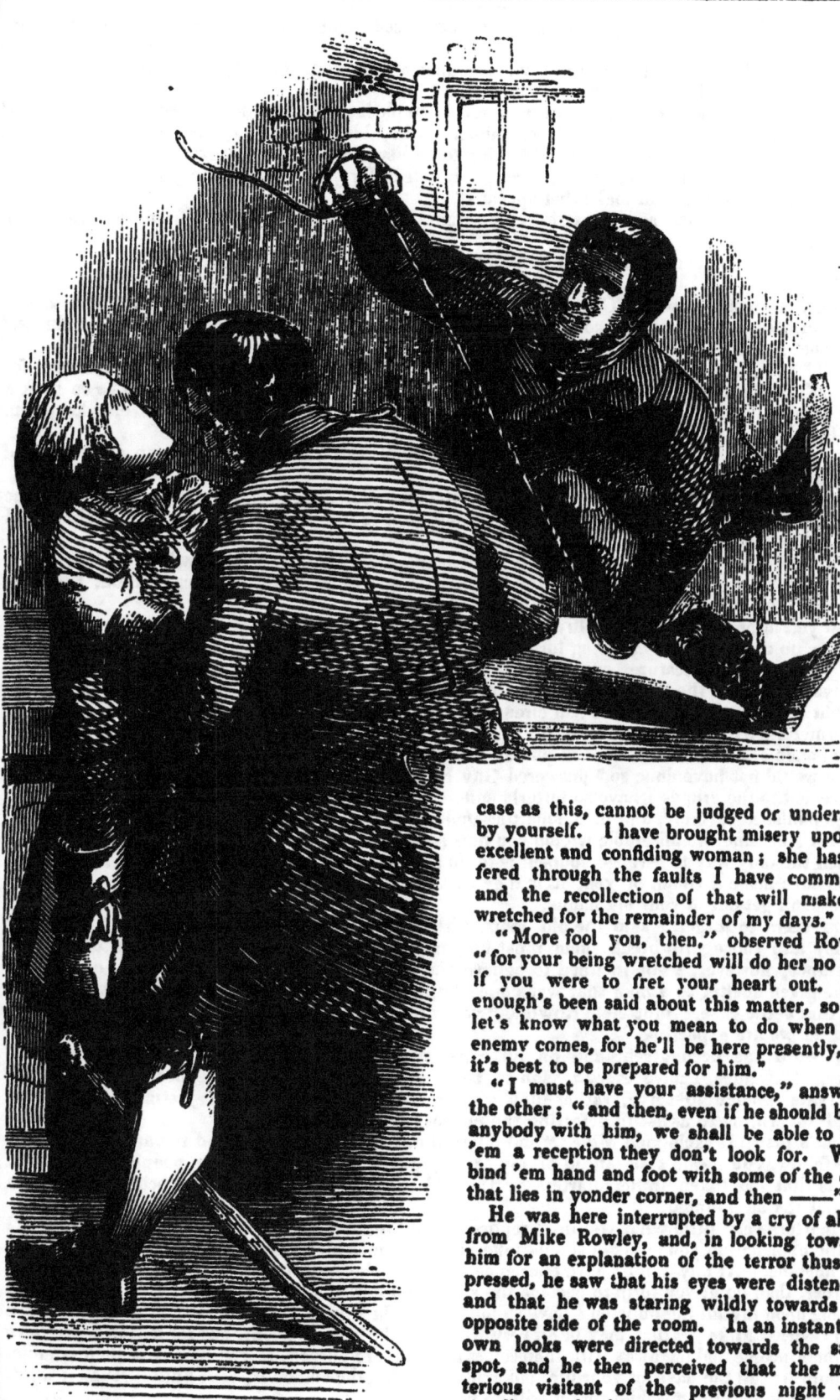

case as this, cannot be judged or understood by yourself. I have brought misery upon an excellent and confiding woman; she has suffered through the faults I have committed, and the recollection of that will make me wretched for the remainder of my days."

"More fool you, then," observed Rowley, "for your being wretched will do her no good if you were to fret your heart out. But enough's been said about this matter, so now let's know what you mean to do when your enemy comes, for he'll be here presently, and it's best to be prepared for him."

"I must have your assistance," answered the other; "and then, even if he should bring anybody with him, we shall be able to give 'em a reception they don't look for. We'll bind 'em hand and foot with some of the cord that lies in yonder corner, and then ——"

He was here interrupted by a cry of alarm from Mike Rowley, and, in looking towards him for an explanation of the terror thus expressed, he saw that his eyes were distended, and that he was staring wildly towards the opposite side of the room. In an instant his own looks were directed towards the same spot, and he then perceived that the mysterious visitant of the previous night was standing at the door and listening to the conversation which had been going forward. On being perceived, however, the old man slowly advanced, and addressing himself to Guy Harrowby, said,—

"Your friend here seems alarmed at my appearance among you, and yet, I suppose, you have told him of my having paid you a similar visit last night?"

"I have," replied the convict; "but the secret, I can pledge my word, will be safe in his keeping."

"Ay, ay, it will be safe enough," exclaimed Mike, bluntly; "but, between ourselves, old gentleman, I don't think it was exactly the thing to be listening to our conversation."

"If I have done so," answered the stranger, "it will be for your own advantage."

"Indeed! and how do you make that appear?"

"By giving such advice as will extricate you from the danger that may arise from the visit of the enemy that it seems you expect here."

"Humph! you know all about what we've been saying then?" exclaimed Rowley.

"I do."

"Then you know," observed Guy Harrowby, "that we have determined to take care of ourselves, and to bind with cords those that come against us, provided they don't happen to be too many for us."

"All that I know," answered the old man.

"Well," exclaimed Mike Rowley! "I don't think we shall have much trouble in the matter; for there won't be more than a couple of chaps to deal with, and one of 'em I know to be as rank a coward as ever lived. It won't take much to frighten him out of his life; or, at any rate, to keep him quiet till he thinks we're clear off."

"Then, I suppose," said the old man to Guy, "that you intend to find some other place of concealment?"

"There's no other way left for me," answered the fugitive; "but where my next lurking-place may be, I know not. My life, however, is a burden to me, and it is only for my wife's sake that I have not before now surrendered myself up to the officers of justice."

"What good would you do by such fool's work as that?" demanded Mike Rowley. "You've had a pretty good specimen I should think of what they do on t'other side the water, without throwing yourself into the same precious pickle again."

"And yet, after all," exclaimed Guy, "it must in the long run come to that."

"I have no desire to hear anything further upon the subject you are talking about," said the old man. "As a fellow-creature, overwhelmed with misfortune, I have been inclined to afford the asylum you need, but the less I know of the reason that has made you a fugitive the better. Here you might have continued to reside had circumstances permitted it; but were I to know too much of your former life, I might consider it my duty to further the ends of justice by surrendering you into the hands of those who are now in pursuit of their victim."

"You would not have done so," answered Guy Harrowby, "had you known all the circumstances that have led to the crimes I have so bitterly suffered for. My first offence, though a mere trifling one, was punished severely, and then, smarting under what I knew to be an injustice, I fell into looser habits, till I became the miserable wretch you now see me."

"Then the only way to revenge yourself is to do all the mischief you can," answered Mike. "If the laws have made a villain of you, it is they that are in fault, and people have no right to wonder that you can't get out of your old habits."

"You seem to forget," said the old man, "that laws were made for the general benefit of mankind, and those who break them must be punished, as an example to other evil doers. In this instance, however, I am inclined to believe there has been too much harshness, or I would not have given shelter to a man that was concealing himself from the officers of justice."

"If that's the case," muttered Rowley, "you are hardly to be depended on when the chap comes that we are expecting."

"My word has been given, and on no consideration will I ever break it," exclaimed the stranger. "Besides, I have every reason to believe that the man who is expected here has his own private revenge to serve, rather than a desire to further the ends of justice, and for that reason I am willing to assist in defeating the purpose he has in view."

"That's just it!" exclaimed Mike; "and if you'll only lend a helping hand towards disappointing the fellow, you needn't be afraid of my saying anything that will open people's eyes about who it is that has taken up his quarters in this old-fashioned crib, and frightened people into a belief that it was haunted."

"It matters very little what you do," replied the old man, "for my days are nearly numbered; and if the explanation you speak of should take place, the mischief you speak of will not be so great as you imagine. At any rate, I have chosen as my home the roof that has sheltered my ancestors; and, rather than be driven forth to become the scorn and derision of my foes, I'll end my life, and thus bring upon myself the oblivion I have so long sought in vain."

"Ah!" cried Mike; "that may be all very well to make a boast about, but for my own part I've no notion of people making away with themselves for the mere purpose of getting out of their trouble. You should live all the days of your life, old gentleman, for, depend on it, your killing yourself won't do other people half the mischief that it will do yourself."

"Granted," answered the mysterious visiter; "but I have chosen this ruinous mansion for my last abiding place on earth, and nothing shall ever force me to quit it while I have life. When I am no more I shall, perhaps, be permitted to find a grave in this, the only place that I have ever loved."

"Why, it's a hundred to one," said Mike, "if anybody knows of your death till long after it takes place."

"Perhaps not," answered the old man; "and yet it is not unlikely that the person you expect here to-night will go forth and spread a report that the supposed unquiet spirit is no other than the dispossessed heir of the place he has chosen for his home."

"If you think there's any likelihood of that," returned Rowley, "the best plan will be to prevent his doing you a mischief."

"In what way?"

"By killing him!"

"Would you commit the crime of murder?"

"Not if it can be helped," answered Mike; "I've no great wish to run myself into danger, but, if this chap should prove very restive, I see no other way that we can get out of the scrape. To be sure we may bind him, as was just now proposed; but that plan would be as bad as any other, for no one would be likely to come to his relief, and then the poor devil would die of starvation; and that would be almost as clear a case of murder as if we finished him at once, by putting a knife into his heart or a bullet through his brain."

"I shall, myself, be here to prevent him perishing from want," whispered the old man.

"Why, so you would," exclaimed Mike; "and, upon second thoughts, I rather think we can't do better than make a prisoner of him. He'd do the same kind turn for us, and I can see no great harm in giving him a little confinement, just to let him see how he likes it himself."

"But," interposed Guy Harrowby, "it must be under a promise that he is not to be set at liberty till we have had plenty of time to get away."

"Leave the management of that to me, and I'll take care that you have no reason to regret my confidence," answered the stranger. "For three days, at least, I'll take care that he remains in this house, and, by that time, you will have had an opportunity of finding some other place of concealment."

"Good," exclaimed Mike; "but how are we to be certain that he won't find means to escape?"

"He shall be conveyed by yourselves to one of the vaults beneath this house," replied the stranger. "Once there, it shall be my care to provide him with whatever is necessary for the support of life; and, at the expiration of that time, he shall have his liberty on condition that he solemnly pledges himself not to divulge to any one the secret of my being here."

"And that he'll be glad enough to do," observed Rowley, "for three days' confinement ought to be enough to tame his spirit; and you'll find him, I dare say, willing enough to promise anything you choose to insist on."

"Remember," said the old man, "there must be no further violence used than may be necessary to place him under the bondage we have been speaking of."

"Why, as for that," replied Mike, "we shall act according to circumstances. I and my friend here can manage him well enough, if he don't happen to be armed; and if he should come prepared for violence, he must take the consequences, however rough our treatment of him may happen to be."

"It shall be my care to prevent his acting rashly in this matter," exclaimed the recluse. "Leave him to my management, at first; and, should he prove deaf to my advice, it will then be for you to act as the urgency of the moment may require."

"All that may be very well for you to say while we are talking the matter coolly over," answered Guy Harrowby; "but I happen to know a little more of this man than you do, and, from what experience I've had, there's no doubt he means to make me his prisoner, at all hazards to himself."

"And you, of course," said Rowley, "ain't quite such a soft 'un as to let yourself be taken while there's a chance of getting out of his clutches?"

"You know me too well to believe that I'll die like a cur," answered the fugitive. "Dangers I have braved in every form, and now that I have succeeded in returning to England, I don't mean to fall into mischief while there's a chance of keeping clear of it. Charles Heathingdon and I have had but a short acquaintance, yet we've seen quite enough of each other to know there's no love lost between us; and, if he will run himself into danger, there'll be small blame to me if he suffers for his folly."

"Rashness will do no good in such a case as this, depend on it," exclaimed the old man. "Your enemy may be crafty and vindictive, but there are still weapons by which he may be defeated, and I believe caution will do more than anything else to deprive him of the revenge he meditates against you."

"Perhaps so," interposed Mike Rowley; "and yet, to my thinking, a man may be a little too cautious. The chap we are expecting here will stand for no repairs, if he happens to fall in with the person he's looking after; and, knowing that so well as we do, it would be madness to stand idle, and give him an advantage over us."

"You have heard my advice," answered the recluse; "and, if you are determined to oppose it, I shall at once decline having anything to do with the matter. In pity for the sufferings of a fugitive, I have given him an asylum till he can procure a better one; he has found shelter beneath this roof, and I believe it is not too much for me to expect that he will comply with the only wish I have ventured to express upon the subject."

"Why, as for that matter," exclaimed Rowley, "it may be all very well for you to smooth things down; but we can't help seeing the affair in another light; and my advice is, that we defend ourselves to the very last."

"Then he whom I have sheltered is ungrateful for the services I have performed."

"No, no," cried Guy Harrowby; "you shall not have that to say of me, at any rate. I have found a friend where one was hardly to be expected, and I will not return his favours with ingratitude."

"Ugh!" growled Mike; "then you've made up your mind to be sent off to the stone jug?"

"Never!" exclaimed the convict.

"How can you help it?"

"By fighting to the last, when I find there's no other way of saving myself."

"Then why not do so at once, instead of waiting till you're grabbed by the enemy?"

"Because I've made up my mind not to act against the wishes of a man that has proved himself my friend," answered Guy Harrowby. "He has given me shelter when it was most wanted; and it would be a poor return, if I should be the cause of driving him away from the place where he wants to end his days in peace."

"You have said well," exclaimed the old man; "and, in return for your submission, I will do all in my power to preserve you from the threatened danger."

"And what can a man of your age do to help us?" demanded Mike Rowley.

"Nothing, by strength of body," answered the recluse; "but much by the power of persuasion."

"Humph! so you think the person we are speaking of may be gammoned by fine words?"

"I certainly think he may be open to conviction," returned the old man; "and, if I should be mistaken, it will then be for you to take whatever course may be necessary for your own safety."

"And that will be to make him our prisoner," said Rowley: "he's coming here for no other purpose than to do the same sort of thing for my friend here; and, if we don't look out pretty sharp, there'll be the devil to pay, and no pitch hot."

"Know you not, then, that rashness will rather injure than serve you?" asked the old man.

"I don't know much about that," exclaimed Mike; "but I'm quite certain that we must have a tussle before this Mr. Heathingdon will own himself beat."

"Perhaps so," replied the other; "but it will be time enough to come to that when we have seen that all other means are of no use; and, upon second thoughts, I have a notion that it will be better for your friend to see his pursuer alone, whilst you and I conceal ourselves in the adjoining room, where we shall be ready to come in to his assistance, if it should be needed."

To this suggestion, after some little demur, the other two agreed, and scarcely had they done so, than sounds were heard proceeding from the lower part of the house, that announced that the hour of peril had arrived. Presently afterwards, a gleam of light was seen glancing up the staircase, when the old man, taking the arm of Mike Rowley, hastily withdrew him to the next room, where they might overhear all that passed, and be in readiness for any emergency that might arise. On the part of Guy Harrowby there was no attempt at concealment, for his mind was made up to offer a desperate resistance, in the event of there being any necessity for it; and, as the footsteps of his enemy approached, he planted his back firmly against the wall, and awaited the result of an interview that was to terminate either in his triumph or captivity. Thus resolved, he saw Charles Heathingdon enter the room, bearing in his hand a lighted lamp with which he had provided himself before he came on this hazardous expedition. At the same moment they recognised each other, and the pursuer, with a cry of exultation, rushed towards his victim, who, however, stood so firmly upon the defensive, that the other suddenly paused in his career, as if awed by the resolute opposition that was opposed against him.

"Have a care how you approach the man you have driven at bay," exclaimed Guy Harrowby. "You have rashly followed me hither, but the advance of another step will end in your own destruction."

"Surrender!" exclaimed the other, gnashing his teeth with rage—"surrender, I say, for I have assistance close at hand, and will never leave this place alive, unless it is to bear you from it as my prisoner."

"And I," answered the fugitive, "am just as resolute to defend myself against the villain that has followed me here. I have never injured you in thought or deed, yet you would hurt me to the gallows for no other crime than that I thwarted the baseness you intended against my wife."

"You did more," exclaimed Charles Heathingdon; "you struck me a blow, and from that moment you made me your determined and implacable enemy."

"The blow you speak of was struck in the defence of her who is dearer to me than my own life."

"It matters little what the cause was, since I am equally determined to be revenged for it," answered the libertine. "The woman made an impression upon my heart that I could not conquer, and the banishment of her felon husband seemed to me a sufficient excuse for the love I proposed her. Your return, however, has defeated my schemes for a time, and it is therefore little to be wondered at if I pursue you to the fate that the outraged laws of your country will accord."

"And what punishment," demanded Harrowby, "does the wretch deserve who would bring infamy and dishonour upon a virtuous and loving wife? You can pretend to feel abhorrence at the faults I have committed, yet have no remorseful feelings for the baseness you have yourself been guilty of."

"What remorse can I feel for having fallen in love with a pretty woman?" demanded the libertine.

"None," answered Guy Harrowby; "for I believe you care nothing for the misery you bring on others, so that your own lustful hopes are gratified. My unexpected return has, however, defeated your baseness, and for no other offence than that you would send me to the gallows."

"Ay, and I will do so," exclaimed the other; "or, for the first time in my life, I shall have to own myself beaten in my projects. Besides, if there was no other reason for the course I have taken, sufficient excuse for it is to be found in the fact that you have returned from transportation before the allotted term had expired, and I am only doing my duty in surrendering you up to justice."

"'Tis well to talk of duty in this matter, when you don't mind breaking it in every other," returned the fugitive. "You would destroy the peace of a family for the gratification of your own base designs, yet cannot pardon an unhappy man who has fearlessly braved all dangers, for the sake of once more clasping a loved wife in his arms."

"You love her!" exclaimed Charles Heathingdon, scornfully.

"I do."

"Then why did you commit a crime that was certain to lead to a banishment from her?"

"If you ask me that question," returned Harrowby, "I reply, that it was because I thought there was no great harm in a poor man helping himself to the wild birds and beasts that were sent by Heaven for the use of one man as much as another. Yet, for snaring a single hare, that was wanted as a meal for a starving wife, I was sent abroad as if I had committed a desperate robbery."

"It could not have been your first offence in that way, or the punishment would not have been so heavy."

"True enough," answered Guy Harrowby; "it was not the first time I had taken game; but there could be no great harm in that, seeing, as I did, that a rich man can shoot and destroy as often as he pleases the wild things that are sent for the use of all people alike."

"Bandy not words with me, fellow," exclaimed Charles; "but yield at once to the fate that neither force nor resistance can avert. My purpose in coming here is well known to you, and I am resolved not to depart except with you as my prisoner."

"Then you have undertaken more than you will ever be able to perform," retorted the convict. "I know the fate that would be certain to follow in case of my being taken, and, rather than the gibbet shall be my end, I'll lose my life in defending myself against whatever power you may have brought for your assistance."

"If that's the case," exclaimed Charles Heathingdon, "I shall call up the man wh accompanied me here."

"Do so," answered the fugitive, "and, when you have put yourself to that unnecessary trouble, I shall be just as resolute in my own defence as when there was only one enemy to deal with."

"You expect then to be a match for two of us."

"Aye, two such as I shall have to cope against," replied Guy Harrowby.

"How can you be sure of that, without knowing who my companion is?"

"I know well enough who it is," answered the convict, "and it will be better for you to place no confidence in a man that will prove himself a rank coward the moment he is required to give his assistance."

"By what means," asked Charles, "have you been able to worm out so much of my secret?"

"It matters not how I have found it out," answered Guy Harrowby. "I know who the man is, and you will do well not to place too much dependence in a chattering barber, who has boasted of what he will do, but may deceive you when his assistance is most needed."

"Be that as it may," exclaimed the libertine, "I will not be thwarted now that I have succeeded in tracing you to your lurking place. I am equal to yourself in strength, Guy Harrowby, and can at least hold you here as my prisoner whilst the man who accompanied me goes to fetch the requisite assistance. You have defied me, and we will now see which of us is to prove conqueror in the contest that is to follow."

Scarcely had these words been uttered than Charles Heathingdon sprang forward with a sudden bound to seize upon his antagonist; the other was, however, not unprepared for the attack, and in a moment they were fast locked in a mortal struggle for superiority. Both were of nearly equal size and strength, so that it was doubtful on which side the advantage lay, for each exerted almost superhuman power and both resolved never to yield whilst a chance of victory remained. At length, however, the foot of Guy Harrowby slipped, and before he could well recover his balance, his antagonist followed up his advantage, and putting forth all his strength, succeeded in throwing his rival to the ground. The suddenness of the fall almost stunned Guy, and as he lay prostrate at the feet of his enemy, the latter knelt upon his chest, and secured him with a firm hold, that the victory now seemed to be completely decided in favour of the libertine.

"Yield," he exclaimed, panting from the exertion he had used. "Yield, I say, for it is in vain to prolong a contest in which it is clear you have no chance."

But the words so boastfully uttered had scarcely left his lips when Mike Rowley flew to the assistance of his comrade, and throwing a cord round the arms of Charles, succeeded in bind-

ing him so firmly that he was immediately deprived of all power of resistance. It was in vain that he struggled to release himself, for Rowley had performed his task in no bungling manner, and at length panting, from the exertion he had used, he demanded to be set at liberty, promising on that condition to depart immediately and leave the victory to his opponent.

"Give you your liberty, indeed!" exclaimed Mike, as he tugged the cord still more tightly; " do you take us for fools, that we should set you free that you may go and raise the neighbourhood before we have time to make our escape?"

"What would you do with me then?" demanded the captive.

"Not quite so badly as you would have done while the chances were in your own favour," answered Guy Harrowby, who by this time had recovered his feet. "You would have handed me over to the officers of justice, but I shall content myself with keeping you here a prisoner for three or four days, by which time I mean to get as far out of your reach as possible."

"Am I to be kept a prisoner here?" exclaimed Charles Heathingdon, with alarm.

"To be sure you are," replied Mike; "what better place would you wish to be in?"

"I would rather be anywhere else than in such a miserable, delapidated building as this," returned the other.

"Ah!" cried Rowley; "you don't like it now that the turn's come to yourself. The place ain't fit to live in when its proposed to leave you here for a few days, but you didn't think anything of it when this poor devil of a friend of mine was to be sent to a gaol, with no chance of coming out of it again till he was sent to the gallows."

"How know you that I was in earnest," demanded the libertine, "when it is just as likely as not that I was only trying to frighten him?"

"If you were only joking, it looked too much like earnest to be pleasant," retorted Guy Harrowby. "Besides, when you got me down just now, and I had no power to help myself, you talked about sending the chap that came with you, for further assistance."

"I did so," answered Charles Heathingdon; "but it was only said to frighten you into submission."

"Then it's our turn now to frighten you into submission," exclaimed Rowley. "The chance has turned all in our favour, and if we suffer ourselves to be talked over, it will serve us right if we get into trouble through it."

"I will do more than make mere promises," returned Charles Heathingdon. "Release me from these bonds, and your reward shall be fifty pounds each."

"A hundred pounds won't do it, nor yet five hundred," exclaimed Mike Rowley. "We've made sure work of it by what's been done, and it will never do to give you a chance of laughing at us for a couple of ninnies. No, no, safe bind, safe find, so here you must remain till a friend of ours comes to set you free, and that won't be till we are far enough beyond your reach."

"Then you mean to leave me in this place, where there is not a whole window to keep from me the chilling winds of night?" said the captive.

"I rather think the place we're going to take you to, ain't half so comfortable as this is," returned Guy Harrowby.

"Where is it?"

"Why, in a vault beneath the mansion."

"Then I am to be left to perish from a miserable death by starvation?"

"No," answered Guy; "we sha'n't be quite so cruel as that, though you don't deserve that we should care what become of you. A person will be left behind that promises to supply you with food and drink, and if at the end of about three days you promise to say nothing about what has taken place, you will be allowed to go where you please."

"I'll never make such a promise."

"Very well," exclaimed Guy Harrowby, in a tone of indifference; "you can do as you please about that, only remember, there'll be no liberty till you do as I have said."

"The best way's to let him find out of his own accord," interposed Rowley. "Three or four days of solitary confinement will serve to bring him to his senses, and then, I'll be bound, he'll tell a very different tale to what he does now."

"Ay, ay," groaned Charles Heathingdon; "it is my evil destiny to be thrown into your power for the present; but my captivity cannot last any long time, and the first use I make of my liberty, shall be to seek out those who have been villanous enough to lay violent hands upon me."

"Why, as for that," returned Guy, "the violence you complain of has been brought on entirely by yourself. You thought proper to come and seek me here, and all that has happened from it is your own fault. Just now I happened to be on the losing side, and I might as well have talked to these old walls as have tried to move your heart to take pity upon me."

"But I would not have left you here to starvation and the horrors of solitude."

"Very likely," answered Harrowby; "but it so happens that you will not be left either to starvation or solitude."

"Who then is to be my companion?"

"That you've got to find out," said Mike Rowley. "I can tell you, however, that there's rats enough in the place to keep you company; and, besides, that there's ghosts and apparitions enough to keep you amused for a month, instead of only for three or four days.

"But neither the one nor the other can bring me food or water when I need them."

"True," answered Guy Harrowby; "but there's a friend of ours that will not let you want for anything, so long as you remain here. He has promised to look after you, and as he lives no very great distance off, he'll pay you visits as often as may seem necessary."

"And set me free at the end of three days?"

"Yes," replied the fugitive; "or sooner than that, if you think proper to make the promise I told you of."

"What! to make no further search after you?"

"Exactly so," answered Guy; "you have seen already that I am not to be so easily captured as you fancied, and the wisest thing you can do, will be to mind your own affairs, instead of running after other people. It's true enough that I have returned from transportation before my time, but when a man has risked so much for his freedom, you may feel pretty sure that he'll not suffer himself to be taken without giving all the trouble he can to those that interfere with him as you have done with me."

"It is your own fault that I have kept up this pursuit after you," exclaimed the libertine. "Had you not struck me that blow in your own cottage, I never should have trouble! my head about the matter, nor have known that you had returned from transportation."

"Humph! then you would have had me stand quietly by, when I saw my wife struggling to release herself from the embrace of a villain? However, let us say no more upon this subject, or I shall lose my temper, which I have no wish to do, seeing that I have managed to get out of the trouble you would have brought me into."

Guy Harrowby now saw that the mysterious old man had glided towards the staircase, and was making signs for them to follow him without delay. The prisoner was therefore assisted to rise from the floor, and, much against his inclination, was forced to accompany those who were about to conduct him to the place of his imprisonment. Charles remonstrated loudly against the force they were using, but his complaints were unheeded, and, after descending to the ground floor of the building, they hurried along a passage, at the end of which was a flight of stone steps leading to the vaults which had been spoken of by the old man. Having got to the bottom of these, they came to a small stone chamber, into which the prisoner was thrust, and then, the door being closed and fastened, they all ascended the steps which they had just before come down, and then proceeded towards the hall, which showed fewer marks of dilapidation than any other part of the building, except that the door had fallen from its hinges through rust and long neglect. Here they stood listening to the loud outcries of the captive, till urged by the old man not to lose the time that was of so much consequence to them.

"Every moment that you stay in this place," he said, "is increasing the danger you ought to avoid. Go, then, and, when to-morrow's sun rises, be as far off as you can from those that will be diligently searching after you."

"I will," exclaimed Guy Harrowby, grasping the hand that was stretched towards him. "Your advice shall not be thrown away upon me; and, should it ever lie in my way to return the kindness you have shown me, I will do so, even though it should be to risk life and limb."

"Enough," said the old man, leading them towards the entrance. "I have done that which, if known, would bring me into trouble; but having myself suffered from the injustice of the world, I have been tempted to assist a fellow-creature, because I thought he was persecuted without cause. So now, farewell, and may your days henceforth be less stormy than those which have passed."

There was a tremulousness in his voice as he gave utterance to these good wishes, but, before Guy Harrowby could make any reply, the old man had turned away, and was lost in the darkness that enveloped the interior of the house. The two men then made their way through the garden, at the entrance of which they were startled by seeing the figure of a human being gliding towards the shadow of the wall, as if some person was lurking about to watch their movements. Rowley, in his alarm, would have urged him to hurry away as fast as possible, but Guy Harrowby was determined to know what the fellow was doing there, and, rushing towards the cowering stranger, he dragged him forth to a place where the light of the moon enabled Rowley to recognise in the supposed spy no less a personage than the barber who had acted as guide to Charles Heathingdon.

"What are you doing here, scoundrel?" demanded the fugitive, shaking the alarmed tonsor roughly. "Tell me why you are here," he added, "or I'll tie a stone round your neck, and throw you into the nearest horse-pond"

"Oh, if you please, sir, don't do that!" cried the trembling barber, as he fell imploringly upon his knees. "I only came to show a gentleman the way to yonder house, and was waiting here till he came out."

"Are you telling me the truth?"

"Indeed I am."

"Then think yourself lucky that you have not been beaten to a mummy, for interfering in matters that don't concern you," exclaimed Guy Harrowby. "The person you brought here was an enemy of mine, and, through you, I might by this time have been in trouble."

"Ah! then you are the person he has been making such a fuss about," said the barber.

"It matters not to you who I am," answered Harrowby; "let it be enough that you have got out of this business without broken bones. So now hurry back to your home as fast as you can, and, above all things, speak not to any one of the adventure you have this night been engaged in. So far you have escaped your deserts; but, if you ever dare even to hint at having seen me, you shall die the death of a dog."

"Mercy on me!" ejaculated the barber; "what a horrible dilemma I'd like to have fallen into. But may I ask, sir, without offence, what has become of the gentleman that I brought to this place?"

"He went away long ago," replied Mike Rowley, wishing to mystify the barber as much as possible.

"Then there goes the reward he promised to give me," exclaimed the other, despondingly. "Here have I been waiting for him in the cold more than an hour, and, after all, he has sneaked off without paying what he promised."

"You've been properly served," said Mike, "and ought to think yourself well off that you have not had a ducking in the pond for what you have done. So now away with you to your home, and don't forget what will happen, if you dare say one word about what you have seen to-night."

The barber jumped nimbly upon his feet on being released from the iron grasp that held him, and ran off, too glad at his own escape to look back after those he left behind.

CHAPTER XI.

GOOD RESOLUTIONS.—THE HALTING-PLACE.—THE CAPTURE.

HAVING, as they imagined, frightened the barber into silence, the two comrades made the best of their way from a neighbourhood that was dangerous to them; and, avoiding those places where they were likely to meet with any one, they directed their steps towards the Isle of Dogs, as a spot where they might better hope for a brief concealment than anywhere else. For some time they remained silent, lest the sound of their voices should be heard; but on reaching a more open place, where they could see some distance around them, they began to consult together as to the plan they should follow in order to make certain their escape.

"If you'll take my advice," said Mike Rowley, after three or four suggestions had been proposed and abandoned, "we shall make our way as quickly as possible to the river side, where it's most likely we shall find a boat moored close to the shore. We may then get over to Greenwich, and have leisure to think of what it would be best to do next."

"Haven't you thought of any place where we may hide ourselves?" asked the convict.

"There's been no time to think much about that," replied Rowley; "but I should think we may find a snug place enough in one of the old pits on Blackheath, for some of 'em are nearly overgrown with gorse, and people might pass near to the place a hundred times without having a notion that any body was lying hid there."

"But how are we to live without provisions?"

"We must take some with us," answered Mike; "and when they are gone I can venture out at night and go into the town for more. You have money I suppose to keep us in idleness for a little while?"

"Ay," he replied, "enough to last us for a fortnight if we manage our matters with care. But when that's gone I don't know where we are to get more, for I can't apply for work now that the hue and cry has been let loose upon me."

"Of course not," answered Rowley; "and so, as there's no other way of doing it, you must make up your mind to commit another robbery when the money is gone."

"I must be hard driven to do that," exclaimed Guy Harrowby, "for I came back to England with a resolution to amend my life, and obtain an honest living for my family by the sweat of my brow."

"Psha!" returned the other; "what fool's notion have you got into your head now? No one of course would give you employment, even if you could apply for it; and, as you don't happen to possess an income of your own, I see nothing else for you to do but to help yourself to money wherever and whenever you may have a fair chance."

"I have myself been afraid it must come to that at last," exclaimed Guy Harrowby; "but, when I think of my wife and child, I make up my mind to suffer anything rather than further misery and shame."

"Misery and shame!" retorted the other; "that I should think has been done already, so you needn't be so particular about stepping on one side when it's to help you to the means of keeping life and soul together. Besides, I've heard you say that your wife ain't afraid of a little work, and if she can support the young 'un for a time, you can get on well enough as far as your own living's concerned."

"Very true," answered Guy; "but if I should get into trouble she would hear of it, and it would break her heart to know that I had fallen again into evil ways."

"Hearts ain't made of such brittle stuff that they break at trifles," exclaimed Rowley. "Besides, you can manage to keep clear of danger, and perhaps by-and-bye a lucky turn may come, and then you may be as honest as one half of the world can boast of being."

"At any rate," answered the fugitive, "I shall not be in any hurry about taking your advice. The money I have will last some time with care, and when that is gone, I will, if still at liberty, venture

once more to the dwelling of my poor Jane, who will make any sacrifice, rather than see me driven to a course that she thinks of with horror."

"But she mayn't happen to have any money just when you are in want of it."

"There is, I believe, little fear of my being disappointed, replied Guy Harrowby, for she had money by her when I saw her a few days since, and all might have been mine, if I could have found it in my heart, to take from her what had cost many a weary and sleepless hour to earn. A part of it, however, I did take, but it was with the hope that I should be soon able to earn some of my own, to return what I had borrowed."

"And after all, it seems you are to be so closely pressed by this Mr. Charles Heathingdon, as I think you call him, that their ain't a chance of your getting any money, but by turning thief."

"If I do turn thief through his means, the day that makes me one shall be the worst he has ever known," exclaimed Harrowby; "as it is, I owe him a grudge, but all that has passed, can be forgot, if he will only keep himself quiet for the future."

"Rather an unlikely thing that, I'm thinking," observed the other, "he has taken a fancy to your wife it seems, and when once a man falls in love, it ain't very easy to drive it out of his head. Beside, I've seen a pretty good specimen of him to-night, and from what passed, I should say, that the first thing he does on getting his liberty, will be to begin a fresh hunt after you, from one end of the country to the other."

" I expect as much myself," replied Guy Harrowby, " though on the other hand, I try to persuade myself, that he will not want to have anything more to do with a man that has defeated him three or four times already."

" Time will show how that me be," said the other, " but he's not the only chap you've got to fear, for there's his precious friend, the barber, who cannot help chattering for the life of him, and if once he talks about what took place to-night, the whole country will be up in arms, and you'll be lucky to keep out of harm's way."

" The fellow is in too much fear of me, to do much mischief, I fancy," replied Harrowby; he heard my threat of vengeance, if anything was said, and if that don't serve to keep him quiet, I don't know what the devil would."

" Why the long and the short of it, is this," said Mike Rowley, " when Mr. Heathingdon gets his liberty again, he'll of course make his first visit to the barber, and between 'em both, I think there'll be more mischief than you expect."

" Then one, as well as the other, must be prepared for what I have threatened."

" Why you don't mean to say that you'll venture back, merely to revenge yourself."

" And why shouldn't I do so?"

" Because it would be throwing yourself in the way of danger, when there's no occasion for it."

" What care I for danger, when I find myself hunted without hope of escape?" demanded Guy Harrowby. " If I must fall at last, it shall be to answer for the blood of the man that drove me to commit crime, when I was most anxious to avoid it."

" That would be poor satisfaction, I think," said Mike Rowley, " when there's other and better ways, for you to get out of this scrape."

" What other, or better way is there?"

" I've told you that already," answered Rowley; " start yourself as a thief, and at any rate you'll have as good a chance of escaping the gibbet, as you have at present."

" If I do so," exclaimed Guy Harrowby, " it shall not be till every other scheme has been tried, and failed. I am not a villain from inclination; suffering and poverty drove me to poaching, in the first instance; punishment followed, as a matter of course, and I left prison with a heart harder and more reckless, than when I had entered it. Then, people that had before pitied me, turned their backs upon the man they thought a confirmed scoundrel, and I was driven again to commit that for which I had been once punished. So you see, Rowley, how I have been driven on, step by step, till I am left to starve, without name, character, or reputation."

" And for all that," exclaimed the other, " you have to thank the infernal game-laws."

" I have," answered Guy Harrowby; " they were made for the benefit of rich men, but how many poor men have they sent to prison, or transportation, I have myself suffered from them, and often have my curses been uttered against those selfish men that punish their fellow creatures for killing the game that they would keep entirely to themselves."

" Well, never mind that now," said Mike Rowley, " for we are getting near the river-side, and I want to know whether you mean to take my advice about crossing over to Greenwich?"

" If a boat happens to be near the shore, I shall certainly do so," answered Guy.

" And suppose there isn't a boat?"

" We must then wait till the morning; when, I dare say, there'll be plenty of people crossing over."

" Ah!" exclaimed Mike Rowley, " I now see what sort of a lodging we are likely to get. It won't be in a house, I can tell you, but under one of the stacks of reeds that stand along the banks of the river."

" Better there than find a lodging in a jail," observed the fugitive, " more than half the night has passed away, and, by day-break, people will want to be crossing over the water, so that we shall be safe enough by the time our enemies begin to make a search after us."

" I should think so," answered the other; " for it's hardly likely there'll be any stir made for these three or four days at least, unless young Heathingdon should happen to get his liberty, which ain't to be expected, after the old chap's promise, to keep him in custody, till we are far enough off."

" You forget, then, that there's another person we have to dread?"

" The barber?"

" Aye," replied Mike Rowley, " he's too talkative a chap to be depended on: and I shouldn't wonder, if, before this time, he has gone and blazoned the affair through the whole neighbourhood."

" What, after the threat we left him with?"

" Our threats won't be of much use, if he's made up his mind to blab the secret," answered Mike; " besides, there's a reward offered for your discovery, and he'll be glad enough to earn it by setting the officers of justice on our track."

" But the fellow seemed frightened at our threats," observed Guy Harrowby; " and I've a notion that he would rather lose the reward, than run the risk of being murdered for his want of prudence."

" I only hope you may be right," said the other, " but, be that as it may, we must keep a sharp look-out, so as not to run into danger while it can be helped."

They had now reached the river-side, but the object they were in search of was no where to be found. There was not a boat moored on that side of the water, and as all hope of crossing over that night was at an end, their next care was to look out for one of the ricks, alluded to by Mike Rowley, beneath which they might find shelter till the return of day-light. In his selection, however, he was so fastidious, that it was some time before a spot was chosen; but, at length, they found one that would afford tolerable shelter for the night, and, choosing the warmest place, they seated themselves upon the ground, glad even, of the rough accommodation they had found. But the night was threatening and lowering, for though at times, the moon shone forth with surpassing brilliancy, huge masses of dark clouds were floating about, occasionally obscuring the luminary, and throwing a gloom around, that was not without its effects upon the spirits of our two fugitives.

"I don't know how it is," said Guy Harrowby at last, "but, somehow or another, I feel as if our escape was not quite so certain as we thought for."

"Humph!" retorted the other, "you are going to grow superstitious, I suppose, when there's most need for exerting yourself."

"You may call it superstition, Mike," answered his friend, "but a man can't help these notions coming over him, when he knows the danger that a discovery must lead to. Go where I will, I shall meet with people that would be glad enough to earn the reward that has been offered for my apprehension."

"Very likely; and the only way to disappoint 'em is to keep yourself out of sight, till there's a chance of getting a passage for yourself over to Holland, or elsewhere."

"And so leave the wife and child that I have risked so much to see once more?"

"Why, what a milksop you are growing, Guy!" exclaimed his companion impatiently. "The old woman, and her kid, are well enough provided for, and if you can't live without 'em, why, they can follow you, when you're safe in another country."

"That is to say," answered Harrowby, "if I should be lucky enough to escape the search of my pursuers."

"And I don't see anything to prevent it," returned the other; "you've only got to keep yourself snug for a time, and as soon as a good chance offers, I and your other friends will manage to get you on board some ship that's just ready to sail."

"Which can't be done without the risk of discovery."

"Of course, it can't; but you must take your chance about that, and I've a notion that you'd be puzzled to think of a better plan than the one I've proposed."

"I can think of nothing but the danger that threatens me on every side," answered Guy Harrowby. "Till the present time, I never knew what cowardice was, but now, the more I try to think of some scheme to defeat my enemies, the further do I seem from the object I have in view. However, I have a staunch friend in you, and whatever advice is given, I shall follow it, whatever the consequence may be."

"You may do that, old chap, without much fear," exclaimed Mike Rowley, "for I've been at hide and seek myself before now, and my experience that way will be of service to you when it's most wanted. I know all the dodges of the chaps we've got to deal with, and shall be glad to pay 'em off some of the old scores that are standing between us."

"But they may be too much for you after all," observed the fugitive, with a ghastly smile.

"It will be time enough to think of that when the evil hour comes upon us," returned Rowley. "I don't often suffer myself to ponder over the bad luck that may happen, and when I do happen to find myself prosing, I get out of it by thinking of the many lucky escapes I've had in the course of my life."

"Let us hope we shall be no less fortunate on the present occasion," exclaimed Guy Harrowby, "I have myself got out of some awkward dilemmas, yet I can't help fancying that, in the long run, I shall find myself outwitted by those that I most want to avoid."

"Likely enough," answered the other; "but I don't see what good it will do you to be making yourself unhappy about it. The only thing you've got to do is to be as cunning as the people you're afraid of, and, by and by, they'll begin to grow tired of looking after you; and then, if you'd rather live in England than anywhere else, it may be easily done by changing your name, and putting on a good disguise."

"Maybe so," returned Guy; "but every thing will depend upon how we manage this affair of ours to-night. We may have people already after us; and, if that should be the case, we have no chance of escape, seeing that there is not a boat near to carry us over to the other side of the river."

"How do you know we shall want one?"

"I'm only looking to the worst side of the question, that we may prepare ourselves against it," replied Guy Harrowby.

"You think, then, we might have found a better place than this to pass the night in?"

"That remains to be seen," answered the fugitive. "This spot will suit our purpose well enough, provided there's no hue and cry after us; but if the enemy should happen to lie upon our track there's no chance of ever being able to retrace our steps, whilst before us all hope of retreat is cut off."

"But there'll be plenty of boats going over to the other side as soon as its day-light."

"Very likely, and some of the people that are going over may happen to recognize us; and then a very pretty dilemma we should be in."

" Not so bad as you fancy," replied Mike Rowley; " for, even if it came to that, you and I are able enough to show 'em what hard fighting is. For my own part, I've made up my mind not to be taken very easily ; and if I should be taken off to a prison, it will not be till some of my enemies have been made to smart for interfering with business that they have nothing at all to do with."

" It would be madness to offer resistance," answered Guy, " unless there was a certainty that it would lead to our escape. Against two or three I should be willing enough to show fight ; but as for more than that number, I should think twice before I rushed into a fray that would end in no good to ourselves."

" Do you think, then, that I've not as much reason as yourself to keep out of the way of mischief?"

" You may have as much reason for it," answered Harrowby ; " but I've a notion you wouldn't mind the chance of getting into a scrape if you took it into your head to be revenged upon the persons that might come in search of us."

" Humph ! then you, I suppose, would run away from 'em like a coward ?"

" Coward's an ugly name for a man that never did anything to deserve it," retorted Guy, abruptly; " I've stood upon my own defence before now, and will do so again when there is occasion, but I hold it no sign of bravery to run into danger where it can be avoided."

" Ah ! then, you'll turn upon 'em if there should seem to be no other way of getting away ?"

" Decidedly, I will."

" That's enough, old fellow !" exclaimed Mike Rowley, " you and I shall begin to understand each other by and by ; and, if we should get into a bit of a scrimmage, I shall know I've got a chap with me that may be depended on. So never mind what I said just now about cowardice, for that was only meant to try what sort of metal you are made of."

" My courage is not what it used to be," returned Harrowby ; " but I've still enough left to serve our purpose if there should be any occasion for showing it."

" And why haven't you as much pluck now as you used to have ?" asked his companion.

" Because I seem to be always haunted by the man I killed to escape from over the water," answered Guy; " day and night, be where I may, the image of the dying wretch stands frowningly before me, as if to warn me that the time is drawing near when I shall have to answer for his death by my own."

" D—n it, man ! why, you ain't fool enough to believe in a parcel of nonsense like that ?"

" Murder ain't quite so soon forgot as you may fancy," returned Guy gloomily. " I myself didn't think much about what I'd done till I escaped the dangers of my sea voyage ; but as soon as my mind was clear of all that trouble it went back to former times, and then the horrors of that moment seemed to be acted over again."

" Then why don't you drink deeply when such foolish notions come over you ?" demanded his companion. " Brandy would even give you fresh courage, and make a man of you."

" I've tried it," answered Guy Harrowby ; " but it only served to madden me the more."

" If that's the case, I don't know what's to be done !" exclaimed Rowley. " For my own part, I've always found it the best way of getting rid of the blue devils ; and, when I've had enough of it, would fight against a dozen fellows rather than suffer myself to be taken to a prison."

" But all your fighting would not do any good in the long run."

" Very likely not ; but I should have the satisfaction of knowing that I hadn't given myself up like a coward. However, it's no use talking to you about that I see, Harrowby ; so, as the day's just beginning to break, suppose we go down to the ferry and wait till the first boat goes across."

Guy willingly assented to this proposition, and they rose to take their departure ; but, before they had advanced a single step from the spot, a sound of quick tramping was heard, and in another moment they were surrounded by seven or eight men, amongst the most conspicuous of whom was their former acquaintance, the barber. The attack was so sudden and unexpected that no resistance could be offered ; and both Guy and his companion were secured and bound before they could recover from the consternation into which they had been thrown."

" What's the meaning of all this ?" demanded Harrowby, who was the first to speak.

" You'll know all about that in good time," answered the barber. " We've found you, and shall get the reward, which is all we want or care about."

" Your reward shall be something that you won't forget in a hurry," exclaimed Mike ; " for when I get free again, which won't be long first, I'll not forget to pay you for the trouble you've been taking in this business."

" There's not much fear of your being set free again in a hurry," retorted the constable, who was at the head of the victorious party ; " you are pretty well known for a bad 'un that ought to have got his desserts long enough ago ; and as for your companion, he's an escaped convict, so his doom's pretty well settled, unless he should have the devil's share of luck and his own too."

" Who told you that I am an escaped convict?" asked Guy.

" This chap, sir," answered the constable, pointing to the barber. "

" And how should he know anything about it ?"

" I've never asked him the question," replied the constable, " but I dare say he won't mind telling you, if you've any very particular wish to know."

" He don't want to be told by me how I know it," said the man of lather ; " he knows I heard all about him from the gentleman that has been looking after him, and as I heard there was a spanking reward offered for his discovery, I should have been a fool to let him escape whilst there was a chance of putting money into my pocket."

"The person you speak of is my deadly enemy," replied Guy Harrowby, "and the information he has given was only done to complete his own evil designs against me."

"We shall see all about that at the examination before a magistrate," said the constable. "You and your comrade will be locked up in the cage for the present, and by and by, you'll be carried before his worship, who'll do as he likes about believing the stories you tell him."

"I'll tell you what it is, my fine fellow," exclaimed Mike Rowley, in a swaggering tone, "you may think it all d——d fine to make prisoners of respectable men like us, but you'll find your mistake out by and by, and then a fine scrape you'll all find yourselves in. Mind, I've warned you not to touch us; and if, after that, you choose to put us into the cage, it'll be our turn afterwards to make you smart for it."

"Oh, as for that," retorted the official, "we've lived too long in a wood to be scared by an owl. We know well enough who you both are, so you may as well go with us quietly; for if you should be rumbustical, we've got handcuffs with us to keep you a little in order."

"Aye," rejoined the barber, "and if they ain't enough, we've three or four loaded pistols among us; and, what's more, we sharn't mind using 'em, if we should be driven to it."

And as he said so, he pulled out a huge weapon and flourished it about, by way of proving that the boast he had made was not a vain one. This had a marked and instantaneous effect upon Rowley, who, in spite of his vaunted courage, had no great inclination to sacrifice his life when the odds were so greatly against him. He therefore touched Guy upon the arm, and said, significantly—

"I think, as these chaps are pretty civil, we may as well go with 'em quietly, for we know our own innocence, and of course it'll be all right as soon as we've explained matters to the magistrate."

"Of course it will," answered Harrowby, with a faint attempt to smile; "we can explain matters to the satisfaction of the magistrate, who'll order us to be immediately released, and then all we shall have to complain of will be the short imprisonment we've suffered."

"It won't be all I shall have to complain of, though," exclaimed his companion, "for these chaps shall learn what it is to take up respectable men, and put 'em into the cage for nothing."

"We ain't much afeard of your proving your respectability," observed the barber, "or the gentleman that told me all about your comrade must be given to telling lies."

"And even if you should turn out to be innocent," interposed the constable, "we've only acted on information that was given us, and there's no law to punish us for doing our duty. So come along with us, my fine fellows, and to-morrow will show what sort of a story you can tell his worship."

As all resistance would have been in vain, neither Guy Harrowby, nor his associate, thought proper to offer any further opposition; and they moved forward, each well guarded to prevent the possibility of an escape. Not a word was spoken by any one as they went along, for the prisoners were kept separate to prevent any attempt being made at escape, and neither of them felt inclined to say anything to those who were accompanying them, lest their words might afterwards be made use of against them. At length, after a sharp walk of half an hour, they reached the cage, the door of which having been opened by the constable, they were thrust in, and the place having been made secure, their captors departed, exulting in the thought of having made sure of a large reward for their services.

Sullen, and somewhat alarmed at the unforeseen dilemma in which they were placed, Mike Rowley seated himself upon the stone bench, to meditate gloomily over the probable consequences of their detention. Guy Harrowby had even more reason to feel alarm for the future, but he assumed an appearance of cheerfulness, and even ventured to express a hope that no proof would be brought against them at their approaching examination. To this his companion listened for some time without making any reply, but at length he exclaimed, impatiently—

"It may be all very well for you to think lightly of this affair, but I can't see my way out of it quite so clearly as you seem to do. The beak won't believe a word we say, and if, as you say, no evidence is brought against us, he'll remand us till another day to give an opportunity for raking together all they can to commit us to prison."

"And if they do," retorted Harrowby, "I don't see that grumbling will get us out of the dilemma."

"It's all very well to take it so easy," exclaimed Mike Rowley, "but this cursed piece of bad luck wouldn't have happened to me if it hadn't been for my d——d good nature in going to look after you in that old tumble-down house."

"Well," replied Guy, "I'm sorry for your sake that it's happened, but you must own its no fault of mine. Besides, I'm the only person they wanted, and when the charge has been proved against me I don't see that they'll want to keep you for merely being found in my company."

"Won't they!" exclaimed Rowley, "only catch 'em letting me off so easily, that's all, after the number of times they've been trying to lay me by the heels. There's half-a-dozen charges they can bring against me if they like, and the very least of 'em would be enough to send me over the water for seven years if I'm found guilty."

"And sooner or later, I suppose, you expected that to happen?"

"Yes, but the longer it was put off the better I should have liked it.   Besides, it's d—d provoking that it should have happened through trying to serve a friend."

"You're right there," answered Guy Harrowby; "but what can't be cured must be endured. We are both of us in a pretty fix, so the only way is to trust to our good fortune, and who knows but some piece of luck may turn up for us when we least expect it."

"That's a cool way of looking at it, however," grumbled Rowley.   "It's all through you that I've got locked up in this infernal place, and yet you want to console me with the hope of good luck when the worst that could happen has sent us to this place."

"I only want to keep up your spirits instead of seeing 'em so downcast," answered Guy, vainly endeavouring to soothe the irritation of his companion.   "Maybe, I've been the cause of getting you into this scrape, but at any rate it was no fault of mine, so I don't see why you should be so confoundedly cross with me about it."

"Transportation, or at least a chance of it, is enough to make a fellow grumble."

"Exactly so ; but I suppose it would have been your fate sooner or later?"

"I'm not quite certain about that," answered Mike, "for I have had the luck to keep out of harm's way for the last two or three years, and I began to think all was as right as a trivet, when all of a sudden I find myself clapt into this infernal hole."

"But do you think there's no chance of our getting out of it?" demanded his companion.

"What chance is there of moving those bars from the window?" asked Mike Rowley.   "Besides its now quite daylight, and there's people enough about to raise an alarm if we should attempt to escape."

"It would be worth trying at any rate," observed Guy, tugging violently at the bars, which however remained firm and immovable in their sockets.   Rowley watched him in silence for some few moments and then burst out into a derisive laugh.

"You see," he exclaimed, "what a chance we have of getting out of this place.   Sometimes, indeed, I should have been better provided than I am at present.   But as ill luck will have it, I've left my file behind me, or these bars should not have kept us here so long."

"Everything seems to be against us," cried Guy Harrowby, sitting himself down in despair.

"Aye, and matters will get so for us, I'm thinking," returned the other ; for they've got us safe enough now, and there isn't a chance that I can see of giving 'em the slip.   However your situation is worse than mine, old fellow, for they'll hang you as sure as you've got a neck, whilst they can only send me abroad for a few years, to come back again a greater villain than I go away!"

"And if they do hang me," answered Harrowby, "there'll be an end of the trouble that have pursued me through so many years of my life.   The thought of being hanged like a dog aint a very pleasant one to be sure, but I suppose there's no help for it, and the only way is to resign myself to it with as good a grace as I can.   In short, Rowley, I've no wish to live if it wasn't that I know the endless misery that a shameful death would bring upon my wife and child."

"Psha! they'd forget all about that, sooner than you think for."

"They might, if left to themselves," replied Guy, "but the world won't let 'em forget it so easily ; for there'll always be some one to remind 'em of the disgrace I brought upon my family, and thus keep up a remembrance that must poison the remainder of their existence.   Besides, when I'm gone, my poor Jane will be thrown entirely upon the mercy of the scoundrel that has already tried to take advantage of my absence."

"As for that matter," exclaimed Rowley, "I don't see that she'll be worse off than she's been while you were thousands of miles away from her.   By your account she's virtuous enough, and that being the case she'll always find friends among people that aint quite so bad as this Mr. Charles Heathingdon.   By the by, I only wish we had him here just now, for I feel just in the humour to pay him off for the scurvy trick he's played us to satisfy his own spite."

"Be content to let matters take their own course," returned Harrowby, "he must always be the reckless devil he is now, and when he comes to think over the bad things he's been guilty of, he'll have such an uneasy conscience of his own, that no one need envy him of it."

"Conscience wont trouble him much, depend on it," exclaimed Mike Rowley.   "The fellow, I dare say, thinks he's only doing his duty in hunting you to the gallows, and as for the little affair of gallantry with your wife, great folks are so in the habit of doing such things, that he'll rather be praised than blamed for what has passed."

"Only by those that are as bad as himself," answered Guy.

"Well, and what more does he care about?" demanded the other, "his companions are of course picked out from such people, so that he's not likely to hear any remarks that would be unpleasant."

"But I have heard that his father and brother are men of very different character to his own, and from them, perhaps, he'll hear truths that he wont like."

"I'll be bound he wont care a straw for what either of 'em may choose to say."

"Not just at present," answered Guy Harrowby, "but by and by he may think of the past a little, and then the reproaches he hears will sting him to the very heart."

At that moment, footsteps were heard outside, and presently afterwards a face was seen peering in between the bars that guarded the prison.   The inquisitive personage was no other than the barber, who nodding familiarly to them exclaimed :—"Good morning to you, gentlemen ; I hope you've spent time comfortably since I saw you last."

"So comfortably, you infernal rascal," vociferated Mike Rowley, "that if I could only get at you, you should remember the scurvy trick you've played us as long as you live."

"Really, my good fellow, I don't know of any scurvy trick that I've played you," answered the tonsor. "I knew you to be a couple of bad 'uns, and, of course, it was my duty to have you locked up as soon as possible."

"Duty!" retorted Guy Harrowby; "why, it was the reward that tempted you to go and lay an information against us. But I told you beforehand to look out for yourself, if anything happened to us through your means; so you may prepare for something that wont be very pleasant, before you are many hours older."

"That is to say if you ain't locked up."

"Locked up or not," answered Guy, "you won't get off the punishment I told you of. I may not be able to do it myself, but I have plenty of friends, and they'll take care to revenge the imprisonment of their friend."

"Oh, ho!" exclaimed the barber, "if that's the case, I shall tell the magistrate what you say, and claim protection from the court. He'll take care to keep you fast enough, when he hears what couple of scoundrels are before him."

"Scoundrel," vociferated Mike Rowley, "'tis well, old chap, that my arm can't reach you, or I might, perhaps, have a murder to answer for presently."

"And then you'd be hanged, instead of only being transported."

Guy Harrowby saw that the ire of his companion was becoming ungovernable, and anxious to put an end to the wordy warfare, he suggested the propriety of letting the matter drop.

"All you can say," he added, "won't do us any good, while some word may escape that will be brought against us when the examination comes on."

"What's that you said about escaping?" exclaimed the barber, who had only caught the sound of a single word. "You think of getting out of this place, do you, my fine fellow? you'd give us the slip after all the trouble we've had to find you, and prevent my receiving the reward that has been offered for your apprehension; but you will be disappointed, for I shall run off to the constable and tell him what you're up to, and he'll send people to watch the place till its time for you to go before the magistrate."

And with these words he bolted away, leaving the prisoners once more to themselves.

"If we hadn't been a couple of fools," exclaimed Mike, "that fellow would have been locked up with Mr. Heathingdon, in the old house. I'd a good mind to propose it at the time, but was afraid the delay might do us more harm than good."

"Its no use talking about that, now that he's done us all the mischief he can," answered Guy, "we have been caged by him, and whatever our fate may be, we must put up with it quietly."

"You, perhaps, may take it quietly," returned the other, "but for my own part I don't half like the prospect before us. Young Heathingdon too, has, I dare say by this time, got out of the place we left him in; and by and by we shall have the pleasure of seeing him get into the witness-box to give his evidence against us."

"And I dare say, sooner or later, the same thing would have happened," exclaimed Guy Harrowby, "he has sworn to be revenged for the blow I struck him, and was determined never to give up his pursuit till he had brought me to this perilous situation."

"Well, he's stuck to you like a leech," observed the other, "and I dare say chuckles to himself at what he's done; but let him look out for himself, that's all, for our people will owe him a grudge for this, and they won't forget to pay him either, before he's many days older."

"And what good will that do us?" demanded Guy.

"Not much, perhaps, but we shall have the satisfaction of knowing that the chap will get his desserts."

"Aye, and our friends may very likely get themselves into trouble through it."

"Oh, leave 'em alone for taking care of themselves," exclaimed Mike Rowley, "they know the sort of customers they'll have to deal with, and will so manage matters that no one will know where the blow comes from."

"Do you think they'll take his life then?"

"Its quite likely they will," answered Mike. "The fellow has made himself a little too busy in this matter, and they'll not be satisfied till they've given him his full desserts."

"For which the chances are that they'll be hang'd."

"How can that be if its not known who does it? They wont go and 'peach against themselves, you may be sure, and of course they'll contrive the business so that there shall be no witnesses by when they go to work."

"That may be," answered Guy Harrowby, "and yet, how many men have been hanged for murder on what they call circumstantial evidence."

"I see then," exclaimed Mike, "that you don't want your enemy to be punished for what he's done."

"Not if it will bring risk upon those that have served me," replied Harrowby. Besides, Charles Heathingdon, as well as ourselves, needs time to repent the evil he has done, and I would not encourage our companions to lay violent hands upon him."

"But suppose they choose to do it without asking your opinion?"

" If they do that," returned the convict, " I shall not have to answer for any thing to follow."

" Humph ! you're growing sentimental."

" I've gone through enough sufferings to make me think very differently to what I used to do," replied Guy.

" But that needn't make a milk-sop of you."

" I'm not one, that I know of, though I don't want to be guilty of another crime, now that my days seem to be drawing so near to a close," answered Guy. " They'll send me to the gibbet for the murder I committed abroad, and the little time that is left me, should be passed in repentance for the evil deeds I have done."

" So, then, you've made up your mind to be hanged?"

" What else have I got to expect ?" asked Harrowby, gloomily. " The death of the keeper must have been known in England long ago, and as there can be no doubt as to who caused it, I've made up my mind for the worst."

"You don't think that our friends will attempt to rescue us?

" I think they'd be mad to do it," answered Guy, " for they'd be sure to fail, and get themselves into a scrape, without serving us in the least."

" That is, if they were fools enough to attempt a rescue, without bringing a strong party to help 'em."

" No party," answered Guy Harrowby, " would be strong enough to beat those that will have charge of us. However, this is a useless subject to argue about, because our friends know nothing of the situation we are in, and even if they did, they'd hardly risk their own liberty for the sake of getting us out of our difficulties."

" But I happen to know they would though," replied the other, " for Dick Fordham and Snatch may expect to be in the same sort of quandary themselves some day or another, and, if they wont help a friend in need, they must look for assistance when it comes to their turn to want it, and as for their not knowing of our being in limbo, I'll be bound some of 'em have been down to the old house to see what has kept me so long, and then they'll be sure to hear that we're locked up in this confounded place."

' And when they do hear it," observed Guy," the wisest thing they can do will be to get away as fast as they can, lest they should be suspected of being our comrades."

" Only let me catch 'em doing such a thing, and see how I'd serve 'em out for it," exclaimed Mike Rowley. " I know enough to lag both of 'em, and, it should all come out if they deserted me, when I want their help."

" What ! turn informer against your friends? "

" Pretty friends they'd be, if theywere to do as you've said," exclaimed the other. " It aint the way I'd serve them if they get into trouble, and I don't expect to be left in a hobble while there's a chance of getting me out of it."

Just then they heard a key turning in the lock, and a moment afterwards the door being opened in walked the constable with three or four men that he had brought with him, to assist in guarding the prisoners.

" Now then," he exclaimed, " its time to be off to the police-office, for the magistrate sits at ten, and it wont be far from that hour when we get there ; so eat your breakfast and be quick about it, or you'll be obliged to put off your meal till after the examination."

Whilst he was speaking, the man uncovered a basket that he had brought with him, and handed it to the two prisoners, who were too much in need of refreshment to refuse it. Whilst they were occupied in discussing their breakfast, the constable proceeded to give what he conceived to be very necessary directions to those who were to assist him.

" You'll keep a sharp look out, my lads," he said, " to see that no attempt is made to rescue these two chaps, I've heard that some very suspicious persons have been seen lurking about this neighbourhood for the last hour or two, and as its likely enough that they're friends of these men, we must be prepared in case they mean to play us a trick."

"What sort of men were they ?" asked Mike Rowley, who at once fancied he saw a chance of escape.

" Ask no questions and you'll hear no lies," retorted the constable. " Besides, I haven't seen the fellows myself, so I can't be expected to know much about 'em."

Having said this, the official maintained a dogged silence, whilst the others concluded their meal, and when that was over, he led his prisoners from their cell, and conducted them through the streets towards the office where the examination was to take place. As they passed along, Mike looked wistfully about him, and at length, to his no small satisfaction, saw Fordham and Snatch following them at no great distance off.

CHAPTER XII.

THE POLICE OFFICE.—THE EXAMINATION.—THE RESCUE.

When the two prisoners entered the police office, they were immediately placed at the bar, though the magistrate had not yet taken his seat on the bench. The place, however, was filled with persons anxious to hear the examination, for a report had been spread abroad, that two desperate characters had been taken in the neighbourhood, one of whom was charged with the double crime of murder

and returning from transportation before the period of his punishment had expired. All eyes were consequently directed towards the two prisoners, who could hear the eager inquiries among the spectators, as to which of them was the man that was accused of killing his guard. This was a question, however, that nobody could satisfactorily answer, and the buzz of eager excitement continued to increase till the entrance of the magistrate, when a dead and solemn silence ensued. Upon seating himself, Mr. Thornley, the magistrate, directed a scrutinizing glance towards the two men before him, and then, as if he knew nothing of the affair, asked the constable, what charge he had to make against the prisoners.

"Please your worship," said the constable, "this one," pointing to Mike, "is a known thief, that we've been looking for a long while, and the other, is Guy Harrowby, a returned convict, that murdered his guard to make his escape from Van Dieman's Land."

"We will proceed with his examination first then," exclaimed the magistrate, and then addressing himself to the prisoner, inquired if it was true that his name was Guy Harrowby."

"It is, your worship," he replied.

"Then that part of the charge is disposed of," said the magistrate, "and it now only remains to prove that he is guilty of the more serious crime of murder. Have you any evidence here against him?"

"Yes, your worship," answered the constable, who at that moment saw Charles Heathingdon enter the court; "here's a gentleman just come in that I believe can say something about the murder."

"Let him stand forward."

Charles Heathingdon entered the witness box, and having been sworn, was asked what he knew of the prisoner. "I know his name to be Guy Harrowby," he replied, "and that he has returned from transportation before the period of his punishment had expired."

"The prisoner has admitted thus much," said the magistrate, "and it now, therefore, only remains to inquire into the alleged murder. Can you give any evidence, sir, to prove the crime you charge him with?"

"At present I am not prepared with witnesses," replied the other; "but if your worship will remand him for a few days, I have no doubt I shall be able to collect all the evidence that will be required."

"Upon the other charge I can remand him," said Mr. Thornley, "but not for the more serious one. That, however, will answer the purpose, and perhaps by this day week you will be able to collect the necessary witnesses. Have you anything you wish to ask this gentleman, prisoner?"

"No man is bound to convict himself," answered Guy; "so I shall not say anything till I see what sort of a turn this affair is likely to take."

"Why don't you tell his worship that the charge is only brought against you out of spite?" suggested Rowley.

"And if it be so, there's reason enough for it," exclaimed Charles Heathingdon. "I suffered violence from them last night, and was locked up in a dark vault, in order that they might escape from my pursuit."

"Where was the place you speak of?" asked Mr. Thornley.

"I am hardly certain about that," replied Charles; "but you may know the place when I tell you that it is a large ruinous mansion—that the superstitious of this neighbourhood report to be haunted."

"I know the house you mean," returned the magistrate; "and now, sir, may I ask how you happened to go there?"

"I went because I had pretty certain information that Guy Harrowby was concealed there."

"And you found your suspicions correct?"

"Yes; both he and the other prisoner were there."

"Did you attempt to capture them without assistance?"

"I did, because I had no reason to believe that there were two persons in the house."

"And they laid violent hands upon you?"

"They bound me," replied Charles Heathingdon: "and under the guidance of a third person, I was conducted to a vault under the house, where I was locked in."

"Who was the other man you speak of?"

"That I know not, but his appearance was very remarkable; and from some few things that transpired, I fancy he has taken up his abode in the house."

"This must be immediately inquired into," said the magistrate. "There have been strange rumours about the place being haunted, and the story you have been telling me seems to promise a clue to the mystery."

"Whenever the search takes place I shall be happy to accompany your people," answered Charles Heathingdon.

"Have you any charge to prefer against the old man that assisted these two prisoners?"

"No," replied the other; "the ends of justice will be sufficiently answered by the punishment of the men who are now standing before you."

"I know not whether I am correct in my suspicion," said the magistrate; "but there seems to me something more in this affair than I can at present fathom. You have, if I mistake not, some other motive in view besides bringing the man Harrowby to justice."

"What other motive can I possibly have?" exclaimed Charles. "I am perfectly well satisfied of the identity of Guy Harrowby; he is guilty of both the charges brought against him, and the course I have adopted has been actuated solely by an anxious wish to bring so heinous an offender to justice."

"Your worship," interposed Harrowby, "my accuser never would have taken all this trouble in the affair but to serve his own feelings of revenge. He has tried to undermine the virtue of my wife, and because I struck him to the earth for a villanous libertine, as he is, he has sworn never to give up the pursuit till he has brought me to the gibbet."

"All this has nothing to do with the case I am inquiring into," said the magistrate. "The witness may have acted in the dishonourable way you speak of, but the evidence he has to give will not be the less important on that account."

"I have another witness in court," said Charles Heathingdon, "if you wish to hear what he has to say."

"Let him stand forward."

The barber here bustled through the crowd, and having made his way to the witness-box, took the oath that was administered to him by the proper official.

"What is your name?" asked the magistrate's clerk.

"Timothy Goggles."

"What are you?"

"A barber."

"Have you any information to give respecting the inquiry now before the court?"

"I know that these two men locked Mr. Heathingdon in a vault under the haunted house, and that he'd have been left there to starve if it hadn't been for me."

"That's false, your worship," exclaimed Guy Harrowby; "for the old man you've heard of promised to supply him with food, and to set him at liberty at the end of two or three days."

"Pray what was your motive for making him your prisoner?" asked Mr. Thornley.

"We had no other reason for it than to secure our own escape," replied Guy. "He came for the purpose of apprehending me, and as the advantage happened to be against him, we locked him up, and then made the best of our way out of the house."

"Yes," exclaimed the barber; "and meeting with me in their way, I had very nearly been served worse than Mr. Heathingdon was."

"I suppose they thought better of it?"

"They did, your worship; but at one time they talked of throwing me into a horse-pond."

"A mere threat to frighten you perhaps."

"I don't know how that may have been," replied Timothy Goggles; "but I suppose they were in a hurry to get off, for after a time they went away, threatening all sorts of violence if I said anything about 'em."

"Notwithstanding which, you very properly gave the information that has led to their capture."

"I lost no time about doing that, your worship," exclaimed the barber; "and, whilst I and others went in pursuit of the two men, others proceeded to the old house, and set Mr. Heathingdon at liberty."

"Was the old man that has been spoken of seen by any of the people?"

"No, you worship."

"Can anybody give information as to who he is?"

"I've made inquiries about it," said the constable, "but no one has ever seen a person of his description."

"The probability is," said Mr. Thornley, "that the man is some mendicant, who has sought shelter there, knowing that the house is uninhabited. Or it may be some criminal, hiding himself from justice, and expecting to find a safe refuge in a place that is reported to be haunted."

"If that's the case, it wont be long before we have him, your worship," said the constable. "Mr. Heathingdon has given a full description of what sort of person he is, and there are men in all directions making inquiries after him."

"Has the house been thoroughly searched?"

"Not yet, I believe."

"Why was that not thought of before any other steps were taken?" asked Mr. Thornley.

"It was thought of," replied the constable, "but the people hereabouts are all such cowards, that no one can be found to enter the haunted house."

"But it is my desire that it is done without delay," exclaimed his worship peremptorily. "Any number of persons that may be deemed necessary will be pressed into this service, and the first man that refuses shall feel that I have authority to enforce my orders."

"I'll take care that it shall be done immediately."

"Do so," exclaimed Mr. Thornley, "and let it be remembered, that it will be your duty to accompany them."

The constable appeared to be quite chop-fallen, as this latter direction was given; but, the tittering of the bystanders brought him a little to his senses, and bowing to the magistrate, he promised that his orders should be fulfilled. This part of the business having been disposed of, Mr. Thornley inquired of the accuser if he had any further statement to make, relative to the man under examination.

"There is one other charge I have to make against him," answered Charles Heathingdon. "I closely pursued the prisoner immediately after his escape from the cottage where his wife lives, and having overtaken him at a lonely spot a few miles from London, I attempted to secure him, but being overpowered, he bound me to a tree, and then escaped after discharging a loaded pistol at me."

"That's false, and he knows it to be so," exclaimed Guy Harrowby. "The pistol he speaks of was one of his own, and I fired it in the air to prevent his afterwards making use of it against me."

"I am bound to receive the evidence of this gentleman as it is given on oath," said the magistrate. "The charge will not be tried if the principal one is sustained, but it will form the subject for a separate indictment in case both the others should fail."

"At any rate," exclaimed Guy Harrowby, "there's only his own word for it, your worship, for there was not another person present at the time when he overtook me."

"It will be for the jury to say what degree of credit they place upon his evidence," said Mr.

Thornley. "I sit here to do equal justice between both parties, and it is my duty to hear every statement that either side may have to make."

"He has purjured himself," exclaimed Guy Harrowby, "but it is only of a piece with the rest of the villany he has practised against me. He now accuses me with having attempted to shoot him, and even if I had done so, it could not have been much wondered at, after the provocation he gave me."

"No provocation would excuse such an act as that you are charged with," said Mr. Thornley. "The person who lays this charge has only done his duty, in procuring your apprehension, and nothing that you can impute to his motives will benefit your own course."

"Is it nothing, then?" asked Guy Harrowby, "if I can prove that he has done it from revenge?"

"It may be used in your defence, when the proper time arrives," answered the magistrate, "but should the charge of murder be sustained, it will matter very little what the motives were that led to your apprehension. It is the duty of every one to assist in the punishment of those who have been guilty of crime, and Mr. Heathingdon has performed a service to his country, if it should be proved that you have committed the crime he accuses you of."

"As your worship is about to remand the prisoner for a week," said the libertine, "I shall be able to collect as much evidence as will be sufficient to warrant another delay. There are some witnesses, however, to be brought from Van Dieman's Land, so that it is possible the trial will not come on for some months hence."

"And am I to be shut up in a prison all that time, on such a charge as this?" asked Guy Harrowby.

"At present I am not prepared to say what course will be pursued," answered the magistrate." After the next examination, your case will be laid before the Secretary of State, who may think it advisable for the convenience of the witnesses to send you for trial to the place where the alleged crime was committed."

"And shall I have to go over there?" asked Charles Heathingdon, not much relishing the idea of so long a voyage.

"Unless your evidence is of more importance than it seems to be at present, I think there will not be any occasion for it," said Mr. Thornley. "Of the murder itself you know nothing, except from hearsay, and you can state nothing more, than that you gave him up to the hands of justice as soon as possible after you became aware that he had returned to England?"

"But suppose," said Guy Harrowby, "this charge of murder should not be proved."

"You would then be tried for escaping from the place you were transported to, an the punishment for that is the same as if you were convicted of the murder."

"Then the law's a most infernal one," exclaimed the prisoner, for where's the man, I should like to know, that wouldn't escape if he had an opportunity?"

"I'm not placed here to answer questions of that kind," replied Mr. Thornley. "Those who break the laws must submit to the punishment awarded to their offences; and no excuse can be urged for evading the consequences they have brought upon themselves. Neither have you any just ground for complaint against Mr. Heathingdon, who has acted very properly, in placing you at that bar, to answer the charges he has brought forward."

"It was not very proper though, I should think, to try and corrupt the mind of a virtuous woman," exclaimed Guy Harrowby; "he took advantage of my absence, and being defeated by my unexpected return, he, in revenge, has resolved to hunt me to the gallows."

"Revenge, I apprehend, has nothing whatever to do with so serious an affair as this," observed the magistrate; "he has, I have no doubt, been actuated by higher motives, but whether that is the case or not, he has done no more than perform a solemn but imperious duty."

"A duty it may be called by some people," exclaimed Guy, "but what would have been said if I had slain him upon the spot, when, upon returning home, I found my wife struggling to release herself from his arms?"

"There are laws to which you might have appealed."

"An outcast, like myself, has little to expect from either law or justice," returned Guy Harrowby. "A poor man is hardly believed when he brings a charge against a rich one and the only wonder is, that I didn't kill the villain in the rage that had over-mastered me."

"The truth is, your worship," said the libertine, caring little what falsehood he uttered to hide his own delinquency, "this man has taken a strange notion into his head that I wish to deprive him of the affections of his wife. There is, however, no foundation for such a suspicion; and I hope my word will be taken, when I solemnly declare that I have no improper feeling towards his wife."

"How was it then," demanded Guy, "that I found you trying to carry her off?"

"I don't know that there's any occasion for me to answer that question," returned Charles Heathingdon. "If you would know, however, why I was in your house, it is easily explained, by my stating, that I happened to be walking near the place, and entered it for the purpose of resting myself."

"Which you have done on former occasions," said Guy, "though my wife, suspecting your designs, has requested that you would keep away from the house."

" She had no right to impute evil notions to me, when my visits were perfectly friendly," answered the libertine, still determined to keep up an appearance of innocence.

" These disputes must not be suffered to take place in my presence," interposed the magistrate, " you," addressing himself to Charles Heathingdon, " best know, whether there is any foundation for this man's jealousy, but, whether there is or not, can have nothing at all to do with the case that has been brought before me. I have listened attentively to everything that bears upon the charge, and as sufficient preliminary evidence has been brought forward, I have granted the remand you ask for."

" And I," said Charles, " will not fail to make good my promises of collecting together as many witnesses as the interval will allow of. Proof at any rate, of his former conviction shall be forthcoming, so that there shall be no difficulty in committing him for trial as a returned convict."

" Unless," observed Mr. Thornley, " he has received a commutation of his punishment."

" If that had been the case," said Charles Heathingdon, " it is only fair to presume, that he would have produced the written document, in order to get rid of this charge at once."

" We are not to judge too hastily, without knowing the motives of the man," returned Mr. Thornley. " He may have reason for keeping such things back, in order to produce them when they will be of more service to himself. At all events, it is not my business to interfere with advice, and the prisoner will therefore either answer your question, or remain silent, as he may think proper."

" I shall not satisfy him just yet," exclaimed Guy, for I know he is anxious to hear all he can, that he may afterwards make use of it against me."

" You act properly enough there," said Mr. Thornley, " and now, as I have expressed my determination to remand this case, I may suggest to you, that it would be well to engage professional assistance, against the next time you are brought before me."

Then desiring the other prisoner to step forward, he asked if there was [any specific charge against him.

" Yes, your worship," exclaimed the constable, " I charge him with being a known thief."

" That's rather too vague a charge, to occupy the time of the court with," said Mr. Thornley, smiling at the pomposity with which the words had been uttered. " I cannot punish the man merely because you believe him to be a thief, but if he has committed a robbery that you are prepared to prove, I am ready and willing to go into the case at once."

" Why, I don't know anything about it myself," replied the constable, " but his name's well known to the police, and if he havn't done anything worse, there's no doubt that he was aiding and assisting the other man to escape."

" Are you sure that he was doing so ? "

" They were both together, your worship, when we took 'em into custody."

" That may be," replied Mr. Thornley, " and yet it is possible enough, that this man may not have known that he was in the company of an escaped convict."

" No more I did your worship," exclaimed Mike Rowley, glad of the chance he saw of getting off. " We met quite by accident like, and as both were going the same way, we chatted together along the road till we sat down to rest under a reed stack, where the officers pounced upon us, and we were carried off to the cage."

" Where did you meet with the prisoner ? " asked Mr. Thornley.

" In the old house that they say's haunted."

" How was it you went there ?"

" How was it, your worship ?" said Mike, a little puzzled what reply to make to this question ;— " why, you see, I'd no money to pay for a lodging, I thought I couldn't do better than have a night's sleep in the old house ; so when I got there, I meets with this man, and we were comfortable enough till the gentleman came and disturbed us."

" I really think, sir," interposed Charles Heathingdon, " that if you will remand this case as well as the other, we shall find that these two men have been acquainted with each other longer than they are inclined to acknowledge."

" Perhaps so," answered Mr. Thornley ; " but unless any crime can be proved against this other prisoner, I have not the power to keep him in custody. Show me that he has broken the laws, and you will find me willing enough to lock him up till we can make a case against him."

" At any rate," said Charles, " I can charge him with having offered very violent resistance when he found that I was resolved to take him as well as his companion."

" And if he had been guilty of no crime he was fully justified in offering resistance," returned the magistrate. " The man says he entered an empty house to get shelter for the night ; and, as no evidence has been brought to prove that his assertion is false, I must order him to be immediately discharged from custody."

" Give me time to do it," exclaimed Charles Heathingdon ; " and I'll undertake to bring a case against him that will secure his conviction."

" You are really asking too much of me," returned the magistrate. " Before I can remand a man I must have clear evidence that he has been guilty of crime ; for no man, according to law and justice, is to be deprived of his liberty merely because another man thinks he can make a charge against him."

" I don't know much about these things, to be sure !" exclaimed Charles ; " but it seems to me

that there is a most extraordinary leaning in favour of a man that is well known to be of bad character."

"I'll not sit here to be insulted, nor hear my motives impugned," retorted Mr. Thornley warmly. "Your case has received every attention from me; but I am not to be turned from the path of duty merely because it is your wish to have this man locked up. I have no right to remand him; and, if I did, there is a law by which he might teach me not to exceed my duty in future."

"Then I suppose the next thing will be that he revenges himself for the part I've taken against him."

"Has he uttered any threats to that effect?"

"No."

"How then am I to interfere?" demanded Mr. Thornley. "You shall have the protection of this court if it is considered necessary; but it cannot be till after some threat of violence has been uttered."

"He's got nothing to fear from me, your worship," said Mike Rowley; "for I'm as harmless as a worm, and wouldn't do the gentleman an injury on no account, though he has tried it on pretty stiff to get me into quod."

"Well, mind you are as good as your word!" exclaimed Mr. Thornley. "It seems you don't bear a very excellent character among the police, but this may prove a useful lesson to you, and I hope the present occasion is the last in which you and I shall be introduced to each other."

"You may depend upon that, your worship," answered Mike Rowley, with a low bow. "This is the first time in my life that ever I was in trouble, and I'll take care it shall be the last, if the police will only let me alone."

"What do you mean by the police leaving you alone?" asked the magistrate.

"Why," replied the other, "I hope it won't be taken amiss if I happen to sleep in an empty house again."

"Go, and earn your living like an honest man," said Mr. Thornley; "and you may have a comfortable house over your head without prowling about to find a sleeping place where you can. I'm afraid there's too much truth in what has been stated against you; but you are a cunning fellow, I can see, and know how to keep out of harm's way as well as most people. Get work, I say, or you'll be very likely to be brought before me or some other magistrate on a more serious charge than the present."

"It's very easy to advise me to get work!" exclaimed Mike Rowley; "but it ain't everywhere that a man can get a situation when he wants one. There's nothing would please me better than hard work; but if one can't find employment, what's a poor devil to do?"

"If you've never done anything to forfeit your good character, there's plenty of employment to be found," said Mr. Thornley. "However, you are discharged, so now leave the court, and mind I never see you here again under a charge."

Mike Rowley bowed his thanks, and muttering something as he passed Guy, hurried out of the place to seek his companions, who he had seen lurking about as they were going to the police office. When he was gone, the magistrate, addressing himself to the other prisoner, said—

"The accusation brought against you, Harrowby, is of a more serious character, and I have therefore ordered the case to stand forward for a week, that we may see what evidence can be collected in the mean time. If you desire the assistance of a legal adviser, he can have free access to you, so that you may be prepared to meet the heavy charge you will have to encounter."

"Please your worship, what prison am I to take him to?" asked the constable.

"Take him to the cage where he was confined last night," answered Mr. Thornley. "Of course you, or some one else, will remain with him to prevent communication with all persons, except his attorney."

The court now broke up, and after the magistrate and witnesses had retired, Guy Harrowby was led out under the same strong escort that had guarded him there. On their way, however, the party gradually diminished, as one by one they dropped off to return home, so that at last there was only the constable and another man left to take their prisoner back to the cage. Guy now began to think within himself that it would be no difficult matter to effect his escape from such trifling odds, and he was considering how it could be best done, when, in a lonely part of the road, they were attacked by three men, who knocked down the constable and his assistant, and forced Guy Harrowby along with them for a short distance, when they all separated upon a hastily given hint that their place of meeting was to be at Doublechalk's, the Wapping landlord.

CHAPTER XIII.

THE DEN.—DRIVING A BARGAIN.—THE LOFT.

Of the three persons who had rescued the prisoner, Richard Fordham was the first to reach the place of assignation, for he knew all the bye ways and near cuts, and was, besides, gifted with more activity of legs than the rest of his associates. On his arrival, however, he was fairly out of breath, and having ensconced himself in the room to which we have already introduced the reader, he ordered a foaming pot of porter to be brought, and at the same time requested to be favoured with the landlord's company, as he had something particular to say to him. Doublechalk was not long in obeying this summons, and seating himself close alongside his guest, he remained silently attentive to the communication that was to be made.

"You know all about that concern of Guy Harrowby's," said Fordham, hardly above a whisper, "and as he belongs to our party, I shall expect that you'll do just as much for him as you would for any of us. He's a right sort of a chap, and mustn't be lost for the want of a friend to get him out of his present scrape. You must know that we've got him out of the clutches of some people that were taking him to the cage, and as there'll be a hot search for him directly, you must find some place to hide him in, or he's as safe to be scragged some of these fine mornings, as that I'm now telling you so."

"What devilish piece of mischief do you want to get me into now, Dick Fordham?" asked the landlord, looking rather black, as he saw there was no little risk to himself, if he interfered in a matter like this.

"There's no mischief likely to happen if you do as I tell you," exclaimed the other. "Guy Harrowby is in trouble, and I'll do all I can to get him out of it, if you'll only give him some corner in your house, where he may hide himself till there's a chance of getting him over to Holland, or some other part of the continent."

"Are you mad to think I'll run the risk of having him found on my premises?" demanded the alarmed host.

"Mad or not, I was never more serious in my life," answered Dick Fordham. "You've got plenty of places where he can hide, and if you refuse to let him stay in your house, you needn't expect to see either me or any of my companions in this precious crib again."

"But they'll be sure to come here to look for him."

"I dare say they may," returned Dick, "but you may put him where the police will never think of looking. For instance, there's the loft where Harry Martin was concealed three weeks before we got him away; and, though it aint a very comfortable place to pass one's time in, it has the advantage of not being very easily discovered."

"But, it mayn't always escape the prying eyes of those that favour me with a visit," exclaimed the host. "Besides, this friend of yours has never been much of a customer of mine, and I don't see why I should run the risk of being ruined to serve him, when he's being hunted like a hare."

"You wont do what I've asked then, Tom?"

"I'd rather have no hand in the business," replied Doublechalk, "for the truth is, I've had the police too often here of late, and now that they've found their way here, I suppose they'll fancy that every chap that is wanted, has found a hiding place in my house."

"What of it if they do?"

"What of it? Why I shall lose my character, and then I may as well shut up business."

"Ho, ho, ho!" shouted Dick Fordham; "you lose your character, indeed! Well, if you do lose it, I hope you'ill find a better one, for people have given you a most rascally name for this long time past."

"What can they have to say against me?" demanded the landlord.

"In the first place," replied the other, "they say your house is a notorious den for thieves; and, secondly, there are some very strong rumours abroad, that you are a receiver of stolen property, so I leave you to guess what sort of a character you've got, to be so much afraid of losing."

"Aye, aye," replied Doublechalk, "I know all about what you've been telling me, but it don't matter much to me what they say, as long as they've no proof."

"And you are cunning enough not to let 'em have that."

"Of course I am, for the goods your people bring here are moved away as soon as the bargain's struck, or else put up into the loft you were speaking of just now, where they are not likely to be found very easily."

"Then why can't you let Guy Harrowby be there a little while?" asked the other.

"Because I don't see any good that I've to get by it," replied Doublechalk. "When favours are wanted, it's worth while to pay for 'em, but I haven't heard a word from you yet upon that subject."

"Oh! you want to be paid then, it seems," replied Dick Fordham. "You forget the money that I and my comrades are always putting in your pocket; and refuse a favour, though I ask it for a friend. But never mind, old boy, you and I shall square accounts upon this affair I see, and then you'll have no more offers from me or my friends, when we've a bargain to get rid of."

"We won't talk of that at present," said the landlord: "but, just wait patiently, will you, till I've seen your friend, and hear what he's got to say for himself. We may arrange these little difficulties when we're all together to argue the matter."

"Oh!" said Fordham, "I thought you'd begin to see matters in another light, when I talked about conveying our favours to some one else. Our dealings are too profitable on your side to be lost for a trifle, so tell me at once, old fellow, that Guy Harrowby shall have a lodging here, and then I promise you the next good swag that I happen to get hold of."

"We shall see about it presently," replied the landlord, evidently relaxing from his former resolution. "You know I've a tender heart, Dick, and——"

"Aye, aye," interrupted the other, "there's a soft place in your heart, I dare say, but the only

way to get at of it is through your pocket. Poor Guy might have been hanged for ought you care, if it had not been that you was afraid your business would suddenly fall off."

At this period the conversation was broken off by the arrival of Sam Snatch, who, panting and puffing from the exertion he had used, seated himself by the side of the other two.

"Well, is it all right?" demanded Fordham, eagerly; "has Guy managed to distance his pursuers?"

"How should I know, when I've had quite enough to do to get clear off myself?" returned the other. "I've had a confounded long run of it, and after all, I dare say, we shall all get into a scrape about this business, for they'll be sure to know who it was that rescued the prisoner."

"Humph! so you are turning coward as well as old, Doublechalk!"

"I don't know that there's much cowardice in a chap thinking a little of himself," retorted Snatch.

"That's just the sort of argument I've been holding," said the landlord. "Dick Fordham wants me to let his friend conceal himself in this house, but I don't altogether fancy the notion of being found out."

"Nobody ever supposed that you'd serve any one but yourself," exclaimed Snatch, suddenly veering round to take part against the landlord. "You're civil enough to us all the while that we're good customers, but the moment we ask you to do us a favour, you begin to find excuses for getting off it."

"Why, you were doing just the same sort of thing yourself just this minute!"

"Ah!" answered Sam, "that was because I had run myself into an ill-humour. But I'll never leave an old friend in the lurch while I can do him any good; and what's more, I'll cut the acquaintance of any man that refuses to do me a favour when I ask it."

"There," exclaimed Dick Fordham to the landlord, "you see I'm not the only one that would be offended by your refusal, so now you know what you've got to expect if our friend is to be refused a lodging here."

"Haven't I told you already that he may make a bed up in the loft, if he likes?" retorted Doublechalk, "I'm always obliging to my customers, as you well know, Dick, and I'm sure we're not going to quarrel now, after the long time we have been acquainted together."

"No, you can come to, I see, when there's danger of losing nearly all your business," said Fordham; "but hang such hollow friendship say I, for it's always my maxim to oblige anybody without been badgered into it."

"But I've made a promise, and that ought to be enough."

"I know you've made a promise," said Dick, "but was it done heartily and freely? You talked about Guy Harrowby not being much of a customer of your's, as if that was any reason why a man should be suffered to be dragged off to prison!"

"And that, too, with the certainty of being hanged," shouted Sam Snatch.

"Poor devil!" exclaimed the landlord, "I'm sure I'd do anything to save him from such a fate as that. And if you ask me why I'm so tender-hearted upon that subject, I reply, that it's because the gallows has already robbed me of too many of my best customers. Why, in less than ten years, I can reckon up no less than seven fine young fellows—all of the right sort—that have been sent out of the world by the hands of Jack Ketch."

"And yet you'd have been hard-hearted enough to have refused a shelter to Guy Harrowby."

"That's because he and I have never had any dealings together," answered Doublechalk, "however, I've changed my mind upon that subject, and you've my promise that he shall stay here as long as he likes."

"But," asked Dick Fordham, "may we depend upon your not giving the officers a hint where he's hiding himself?"

"Is it likely that I should do that, when the place where he's going to be is nearly filled up with things that would lead to a discovery of my own dealings, with such men as yourselves?" demanded the host. "No, no; I've too much reason for keeping that place secret; to send officers into it, even if a large reward should be offered for the discovery of your friend."

"Well," observed Dick, "I see there's reason enough for keeping your word, so I shall depend upon there being no tricks played. But I wonder what keeps Guy so long, for he had no further to come than we had, so that he ought to have been here by this time."

"He don't know his way quite so well as we do," replied Sam Snatch, "poor devil! he's been abroad so long that he's quite forgot the streets and turnings of London."

"Perhaps he's been nabbed again," suggested Doublechalk, "and if that's the case, I shall be saved the trouble of finding him a lodging."

"That's all you think about," exclaimed Dick Fordham. "The poor fellow may be hanged, for aught you care, so that you're to have no trouble with him. But for my own part, I hope he's not been nabbed, for if he has they'll never give us such another chance of getting him out of their infernal clutches."

All further doubt and uncertainty upon this subject was here put an end to, by the arrival of Guy Harrowby, and Mike Rowley, who, though taking different routes, had arrived at their place of destination just at the same time. They were both nearly exhausted with running, yet Fordham was too anxious to know how they had got on, to wait till they had recovered breath.

"What the devil made you so long after us?" he asked. "Did the chaps we left behind get on your trail, or did you lose your way in coming here?"

"There was a little of both happened, as far as I'm concerned," replied Guy; "for I hadn't got very far before I heard a loud shouting from some people that were in pursuit; and, as they seemed to gain upon me, I bolted into a house that was unfurnished, and laid myself down upon the ground, lest they should take it into their heads to look in. However, they ran past the place, and as soon as they were beyond hearing, I crept out, and took all the darkest and least public places that I could find. But not an inch of my way did I know, and as it would have been dangerous to ask any one, I was obliged to blunder about till I came to a place that I knew something of."

"And did you hear anything more of the chaps that were after you?" asked Fordham.

"No," he replied; "they seem to have turned off in another direction after they had passed the place where I was."

"Then you've been pretty lucky, after all."

"Aye, if you can call it lucky, when I don't happen to know of a place where I may hide myself."

"Make yourself quite easy about that, old chap," said Dick Fordham, "for the landlord here has a snug corner to stow you in, and it would puzzle all the officers in London to find you there. The fellow, to be sure, warn't very willing at first to let you be here, but we've brought him to reason at last; and, what's better than all, I believe he understands that it wouldn't be to his own interest to let the officers know where you are."

"No, no, you'll be safe enough here, I can promise you," said Doublechalk. "Your lodging, however, won't be a very comfortable one; though, I dare say, that won't matter much, since any place is better to live in than a prison."

"Anything will do that keeps me from a fate that I'm afraid to think of," answered Guy.

"Aye," observed the landlord, "the notion of being hanged aint a very pleasant one, it must be confessed."

"To me it's not, at any rate," exclaimed the convict; "though, why I should live on in this state of uncertainty and misery, I know not. But so it is; and eager enough was I to take the opportunity of escaping, though it was with the certainty that I should find no rest or quiet, go wherever I might."

"Why, the truth of it is," said Dick Fordham, "we none of us fancy the idea of dangling on a rope; and, for my own part, I never yet knew the man that wouldn't escape from that fate if he could. However, you may thank your own good fortune that we've found a snug place for you to hide in, and in a few days, when things begin to grow quiet again, we'll see what can be done towards getting you out of this country, for I see plainly enough that they'll never leave you alone while you stay in it."

"And how soon afterwards," asked Guy, "will it be before my wife will follow?"

"Why that must depend upon circumstances," replied Fordham; "but she must not be too close upon your heels, for there'll be plenty, I dare say, watching her movements, and it would be as well not to let anybody know where you go to, for fear of accidents."

"They can't touch him when he's in a foreign country," interposed Mike Rowley.

"I know that as well as you do," exclaimed Dick; "but I suppose it wouldn't be very wise to let this Mr. Charles Heathingdon find out where he's living, when we know the revengeful feelings he bears towards him."

"But when he finds that I'm far away," said Guy, "I'm afraid he'll take the opportunity to repeat his insulting proposals to my wife."

"Leave all that part of the business to my management," said Fordham, "and I'll take care you shall have no reason to be sorry for it afterwards. The young squire will find a tough customer in me, I can tell him, for I've no reason to be afraid of his spite, as you have; and if he dares make love to her again, I'll give him such a towelling as he shall remember to the last day of his life."

"If that aint a handsome offer, I don't know what is," exclaimed Sam Scratch, in ecstacies. "So, after all, Harrowby, you've got a little luck left; and you may now go abroad as soon as they'll let you get there, and have your mind quite easy about your wife."

"Perhaps," observed Guy, "I may not find it so easy to escape as I fancied."

"For my own part, I don't see anything to be afraid of now," exclaimed Mike Rowley. "The place where you're going to hide in is a safe one, for I tried it myself once, when I was in a bit of a hobble; and, though I could hear the traps searching about for me in the room underneath, they never found out the place you enter by; and after waiting till they were tired, they went away, and never came to look for me in this house afterwards."

"If it wasn't a pretty safe place," said Doublechalk, "I should have been a ruined man long before this time: for it's the room where I store up some of the things I buy upon the cross; and if the goods were seen they'd be sure to be traced to their right owners, and then I should have to pay, or visit the country you have just escaped from."

"And how long," asked Harrowby, "am I likely to be a prisoner in that room?"

"As long as they think proper to keep a look out for you," replied Dick Fordham.

"And that may be for months."

"Ah, no! not so long as that either," returned the other: "we must beat them off, if we can, by cunning; and the best way that I know of for making 'em give up the search, will be to spread a report that you've made your escape out of England."

"Capital!" exclaimed Snatch; "upon my life, Dick, you're the best chap I know of at thinking of schemes to get people out of their troubles."

"What's the use of a fellow that's got no wit at his finger ends when he needs it?" demanded the other. "I've been in too many scrapes myself to be much of a sleepy one; and the more pinching the danger is, the sooner comes some thought or another into my mind for getting out of it."

"At any rate, Dick," exclaimed the convict, "I've found you a friend when there was most need of your services; and, if it should ever be in my power to return your kindness, you shall see that I'm not ungrateful."

"As for that," said the person he had addressed, "I don't care whether you ever think of it afterwards or not. If I do you a service, it's because it suits my own humour; for I shouldn't like to see you hanged, while there's a chance of cheating the executioner."

"There, we're all of us of a mind," exclaimed Snatch; "and, what I hope is, that when it's my turn to get into a scrape, I may find Dick Fordham just such a friend to me as he's been to you."

"And that you shall, if you do nothing to affront me in the mean time," returned the other; "I'd as soon save you from the gibbet, as any one else, if I saw there was a chance of your being scragged."

"I'll tell you what it is, gentlemen," exclaimed the landlord, "if we keep your friend talking here much longer, he'll be very likely to fall into the hands of his enemies; for I shouldn't wonder if this is one of the first places they come to look for him in; and it would be of no use to show fight, for they'd call further assistance; and then, I'm thinking, it would be all pretty well over with this chap."

"You're right enough there, old fellow," said Dick Fordham; "and I've been thinking the same thing myself for some time, though I did not like to break up a party that was so snug and comfortable. However, Harrowby, the long and the short of it is, that you must mizzle to your den, for fear we should have any awkward visitors to spoil your harmony."

"I'm ready to go," replied Guy, rising from his seat.

"Then here's off," exclaimed the landlord, following his example; and taking a candle from the table, he desired Harrowby to follow him in silence. The latter obeyed this injunction, and having shaken hands with his companions, he accompanied Doublechalk, who led the way into a small room, adjoining which, there was a staircase leading to the upper portion of the house. This they ascended with as little noise as possible, till they reached an attic; where the landlord paused, and giving the light into Guy's hand, opened a closet door, and with the assistance of a chair, slipped back a sliding panel that was so contrived as to appear like the regular ceiling, belonging to the cupboard. Having made this opening he scrambled up, and then called to Guy to follow his example with as little delay as possible. This, the fugitive prepared to do; and mounting the chair, with the light still in his hand, he could see just enough into the loft to perceive that it was a low-roofed place, nearly filled with goods of various descriptions, and without any visible aperture through which the light of day could make its entrance. Giving the candle into the hands of Doublechalk, who was ready to render him assistance, he contrived, though not without some difficulty, to scramble up, and soon found himself in the place where he was to find concealment, though for how long a period was uncertain.

"You see what sort of a lodging you'll have," said the landlord, moving the light about to show the extent of the loft from one end to the other. "The quarters aint very comfortable ones as you see, but I think you'll be safe enough in 'em, and that's everything that can be wished for by a man in your situation.

"They'll do well enough for the purpose I want 'em for," answered Guy Harrowby. "A few days' concealment will, I hope, be sufficient; and then I may leave my lurking-place—to wander, I know not where."

"Whatever you do," exclaimed Doublechalk, "don't let anybody hear you walking backwards and forwards, for there's often some of my people in the room underneath, and if there should be any sounds, that they're not used to, its a hundred to one but they fancy the place is haunted; and then if a search takes place, you'll be done for, as sure as a gun."

"Must I take no exercise then?"

"Why, you must have a little," I suppose, replied the landlord, "but it must be managed as cautiously as possible. I should advise you to take your shoes off, when you walk about; and even then you must tread gently, for these old boards creak at almost every step, and if that was heard down below, there'd be a rare to do in the house directly afterwards."

"And how am I to be supplied with food?" asked Guy.

"You must leave that to my management," answered the other. "In the morning I'll contrive to come here when my absence is not likely to be noticed, and I'll bring you enough to eat and drink to last you for three or four days afterwards."

"Then I shall have no society—no one to speak to, all the time I'm here."

"Why, I believe there's rats enough to keep you company, if you don't think proper to drive 'em away."

"And how is the place in the day time?" inquired Guy Harrowby. "Is there any light to cheer the solitude I'm doomed to?"

"I can't say much about that," replied Doublechalk. "There's no windows to the place, as you may see by looking round, but there's plenty of chinks and crannies, and they let in as much light as you'll want. Then, if you'd amuse yourself, there's a lot of old books in yonder corner; they may be pleasant reading for ought I know, but I've never looked into any of 'em, though they'd been in my possession a long while."

"They'll serve to pass away some of the weary hours at any rate," observed the fugitive.

"And then, by way of a change," continued Doublechalk, "you can examine the stores that are heaped up about the loft. You'll find a variety I can tell you; though, it must be confessed, the things I keep here aint of much value."

"Will any of my companions that are now down stairs, be able to come and see me here?"

"The devil a bit must they come," exclaimed the landlord.

"Why not? Surely you're not afraid of men that you are in the constant habit of trading with?"

"No, I'm not afraid of 'em, as you say," answered the other; "because, they've so often found the place useful to themselves, that they'll never split about it, lest they should happen to want the use of it again. But the truth of it is, I can't be sure of the people I have about me, and if they should once get a notion that there's a hiding place in my house, it's likely enough I should have the officers down upon me directly."

"In that case," exclaimed Guy Harrowby, "I must put up with the solitude, rather than bring any risk upon you. But, at any rate, I suppose I shall see you at least once in the course of the day."

"That'll depend upon circumstances," answered the host; "for I must not promise to pay you a visit, except when I can do so without fear of being seen by any of my people. But I'll come as often as I can, since I know you'll find yourself dull enough here; and it'll need a little change to make the place at all bearable."

"Perhaps my stay here will not last any long time," said Guy; "and, to my mind, the shorter it is the better, for it is not the cheerlessness of the place alone that I mind, but the uncertainty and continual dread that I shall be in that will be most hard to bear."

"As for dread, I don't think there's any occasion for you to feel any," exclaimed Doublechalk; "for my house has been searched a good many times, from top to bottom, and never yet has anybody thought of there being a lurking place up here. They always open the closet door below, to have a look if any thing's there, but the sliding panel above is made to look so much like the ceiling, that they've always gone away without making any discovery. But I must leave you now, so good night to you; and in the morning, I'll be here again, to bring you something to eat and drink."

Doublechalk then descended through the opening, and when the panel was again closed, the fugitive found himself involved in utter darkness.

CHAPTER XIV.

WHEN Charles Heathingdon left the police office, he returned with all speed to his hotel in town, so that he knew nothing of the subsequent escape of Harrowby, and the present defeat of the evil designs, he had been at so much pains to plot against the object of his displeasure. Having therefore, as he imagined, succeeded in securing the destruction of his victim, his next resolution was to return home into the country, in order to seek another interview with Jane Harrowby, and gather from her any information that might be of service at the next examination. After taking a luncheon, he desired his horse to be got ready for an immediate journey; and within a very brief period afterwards, he was retracing the road which he had come a few days before, when in headlong pursuit of Guy Harrowby. Anxious to make his journey as short as possible, he urged his horse to its utmost speed; and, just before dark, he found himself within his paternal domains, though without having yet formed any specific plan, by which he was to be guided. A ride of less than a quarter of an hour, brought him to the mansion; where being quickly attended by a groom, he threw himself from the saddle, and ascending the steps, passed through the hall and entered the library. Here, to his surprise, he found his father, who had returned home during his absence, and to whom his sudden departure had occasioned no little surprise.

"So," exclaimed Colonel Heathingdon, laying his book upon the table; "you have returned home at length, to account, as I suppose, for your leaving this house so suddenly a few days since."

"I was not aware till now," answered Charles, haughtily, "that it was necessary for me to explain my motives every time that it is my pleasure to leave home."

"It would have been but an act of courtesy to have done so, at any rate," exclaimed his father; "I came home yesterday expecting to find you here, and the first news which greeted me was, that you had gone off in a great hurry, nobody knew where, though the general supposition was, that you intended visiting London."

"Was it requisite, sir," demanded Charles, "that I should inform your servants where I was going to?"

"Certainly not," answered his father; "but your brother Edward might have deserved your confidence, and if he was not worthy to be trusted with so important a secret, there is Major Carfield who, as my most intimate friend, should have been told where you were going, and when you might be expected to return."

"My brother," said Charles, "being younger than myself, I certainly should not consult in a matter of this kind; and, as for Major Carfield, he takes too much upon himself already, for me to consider him as a friend or an adviser."

"That is to say, he sees your faults, Charles, and has honesty enough to reprove them."

"You are severe upon me, sir," exclaimed the young man, shrinking from the stern glance that had been directed towards him.

"Not so much so, as I fear you deserve."

"Then some enemy has been at work to injure me," exclaimed Charles. "In all probability I am indebted for this anger to Major Carfield, and if my suspicions should prove to be well founded, I'll teach him to be less busy with his interference in future."

"You are quite mistaken in attributing any interference to the excellent friend you have named," answered Colonel Heathingdon. "What I have heard has been from common rumour, and the stories whispered about, Charles, are anything but to your credit."

"What does all this mean?"

"You do not mean to deny, I suppose," answered his father, "that you have made dishonorable overtures to a female of humble rank in this neighbourhood?"

"I suppose, sir," said Charles, a little confused, "you are alluding to a little affair of gallantry with a poor cottager that lives on the borders of your estate?"

"The poor cottager you speak of," exclaimed his father, reproachfully, "has the merit of being honest, and industrious; above all else, of irreproachable virtue."

"You may know her character better than I can pretend to do," replied the young man, sarcastically; "my acquaintance with her has not been of very long duration, so that I can scarcely be expected to have found out all the excellent qualities you have enumerated."

"I have never yet seen the female that I am aware of," exclaimed Colonel Heathingdon; "but my neighbours are loud in their praise and I therefore suppose she is all that has been represented."

"Whatever they may say in her favour," answered Charles, "there is no one, I believe, that can speak well of her husband."

"In that respect," said the elder gentleman, "I believe she has been most unfortunate. The man, if I understand rightly, has been transported?"

"He has," answered Charles; "but the punishment does not seem to have had a very beneficial effect upon him, for he has since committed a worse crime than that for which he was banished from his native land."

"Indeed! what has he done now?"

"Murdered his guard, in order to escape the more easily from the place he was sent to."

"This is bad news for his wife," exclaimed the colonel; "but I suppose he has been taken and punished for the dreadful crime he has been guilty of?"

"So far he has contrived to escape the vigilance of his pursuers," answered Charles Heathingdon; "and the most singular part of the affair is, that he is now in England where, for some days, he has eluded the vigilance of those, whose duty it is; to take him into custody."

"Is he still at large?"

"No; but he was, till a few hours since, when I traced him to his lurking place; and, through my means, he is now likely to meet with his deserts."

"And, pray Charles," asked his father, "may I ask, what motive you had for taking so much trouble upon yourself?"

"I had but one motive, sir," he replied; "and that was the performance of a public duty."

"I hope you may always be guided by the same impulse," exclaimed the colonel; "but I am afraid, Charles, there was something besides the sense of public duty that has impelled you to become a sort of amateur thief-taker."

"What motive do you think I can have had?"

"Most sincerely do I hope my suspicions are unfounded," answered his father; "and yet, I have a lurking suspicion that you would get rid of this unfortunate man in order that your designs against his wife, may have no obstacle."

"Your opinion of me is not a very flattering one," said Charles; "but, at all events, I have the satisfaction of knowing that I have performed an important service, in apprehending so great a villain, as this Guy Harrowby."

"Has he been examined yet before a magistrate?" asked Colonel Heathingdon.

"He was under examination, to-day," answered Charles; "and, as I was not prepared with all the requisite witnesses to support my charge, he has been remanded for a week, by which time I shall be better prepared with evidence of the murder he has committed."

"You have managed this affair skilfully," observed his father; "though, I am afraid, it has been done to throw the wife more completely in your power."

"Really, sir," retorted the young man, "you seem to take a great deal of interest in this woman, considering you have never seen her."

"My interest in her behalf," said Colonel Heathingdon, "has been excited by the danger she is threatened with; she has become the object of a libertine's lawless passion, and my anxiety for her honour, as well as your own, makes me dread the consequences that may follow from your own thoughtlessness."

"This is not the way you used to think of me, sir," exclaimed Charles; "till Major Carfield became a frequent visitor, I was honoured with some of your regard. Now, however, I am to receive nothing but your reproaches; and it is not, therefore, to be wondered at, if I attribute the change to the meddling interference of an enemy."

"Major Carfield, at all events, is not the enemy you take him for," answered his father; "he has never once spoken to me upon the subject of your errors, and you will, therefore, do well to think more kindly of him in future."

"That I can never do," replied Charles; "for, it is very easy to see, that he treats me with coldness and disdain, whilst my brother receives nothing but kindness from him."

"Perhaps it is your own fault, that the difference is made," observed Colonel Heathingdon. "The dispositions of your brother and yourself are widely different; and the major has

too much rough honesty to conceal the feelings with which he observes your unlicensed proceedings."

" What has he to do with me ?" demanded Charles ; " and, why am I to pay more deference to him, than I do to you ? "

" So, your dislike to the major, then, arises from a feeling of jealousy that is unworthy of you."

" Indeed, sir, you utterly mistake me," exclaimed Charles ; " I feel too little respect for Major Carfield, to care for the slighting way in which he treats me."

" If he knows anything of your imprudent love for the convict's wife," said the colonel, " you owe him some thanks, for the silence he has maintained upon the subject. He has never mentioned it to me, though he might have felt justified in doing so, when he knew how important it was that you should be stopped in your career, before further mischief comes of it."

" Pray, sir," exclaimed Charles, " if you have not heard this from the major, may I be permitted to inquire what other person has made himself so busy with my affairs ? "

" It is not from one person alone, but from many, that I have heard of your frequent visits to the cottage of Jane Harrowby," replied his father ; " the scandal is pretty well buzzed about the neighbourhood, I can assure you, and your conduct is severely commented upon, since it is known that you receive not the slightest encouragement from her."

" How do people know that ?"

" Because, I suppose, she has told them so," answered Colonel Heathingdon ; " the woman is, in my opinion, perfectly justified in exposing this affair, since her own character can be upheld in no other way."

" Her character ! " exclaimed the young man, " what character can the wife of a convict have to uphold ? "

" One that is most precious to her—the character of a virtuous and faithful wife," answered the colonel. " I have heard her spoken of in the highest terms of praise, and as a proof of the estimation in which she is held, the people hereabouts give her constant employment, by which she obtains a creditable living for herself and child."

" I believe they do give her work," replied Charles ; " but public benevolence has been misapplied before now."

" You mean to infer, then, that it has been misapplied in the present instance ? "

" That remains to be proved," answered the young man.

" It is most ungenerous of you, Charles," exclaimed his father, angrily, " to throw even the shadow of a suspicion, upon one who has been left so exposed as this poor woman. She has been known in this neighbourhood, I believe, from her birth ; and, surely, if she had ever failed either in her duty or morality, there would have been some one besides yourself to assail her with detraction."

" I little thought to offend you by a mere suggestion," said Charles ; " the subject however, seems to be one upon which we are not likely to agree, and therefore we had better say no more about it."

" The less the better," exclaimed Colonel Heathingdon ; " but before you leave me, Charles, I must have a promise that you will discontinue your visits to the cottage of Jane Harrowby."

" That's a promise, sir, that I cannot make just at present."

" Why not ? "

" Because I have some few questions to ask her, that may lead to important discoveries against the next examination takes place."

" Do you then expect that the wife will say aught that may prove injurious to her husband ? "

" Not willingly, I dare say," replied Charles ; " but there are ways to put my questions that will disarm suspicion, and even the slightest hint that escapes her lips may prove of vast importance towards procuring the conviction of Guy Harrowby."

" Charles, Charles ! " exclaimed his father ; " I really begin to grow ashamed of acknowledging you for my son."

" For what reason, sir ? "

" Because your conduct is calculated to bring disgrace, not only upon yourself, but upon all who are in any way connected with you. From motives of revenge you have hunted this unfortunate man into a prison, and now would procure his conviction through the instrumentality of his wife."

" I see nothing to be ashamed of in what I have done," answered the young man ; " Guy Harrowby is a murderer, and it is the duty of every one to give his assistance towards bringing him to punishment."

" But would you have taken all this trouble except for purposes of your own ? "

" Probably, not," answered Charles. " The man struck me to the earth not many nights since, and I shall never be satisfied till my revenge is completed."

" Where did this occur ?"

" In his own cottage."

" He has ventured to show himself there, then ?"

" Yes."

" I see how it is," exclaimed Colonel Heathingdon ; " the wretched man found you trespassing in his cottage, and judging the motive of your visit he struck you, as anybody else would have done, to the earth."

" He did so, and fled immediately afterwards," answered Charles. " My determination, however, was soon formed, and following in his track, I never relaxed from my exertions till he was safely locked up."

"And now, in cooler moments, do you feel no remorse for the course you have pursued?"

"I see no reason for regret, sir," replied the young man. "In the first place, as a murderer, he deserves little pity; and, secondly, the blow he struck me must and shall be revenged."

"As for the blow," exclaimed the colonel, "I think you have reason to be thankful that the punishment he inflicted was not of a more serious description. The man, you say, has blood already on his hands, and meeting you as he did, the assailer of his wife's honour, it would hardly have excited surprise if he had laid you at his feet a lifeless corse."

"There are no thanks to him that he did not do so," answered Charles; "for the villain seized a loaded gun that was hanging over the mantelpiece, and would have shot me but for the interposition of his wife."

"And yet that is the woman you would make a widow of," exclaimed the colonel, bitterly.

"Yes, sir, when it is to punish an assassin."

"I see, Charles, that all argument would be thrown away upon you in your present humour," said his father; "the conversation we have had this night has given me more pain than anything that has occurred for a long time past. Leave me for the present, and reflect upon the course you have pursued, and are still inclined to follow. To-morrow I will see you again, and by that time I hope you will have made up your mind to pay no more of those disgraceful visits to the cottage of Jane Harrowby."

Charles Heathingdon still lingered; but his father impatiently waved his hand to urge his departure, and the young man left the room deeply mortified at the reproof he had been compelled to hear. Nothing that had been said, however, was of sufficient weight to change the determination he had formed; and in defiance of the last wish uttered by his father, he left the mansion, and proceeded by the road which led towards the cottage of the convict's wife. But though his resolution still remained unchanged, his haughty spirit felt deeply mortified by the severe rebuke he had met with; and as he walked onwards, he thought over various schemes by which he might ascertain who it was that had informed his father of so much of what had occurred during his absence from home. In his own mind he felt quite certain that it was Major Carfield who had made himself so busy with his affairs; and, notwithstanding the assurance of his father to the contrary, he determined to try by every means in his power to ascertain how far his suspicions were correct. At length he reached the cottage-door, and raising the latch, entered the humble room in which Jane Harrowby was still occupied with her daily labour. She started on perceiving who her visitor was, and letting fall the work upon which she was engaged, asked, in terrified accents, the object of his visit at so late an hour.

"Be not alarmed," he said, with forced tranquillity; "for I am here on no unfriendly visit. I have news for you, Jane—news of your husband."

"My husband! oh, say if he is well."

"He is well enough in health," answered the libertine, "but is now plunged in the deepest affliction. In short, to keep you no longer in suspense, he has been arrested, and is at this moment in a prison."

"Oh, heavens!" she cried, burying her face in her hands; "then he is lost to me for ever."

"I don't know that matters are quite as bad as all that," returned Charles Heathingdon, with affected pity; "its a bad affair enough, it must be confessed, but he is not without friends; and I, who rank myself among the number of them, will do all in my power to save him from the punishment of his crime."

"You, do aught to save him!" exclaimed Jane in a tone of doubt and astonishment.

"Aye, have you any reason to believe that I would not exert myself in his behalf?"

"You are his foe," she replied, "and would rather give your aid to crush than to save him."

"Why do you look upon me as his foe?"

"There are too many reasons for my doing so," she replied.

"Name any one of them."

"I will name the first that comes to my mind," answered Jane; "you profess to love me, and therefore cannot but regard my husband with dislike."

"There you are mistaken," he replied; "for the love I bear towards you, Jane Harrowby, will urge me to do all I can for the preservation of your husband."

"It is in vain for you to tell me so," she exclaimed; "because, I well know it to be impossible. Nay more, Mr. Heathingdon, I feel well assured that this visit to me to-night bodes me no good. You have a purpose in it, and that purpose I have yet to find out."

"What purpose do you imagine I can have?"

"A short time will most likely prove that," answered Jane; "at all events you know your presence here is at all times most unwelcome to me, and your choosing so late an hour convinces me that my suspicions are not without foundation."

"I came," he replied, "to tell you of the misfortune of your husband, and to see if you have any suggestions to make by which I may do him a benefit."

"Such at least, is the shallow excuse by which you think to impose upon me."

"You are determined, I see, not to give me the credit of good intentions," exclaimed Charles Heathingdon.

"Alas!" she replied, "have I not seen too much reason to believe the contrary?"

"It is a foolish prejudice that you would do well to get rid of as soon as possible,"' he replied. "Have I not offered to place you in a situation far above the one you at present occupy, and is not that of itself a sufficient proof of the regard in which I hold you?"

"You have done so," she exclaimed, reproachfully; "but what was the sacrifice I was to make for it in return. I was to become your mistress—to forsake husband, child, and all, alas, that is most dear to me, to sell myself to one that I loathe and detest!"

"Take care how you anger me with words like these," exclaimed Charles Heathingdon; "hitherto you have found me a supplicant for your slightest favour; but my temper will not endure an insult, and if once we separate in wrath, you will from that moment find in me an implacable foe."

"Be it so," she calmly replied; "let your wrath fall upon me alone, and I will endure it without complaint."

"It will not fall upon you alone," he exclaimed; "because I know the sufferings would be far increased if my vengeance falls upon your husband. I will even do all I can to assist in procuring his conviction, and the death he will then suffer upon the gibbet will have been caused by your own scorn towards myself."

"Monster!" she wildly cried, "is it to drive me to madness, that you conjure up those frightful images before my eyes?"

"It is rather to bring you to your senses," he replied, with cold sarcasm; "I would have you perceive the consequences of your own folly in order that you may see which is the better plan for you to adopt."

"You believe me to be friendless," exclaimed Jane; "and, coward-like, would take advantage of my helpless situation. But I have heard your father has arrived at his mansion, and strangers as we are to each other, I'll seek an interview with him to-morrow, and implore his protection against the evil doings of his profligate son."

"Indeed!" retorted the other with a sneer. "It's well I know your intentions, Jane; for being thus prepared, I may take precautions to avert the mischief you would do. On presenting yourself at the house, you will be turned from the door by the servants."

"In that case, I'll wait, patiently, till I can meet your father in his walks."

"Your patience must be inexhaustible, then," he replied; "for Colonel Heathingdon never leaves the house, except to take exercise in his own gardens. Nor would a letter to him do, for it is always my task to open all that are sent to him; so, you may well imagine, that one from you would never reach its place of destination."

"It is certainly something to exult at the success of your own villany," cried Jane Harrowby; "but you may yet find out, that the deepest laid schemes do not always end as may be expected. I have said that Colonel Heathingdon shall know of his son's worthlessness, and I will find a way to do so, in spite of all the cautions you may take to defeat my object. Nay, if everything else fails, I'll make my story known to the rector, who, I know, is a frequent visitor at the mansion. He will not refuse to assist me, and through him I will make known the infamous propositions you have made to me."

"All this," exclaimed Charles, "is but an idle waste of words. My father has already been informed of my frequent visits to this place, and in a conversation that I had with him, scarcely an hour ago, I admitted the charge, and asserted my own right to do as I pleased. We parted in anger; but there's no doubt, when we meet again to-morrow, he will be all sunshine and good humour."

"Perhaps so," answered Jane Harrowby; "but it will be in the expectation that his son will not be insensible to the advice he has given him."

"His wrath was but the spirt of a moment," replied Charles; "and, as usual, will not last any long time. You see, therefore, how little dependence is to be placed upon him, and I now ask, for the last time, if you will purchase life and liberty for your husband, by accepting the proposal that I have so often made before?"

"What power have you to bestow life or liberty upon him?" demanded Jane. "If, as you tell me, he is in prison, there is no help for him, and it will only remain for me to do all that a wife can, to save him from a death of shame."

"But the murderer, when once committed, is never spared from the gallows."

"And who is there to prove that Guy Harrowby has been guilty of shedding man's blood?" demanded the unhappy wife. "You are the only person that has dared bring such a charge against him, and I know your motives for doing so, too well, to believe the falsehood."

"I have uttered no falsehood about it," exclaimed the libertine; "for, as surely as I now tell you so, your husband only effected his escape by murdering the man that was placed as a guard over him."

"What proof have you of it?"

"Guy Harrowby will know all about that in good time," answered Charles; "at present, I have left him in safe custody, and in a week hence, I shall have all the evidence that will be necessary to secure his committal for trial."

"And you are villain enough to exult in bnging him to a death of shame?"

"Have I not reason to exult in the success of my plans?" he exclaimed. "Think you, Jane. I have forgot the blow he struck me in this very cottage, or that I shall spare my victim now, that I find I am hated by both himself and his wife?"

"The hatred you speak of has been occasioned by your own fault," she replied; "had you never bestowed your withering love upon me all the rage and malice you have shown would have been spared."

"A man cannot help falling in love," exclaimed Charles; "nor is he to be reproached for it by the woman that has caused his misery. The acquaintance that has commenced between us is as disastrous to me as it has been to yourself, for I am no longer what I was; and if matters continue much longer in this way, I shall lose the respect of all that I most value."

"Then, why not break the chain at once, and release yourself for ever from its thraldom?" she demanded.

"How is it to be done?"

"That question can best be answered by yourself," she exclaimed. "You know my resolution, and you will find it unalterable, so the best plan you can pursue is to leave this part of the country; and, in the course of time, you will learn to despise the unfortunate Jane Harrowby, instead of harassing her as you now do by your hateful propositions."

"No," he replied, after the pause of a minute or two; "I cannot leave this place, even though my remaining in it should bring misery upon my future life."

"Then there is but one other alternative," answered Jane Harrowby; "I will myself quit the neighbourhood, though I know not of any other place where I may meet with the kindness I have here."

"It will be useless for you to do so," exclaimed Charles Heathingdon; "for, go where you will, I shall follow without delay. You will think mine a perverse spirit, Jane, and perhaps it is so; but I have been unused to contradiction all my life, and cannot now submit to be conquered by a woman."

"Have you forgotten, then," she asked, "that the world's respect depends upon your conduct in this matter?"

"I am well aware of all that," he replied; "but my heart is too stubborn to yield, even though I see the trouble my wilfulness must lead to. Even the warnings of my father are thrown away, and I rush onward to my ruin with all the frenzy of a madman."

"That is because you will not give yourself time for a little calm reflection."

"I have tried to reflect and to be calm too," he replied; "but, the more I think, the further do I seem from convincing myself that this love of mine must be conquered."

"Surely you cannot reflect upon the wide difference between our situations in life?"

"I have thought of it though," he exclaimed; "yet, still the same wild phantoms follow me. You, Jane, I know, deem my love to be nothing more than that of a libertine, who seeks only the gratification of his passion. I, however, know that my regard is of a more holy kind; for, had there been no obstacles in the way, I would have made you my wife rather than have sought a partner from among the fairest daughters of our haughty aristocracy."

"Let us speak no more upon this subject!" exclaimed Jane earnestly. "Your words are wild and meaningless, and we have already suffered this interview to grow to too great a length. Leave me, I beg, and let this be the last occasion that we shall ever meet each other."

"No," he cried, "we will not part so easily as that. You shall go with me, Jane; by heaven, you shall! so resist me not; for, were the great fiend himself to appear, I would not be thwarted in my object."

He advanced to seize her; but Jane Harrowby foresaw his design, and reaching down the loaded gun that hung over the mantel-piece, she retreated a few paces, and then presented it at him.

"Mr. Heathingdon!" she exclaimed; "I am armed, as you see, for my own protection, and will not hesitate to fire if you advance another step towards me. Leave the house, I command you, or I shall presently be guilty of shedding the blood of a fellow-creature."

"Nay, hear me," he cried; "and do not that in haste, which you will afterwards have to repent of."

"I am firm and resolute in my demand," she returned, in the same tone of determination. "You have thought proper to invade the privacy of my own humble home; and, having none here to protect me, it only remains for me to show that I am not to be intimidated by the insolence of a heartless libertine. Begone, I say to you once more, and tempt me not to commit a deed that at any other time I should have shuddered at."

"Will you not hear reason, Jane, and ——"

"I will hear nothing that you have to say," she replied, interrupting him. "Already I have endured your presence here too long; and now, for the last time, I desire you to remain no longer beneath this roof."

"Your command shall be obeyed," exclaimed Charles, alarmed at the determination with which she had addressed him. "For the present, I take my departure; but it will only be to return here again at no distant period."

He turned angrily away, and rushing through the door, was lost in the darkness of the night.

CHAPTER XV.

THE THIEVES' RESORT.—INTERRUPTION.—A CONSULTATION.

It was fortunate for Guy Harrowby that he followed the suggestion of the landlord; for he had not left the parlour any very long time, when an altercation was heard at the bar; and in a few minutes afterwards, our old friend the constable, and three other men, entered the room. A hasty glance round, however, served to convince them that the object of their search was not there; and they were retreating, when Mike Rowley called them back, to enjoy a little fun at their expense.

"Where the devil are you off to, in such a hurry, old fellow?" he exclaimed. "Do you scorn to drink with an old acquaintance, that you bolt off as soon as you're come into the room?"

"Why, hang me, if it aint that infernal scoundrel that got discharged this morning, when everybody thought he was safe booked for three months, at least," cried the constable, opening his eyes with astonishment.

"Yes," replied Mike; "I'm the identical chap you was so kind as to take care of last night. But it was no go, old fellow, for the magistrate know'd more of the law, than you and I put together; and he saw that he got into the wrong box, if he sent me to limbo, when I hadn't been doing anything that deserved it."

"Well, never mind about that," returned the official; "for if I put you to a little inconvenience, it was only in the way of doing my duty. I made a mistake, I suppose, and it was lucky for you that you'd a sensible magistrate to go before, for there's some of 'em that would have sent you off for three months, with hard labour."

"What for?"

"Why, for being a suspicious character."

"There now," exclaimed Mike Rowley, appealing to his friends; "what man can ever consider himself safe, if they look upon me as a suspicious character. By and by, I supposes they'll want to be scragging me, because they may take it into their heads that I aint quite what I ought to be."

"That's the blessed injustice they always deal out to poor hard working fellows like us," chimed in Sam Snatch. "If we're seen walking ever so quietly, in the public street, there's some people that will take it into their heads that we are wanting to pick pockets; and if we are found sitting in a house like this, there's always some d—d good natured friend or another that's ready to swear we belong to a set of thieves."

"As for that," returned the constable, "I should say as much of you, by the look of your mug."

"You'd better say that again, young fellow;" exclaimed Snatch, striking his fist very hard upon the table; "you're one of those chaps, I suppose, as won't let quiet chaps like us, alone; but if you come any of your imperance here, you'll be likely to get what you won't much fancy."

"Indeed, and what's that?"

"A d—d good thrashing," he replied, with another blow upon the table. "Ah! you may laugh, but there's enough of us here to do it."

"And there's enough of us to prevent it," answered the constable. "At any rate, we're four to your three, and if that aint sufficient, we can call in plenty of assistance, out of the street."

"What's the use of making a rumpus about nothing?" interposed Dick Fordham, who foresaw that a row was brewing, which would do them no good. "The gentlemen that have just come in don't want to interfere with us, seeing as they do, that we're not the people they're looking after."

"At present you are safe enough," answered the constable; "but I know every one of you, and I'm most confoundedly mistaken if all of you won't be out to another country, before you're much older."

"What reason have you for saying that?" demanded Mike Rowley, with alarm.

"Because I happen to know that every one of you are thieves," answered the other.

"The devil you do! Then why not take us up, and carry us before the beak?"

"I've had you there once already to-day," replied the constable; "and you had the good luck to be discharged, because I couldn't bring anything clearly home. However, it won't be long first, I dare say, before I, or some one else, gets hold of you again."

"What for?" demanded Snatch, with assumed simplicity. "Mustn't honest people walk about the streets without being laid hold of, and dragged before a magistrate, by such infernal meddling fellows as you?"

"Aye, you don't like us chaps, I know," retorted the constable. "We're a little too daring for you, and often spoil sport, when you've made up your mind to have a good haul."

"Do you take us for thieves then?" asked Mike Rowley, with well feigned indignation.

"I happen to know that you are one," replied the other, "and I've a pretty good notion that your companions are not much better. However, I've no business with any of you to-night, so you may make yourselves quite easy, till we have the pleasure of meeting next time."

"Confound it," exclaimed Fordham, "what's the use of carrying the joke so far as this? If these gentlemen are going to sit down and enjoy themselves, they are welcome to our company; if not, they can go away about their business, and leave us just as they found us."

"Our business," answered the constable, "is, I rather think, over for to-night.'"

"What," said Snatch, "you can't find some chap, that you're looking after? Isn't that about the ticket?"

"I dare say you know as much about it as I do," said the official. "The prisoner that we had in custody to-day has escaped; and there'll be a devil of a row about it, if we don't get hold of him again."

"Why you don't mean to tell me," exclaimed Mike Rowley, with well dissembled disguise, "that my fellow-prisoner has managed to escape out of your clutches."

"He has though," answered the other; "and for all your pretending to be so much surprised, I've a notion that you had a hand in helping him to escape."

"Nonsense! you never can think that?"

"Indeed, but I do though."

"What an idea!" exclaimed Mike Rowley, again appealing to his comrades. "You hear what this chap says, and yet every one of you can swear, that I came straight here after leaving the police office, and that I've never been out of your sight from that time till now."

"Oh yes," returned Dick Fordham, "we can swear that, I should think, with a very good conscience."

"Well, at any rate, I'm not bound to believe you," exclaimed the constable; "and, what's more, I give you all fair warning, that I mean to inquire into this affair till I've sifted it to the very bottom."

"And very right too," interposed Mike Rowley; "you, of course have got all the blame of it, and we, knowing our own innocence, can have no fear of getting into any trouble about the affair; so you can take me before his worship again if you like, and then I can talk to him a bit about the hardship of a man like me being charged twice with doing wrong in the course of a week."

"Ah!" exclaimed the constable, "you've a nice way of wheedling people over—you have. Anybody but yourself would have got sent to prison this morning after what I told the magistrate about you; but somehow or another he was in one of his tender moods, so you got discharged, and all through that I've lost my prisoner."

"Then you still think I had something to do with it?"

"Not only you," replied the other, looking all of them full in the face, "but I've a pretty strong notion that every one here present had a hand in it."

"Then why don't you take us all up without making any further fuss about it?" demanded Sam Snatch.

"Because I want to be a little more certain of being right before I do that," replied the constable; "there were three men, pretty much like yourselves, that came and knocked us down when we were in a lonely part of the road; and, before we could say Jack Robinson, the prisoner had flitted, and he and his three companions were clean out of sight by the time we had recovered ourselves."

"And serve you right, too, if you couldn't take more care of your prisoner," exclaimed Fordham; "you should have had more people to guard him, and then you wouldn't have been in such a precious pickle as you are."

"There were enough of us when we left the police office," answered the constable; "six stout chaps ought to have been enough to take care of one prisoner, and so they would, only that the fellows slipped off one by one as they got near their homes, and when we were attacked there were only two of us besides the man we had in charge."

"And the prisoner would, I should think, have been able enough to beat the pair of you, if you're a sample of what t'other chap is," exclaimed Dick Fordham; "however, as I don't want to be personal, suppose we change the subject, by your telling us what brought you here to-night?"

"I came to see if the prisoner was here."

"And what the devil made you think he could be in this house any more than another one?"

"I had a very good reason for it," replied the constable.

"This house, as of course you know, don't bear a very good name, for its said to be the resort of thieves and other bad characters; and, besides that, I heard that Guy Harrowby had been here not very long ago."

"I can't say how that may be," exclaimed Fordham; "but if he has been here, its the very reason why he should not come again, whilst the pursuit after him lasts. Of course, he'd have been a fool to expect concealment where people were sure to come and look for him before they went anywhere else."

"Its all very well for you to tell me that," returned the other; "but I aint to be gammoned quite as easily as you seem to think for. He may be here now for aught I know, and I've a great mind to search the house from top to bottom before I go away."

"And I would too, if I was you," said Fordham; well convinced that the search would prove a fruitless one.

"There's nothing like being satisfied when there's a doubt upon one's mind, and as I know the ways of the house better than you do, I don't mind shewing you over it, so that there shan't be a nook nor a cranny that you don't poke your nose into."

"You're only jeering me I find," exclaimed the official, as he observed a broad grin upon the countenances of all the men. "You'd like to catch me putting myself under your guidance, I dare say;—but I'm a little too wide awake for that, so I shall put off the search till another opportunity; and, in the meantime, people will be stationed round the house, so that all who go out or come in, will be seen and marked."

"I don't care what arrangements you make, my fine fellow, so that you don't interfere with me," said Mike Rowley. "You've had me in your custody once, and I'm not likely to forget it in a hurry; but if you lay hold of me again, it may lead to something rather unpleasant between us."

"I don't want to have anything to say or do with you any more," exclaimed the constable. "You've had warning enough I should think, to mend your ways in future; and now, if you choose to do good instead of harm, there's a capital opportunity of doing so at once."

"How do you mean?"

"Why, by helping me to find the man I'm searching for. You know him, and I dare say are well enough aware of the place where he's hiding; so, if you like to give him up to justice, you shall have half the reward."

"Oh! you think to tempt me then by the offer of blood money?"

"Psha!" exclaimed the constable, "what's the use of making such a fuss about nothing? Its your duty to tell where he is, even if no reward was offered; and, surely, there can't be any very great objection to earning a sum of money, when it's to give up a man that's charged with murder."

"But this chap and I were friends together for a little while."

"I know it," returned the other; "but what odds does that make in a matter of business like this. He very nearly got you into a scrape through your being taken with him, so I should think there was an end of your friendship for a man, that you said, was almost a stranger."

"All this blarney won't do any good with me, I can tell you," exclaimed Mike Rowley; "the prisoner has escaped, and I can only say good luck to him, for he was a trump of a fellow whilst we kept company, and I should be sorry to hear of any harm coming to him."

"Very well!" returned the official, "you can do as you like about it of course; but mind this, my fine fellow, you'll make yourself liable to a severe punishment if you harbour or assist to conceal a man that is charged with having committed a murder."

"Oh! I'm not to be frightened by anything the big wigs can do," returned Rowley, snapping his fingers; "they'd be glad to hang me as well as him I dare say, but how am I to know that Guy Harrowby is guilty of murder till after the jurymen have returned their verdict?"

"At all events, you know that he is charged with the crime."

"Yes, but I've heard it said, that every man is supposed to be innocent, till he has been found guilty."

"What's the use of argufying this matter any further?" interrupted Dick Fordham; "you've said that you'll have no hand in giving up a poor devil to the gallows, so 'tother chap ought to see by this time, that he aint likely to get much good out of you, if he keeps on talking for a month. He sees the man he's looking for aint here; but, as I told him before, if he'd like to have a regular rummage over the house, I'll go with him and shew him the way."

"I'd rather be excused from trusting myself to your care," replied the constable.

"Oh, you're afraid I should play you a trick then?"

"As for being afraid," returned the other, "I've as good a share of courage as most people, but when chap's like you are so d——d civil, I always think there's something in the wind, so I shall put off the search till we can come in greater force."

Doublechalk, who had just left the fugitives in the loft, returned into the room whilst these latter words were spoken; and, glancing inquisitively at the constable, he at once guessed the object that had brought him there. He, however, affected ignorance upon that point; and addressing himself to the unwelcome intruder asked him, "what it was he wanted?"

"We want somebody that we're not very likely to find, it seems," replied the functionary; "a prisoner has escaped out of my custody, and I thought it was not at all unlikely, that I might meet with him here."

"I don't harbour bad people," exclaimed the landlord, sharply; "so this is about the last place in the world where you might have expected to find a thief."

"The man I'm looking after is worse than that," returned the other, "for there's a charge of murder against him; and, if I don't meet with him before this day week, I shall be likely to find myself in the wrong box."

"What's the name of the man?" asked the landlord.

"Guy Harrowby."

"Humph! don't know him;—never heard the name before."

"You do know him though; for he's been in this house two or three times very lately."

"I don't know him by that name then," answered Doublechalk; "a great many stranger's come into this house in the course of the day, and it isn't for me to ask who they are, or where they come from."

"The truth of the matter is," said Dick Fordham, "this man's got a notion, that the fellow he's after is concealed in this house."

"Concealed in my house!" exclaimed the landlord, indignantly; "I should like to catch myself helping evil-doers to escape from justice. No, no, Mr. Constable, if he'd shown himself here I'd soon have given him up, and no mistake."

"I don't know how that may be," returned the other, "but it seems my visit here's no go; and that being the case, I shall wish you all a very good night."

"Oh, good night to you old fellow," exclaimed Sam Snatch; "but I say my cove, when will you come again, and stay a long time."

"It won't be long before I'm here again, I dare say," replied the other; "I've a notion now, that the man's concealed somewhere about the place, only I don't like to risk my own life when there's such a bad lot about me."

The constable, and his attendant satellites, marched themselves off as soon as he had given utterance to this; and, as soon as they were fairly out of hearing, Mike Rowley burst forth into a boisterous fit of laughter.

"What are you making such a row about?" asked Dick Fordham; "was there anything very funny in the fellow calling us a bad lot?"

"It wasn't that," replied Mike, "but, for the life of me, I couldn't help laughing to see them chaps go away; when, all the while, the man they were looking after was in the house. By the bye, Dick, I thought you was rather mad, when you offered to show the constable over the house."

"You don't suppose I should have done it if there'd been a chance of his taking me at my word," answered Fordham; "I knew well enough that he'd be afraid, and, at any rate, the offer I made was likely to give him a notion that Guy Harrowby was not here."

"I left him snug enough in the loft, just now," observed the landlord; "but I don't think he likes his quarters much, for he seems to think his lodging aint the most comfortable one he was ever in."

"At any rate," said Mike Rowley, "its better than the cage they put us into last night. We'd nothing but the bare benches to sleep upon there; but, where he is, he may find plenty of things among the lumber to make a tidy bed of."

"And when he wakes in the morning," observed Fordham, "he'll have the consolation of knowing that he's got a fair chance of cheating the hangman."

"Do you think there's any truth about the murder they talk about?" asked Doublechalk.

"How should I know anything about it?" asked the other; "it happened too far off to be much talked of here, but I fancy I've a recollection of hearing some time ago, that one of the convicts had murdered his keeper and afterwards escaped into the bush."

"Then, I'll bet a pound, Guy Harrowby was the man," exclaimed the landlord; "though, why he should have been such a fool as to come to England I can't think, since he was sure to be nosed out by some of the people."

"I know all about that part of the business," said Mike Rowley; "for he told me a long rigmarole while we were together last night. It seems, that being transported went against the grain, for he didn't like being parted from his wife; so, from the time he reached the place, he was always planning how he might get away."

"And as there was no other way," said Snatch, "I suppose he killed the guard, and then bolted."

"I dare say that was it," replied Mike; "but I didn't like to ask him too many questions about it, because, the less we know of these matters the better."

"So it is," returned Sam; "for, if we know nothing, there can't be any fear of blabbing the secret."

"A very sensible observation that of yours," exclaimed the landlord; "but your remarks are always excellent, Sam, and it's a pity your father hadn't made a lawyer of you."

"I'm a thief, and that's about the same thing!" he replied.

"Good again," exclaimed Doublechalk; "upon my life Sam, you're the sharpest chap in the company."

"Not quite so sharp as yourself though," retorted Snatch; "for your remarks are rather cutting!"

"This is d——d nonsense after all," interposed Dick Fordham; "for all this wit, as I suppose you call it, won't assist the poor devil that's up in the loft; he may be safe where he is for a little while, perhaps; but we ought to be ready with some plan to get him clear out of England, as soon as the search after him begins to grow a little cooler. What say you, Doublechalk, have you any bright thought upon the matter?"

"Not I," replied the landlord; "all I care about it is that you'll get him out of my house as soon as possible."

"You needn't be afraid of our doing that," returned the other; "for Harrowby won't care how soon he gets out of that infernal dark hole of yours; and, as for ourselves, we shall be glad to get him abroad, because as long as he remains in England we shall be doing very little in our own way of business."

"And where do you think of taking him to?"

"That's not quite certain yet; but I rather think we shall try and get him over to Holland."

"Holland!" exclaimed the landlord; "why I thought that was where he came from when he landed here a few days ago."

"So it was, and a d——d fool he was that he didn't stay there. But no—he must needs come to England to see his wife, as if she couldn't have gone over there to him."

"Why," exclaimed Doublechalk, "it seems as if he wanted to throw himself in the way of danger."

"I don't know that he was quite such an ass as that," said Dick Fordham; "but if he had given the matter a moment's thought he might have been sure that he couldn't be in this country many hours without a regular hue and cry being raised after him. However, he sees his folly now, I dare say, so all we've got to do is to get him out of his trouble as well as we can."

"I'm thinking that won't be quite so easy as you fancy," observed Mike Rowley; "the fellow that was here just now seemed to have a notion that he was lurking somewhere about this house; and, as that's the case, he's likely enough to come back here with about a score of the police."

"And if they do, what have we to fear?" asked Fordham. "They may search the house from top to bottom, perhaps; but, when they've put themselves to all that trouble, they'll not be a bit more forward than they are now."

"It may be all very well for you to take it so easily, about searching the house," said the landlord; "but it won't be very pleasant for me, I can tell you, to have a parcel of fellows rummaging the place from top to bottom. Besides, how the neighbours will talk about it when its known that I've had a visit from the police."

"Well," returned Sam Snatch, "it won't be the first time they've had to talk about that sort of thing."

"May be not; and yet I can't say that I feel any the more comfortable on that account."

"What's the use of grumbling when you can't help yourself," exclaimed Mike Rowley; "the man's in the house, and you can't get rid of him, unless you take it into your head to turn him out neck and crop."

"I should like to see him do it, that's all," said Fordham. "He can try it on if he likes, but it would be the worst day's work he ever did for himself; for it wouldn't be long afterwards before he found himself under lock and key in Newgate. We happen to know quite enough of his goings on to send him there without much trouble."

"Gentlemen," exclaimed Doublechalk, "if you're going to get up a quarrel, the sooner we part the better. It's quite late enough for me to close the house; and then, if the police should come and find the place empty, the appearance of matters will be all in my favour."

"Well, old fellow," returned Dick Fordham, "I don't know but what you're right as far as that goes; so, for the sake of appearances, as you call 'em, we'll relieve you from the honour of our company. To-morrow we shall pay you another visit, and mind we hear a good account of our comrade, Guy Harrowby."

They then drained their glasses to the bottom; and, bidding the landlord good-night, left the house one by one, so as to excite as little observation as possible.

CHAPTER XVI.

A JOURNEY.—LODGINGS TO LET.—AN ENCOUNTER.

THE day following the return of Charles Heathingdon into the country, Jane left her cottage to the care of a female neighbour; and, with her child, took a place in the carrier's waggon, in order to reach London that she might be near her husband, who was, according to the libertine's account, in prison on a charge of murder. The money she had saved was sufficient, with prudence, to last some little time; and, though her presence might not be of any real advantage to Guy, it would at least be some consolation to have her near him, and to have interviews with her as often as the rules and discipline of the prison would permit.

Her journey, to one so anxious as herself, was a most tedious one; for the vehicle moved lazily along the road, and the waggoner stopped so often on the way, that it was not until nine o'clock on the following morning that Jane Harrowby found herself in the busy streets of the metropolis. The place where the waggon put up at was in the Old Bailey; and, after having paid her fare, she walked on, without knowing whither, in search of some place where she might procure a lodging for the time she was to remain in town. Passing the gloomy walls of Newgate, she crossed Smithfield; and, on reaching St. John's Street, arrived at a decent looking house, in the parlour window of which was a bill, announcing that there was a room to let. As this seemed likely to suit her purpose, she knocked at the door, which was opened by a portly dame, who, on learning her errand, invited her into the front room, which she informed her visitor was the one she had to let.

"It's a nice airy place, ma'am," she said, throwing open the window; "and, as you seem to have come from the country, I should think it will be just the thing."

"I have no fault to find with it," answered Jane, "if the rent happens to be within my means."

"The rent's a mere nothing," returned the female; "seven and sixpence a week won't be considered too much for a first-rate situation like this."

"It's more than I intended to give," replied Jane Harrowby; "but as I have neither time nor inclination to search further, I will take it for the little time I am likely to remain in London."

"Can you give me a reference?"

"I am a stranger in town," answered Jane, "and all I can do is to pay you the first week's rent in advance;" and taking a small purse from her pocket, she handed the amount agreed upon to the landlady, who, though she took the money, was still inclined to ask more questions.

"You are a married woman, I suppose," she said; glancing her eye suspiciously towards the sleeping child.

"I am."

"Has he come to London with you?"

"No," answered Jane, falteringly, as she found herself compelled to use the language of deception; "he remains at home, as the business I am on can only be done by myself."

"I forgot to ask your name."

"It is Simmons," answered Jane; pronouncing the first that came to her mind, for she well knew that the name of her husband had by this time become notorious, and that it was therefore necessary to use an assumed one.

The landlady now seemed to have fairly exhausted all her questions, and by way of excuse for remaining in the room, she took up her apron, and dusted the tables and chairs. At last, finding that her new lodger was not likely to be very communicative, she inquired, "whether she intended to take possession of the room from that moment."

"I would do so," answered Jane, "if you have no objection."

"Oh, as for objection, there can be none," replied the woman; "you've paid rent for your apartment for a week, so of course you can take possession from this moment, if you think proper. Shall I send my girl out to get anything for your dinner, Mrs. Simmons?"

"To-day I shall not have to trouble you," returned Jane; "I have some cold meat left that I brought with me from home, and I believe there is also bread enough to last me till to-morrow. Indeed, I shall be so little in the house, that scarcely any attendance will be required."

"Well, now," exclaimed the landlady, as she perceived a tear glistening in the eyes of the poor creature before her, "as sure as my name's Margaret Toddy, there is something weighing heavily on your mind?"

"There is," replied Jane, with a sigh; "but I must endure it without complaint, since I have not one friend in the world to whom I can look for help or consolation."

"Humph! you can't have a very good husband, then, if you're without so much as a friend."

"I have no complaint to make against him," answered Jane.

"Ah!" exclaimed Mrs. Toddy; "I see how it is—you are one of those meek, quiet wives, that will put up with anything rather than show a proper spirit. When my poor dear husband was alive, I always let him see that I wasn't to be trampled upon; and, from being a little rumbustical and overbearing at first, I brought him down to be as quiet as a lamb. But mind, Mrs. Simmons, I haven't a spark of curiosity about me, so don't suppose I want to pry into any of your family secrets. No, no, I pride myself upon minding my own business, and leave others to do the same by theirs."

"Do you know," asked Jane, without making any reply to the latter observation, "where, or how I can see a newspaper?"

"They'll lend you one from the public-house over the way," replied Mrs. Toddy; "it will be one day old, to be sure, but I dare say that won't much signify—that is, if you only want to read over the police news, and the accidents and offences, for amusement."

"It is for something more than that," replied Jane, who expected to find in the paper something that would give information respecting her husband.

"Ah," rejoined the other, "then, I dare say, you'wish to look over the advertisements for a situation, or something of that sort."

"Yes, yes, that's it," exclaimed Jane, hurriedly; as she began to grow weary of so many questions.

"Well, now, only to think that I should have made such a near guess at the truth," cried the landlady; "not that I'm at all curious, or wish to mind other people's affairs instead of my own; for I scorn them as is meddling, and wouldn't, for the world, pry into things that don't concern me. By the by, Mrs. Simmons, I haven't asked you yet what part of the country it is that you come from?"

"Nor do I think proper to inform you," answered Jane with more spirit than she usually manifested. "You were just now boasting of having no desire to interfere with other people's business, and yet with the same breath you —"

"There now!" interrupted the old lady, "I declare if I haven't given offence without meaning it. I thought there could be no great harm in asking about where you came from, and yet it seems you don't like it."

"I have not the slightest objection to your asking as many questions as you please," returned Jane, "but it must be left to my own inclination whether I answer them or not. The business that has brought me to London is of a very peculiar nature, and there are reasons for my keeping my presence here a secret for the present."

"Very good, Mrs. Simmons, very good," exclaimed the landlady, endeavouring to conceal her chagrin; "I don't want to give you any offence, I'm sure, so we won't say anything more about this affair. But where there's mystery, there's always doubt, because people can't help their thoughts, though it aint always right, perhaps, to speak 'em out."

Hereupon, Mrs. Toddy walked out of the room under no little excitement, and Jane felt well pleased that she had got rid of an incessant clack, that at the present moment was most intolerable. Already she almost began to regret that she had pitched her quarters with a person who was so inquisitive in the affairs of her lodgers, but it was now too late to retrace her steps, and the only thing she could do was to be guarded in all she said, and to leave the landlady with no more information than she had at present obtained. During this period of temporary quiet, she took from her basket the humble meal she had brought with her from home, and was helping herself sparingly to it, when Mrs. Toddy re-entered the room. To all appearance, she had quite forgotten the momentary anger that had been caused by disappointed curiosity, and, holding out a newspaper to Jane, she said,—

"So, I see, some of our police officers have been making a very pretty mess of it, for they've suffered the escape of a man that had been examined before the magistrate for murder, and the fellow has made such good use of his chance, that no trace of him has been found yet."

"What is the man's name?" demanded Jane, gasping between astonishment and doubt.

"Guy Harrowby."

"Ah! then he will be saved!" cried Jane, clasping her hands convulsively.

" Saved ! " exclaimed the landlady. eyeing her with surprise " why.you don't think it's right that a murderer, like him, should get clear off when he deserves to be hanged ? "

" I knew not what I said," answered Jane, endeavouring to recover her composure, " the man may be innocent, for aught we know, and, surely, if he is guilty, it would be better that he should live to repent past crimes than perish, ere he has had time to obtain pardon for the evil he has committed."

" Mercy's all very fine to talk about," returned the landlady, " but I don't see why one man should be suffered to escape any more than another. Now, this one seems to be a terrible bad fellow, and all I hope is, that it won't be long before they get hold of him again."

" And I," " sighed Jane, " hope he may find some kind Christian that will conceal him till the search is over."

" Why, bless your simple heart," exclaimed Mrs. Toddy, " he's no more chance of getting clear off than I have of going to pay a visit to the Pope of Rome."

" What reason have you for thinking so ? "

" Because I see there is a reward of fifty pounds offered for his apprehension," answered the landlady; " besides, the officers seem to be pretty close after him, for they've been to a public-house in Wapping, where, it's well known, he has been, three or four times, lately."

" And he was not there when they went ? "

"They didn't find him there," answered Mrs. Toddy," but it's supposed he aint very far off, and some of the police, in plain clothes, are watching all about the neighbourhood."

"Does the paper mention the name of the public-house?" asked Jane, with as little appearance of anxiety as she could command.

"Yes; it's called the Seven Horse Shoes."

Jane Harrowby made no reply to this, but resolved to lose no time in paying a visit to that place, as being the most likely where she might obtain some clue towards discovering her fugitive husband; at any rate this seemed to be the only course that lay open to her, and, in a manner to avoid as much as possible the chance of having her purpose suspected, she inquired in what direction Wapping was to be found.

"Oh, quite at the east end of London," answered the old woman; "if you're going there you'll have to pass over Tower Hill, and then it won't be long before you reach Wapping; but it's a nasty place for strangers to visit, so I wouldn't advise you to go there after dark."

"Why, do you suppose I am going there?"

"Because you asked the way to it; and seem so anxious, ever since I told you about the man that is supposed to be hiding himself there."

"You are mistaken in supposing that I am anxious upon a subject that concerns me not," answered Jane; "I pity the man you have been speaking of, as I should any one else; but pity is of little use to a poor wretch in his forlorn and miserable situation."

"All I can say about it is—that if he has murdered any one—he deserves to be hanged for it."

"But," answered Jane, "from the little I have read of this account, there appears to be no proof that he has been guilty of the crime of murder; the charge may be a malicious one, brought against him by some enemy to satisfy his own revenge."

"I don't know how that may be," returned Mrs. Toddy, "but it's not very likely that he's innocent when he escapes rather than stand his trial."

"How was the escape contrived?" asked Jane, who had only glanced over the printed account.

"Oh, by means of some of his friends, I suppose," replied the landlady; "after the examination they were going to lock him up in the cage, when—all of a sudden—out rushed, I don't know how many men, who knocked down the constables and got the prisoner clear away before the poor fellows could pick themselves up again."

"When did this happen?" asked Jane.

"The day before yesterday."

"And he has not yet been found?"

"I don't know what to-day's paper may say about it," she replied; "but, when this account was published, no one seemed to know where to look for him."

A knock at the street door now called Mrs. Toddy out of the room; and putting by the remainder of her meal, for which she had no appetite, Jane Harrowby wrapped a shawl around her sleeping infant, and left the house, after informing the landlady that she should return home at an early hour in the evening. Unused, as she was, to the streets of London, she found no little difficulty in finding her way to the place she was in quest of; but, having inquired in some of the shops as she went along, she at length reached Tower Hill, where she again paused, uncertain which way to proceed. Whilst she was thus standing still, a gentleman approached, who, uttering her name in a tone of surprise, advanced at a more rapid pace; and, to her consternation and alarm, she recognised the form and features of Charles Heathingdon.

"Good heavens!" he exclaimed, "how is it that I find you at this distance from your home? What extraordinary whim is it that has brought you to London?"

"To save my husband, if possible, from the arts of his cruel persecutor," she replied. "I have come to seek him whom you would destroy; and, if I cannot save, to at least die, ere they lead him forth to execution."

"Be advised by me, and return to the country without delay," exclaimed Charles: "your presence cannot possibly be of service to him, though it may do him more mischief than you are aware of."

"Mischief I will NOT do him," she replied; "but it may not be out of my power to do him a service, in spite of all the schemes of villany you have formed for his ruin."

"You are still as much prejudiced against me as ever, I see, Jane," he exclaimed, whilst his lip curled with a bitter smile.

"Mine is not an idle prejudice," she replied: "the evil that you have done to me and mine is greater than you can ever repair. You profess to love me, though my vows are already given to another; and, when I reject your proposals with the scorn they deserve, you turn your vengeance against my husband, though you well know that the consequences must be fatal to him."

"Your anger on that account," exclaimed Charles, "may now cease; for your husband has escaped, and, for the present, all trace of him has been lost."

"I know he has escaped," she replied; "and my earnest prayer to heaven is, that he may no longer fall into your power."

"Perhaps you know where he is."

"Alas! I know no more of him than you do."

"You would save him, I suppose, from the danger he is threatened with," said Charles Heathingdon.

"Aye—if the sacrifice of my own life would do it."

"There's no reason for so great a sacrifice as that," exclaimed the libertine: "you know the terms I have already proposed, and they are still open for your acceptance. Promise to become mine, Jane Harrowby, and your husband shall not want for assistance to get out of England."

"Away! let me pass on," she exclaimed, endeavouring to press forward. "Let me pass, I say, or I'll claim assistance from the first person that approaches."

"Moderate your anger," he said, "and do not commit yourself by doing that which you will afterwards repent. You may expose me to whom you please, but remember, it will be repaid with interest. Guy Harrowby has only escaped for a time; in a few hours he may be in custody again: whatever follows will be through your own fault."

"I know," exclaimed Jane, "you will appear against him, and do your best to procure a conviction; but the moment of your triumph shall be that also of your disgrace, for I will myself stand forward in the witness-box, and proclaim your shame to all around!"

"What can you say to injure me?"

"I can make known to the world the base propositions you have made to me," she replied.

"Psha! People have too much business of their own to attend to, without caring about mine or yours."

"But I will tell them the terms upon which you offered to assist in the escape of my husband."

"Which I," he replied carelessly, "shall take especial pains to contradict, and we shall then see which side obtains the most credit for telling the truth. Why the very fact of my being the first to denounce your husband, will be sufficient to prove that I am not likely to have suggested any connivance in favouring his escape from England."

"So you may flatter yourself," she exclaimed, "but do not believe that falsehood will be triumphant over truth."

"I see no reason why I should fail," he replied, "for there is not a single witness that can be brought forward to prove that I ever made such a proposition. So you see how utterly hopeless your case is, and how easily I shall be able to thwart the mischief you would do me."

The heart of Jane Harrowby was too full for utterance, and, pressing the infant still more close to her bosom, she made another effort to pass on, but the libertine was determined to detain her still longer, and grasping her tightly by the arm, he exclaimed:—

"It is in vain that you seek to avoid me, because I am determined to take the present opportunity to point out the helpless situation to which you are reduced. You have come to London, I suppose, in search of your husband; you would assist him to evade the terrible fate that hangs over him, and yet you refuse to adopt the only means by which you can hope to benefit him."

"I entreat you to let me pass on," gasped Jane; "if there is one spark of kindness or honour in your heart, you will detain me here no longer against my inclination."

"Promise that you will meet me again," he said, "name the time and place, and you shall depart without further hinderance."

"I will make no promise of the kind," she replied, "for I will not owe even my deliverance to a lie."

"Then it is your own fault if I persist in my resolution," answerered Charles Heathingdon, "the offer I have made you is a perfectly fair one, and you can no longer blame me for the course I am pursuing."

"I may at least ask by what authority you presume to detain me here against my will."

"Authority," he replied, "is out of the question, when I do not profess to have any other than my own will and pleasure; besides, you profess an anxious desire to save your husband from the penalty of his crime, and the object of my present interview is to offer terms by which he may escape a fate that is otherwise inevitable."

"How know you that it is inevitable?" she asked; "my husband is at present as free as you yourself are;—he is not without friends to assist him in this dreadful hour of need, and I feel assured, that there is yet a chance of his escaping death without your aid."

"It's a poor hope if that's all you have to depend on," exclaimed the libertine. "He may have friends as you say, to assist him to escape, but on the other hand, we have vigilant officers to look after him; he has found a temporary hiding place, I dare say, in some obscure place or another, yet he cannot remain concealed for any long time, and the first time he ventures out of doors he will fall into the hands of those that are lying in wait for him."

"All that he is perfectly well aware of," replied Jane, "and he will therefore not venture out of doors, till he can do so with tolerable safety."

"Perhaps you know where he is?"

"Would to heaven I did, for it is likely a woman's wit would be a match for your villany."

"Fair words, and more courteous language if you please," exclaimed Charles Heathingdon, "I would argue this matter in all friendship of spirit, yet you treat me as though I were your greatest enemy."

"You are the enemy of my husband, and therefore cannot be any friend of mine," she replied; "you profess indeed to love me, yet persecute me with all the cruel rancour of a fiend."

"Can you not find a better term for my passion?" he asked, "or am I still to endure the hard names by which you choose to designate my motives. You have been at some pains, Jane, to draw upon yourself the anger of a man who professes to love you, and I may therefore take some credit to myself, that I have so far abstained from a course that may after all be found necessary."

"I have little courtesy to thank you for," she replied.

"Perhaps not," exclaimed Charles Heathingdon, "but that has been more your own fault than mine. Had you treated me with the least show of kindness, your husband would not have been in his present dilemma."

"Must I again ask you to suffer me to pass on?" she cried; "am I your prisoner, Mr. Heathingdon, that you presume to detain me here against my will? Make way for me, I say, or I will appeal to some passenger to protect me from further insolence."

"Tell me first when and where I shall next see you."

"It is my most earnest prayer," she exclaimed, "and shall be my endeavour to avoid any meeting in future. It is through you that I have been forced to leave my home to come in search of the man whose destruction you have resolved upon—it is through you that I have been cast into the very lowest depths of misery and despair, and so loathsome have you now become to me, that I would flee even to the very ends of the earth, rather than again find myself in your presence."

"Beware how you excite my fury," exclaimed the libertine, in a low, but deep tone of voice: "it is in your power to make me the deliverer of your husband, and yet knowing all that, you rail at me, instead of endeavouring to obtain the valuable services it is in my power to perform."

"Had you a spark of generosity," she replied, "you would perform them without requiring any sacrifice to be made. You say it is in your power to save my husband from a dreadful fate, yet would drive him to the gibbet, because his wife has virtue enough to reject, with scorn, your infamous proposals."

"Your scorn it is that has driven me to what I have done," exclaimed Charles Heathingdon. "My attentions have been received with the bitterest reproaches, and I have met only scorn and invectives where I expected at least some little show of civility. Yet, for all that, Jane Harrowby, you shall not turn me from my purpose—I'll haunt you like your own shadow, and, go where you may, there also will I follow."

Just then three or four persons were seen approaching, and taking the opportunity their presence afforded, Jane made a sudden spring forward, and in an instant was beyond his reach. The libertine gazed after, and then turned away, muttering at what he called her insolence and perverseness.

CHAPTER XVII.

TRAVELS IN THE EAST.—THE PILGRIMAGE SUCCESSFUL.—A GALLANT OFFER.

TERRIFIED as she was, lest she should be pursued by her tormentor, Jane Harrowby relaxed not her speed till she became so exhausted by the exertion, as to be compelled to pause a few moments to recover herself. To her own infinite gratification she discovered that no attempt had been made to follow her, and having sufficiently recovered herself, she proceeded with more confidence to search for the house she had come in quest of. The place in which she now found herself was one of the filthiest and lowest in the neighbourhood of London; crowds of wretched-looking people were thronging to and fro. The gin-shops sent forth their shoals of drunken and disorderly persons, and language of the coarsest and most filthy description met her ears at every step she took. Under any other circumstances, Jane would have turned back in disgust; but the object she now had in view was of such paramount importance, that she still proceeded onwards, though without knowing whether she was going in the right direction or not. At length, meeting a decent-looking woman, she stopped her to inquire the way for the "Seven Horse Shoes," at Wapping; and having received from her a clear and satisfactory direction, she again went on, though with anything but confidence in the success of her mission. A quarter-of-an-hour's walk brought her to the door of the public-house she was in search of, and there she paused a minute or two; for the place looked like a resort for bad characters, and the sounds of drunken revelry within made her fearful of meeting with insult from the dissipated wretches who were there congregated. Upon consideration, however, there was no alternative: it was the only place she knew of where there was a likelihood of hearing anything of her husband, and that consideration alone induced her to enter the forbidding-looking place. Perceiving that there was a room forward, she hastened there; and finding it empty, rang the bell, which was answered by the pot-boy, who she desired to send his master to her, as soon as he was disengaged. The lad stared at her with stupid surprise, and then turned away, thinking, no doubt, his master had got a queer sort of a customer. Sooner than she expected, the landlord entered the room, who, after eyeing her with suspicion, inquired what was her pleasure?"

"My errand," she replied, timidly, "is to ask if you can give me any information of a man named Guy Harrowby?"

"Guy Harrowby!" exclaimed the landlord; "who are you that have come here to ask about him?"

" His wife."

" Indeed ! and how am I to know that this aint some trick of the officers to find out where the fellow is ?"

" On my honour, I have told you nothing but the truth," exclaimed Jane, earnestly.

" How can that be," demanded Doublechalk, " when I've heard him say his wife lives somewhere down in the country ?"

" I do live there," she replied ; " but hearing that he was in prison on a charge affecting his life, I came to town with my child to see if anything could be done for him."

" You've heard, I suppose, ma'am, that some of his friends managed to rescue him from the constable."

" Yes," she replied, " I have heard that he is again at liberty, and, as the report stated that he had been seen in this house on three or four occasions, I came here thinking you might be able to tell me where I can find him."

" I can't give you any information about that," exclaimed the landlord. " Guy Harrowby don't trust me with any of his secrets, and, even if he had, I shouldn't blab 'em to a person that I never saw in my life before."

" Do you think, then, his wife would betray him ?"

" How do I know that you are his wife ?" demanded the other sharply. " It would be easy for any other person besides yourself to tell me as much, and if I was fool enough, for ought I know Guy Harrowby might soon afterwards find himself in prison again."

" You do not deny knowing where he is, then ?"

" Why, as for that," replied Doublechalk, " I dare say, if I happened to want him for anything, I should have much trouble to find him out."

" Is he far from this place ?"

" Humph ! not very far."

" Can I see him ?"

" I should say no, most decidedly," answered the landlord. " His life depends upon the good faith of his friends, and as I've promised not to tell any one this secret, I mean to keep my word."

" For which I give you my thanks," exclaimed Jane. " He is, I see, not so deserted by his friends as I imagined, though I could wish you would let me see him, if only for two or three minutes."

" But what a deal of mischief might be done in those two or three minutes, my good woman," returned Doublechalk. " There may be some scheme in this visit of yours ; so, as far as I'm concerned, you'll go away from this house very little wiser than you came into it."

" You still suspect me, I see," exclaimed Jane, " and yet, if my motives were unfriendly, you have already acknowledged enough to get yourself into trouble."

" What have I said ?"

" That you know where he is, and are consequently conniving at his escape."

" Ha ! and you mean to inform against me for it, do you ?" exclaimed Doublechalk. " But I thought from the first it was all gammon about your being his wife, so you may go back to those that sent you here, and tell 'em Guy Harrowby is in such snug quarters, that no one will ever be likely to find out where he is."

" Thank Heaven for that," cried Jane, fervently. " You believe that I am some spy sent here to worm out the secret of Guy Harrowby's hiding-place. Such, however, is not the fact, for I am indeed his wife, though most unhappy at the fearful situation in which he stands."

" Well," returned the other, " I should think, if you really are his wife, you can't be very happy. He's in a precious awkward mess, I can tell you, ma'am, for the police are keeping an uncommon sharp look-out, and if they should happen to find him, he'd be hanged, certainly."

" But you say there is little chance of his being traced to the place where he is ?"

" He's all right enough at present," answered Doublechalk, " but the secret's known to three or four people besides myself ; and, as a reward of fifty pounds has been offered for his discovery, there's no saying whether one of 'em mightn't tell where he is, for the sake of the money."

" Then, why not remove him to some other place ?" demanded Jane Harrowby, eagerly.

" Because it can't be done without exposing him to too much danger," replied the landlord. ' People are watching about for him in all directions, and as sure as he ventures out of doors they'll nail him."

" And are you still determined," asked Jane, " that I shall not be permitted to see him ?"

" I see no reason for altering my determination," he replied. " You say you are his wife, and it may be so, for aught I know ; but it's likely any other woman would come with the same sort of story, if there was any trick to be played off against us."

" Can I send a message to him ?"

" Yes—I'll tell him anything you like ; but he won't hear it for some hours, because I don't visit him oftener than need be, for fear there should happen to be inquisitive people watching my movements."

" When shall you see him ?"

" The first thing to-morrow morning."

" You will tell him, then, that his wife is now in town ; and ask if he can suggest any plan by which she may assist him in his present unhappy condition."

"I'll give him your message to a certainty," exclaimed the landlord; "though, for the life of me, I can't see what help can be given by a woman that has got a child to carry about in her arms."

"I can at least bring love and zeal into the cause," replied Jane Harrowby. "My regard for him has been rather strengthened than weakened by the trials and vicissitudes he has unhappily gone through; and, though all else in the world forsake him, he shall yet find that the affection of his wife is unshaken."

"Ah!" exclaimed Doublechalk, "I now begin to believe you really are the wife of Guy Harrowby, for he said you was a trump, and the words you've just now spoken prove you to be one."

"Then, being convinced that no danger is to be feared from me, you will no longer refuse me the interview with him that I have asked for."

"Why, I don't know of any good that you're seeing him would do," answered the landlord. "The more he's visited, the more likely he is to be discovered; and I suppose you don't want to have him locked up in a prison, merely because you couldn't be satisfied without seeing him."

"I will, at all events, wait till you have conveyed my message to him," replied Jane Harrowby. "You can tell him, also, that I am ready to adopt any plan that may be suggested for his escape, either now or at some future period."

"We mustn't be long thinking about it," observed the landlord, "for the pursuit after him is a precious hot one; and I'm afraid, if we don't get him out of England pretty soon, they'll find out where he's hiding himself."

"May it not be so managed," asked Jane, "that he can be removed without further delay? Is there, in short, any reason, why he should not leave the country this very night?"

"Bless your heart, ma'am," exclaimed Doublechalk, "why, there's a thousand reasons why he shouldn't stir away from the place where he no wis, till we've made quite certain of getting him clear off."

"And where do you think of taking him to, when the proper time does arrive?" asked Jane Harrowby.

"Why, that's according as it may happen," answered the landlord. "It must be to some foreign country, though; and, as he arrived here in one of the fishing-smacks that come from Holland, I suppose it's likely enough that he'll go back in the same way."

"But will he be safe there?"

"Oh, yes, he'll be safe enough," answered Doublechalk, "because our officers have no right to take him there, even if they should happen to fall in with him. Besides, I don't suppose he'll want to stop in any one place long together; so that, by-and-by, he and you may find your way over to America, where you may live as well, and, perhaps, a great deal happier than you can here; at any rate they've no infernal game laws, that first lead men into crimes that very often send them, a few years later, to the gallows."

"I care not where we may have to go to," she replied, "so that I can see my husband once more safe and happy."

"Well," returned Doublechalk, "and if you'll have a little patience there's no saying what may turn up. There's plenty of us to get him off as soon as there's a chance of doing it without being found out, and we'll do it too, or by-and-by, when trouble comes to our turn, there'll be nobody willing to help us out of it."

At that moment the voice of Dick Fordham was heard at the bar, and the landlord jumping up from his seat hurried out of the room to consult with his colleague as to what had better be done under present circumstances. Dick, however, was of opinion that the consultation had better take place in presence of the female, and they accordingly repaired to the parlour, where a rough ceremony of introduction was performed by Doublechalk.

"I don't know whether you've ever seen the lady before, Dick," he said, "but this is the wife of our friend Guy Harrowby, and a plucky body she is too, or she wouldn't have come all the way to London for the sake of helping to get her husband out of trouble. And this is their young'un too; the very picture of his father, aint he, Dick?"

"I aint much of a judge of pictures," answered the other, "but I like the woman's kindness for her husband, and, hang me, if I don't do all I can to help her in getting the poor fellow out of his troubles. Have you taken her to see Guy Harrowby yet, Doublechalk?"

"The devil a bit would I do that."

"And why not?"

"Why not? for a very good reason. I wasn't quite sure at first that she was his wife, though she told me she was; and, even if I had been certain about the matter, I don't know that I should have taken her to him, because we never can tell who's watching us, and we might get ourselves and Guy into a mess in no time."

"My chief anxiety was to know that he is safe," exclaimed Jane, "and having satisfied myself that he is so, I can now wait patiently till it may be quite safe for us to see each other."

"If you want to send any message, our host here will take it to him," observed Dick Fordham.

"I've already got one, and he shall have it when I go to him in the morning," exclaimed Doublechalk.

"Why can't you go with it before then?"

"Because I know what a set of devils I've got in this house," replied the landlord. "There's the pot-boy and the servant girl—they both of 'em fancy something out of the way is going on, for the girl has thrown out a hint that she could say something if she liked, and the boy followed me closely this morning, and the secret of that trap-door would have been discovered to a certainty, only that I happened to catch sight of the young gentleman in good time."

"And what did you do with him?"

"What did I do? why, kicked him down stairs, to be sure, and if I'd broken his neck it would have served the young scoundrel right."

"But are you quite certain that he don't know anything about the loft?" asked Fordham.

"To be sure I am," answered the other; "I've never let him sleep in the lower part of the house for that very reason, s... ..... made in the kitchen, where he, of course, can't watch my actions."

"Am I to understand, from what has just passed," exclaimed Jane Harrowby, "that my husband is concealed in some part of these premises?"

"Why it can't be denied without telling a lie about it," returned Dick, "and I don't see that there's any occasion to keep the matter a secret from the man's own wife."

"But I wasn't quite sure at first that it was his wife," exclaimed the landlord. "She came into the house quite unexpected, and when she first began to ask questions about Guy Harrowby, I made certain it was some spy that had been sent to fish out as much of the secret as she could."

"You must have been a d—d fool for your pains, then," retorted Dick Fordham, "for you never saw a spy with such an honest-looking countenance as this woman has got. Why, I could see with half an eye, old boy, that she's one of the right sort."

"Ah!" exclaimed Doubleehalk; "but you see we aint all such cunning chaps as you or there'd never be any mistakes made. For my own part, I always like to be on the safe side, and that's the reason why I didn't at first seem to know anything about Guy Harrowby."

"But you acknowledged it afterwards," said Fordham; "and you might as well then have taken her up to the loft to see the poor devil there."

"Well, as I didn't do it there's no occasion to say anything more about it," exclaimed Doublechalk. "I didn't know who the woman was, nor what her object might be; but now, as we're pretty well satisfied upon those matters, I'll show her up, if she has any particular wish to see him."

Jane paused, uncertain how to act; for, anxious as she was to hold a brief conversation with her husband, there were, on the other hand, reasons why she wished to delay it till another time.

"You will deliver the message I gave you?" she said, addressing the landlord; "and if he should seem surprised at my going away without seeing him, you may say I met Mr. Charles Heathingdon on my way hither, and that the terror occasioned by seeing him has so shaken me that I am afraid to hazard the interview, anxious as I am that it should take place."

"And who the devil is this Mr. Charles Heathingdon that you have told me about?" asked the landlord.

"Oh, I've heard of the fellow from Guy Harrowby!" exclaimed Fordham. "The scoundrel wants to make love to this young woman; and, because she won't give him any encouragement, he has persecuted her husband, and will continue to do so, I suppose, as long as he remains in England."

"Then we should find him an awkward sort of customer if he should have taken it into his head to have watched her to this house," observed Doublechalk.

"I only wish he'd come here just at this moment," said Dick Fordham. "If he did, I'd give him such a d—d good thrashing that it should puzzle his own father ever to know him again."

"What good should you get by that?"

"Never mind what good I got by it so that I gave him what he deserves," answered Dick. "I've heard a little bit about that gentleman, and so have you too, I should think; for it's the chap that's been trying so hard to hang Guy Harrowby."

"The devil it is!" exclaimed the landlord; "then I don't think this is just the sort of place to come to. He'd be murdered among you as sure as a gun, and then there'd be more row about my house than there is at present, and that is quite needless."

"Why, I think it's very likely he'd receive some rough handling," observed Fordham; "but I don't think we should go quite so far as you seem to fancy. The scoundrel don't deserve any mercy from Guy Harrowby nor his friends; but it wouldn't do for us to risk our necks when a good drubbing might, perhaps, answer the purpose quite as well."

"Most earnestly do I hope you will have no opportunity of meeting with him," interposed Jane Harrowby.

"And why not?" asked Dick.

"Because his disposition is so vindictive," she replied, "that I am afraid it would lead to something dreadful. You have seen with what determination he has pursued my husband; and in the same way would he persecute all those that he fancied were in any way concerned in shielding him from justice."

"He might like to try it on, very likely," observed Fordham; "but I rather think he'd find us too many for him in the long-run. Even as it is we owe him something for what he's already done;

and we only want to catch him at some convenient place, and he'll be heartily sickened of meddling with other people again."

"You'd much better leave him alone," exclaimed Doublechalk. "If you serve him out it will do you no good, but it may bring you all into more trouble than you'll know how to get out of. Besides, he can't do any more harm to Guy Harrowby till he finds out where he is; and I don't think there's much chance of his doing that, if we keep matters snug and quiet to ourselves."

"That's a matter that none of us are likely to consult you about," returned Dick Fordham. "It may be all very well for you to give an opinion when you're asked for it, but it's another thing whether we may choose to make any use of it."

"Then, why do you make use of my loft to hide your friend in?" demanded the landlord.

"For a very good reason," answered Dick;—"we don't know of any other place where he'd be so safe, and, even if we did, I fancy we're quite good enough customers of yours to ask such a trifling favour as this is. Why, if you had refused us, we should have left off coming to your house, and I fancy you'd have missed our money before many weeks had passed over your head."

"I'm not finding fault with your custom, Dick," exclaimed the landlord, "but you never seem to think of the trouble the keeping this man here gives me."

"Trouble!" cried Dick Fordham;—"why, you don't mean to say he gives you much trouble, when you only go up to him once a day, just to take him something to eat and drink."

"For which I am never likely to to receive a farthing!"

"Have no fear about that," exclaimed Jane Harrowby; "for, when once we have succeeded in getting him away from England, I'll work my fingers to the very bone but what I'll repay you for all the trouble and expense you have been at for my husband."

"I thought you were going to join him abroad, as soon as he gets over there?" observed the landlord.

"It won't be as soon as he gets over, though," exclaimed Dick Fordham; "for I shall do my best to persuade her to stay where she is, till we know how Guy is likely to get on, and where he may think proper to settle. When that's all clear and straightforward, she can go over to him, and live a little more quietly than she has been able to do for some time past in England."

"If it should be his good fortune to reach some foreign country in safety, I shall be most willing to listen to the advice of my friends, as to what it may be best for myself to do. It is most likely that I should remain here for some time, and in that case I can have as much work as I can take from the ladies, who have all along been my friends. So, you see, there is every chance of your being paid, not only for any expense you may be put to, but for the trouble and risk that his presence here may have brought upon you."

"There, old greedy, will that satisfy your avarice?" exclaimed Dick Fordham; "the woman's willing enough to pay you, you see, and even if she hadn't it in her power, there's plenty of us to subscribe it among ourselves."

"Well, as that's the case, I don't care how much longer he stays here," returned the landlord; "I only want to get a living by my business, and yet you seem to think me greedy, for merely looking after my own interest."

"But I," said Jane, "feel most grateful for the assistance you have given my husband, when, but for the kindness of his friends, he must at this time have been in the hands of the law. It is now nearly time for me to go, and some time in the course of to-morrow I will come to see my husband, if nothing in the meanwhile should happen to prevent it."

"Well, don't be in such a hurry about going," said Fordham; "because, if you've no objection to it, I'd offer my services to walk with you part of the way. You may trust me, ma'am, upon my word, for I should be ashamed of myself to behave in the way that Charles Heathingdon does."

"Your offer is a very kind one," replied Jane; "and I have every confidence in the motive that has urged you to make it, but I can find my way back more easily than I came here, and as it is not yet quite dark, there is very little fear of my meeting with any interruption."

"There is quite as much fear now as when you were coming here," observed Fordham; "you didn't think of meeting with young Heathingdon, I dare say, and yet you come bounce upon him. But I suppose he'd been hereabouts, watching to see if he could catch sight of his victim, and was going home again when you met him."

"Then there can be no fear of seeing him as I go back," exclaimed Jane Harrowby.

"I'm not quite sure about that," answered Dick; "for he may take it into his head to come and have another look about the place, and if so, you might just happen to fall in with him again, and it's a hundred to one if you get off so easily as you did the last time. So you'd better take my offer, ma'am, and I'll undertake that you shall reach home quite safe."

"Indeed, I would rather go alone."

"Ah!" exclaimed Dick, "then I begin to see how it is now—you're ashamed to be seen in the streets with a chap like me; and, to speak the truth, I don't much wonder at it, for I'm pretty well known, and those that see us together wouldn't form the best opinion of you. But that wouldn't matter much either, for I suppose you're not known to many people in London, so that, whatever they may say or think, won't do any harm."

"It was not from any feeling of shame that I refused your offer," answered Jane Harrowby' "but that I see no occasion for the protection you have been kind enough to offer. I came here alone, and can return in the same way, without much fear of being interrupted in my way."

"How do you know this Mr. Heathingdon may not be laying wait for you?" he asked.

"I must take my chance whether he does so or not," she replied. "It is, I think, scarcely likely that he will risk the uncertainty of a meeting, and, even if I should see him, there are always people enough in the streets that would give their services to a female, to protect her against the insolence of a ruffian."

"Then you won't accept my offer?"

"You've heard her say she won't, and that ought to be enough," interposed Doublechalk. "The young woman is right not to trust herself under the care of a stranger, and the best thing you can do, is to let her have her own way."

"Oh, if she don't like to accept my offer, there's an end of it at once," retorted the other.

"At all events, I refuse it, with gratitude for the kindness you intended," answered Jane; "but there's no more danger of any person interfering with me now, than there was when I came; and, when the world is so censorious, it is better not to give occasion for ill-natured remarks."

During the time that Jane Harrowby was giving utterance to these words, she rose from her seat, and having wrapped her shawl round the child, she took leave of her newly-formed acquaintances, and quitted the house to return home.

"That seems to be a decent sort of a body," observed Doublechalk, as soon as she was out of hearing. "At first, I wasn't much inclined to believe that she was the wife of Guy Harrowby; but I don't think that anybody else would have taken so much pains in this matter as she has done."

"Why, of course, she's his wife," returned the other, "and a good faithful creature she seems to him too. She's got her share of trouble though, and I'm afraid she'll see a great deal more of it, before she's many weeks older."

"What! if we get Guy out of the country?"

"Getting him away won't save him from being followed up by Mr. Heathingdon," answered the other; "and, besides that, there'll always be people enough to twit her with being the wife of a man that's charged with being a murderer."

"Then she must get over to her husband as soon as possible," replied Doublechalk. "We shall have no trouble to do that, and when she's in a foreign country, nobody will know her; so, of course, there'll be no fear of anyone telling her of her misfortune. And the poor thing deserves to have her mind more at rest, for I never saw a woman so cut up about her husband's troubles as she is."

"We mustn't think of letting Harrowby go yet, though."

"The sooner he leaves us the better," returned Doublechalk, "for there's no saying whether that infernal constable mayn't pay us another visit; and, if he should happen to pay us another visit, he won't be got rid of quite so easily as he was the last time. He has a notion that he's concealed somewhere in the house, and though the loft has never yet been found out, it's no reason why it shouldn't, if they're determined not to go away without their prisoner."

"You needn't throw cold water upon it in that way," exclaimed Dick Fordham. "For my own part, I see no reason why they should find him, and I for one wouldn't mind shooting the first man that attempted to enter the loft."

"And a very pretty scrape I should get into if anything of that sort was to take place in my house," returned the landlord. "They'd take me up for harbouring a murderer, and then I should be transported, as a reward for interfering in matters that don't concern me."

Fordham was about to exclaim against the alarm that had been thus expressed, but not wishing to cause a quarrel just then, he rose hastily and took his departure.

CHAPTER XVIII.

THE RETURN.—A FRIEND IN NEED.—THE PERSECUTOR.

SOMEWHAT consoled at having received information respecting her husband, Jane Harrowby returned to her lodgings, where she found the landlady arranging the bed preparatory to her coming home. Everything, in short, was made as comfortable as circumstances would permit, in the one room occupied by the convict's wife; and she congratulated herself upon having fixed her temporary abode in a place where she might hope to meet with that kindness, which could alone mitigate the anguish it was her unfortunate lot to endure. Having laid down her sleeping child, she supped off the remains of what she had brought from home; and, during the meal, Mrs. Toddy returned to the room to say "good night!" and fish out any secrets that her new lodger might be inclined to reveal.

"You seem tired, my dear Mrs. Simmons," she said, throwing herself into a chair; "but, perhaps that aint to be wondered at, for I dare say, by the time you've been out, you've had a long walk; and dragging about with you a heavy child like that, is enough to fatigue a stronger person than yourself."

"The place I've been to is further off than I expected," replied Jane; "but, had the distance been twice as much, I should not have regretted the fatigue I have endured."

"Humph! been to see a friend, I suppose?"

"I have been to inquire about one," answered Jane; "but the persons I saw were quite strangers to me."

"Then of course they couldn't give much information about what you wanted to know?"

"I gathered quite sufficient for my purpose," replied Jane Harrowby; "and my mind is all the happier since it has been released from its load of anxiety and doubt. There is, however, a secret connected with it which, for the present, I dare not reveal; so you will not be offended, I hope, at my saying as little as possible upon that subject."

"Lor' bless you, my dear creature!" exclaimed Mrs. Toddy, "I'm not at all curious, and never want to be prying and meddling with other people's concerns. To be sure, I may have thought there's a little mystery connected with you, but, as it's no business of mine, I shan't inquire into it unless it should appear that my assistance may be of any service to you."

"A thousand thanks for this kindness to a stranger," cried Jane, in the fulness of her gratitude. "Your advice and opinion may be of the greatest service to me; and, perhaps, to-morrow, I may tell you the cause of my visit to London."

The answer of Mrs. Toddy was cut short by a loud double knock at the street door, and the old lady bustled out of the room to see who it was that had paid her a visit at so late an hour. Jane had no desire to listen, but she could plainly distinguish the voice of a man, though he spoke in a subdued tone, and it seemed to her that the sounds were familiar to her ear. This circumstance occasioned no little uneasiness in her mind, lest anyone should have taken the trouble to trace her out, and her thoughts were busily occupied in endeavouring to guess who it could be, when she heard the street door closed, and directly afterwards Mrs. Toddy again came into the room.

"Well," she exclaimed, "I've got rid of him at last; but I've had the greatest difficulty in the world to persuade him that you are not the person he supposed was lodging in my house."

"Who is he?" demanded Jane anxiously.

"That's more than I can say," answered the landlady, "for though I tried my hardest to get at his name, he seemed determined not to tell me."

"What aged person does he appear to be?"

"I should think about one or two and twenty!"

"Then I am afraid my persecutor has again discovered his devoted victim!" exclaimed Jane in accents of terror.

"I don't think you need be much afraid of it's being anyone that knows you, Mrs. Simmons," replied the landlady, "for he didn't call you by that name at all."

"What was the name he asked for me by?"

"Mrs. Jane Harrowby."

"And what reply did you make?"

"I told him there was no person of that name in my house."

"You told him wrong then," exclaimed Jane, on seeing that all further disguise would be useless. "He that I would have avoided above all other men has traced me; and even here I shall be no longer safe from his persecution."

"The gentleman seems to have taken a good deal of trouble about it," observed Mrs. Toddy, "for he told me that he had followed you a long distance, and, after seeing you enter this house, he walked up and down some time before he knocked at the door to ask if he could see Mrs. Harrowby; and when I told him there was no such person living here, he replied that it was no use telling him such a falsehood, for he had seen you enter the house not half an hour before, and he was determined not to leave the place till he had spoken to you. And then he told me that you are the wife of a returned convict, whose escape from the officers a day or two ago has made such a stir."

"He told you the truth there," sighed Jane; "though why he should have exposed me I know not."

"If it was to do you a mischief he was never more mistaken in his life," exclaimed the landlady; "for a woman can't help the faults of her husband, and she ought to be pitied instead of being scorned in the midst of her troubles."

"You will not think the worse of me, then, for what you have just been told?"

"I should think not, indeed!" answered Mrs. Toddy. "Thank goodness, I've got a heart that can feel for the misfortunes of my fellow-creatures; and I shall be likely to tell this gentleman a little bit of my mind when he comes here again to-morrow."

"Did he say he should come to-morrow?"

"Oh, yes," replied the landlady; "he's determined to have some conversation with you, and so he shall, if you've no objection; but it shall only be in my presence, now that I know what sort of a chap he is."

"How have I deserved all this kindness?" cried Jane. "We were strangers to each other till a few hours since, and yet I have received from you all the attention that could have been bestowed upon me by a mother."

"And a parent I'll be to you, as far as protection goes," returned Mrs. Toddy; "for this gentleman, as he calls himself, seems to bear you no very good will, and I'll soon let him know that you're not quite so friendless and unprotected as he may fancy. But you haven't told me yet, my dear, what it is that has made him your foe?"

"It is because I would not listen to the dishonourable proposals he was base enough to make during the absence of my husband from this country."

"The villain! and now, I dare say, he wouldn't mind what he does to be revenged on you."

"He still professes to love me," replied Jane, "and follows me from place to place, though he well knows the scorn with which his addresses have been received."

"Then, why don't you apply for the assistance of the police?"

"For one reason that must ever be paramount," she replied: "even now he is pursuing my unfortunate husband with the most relentless hatred, and I would not add to his vindictive feeling by doing as you have said."

"Oh! but I shouldn't think anything about that," exclaimed Mrs. Toddy, "for, if he should come any of his cantankerous tricks, there's always protection to be found in the law, and he'll soon be taught that his gallivanting with married women aint to be allowed."

"What is there to prevent his annoying me as he has already done?" asked Jane; "he is the son of a rich man, and I the wife of a poor one, who has forfeited all claim to protection, and who, indeed, cannot leave the place where he is concealed without bringing himself to a death of shame that I shudder to think of."

"I don't want to throw cold water upon the matter," exclaimed the landlady, "but I must say

I see but a poor chance of his hiding himself for any long time from the police. They'll be too much for him before long depend on it, so the best thing you can do will be to make up your mind for the worst that may happen."

"I cannot do it," she replied, the tears rushing to her eyes as she thought of the danger that was thus hinted at. "I have encouraged hope when there was less chance of his escape than there is at present, and at this moment I believe that, with the assistance of his friends, he may be got out of England, and then all further danger will be at an end."

"How is he to be got away when there's so many people looking after him?" asked Mrs. Toddy.

"His friends are zealous in his behalf," replied Jane, "and with caution they may be able to carry their plans into effect. He can remain where he is too, as long as he pleases, and, from what I understand, the place is not very likely to be easily discovered."

"Then he'll be a foolish fellow to leave it."

"There is no way of helping that," answered Jane, "for the person in whose house he is concealed is afraid of its being known that he has given shelter to a fugitive from justice."

"Aye, and well he may be," exclaimed the landlady, "for they'd be sure to transport him if they found him out doing a thing like that."

"There is no chance of there ever doing so."

"So we may fancy," replied Mrs. Toddy, "but officers of justice are used to business of this sort, and they go about inquiring of one or another till they get hold of a clue, and then it's not long before they nose out the poor devil they are looking after."

"Most earnestly do I pray that in this instance they may be disappointed," exclaimed Jane.

"Do you think your husband repents the past, and would do better in future?"

"I am sure of it."

"Then it would be a pity if the chance wasn't given to him," exclaimed Mrs. Toddy; "and yet, when I come to think of it, they say your husband has been guilty of a murder, and if that should be the case, he deserves to die on the gallows."

"Like yourself, I have heard the report," answered Jane, "but from his own lips I know nothing of it."

"And if you had, it's not very likely that you would tell it to anybody, for fear they should speak of it again."

"He has too many enemies already without my doing anything against him," answered Jane. "It is my duty to do all I can to save my husband, and never will I give utterance to one word that might serve to endanger a life that is now more precious to me than ever."

"Upon my word, ma'am, you're a pattern of a wife," exclaimed the landlady; "and, in spite of what they say he has done, I do hope he may contrive to get clear away from his enemies. Not that I care much about himself, because I don't think he can be any very great shakes, but you seem still to love him as much as ever, and I fancy it would break your heart if they were to hang him after all the trouble that has been taken."

"It would indeed," sighed Jane.

"Yet you ought to prepare yourself for it, in case the worst should happen," answered Mrs. Toddy.

"What! resign myself to the thought of my husband's life being sacrificed to the offended laws of his country?"

"If there's no help for it, all the fretting in the world will do no good," replied the landlady; besides, there's your poor child ought to be thought of, for, if father and mother were both dead, he would, I suppose, have nothing better than the workhouse to look to?"

"That would indeed be his fate," cried Jane, "and many a moment of bitter anguish does the thought cause me. For his sake, therefore, I will endeavour to support my spirits, and the more so, as I am not without hope that my husband will find means to get out of the country before the place of his concealment is discovered."

"And you, I suppose, would go over with him?"

"I should follow as soon afterwards as might be convenient," replied Jane Harrowby. "Probably in a few weeks we should meet again, to find that happiness abroad that has been denied me in my own country."

"Well!" exclaimed Mrs. Toddy, "for my own part I can't think how you can feel any regard for a man that has been guilty of killing a fellow-creature."

"I never have nor can believe that he is guilty of a crime so fearful as that," replied the faithful wife. "He may have been unfortunate enough to have deprived a human being of existence, but, if so, it must have been by accident, since it never was his nature to be either cruel or vindictive."

"I hope what I said hasn't offended you," exclaimed Mrs. Toddy, "but I'm rather apt to speak my mind, and I was thinking that, as the match don't seem to have been a very happy one, it would be a good opportunity of getting rid of an indifferent husband."

"He has never been otherwise than kind to me."

"But he has brought disgrace and unhappiness on you."

"That he has been guilty of serious offences cannot be denied," answered Jane Harrowby, "but want in the first instance led him to commit an offence against the game-laws, and being convicted for killing a single hare, he was punished with as much severity as if he had done a deed

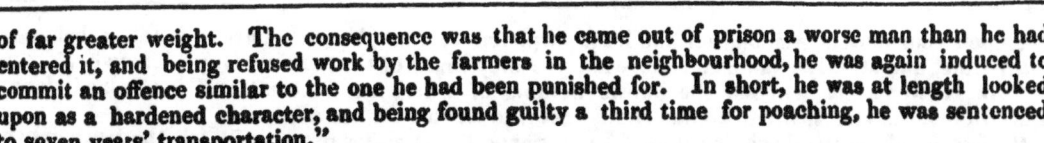

of far greater weight. The consequence was that he came out of prison a worse man than he had entered it, and being refused work by the farmers in the neighbourhood, he was again induced to commit an offence similar to the one he had been punished for. In short, he was at length looked upon as a hardened character, and being found guilty a third time for poaching, he was sentenced to seven years' transportation."

"I see," observed Mrs. Toddy; "and, not fancying the place they had sent him to, he took the first opportunity that presented itself to make his escape and return to England?"

"He did," answered Jane Harrowby; "and for that act he has rendered himself liable to transportation for life."

"He's liable to something more than that, I'm thinking," exclaimed the landlady; "for if they should find him, and the murder be proved, he'd be sentenced to death without the least hope of a reprieve."

"I am myself well convinced that he is innocent of that horrible charge," exclaimed Jane.

"Then how did the report begin?"

"No explanation am I able to give," she replied; "yet in my own mind I feel satisfied he is not guilty of wilfully shedding the blood of a fellow-creature. It has been hinted to me that the person he is accused of killing was the guard placed in charge over him; and if so, a struggle may have occurred when he attempted to escape, and the poor fellow died through an accidental blow."

"It wouldn't matter much how it happened if it can be proved that your husband caused the death of the man," observed Mrs. Toddy.

"At least the crime would not be so great."

"That would not make any difference about the punishment," returned the other. "They'd pronounce sentence of death upon him, and all the interest you might try to make would never save him from the gallows. However, I don't want to make you any more unhappy than you are, so I'll leave you now, and in the morning I'll talk further with you upon this subject."

Mrs. Toddy, who really felt greatly concerned for her lodger, then quitted the room, and Jane Harrowby, fatigued by the exertion she had gone through, retired to bed, in the hope that rest would enable her to accomplish the task she had set herself for the following day. But it was some hours before she could close her eyes in sleep, for many uneasy thoughts flitted through her mind, and it seemed to her that the misfortunes with which she had been afflicted were yet very far from their termination. At length, however, she fell into an uneasy slumber, from which she woke at an early hour, and hearing that Mrs. Toddy was already up, she rose and dressed herself, intending to go out as soon as possible, in order that she might be absent when Charles Heathingdon paid his threatened visit. But in this she was doomed to be thwarted, for just as she had concluded breakfast a double knock was heard at the door, and after a short altercation with the landlady, who would have resisted his coming further than the threshold, the libertine entered the room. His step was firm and resolute, as if he had already made up his mind as to the course he should adopt, and taking a seat he first addressed himself to Mrs. Toddy, and desired her to leave the room, as he wished the interview to be a private one.

"My landlady will remain where she is," exclaimed Jane; "there can be no secrets that she may not hear, for I have told her all that has transpired, even to the persecution I have endured from you."

"Well, she can stay here if she likes," returned Charles, "but it must be on condition that she does not interfere with anything I may say or do."

"Indeed, young gentleman, but that will depend entirely on circumstances," replied Mrs. Toddy; "I've heard that you haven't very honourable feelings towards this poor creature, and I should wish you to understand, that while she remains under my roof she will be protected just the same as if she was my own daughter."

"Your protection is not required," exclaimed Charles Heathingdon, "and I will endure no meddling interference, when my business here is to forward the ends of justice. By-the-by, you are already convicted of a falsehood, for you last night told me there was no such a person in your house as Jane Harrowby."

"And I believed I was telling the truth," replied the landlady, "for she took my lodging under the name of Simmons, and it was not till after you had gone away that she told me what her real name is."

"Has it not struck you," he asked, "that there must be guilt where persons are obliged to have recourse to fictitious names?"

"In this instance I can't think anything of the kind," she replied, "for the poor woman has seen trouble enough, and she has given me good reason for concealing her own name just at present. I needn't tell you she's the wife of a convicted criminal, so that of course the name she bears is better concealed."

"Have you seen anything of her husband?" demanded Charles Heathingdon, looking intently in her face, as if he would read her inmost soul.

"Seen him!" exclaimed the landlady; "do you think it likely that I'd assist to conceal a criminal when I well know the scrape it would be sure to lead me into?"

"Women are generally plotters," he replied; "and I have seen no reason yet why I should not believe you to be as much so as the majority of your sex. At all events, I shall keep a sharp eye upon your movements, and on the least suspicion of foul play, I'll have you taken before a magistrate, and strictly examined as to what you may know of the fugitive, Guy Harrowby."

"As Heaven's my witness, she knows nothing of where my husband is;" exclaimed Jane, alarmed lest the kind-hearted woman should get into trouble on her account.

"Of course," returned the libertine, "I don't expect that either of you will tell the truth when it might turn so much against yourselves. However, I would warn you of the danger you may be running into, for if I have good reason for believing that you know where the fugitive is concealed, I'll take such steps as may appear most likely to extort the secret from you."

"Even if I knew the place of his retreat," said Jane, "is it likely that I would, under any circumstances, betray him to one so vindictive and blood thirsty as yourself?"

"Not willingly, I dare say," he replied, "but there are ways to make even the most obstinate yield. There may, however, be no occasion to resort to extreme measures, for we have vigilant officers engaged in this affair, and, from what I have learnt from them, there is little doubt that Guy Harrowby will be in their hands before many hours have passed over his head."

"God forbid!" exclaimed Jane, shuddering as these words of evil omen met her ear.

"Oh, don't believe a word he says about it," interposed the landlady. "He wants to frighten you, that's all; but take my advice, and don't listen to what he says."

"She may find my words come true sooner than she expects," returned Charles Heathingdon. "The police have received fresh information in the course of last night, and I am in hopes the murderer has been taken and locked up in some place of security."

"And pray," exclaimed Mrs. Toddy, "what reason can you have for taking so much interest in this affair."

"There can be no occasion for me to answer that question," he replied; "because no doubt Mrs. Harrowby has made you acquainted with all the points of this matter."

"She has acquainted me with some few particulars certainly," answered the landlady; "and, if the truth must be told, I don't think they reflect much credit upon yourself. You chose to fall in love with a married woman, and when she treats your addresses with the contempt they deserve, you spit all your vengeance upon the poor creature, because she had virtue enough to remain faithful to her husband."

"Am I to be lectured like a school-boy?" demanded Charles, wrathfully; "I came here to see your lodger, and not to be railed at by an old woman."

"But the old woman knows she's on the right side, and you shan't stop what she's got to say," answered Mrs. Toddy: "you may look as black as you please at hearing the truth, for I'll have my say out, if you were afterwards to kill me for it."

"You will bitterly repent this, depend on it," exclaimed Charles Heathingdon, vehemently.

"Perhaps you may be made to repent before I am," replied Mrs. Toddy. "You think to frighten me, I suppose, but all you can say won't hinder me from taking care that you don't harm this young woman."

"I came here," he exclaimed, "to see Jane Harrowby, and not to quarrel with her landlady. I would know if she is willing to say where her husband may be found."

"Just now you said the secret was already found out," said Jane; "and if any reliance is to be placed on that assertion you surely cannot require the information you ask from me?"

"There is no certainty in what I have been told," he replied. "A large reward is offered for his apprehension, and those that are desirous of earning it are naturally very sanguine whenever they fancy any clue has been found; they may have given too easy credit to unfounded assertions, and to make the capture of Guy Harrowby as certain as possible, I have come here to obtain from you the necessary information."

"Then I rather think you'll go back no wiser than you came," interposed Mrs. Toddy, "for though I haven't known my lodger many hours, I've seen quite enough of her to tell you that neither threats nor persuasions will ever make her betray the man that you want to find."

"She'll do as she pleases about it, I suppose," retorted Charles; "but if she persists in her obstinacy, it will be of more serious consequence to herself than she imagines."

"How can it do her any harm?"

"By forcing me to do that which I would avoid," he replied. "I have sufficient reason to believe that she knows where her husband is lurking, and, in that case, she will be liable to a very severe punishment for aiding and assisting a criminal to escape from justice."

"Indeed!" exclaimed Mrs. Toddy; "and so you would make me believe that there's a law to punish a wife for being so fond of her husband that she will not be the first to turn against him?"

"What I have told you is nothing more than the truth," answered Charles Heathingdon. "So far as I have said she is in my power, and she will, therefore, do well to consider her danger before she decides upon the course she is to adopt."

"There is nothing for me to consider," exclaimed Jane; "I know the duty I owe to my husband, and will not be frightened out of it, whatever persecution you may think proper to commence against me; besides, you have no reason for saying that I know where he has found concealment."

"At any rate, there is good reason for believing it," returned the libertine. "Your coming to London proves as much; and I am determined to find out the fugitive, let it cost what trouble or expense it may."

"And why are you taking so much pains in a matter that, it seems to me, you have nothing to do with?" asked the landlady.

"If this female has made you her confidante, there can be no need for you to ask me that question," answered Charles. "I have offered her my friendship, and have received nothing but scorn and contempt in return for it. She might have made a friend, who would have risked everything in her behalf, but having converted me into an enemy she must take the consequences, and blame herself for them.

"A very pretty notion of yours, truly!" exclaimed Mrs. Toddy: and so, because she has acted like a good and virtuous wife, you are to crush her under your foot. But you'll find me a match for you in this business, I can tell you, Mr. What's-your-name; so don't think you're going to harm this young woman while she's got a friend that will stick up for her."

"Mind your own business, woman, or you will get yourself into trouble," returned Charles, angrily. "My errand here was to further the ends of justice, and if you throw any impediment in my way it will be at your own peril."

"Indeed! And pray what will you do?"

"That which you will remember as long as you live," he replied. "However, I have no wish to involve myself in a quarrel just now, so leave the room, that I may speak without further interruption to Jane Harrowby."

"Leave the room? oh!" exclaimed Mrs. Toddy, indignantly, "things have come to a very fine pass, truly, that I may not go into what part of my own house I like! I shall stay where I am, sir, as long as I please, and if you threaten my lodger any more I'll send for a policeman, and have you locked up for disturbing the peace of my house."

"The experiment would be too dangerous a one to put into practice," sneered the other. "Mrs. Harrowby knows from former experience that I'm a man of my word, and if once I am driven to it, she will find in me an enemy that will never be satisfied till he has crushed her into the very earth."

"Take care that I, or some one else, don't trample you into the earth in return for it," exclaimed the landlady. "You think, because there's only two women to deal with, that you can do as you please, but I can answer for my own spirit, and if you rouse me, Mr. Thingamy, you'll have to own afterwards that this was the most unlucky day of your life."

"Woman," he muttered, "I'll have nothing to say to you."

"I entreat you not to irritate him further," interposed Jane Harrowby. "His malice is already excited against me, and I dread the fury that I—weak and helpless as I am—have not the means of resisting."

"Pshaw! are you afraid of him, then?"

"Not for myself," she replied; "but if I suffer from his persecution, I suffer not alone. My child must either go with me to a prison, or be taken from me to become an inmate of the parish workhouse. You have heard him threaten to charge me with having aided to conceal my husband from the officers of justice, and too well do I know his nature to doubt for a moment that he will perform what he has said."

"Really, ma'am, you pay more heed to his threats than they deserve," exclaimed Mrs. Toddy. "It may be all very well for him to bounce that he'll do this, that, and the other, but I happen to know that he can't send you to a prison; and, to his teeth, I tell him that he has only uttered the threat because he fancies you are to be frightened into saying something that may lead to the discovery of your husband."

"I have threatened nothing more than I can and will do," answered Charles Heathingdon. "I have no enmity against Mrs. Harrowby; for, on the contrary, I have all along offered her my services and assistance; these, however, she has rejected, and you, instead of giving her prudent and motherly advice, encourage her in pursuing a course that can only end in her own misery and wretchedness."

"She has refused to have anything to do with your services or assistance either," exclaimed the landlady; "and that being the case, you had no right to follow her up in the way you have done."

"It matters but little whether I had a right to act so or not," returned Charles. "The purpose I have in view will fully justify me in the eyes of all persons who would see criminals brought to the just punishment of their crimes."

"And is that the reason you give for forcing your company on this poor woman, when you know she can't bear the sight of you?"

"Idle prejudices like hers are not to deter me from my purpose," he replied.

Jane Harrowby now for the first time ventured to look towards him, and, in a reproachful tone, said—

"Can it be called an idle prejudice when I have to complain of conduct such as yours? You have taken advantage of the husband's absence to make dishonourable proposals to his wife; and, because she had virtue enough to treat your conduct with the scorn it merited, you have never ceased to persecute and annoy her. Nay, even her husband becomes the object of your deadliest hatred, and you have resolved to follow up your revengeful purpose till he has been sent to end his wretched life upon a public scaffold."

"That is indeed my determination," he replied, "and nothing but an alteration in your own conduct can ever induce me to abandon it. You, Jane Harrowby, have it in your power to save him from the gallows, and yet you every day become more and more insulting to me."

"Did ever anybody hear villany so coolly uttered?" exclaimed Mrs. Toddy. "When this young woman first told me of your conduct, I could hardly believe but what she must have been mistaken; but you have now repeated it in my presence, and all I can say is, that if I was in her place, I'd go before a magistrate, and ask if there was no protection for a woman against the villanous arts of a libertine."

"And she would be told that there is not," he replied; "besides, her story would not be believed, when it was known that she who made the complaint was the wife of the man I am taking so much pains to apprehend. It would be thought, indeed, that the charge was invented for no other purpose than to bring my name into contempt."

"Not if I went with her to confirm her statement."

"Why, that would make it all the better for me," exclaimed Charles Heathingdon; "for I should then turn round and bring a charge against both of you for conspiring together to do an injury to my character."

"Ah!" returned the landlady; "I see plainly enough that you are capable of doing any dirty act, if it's to suit your own purpose; but in me you've got a troublesome customer to deal with, I can tell you, so mind what you're about, or you may get the worst of it, for all your cunning ways."

"My business here is with you," he exclaimed, addressing himself to Jane Harrowby; "and not with this woman, who has so impertinently thrust herself forward in an affair that she has nothing at all to do with. At present I shall leave you to reflect on what I have said, and this evening or to-morrow I will come again, to learn if you are willing to disclose the place where your husband is concealed; and remember, your obstinate refusal to do so will only involve yourself in trouble without serving the fugitive, who must of necessity be taken, before many days have passed over his head." With this he rose from his chair, and having cast a withering look of hatred towards Mrs. Toddy, walked out of the room and immediately quitted the house.

"That's a pretty sort of a fellow, truly," cried the landlady, as the door was violently slammed. "He thinks to do just as he pleases; and when people won't let him have his own way, he flies in a towering rage, and threatens to do all sorts of vile things. But as I told him just now, he's got one to deal with that don't care a brass button for him, and as for what he threatens to do against you, he had better not try it on, I can tell him, for, as long as you remain here, I'll take care to prevent his plots from doing you any harm."

"Then have I indeed found a friend, when least I expected to do so," cried Jane, in accents of gratitude. "Heaven never deserts the helpless, and I now begin to believe that the evil designs of him who has just left us will not be permitted to be carried into effect."

"Of course they won't, if we mind what we're about," said Mrs. Toddy; "but you must not let him see that you are frightened of him, though, for if once he gets that notion into his head he'll never leave off annoying you."

"How can I help betraying my terror, when I find myself in the presence of such a ruthless enemy?" asked Jane. "He knows well enough that I fear him, or he would not have dared to act towards me in the way he has."

"And he had better not do it again, now that I have taken up your cause in earnest," exclaimed the landlady. "The worthless scoundrel has heard what sort of an opinion I have of him; and he shall find me as good as my word, if he comes here to frighten and annoy you."

"Which he has threatened to do, either to-night or to-morrow."

"Ah! so he says," answered Mrs. Toddy; "but he'll have time to consider the matter over in his own mind; and, when he has done that, I'll be bound he won't be quite so hasty as he was just now."

"Nothing," sighed Jane Harrowby, "will ever turn him from the object he has in view: my husband is the object of his hatred; and never will he give up his pursuit till he has either accomplished his purpose, or discovered that Guy Harrowby has succeeded in making his escape out of England."

"And where are you going to now?" asked Mrs. Toddy, on seeing that Jane was preparing to leave the house.

"To the same place where I heard of my husband yesterday," she replied.

"How very thoughtless of you, to be sure!" exclaimed the landlady, with surprise. "You are almost certain to be met again by the person that has just gone away; and if he should happen to follow you—as he did here, last night—he'll find out the secret, and then the game will be all up with your husband."

"What would you have me to do, then?"

"Keep in-doors for the present," replied Mrs. Toddy, "and wait till you can go to the place you speak of without risk of doing any mischief."

Jane Harrowby felt that it would be no easy task to restrain her impatience; but she knew perfectly well that Charles Heathingdon was likely to lie in wait for her; and that, if he followed her to the hiding-place in Wapping, the capture of Guy Harrowby would succeed immediately afterwards. She therefore yielded to the prudent advice of her kind-hearted landlady.

CHAPTER XIX.

A WAVERER.—THE SURPRISE.—A CHASE ON THE RIVER.

EVERY hour that passed away served to increase the alarm of Doublechalk, lest a discovery should take place, that he had afforded concealment to a criminal, who had been rescued from the officers of justice. The penalty for such an offence was too serious to be thought of slightingly, and after Jane Harrowby had left him, he began to reflect whether it would not be better to give up the fugitive at once, than run a risk that might involve him in so fearful a

dilemma. This course seemed to him the best, and he had almost made up his mind to it, when the thought crossed his mind that if he did so, he should bring upon himself the wrath of Dick Fordham and his comrades; and if once that was excited, his situation would be fully as bad as if he was found out screening a criminal from justice. Sorely puzzled was Doublechalk what to do, for that morning several suspicious looking persons had presented themselves at his bar, some of whom had mentioned the name of Guy Harrowby, and inquired if anything had yet been heard of him. These, he had no doubt, were people who had been sent there to worm out all they could, and he expected that the next thing would be to see a number of the police enter, and insist upon searching over every part of the house. All these notions, unfounded as they might be, gave a great deal of uneasiness to poor Doublechalk, who was still pondering over the subject, when Mike Rowley entered, and beckoned for him to follow into the little parlour.

"Now, old fellow," he exclaimed;—"how gets on the the chap that you've got up in the snuggery above? He's still safe and sound, I suppose? No unwelcome visitor—eh, Tom?"

"He's all right so far," replied the landlord;—"but I've a notion he won't be so much longer, for there's been a lot of queer looking people here this morning, and I fancy they only came to see how the land lays."

"Did they ask anything about Guy Harrowby?"

"Some of 'em did, but you may suppose I didn't appear to know anything about him"

"I'll be bound the danger isn't half so great as you fancy it is," exclaimed Rowley. "'Its not at all surprising that people should speak of a man that everybody is talking about; and yet, you must needs fancy that they came here as spies, to discover whether he's in your house."

"It's enough to make a man frightened when he knows the awkward risk he's running," returned Doublechalk. "You and your comrades can make yourselves easy, because you're in no danger; with me it's quite different; and hang me if I don't repent ever having consented that he should be concealed in my house."

"Well, but it's too late to think about that now, old fellow," exclaimed Mike Rowley; "he is here, you know, and what's more, he must remain till we can contrive to get him away without fear of his being seen by the police."

"That may never be," said Doublechalk, "and as I don't choose to get myself into a scrape for the sake of serving other people, I tell you, once for all, that you must take your friend away to-night to some other place."

"To-night!" exclaimed Rowley, "and suppose we should happen to find out that people are watching round your house?"

"You must take your chance about that."

"Then you've turned against us all of a sudden, and would rather give Guy Harrowby up to justice than hide him from his enemies a few days longer?"

"What's a man in my situation to do?" asked Doublechalk; "I've been willing enough to lend a helping hand up to the present time; but I now begin to see that I shall get into a precious dilemma about this business, and I should be a fool indeed, to ruin myself for the sake of serving a man that I hardly know anything about."

"Why, its not only him that you're serving," replied Rowley, "but me and all the rest of us; for we don't like to see an old pal sent to the gallows so long as there's a chance of saving him from it. However, I know you can't be serious, because it was no longer ago than yesterday that you said he should stay here as long as we liked."

"May be I did say so," answered Doublechalk, "but a man may alter his mind when he sees good reason for it; and that's just my case at this present moment."

"And what do you think Dick Fordham will say when he hears what you mean to do?" asked the other.

"I neither know nor care what he may say about it," replied Doublechalk, "it's the duty of every man to take care of himself before he thinks of other people, and though I should have been afraid to let Guy Harrowby stay here a little longer, I can't do so when I know the danger it will run me into."

"Then why didn't you tell his wife what you was going to do, when she was here, yesterday?"

"Because I hadn't thought so much of the matter then, as I have since," answered the landlord. "As I've already told you, there's been some queer-looking customers in here this morning, and I've a notion there'll be a visit from the police before the day's over."

"It's only fear that makes you think so," retorted Mike Rowley; "the truth is, old chap, you're turning coward, and would desert a friend when he's most in need of your assistance"

"Who'd help me if I was unfortunate enough to get into trouble?" demanded Doublechalk. "It may be all very well for people to talk about friendship and all that sort of thing, but we must look to ourselves a little bit, Mike Rowley, in spite of what the world may choose to say about it."

"How d——d provoking it is that Dick Fordham aint present to hear you talking in this way," exclaimed the other, "he's got the gift of the gab better than I have; and it wouldn't be long before he'd bring you to a different way of thinking."

"He, nor a dozen like him, wouldn't be able to do it."

"Then he'd be revenged upon you somehow or another for turning tail on an old friend," exclaimed Rowley, "so I'd have you alter your mind once more, if you'd save yourself from the vengeance of your comrades."

"He'll be here presently, I dare say, returned Doublechalk, "and the first thing I do will be to tell him, that he must take Guy Harrowby away from this house to-night."

"But I tell you it can't be done if we have reason to believe your place is being watched. You wouldn't turn the man out, I suppose, if it was sure to lead to his falling into the hands of his enemies?"

"I don't think it's likely I should be quite so hard upon him as all that," exclaimed Doublechalk.

"Well, then, I'm pretty sure the house will be watched."

"What makes you think so?"

"Because it's been the case for the last two or three days," answered Mike Rowley; "some of the police are always lurking about the place, for I know some of the chaps in spite of their being in plain clothes."

"Then, they intend mischief."

"Perhaps so," replied Rowley, "but they'll get tired of this sort of work if we can manage to keep Guy Harrowby out of their sight a few days longer."

Doublechalk was considering within himself what sort of an answer he should give to this, when Sam Snatch, panting, and out of breath, ran into the room.

"They're coming!" he exclaimed; "they'll be here in a few minutes, so prepare yourselves with answers to any questions they may put to you."

"Who's coming? Who'll be here directly?" asked Mike.

"The police."

"The police!" exclaimed the landlord, with alarm, "how know you they are coming here?"

"In this way," replied Sam: "as I was coming along just now, I saw about half-a-dozen of 'em standing talking at the corner of a street some little distance from here, so I pretended to be looking into a shop-window, and then I heard 'em talking about Guy Harrowby, and that they had received certain information of his being concealed in this house—and here they are, too; so now look out for squalls, for there'll be a row in the place presently."

"Then, to prevent having awkward questions to answer, I'll go up and hide myself with Guy Harrowby."

Thus spoke the landlord, and the words were hardly out of his mouth, before he was scampering up the stairs. As he disappeared from one door six policemen entered the room, and having glanced round, one of them inquired where the landlord was?"

"I don't know anything about him," replied Mike Rowley, "but I suppose he's gone out, for we haven't seen him to-day."

"Do you happen to know," asked the sergeant, "if a man named Guy Harrowby has been seen anywhere hereabouts within the last few days?"

"I know the chap you mean," returned Mike Rowley, "but it's not very likely he'd show himself, when he must know well enough that your people are looking after him, and if he should be found, there's nothing but the gibbet for him to expect."

"And found he will be before long," said the sergeant, "so, if you happen to know where he's to be met with, you may as well earn the reward that's been offered for him, as any other person."

"He has not been fool enough to let me know where he is," returned Rowley, "and even if he had, I should not have been rogue enough to tell you or anybody else where he is."

"Then you'd assist a murderer to escape, instead of doing what you can to bring him to punishment?"

"I haven't said that, nor anything like it, though you choose to give me the credit of it."

"The truth of it is," exclaimed the policeman, "we have orders to lose no opportunities of finding the man we are in search of. He has been rescued from custody by some of his comrades, and if you can tell me who they are, I can take it upon myself to promise that you shall be well rewarded for your pains."

"Do you take me for a common informer?"

"No; but you might as well make money when it is to be done so easily."

"Well, then, to speak my mind plainly at once," answered Mike Rowley, "I'll see you—and all the lot of you—d——d before I'd sell people for the sake of a paltry reward. The man never harmed me, and I won't injure him for anything that might be offered."

"If I was only sure that you know anything about the man we are in search of, I'd soon find a way to make you alter your tone," exclaimed the sergeant. "I have a pretty good notion that I've seen you in bad company before now, and if I happen presently to recollect when or where it was, I shall not part from you quite so easily as you may have expected. So just remember what I've said; and if it's in your power to give us any information, do so at once, and it will save you a deal of useless trouble."

"How can he give any information if he don't happen to know where the chap is to be found?" demanded Sam Snatch.

"Nobody asked you for an opinion about the matter," exclaimed the sergeant, "and now I come to look at you, young fellow, I rather think this aint the first time that we have had the pleasure of being in each other's company?"

"Ah!" returned Sam, "what an astonishing memory you have got, to be sure. Why, it's five years ago since that little affair that you have been reminding me of."

"Yes, it's five years, sure enough," answered the policeman, "and the most remarkable part of the affair is that you should have escaped hanging so long."

"There is nothing very remarkable about that I should think," exclaimed Sam, "because I've a natural aversion to hanging, and of course Iv'e taken uncommon care never to do anything that might bring me to it."

"Well, do you happen to know where we may light upon this Guy Harrowby, the returned convict?"

"Not I."

"So you would make us believe, but I've a notion you could tell us if you liked."

"Upon my honour, Mr. Sergeant, I haven't seen anything of him for the last three or four days."

"Where was he then?"

"I met him in the street, but where it was I can't at present recollect. However, if you want to——"

"The less you say, Sam, the better it will be," interrupted Mike Rowley. "These chaps are listening with all their ears to everything you say, and it's likely enough that you may presently say something that will put 'em upon the right scent. Now, I know well enough that you don't want to do the poor fellow an injury, so hold your tongue, and leave these men to find the person they are looking for as well as they can."

"I'll tell you what it is, young fellow," exclaimed the serjeant; "you'll presently get yourself into an infernal queer mess if you don't take care what you are about. The man we're looking after is a murderer, as well as an escaped convict, and all persons that assist in concealing him, will be punished as far as the law will allow."

"What the devil's all this row about?" exclaimed Dick Fordham, who at this period entered the room. "Six police in this house all at once! then there must be something fresh up that I haven't heard of yet."

"We're looking after a man that I dare say you know something about," returned the policeman.

"Can you tell me his name?"

"Oh, yes! his name's Guy Harrowby."

"Why, to be sure I know him," exclaimed Dick, "he's a particular friend of mine; that said Guy Harrowby."

"Indeed!" said the serjeant; "then perhaps you'll have the kindness to tell me where we may find him?"

"No I won't."

"Then we must find means to make you,"

"You can't do that," exclaimed Dick, laughing, "for the truth is, I don't know myself where he is just at this moment."

"Where has he been lately?"

"Oh, to a dozen places at least!" replied Dick Fordham; "he don't stop long at any one of 'em for fear some good natured friend should take it into his head to go and inform against him."

"But you could give us some sort of an idea where he is to be found, if you thought proper."

"Humph! and supposing I don't think proper?"

"Why, then, upon my having proof of that fact, it would be my duty to take you into immediate custody."

"Upon what charge?"

"For assisting to conceal a man that has been guilty of crime," answered the policeman.

"Blockhead! haven't you just been told that I know nothing at all about the man you're looking after?"

"I heard you say so," replied the policeman, "but I don't believe you any the more for that. You are all three suspicious characters, and I've a great mind to hear what you'll have to say for yourselves before a magistrate."

"Say for ourselves," exclaimed Mike Rowley; "why we should tell his worship that it's a very hard thing that respectable people like us can't meet in a public-house without the police suspecting us to be thieves."

"The less you say about that the better," returned the serjeant, "for there's enough of us here that know all three of you, and if many inquiries were made you'd very likely be sent to prison as reputed bad characters."

"Ah!" exclaimed Sam Snatch, "you wouldn't have said that, only we wouldn't take the blood-money when you offered it us."

"All I can say is that you are three fools for your pains for refusing a good offer," said the serjeant; "some one else will soon be found that's not quite so particular, and then we shall nab this Mr. Guy Harrowby without being under any obligation to you or your friends."

"I hope you mayn't be able to find him," exclaimed Dick Fordham: "and I tell you plainly, if it was in my power to lend him a helping-hand towards getting clear away, I'd do it in spite of any punishment they'd give me for it afterwards."

"What reason have you for pitying such a villain as he is?" demanded the policeman.

"Merely because I don't believe he's so black as people try to make him out," replied Dick Fordham; "besides, if he has done wrong, it was because he was forced into it by the hard laws that people have made against poaching. They sent him to prison for killing a hare, and from that moment he was never what he'd been before."

"I've nothing at all to do with that," exclaimed the serjeant.

"The man has committed the crime of murder since then, and it's for that, and returning from transportation that we are now looking after him. Surely you don't wish to shield from punishment a man that has wilfully taken away the life of a fellow-creature?"

"I don't know, except from what people say, that he has been guilty of anything of the sort," returned Dick Fordham; "there's been many an innocent man tried before now, and I dare say it can be proved that the guard was killed by a fall, and not by any blow that was struck by Guy Harrowby."

"It's no use your trying to defend him," exclaimed the policeman, "because almost everybody knows that death was caused by a knife, and that the blow was struck by the person we are now looking after."

"So say his enemies," observed Mike Rowley, "but his friends think quite differently, so its no use for you to be trying any longer to make us betray an old comrade."

"We may by-and-bye be obliged to make you all open your mouths upon this subject," exclaimed the serjeant, 'at present I shall leave three men down here to mind that you don't leave the place, and the other two will go with me to assist in searching every part of the house from the cellar up to the very roof itself."

"Roof!" cried Dick Fordham with alarm; "why what the devil do you expect to find there?"

"A loft."

"Nonsense," exclaimed the other, "I've known this house a good many years, but I never yet heard of there being such a thing as a loft."

"Indeed!" retorted the serjeant; "but we happen to have received information that there is a loft, and it was in consequence of that intelligence that we were sent down here to learn if there was any truth in it."

"Then you may take my word for it," said Dick, "that there's nothing above the garret, but the bare roof."

"We shall try whether there is, at any rate," answered the policeman. "It's our business to find that out, and we can't return to the station-house, and tell the inspector that we have not searched the house, in consequence of believing your assertion that there is no loft belonging to this house in which the fugitive could hide himself; we must search the place ourselves, and something strikes me very forcibly that we shall not only find a loft in the place described to us, but that we shall also meet with the man that has given us so much trouble to run after him."

"If you do, it's more than I expect myself," returned Fordham, "the person you want to find knows of course the danger he'd be in if he happened to be caught, so he wouldn't be fool enough to stop in any one place long enough to give any one a chance of informing against him."

"So you may tell me," exclaimed the serjeant, "but it won't put me off from searching this house for Guy Harrowby. So here goes, and when I come down again it will be to tell you that we have secured our prisoner."

And with this boast the serjeant and two of his men went on their exploring expedition, whilst the other three policemen returned below to prevent the departure of Dick Fordham and his companions, till it was known whether they were guilty of conniving at the concealment of a man charged with a serious felony."

We must now follow Doublechalk, who some little time previously had mounted the stairs, and hearing the voices of the policemen as they entered the room he had just left, he lost no time in removing the false ceiling in the cupboard, and scrambling up, closed the opening, and then looked round for Guy Harrowby, who he found sleeping on some of the lumber that had been collected together. Doublechalk lost no time in waking him from the uneasy dreams with which his mind was perplexed and troubled.

"Guy Harrowby," he said, shaking him by the shoulder; "wake up I tell you, for the police are down below, and if they should happen to find their way here, we shall have enough to do to fight our way out of the danger."

"Why should I try to escape from them?" asked Harrowby rousing himself. "Its only avoiding my doom for a few days, and prolonging miseries that grow more and more wearisome. Lead them here at once, and I will surrender myself a prisoner into their hands."

"Certainly that's a very pretty notion of yours," exclaimed the landlord, staring at him with surprise. "So you wouldn't mind giving yourself up to justice, though by acting in such a mad-headed manner you would let the police know that I've been concealing you in my house, instead of giving the officers information where you were to be found."

"I forgot all about that," answered Guy, "and rather than bring you into danger I'll suffer still longer the torments of anxiety, that seem to me almost insupportable."

"Aye," exclaimed Doublechalk, "and you would be still more willing to remain out of danger when you hear who came to make inquiries about you last night."

"Inquiries about me!—then it must be some of those that would drag me from my hiding place Perhaps, your visitor was no other than Charles Heathingdon, the unprincipled scoundrel, to whom I owe so large a part of my miseries."

"You are wrong there," replied the landlord, "for the person I am speaking of is your own wife."

"My wife!—is she in London?"

"To be sure she is; the poor creature couldn't bear the uncertainty she was left in, so she put into her pocket all the money she had been saving, and came up to town, that she might be near in case her assistance might be useful."

"Where is she now?"

"I can't tell you that," replied Doublechalk; "but, I rather think it's somewhere 'tother side of London, for she spoke about crossing Tower Hill on her way here, and meeting with that chap that would take your place, when you were supposed to be far enough away from England."

"You mean Charles Heathingdon?"

"That's the very man."

"Do you know whether he insulted, or offered any violence to her?" demanded Guy, eagerly.

"I'm not able to tell you much about that," answered the other; "but, I believe he kept her a long time in talk, and she wouldn't have got away when she did, but for somebody coming towards them, and then she bolted off, knowing well enough that he wouldn't dare follow her."

Guy Harrowby remained silent for some little time, and then striking his clenched fist on a table, near which he was standing, he hoarsely exclaimed—

"This only adds to the debt of vengeance that I owe to the heartless scoundrel, who would take from me the only blessing that this life affords. I have tried to banish all evil thoughts against him from my mind, but he still pursues his own evil course, and, in spite of all my resolution, I find myself forced to resent the injuries he has tried to inflict on me."

"You know best what ought to be done in a case of this kind," returned Doublechalk; "and, all that I can say about it is, that if it had been an affair of my own, he shouldn't have been alive at this moment, to hunt me out as he has done you."

"You think I have been too forbearing," answered the fugitive; "yet I would avoid committing further crime so long as it may be possible to do so. Now, however, that I see it is in vain to expect any change for the better, he must keep clear from me, or there will be bloodshed between us."

"All I hope is, that you won't happen to meet together in my house," observed the landlord of the 'Seven Horse Shoes.'

"You need have no fear about that," replied Guy, "for I have made up my mind not to remain here longer than the coming midnight hour."

"You have?"

"Aye," he replied, "this hiding and sneaking suits me not, and I'll at once take my chance, whatever it may be."

"Well, it's strange enough that I was going to speak to you upon that subject," exclaimed Doublechalk. "I begin to think you can't remain here any longer with any safety; and, as the policemen are now in the house, I shouldn't at all wonder if they search about till they discover this loft, and then it will be all over with me."

"And with me too."

"Aye, both will get into trouble about it," returned the host, "so I think the best way you can do will be to cut away from this place, as soon as you possibly can."

"It shall be at the time I have said to-night."

"Before then, if you please, Master Harrowby," exclaimed the other. "I've a contrivance for getting you away at once, without much fear of your being discovered."

"How can that be done?"

"Behold!" exclaimed Doublechalk, raising a trap door just above their heads. "This leads to the roof the house, and will afford the means of escape I told you of."

"But if the officers should happen to discover this loft, they'll be sure to seek me on the top of the house."

"There's no doubt of that," replied Doublechalk; "but still, they'll be disappointed, for the trap door of the next house is always left open for the accommodation of myself and friends; and, as we shall fasten it as soon as we have passed through, the police will find themselves completely at fault."

"How do you know your neighbour may be depended on?"

"Because we both happen to follow the same sort of business," replied the landlord. "He's a marine store dealer, and being subject to frequent visits from the officers, he has found my trap-door as convenient as I have his."

"Then you have agreed to assist each other whenever either may happen to find himself in danger?"

"That's it, my boy."

"And supposing we happen to get into his house in the way you have proposed, how am I afterwards to get away without being seen by any of the officers that are in search of me?"

"Much more easily than you fancy," replied Doublechalk; "my neighbour keeps a boat that's always in readiness for an affair of danger like the present. I've often made use of it for myself, and being a pretty good waterman, I'll get you over to the opposite side of the river before any one can suspect which way you have gone."

"Then we had better go at once," said Guy Harrowby, "for if we waste time it may not be so easy to escape as you may imagine."

"There's no hurry about that," returned the landlord, "because they won't find the entrance to this loft without some little trouble; and it will be quite time enough for us to think of retreating when we hear 'em trying the secret panel over the closet beneath; when that's the case, we'll be off, and I'll have you over on t'other side of the water in less than no time."

"And why not go at once?"

"For a very good reason," answered Doublechalk. When they're all up here, it will take 'em some time to scramble down to the bottom of the house; and, whilst they are doing that, you and I shall be far enough beyond their reach."

"The boat is always in readiness, you say?"

"Yes; and the river runs close to the back of the houses, so we shall not have to lose a moment before we dash out into the stream, and then, old fellow, we shall be safe."

"Hark!" exclaimed Guy nudging his companion, "I hear the footsteps of several persons coming up the stairs! The enemy is upon us, and we have not another instant to lose!"

"Stop, at any rate, 'till I give the word to cut," whispered Doublechalk; "we shall have plenty of chance when we see 'em begin to move the sliding panel, so don't speak another word above your breath, but listen to every thing that passes, and we may hear something that will be as a guide to us how to act by-and-bye."

A dead silence now ensued between them, and, in a few seconds, they heard several persons enter the room beneath, and from the few words that were spoken by their pursuers they soon learnt that the fact of there being a loft overhead had, by some means or another, been revealed to them. Guy and his companion heard them groping about in search of the secret entrance, till at length the sliding panel was seen to move, and then, as any longer delay would have been dangerous, they passed speedily through the trap-door, and descended through that belonging to the next house, which they bolted securely to prevent pursuit, and then hurried down stairs to reach the boat which was to convey them across the river. And it was well that they lost no more time, for the serjeant and his men entered the loft just as the others had reached the adjoining house in safety.

"The bird has flown, at any rate," exclaimed one of the men; "and I suppose, as the trap-door has been left open, we shall have to scramble after him over the roofs, at the risk of breaking our necks."

"We must take our chance about that," returned the serjeant, "for as we're so close upon his heels, we'll take him, and pocket the reward that has been offered for his apprehension. So both of you follow me, and remember, dead or alive, Guy Harrowby must be secured."

He then sprung through the trap-door, and being accompanied by the others, an active search was commenced from one end of the row of houses to the other. Nothing, however, could they see of the fugitive; and the next thing they did was to try all the trap-doors, bu every one of them was fastened, and it now became evident that all their trouble had been thrown away.

"What the devil can have become of the fellow?" exclaimed the serjeant, as he wiped the perspiration from his forehead. "He must have got out upon the roof for certain, and yet he's managed to give us the slip, though for the life of me I can't see by what means he's done it."

"Surely," observed one of the men, "he hasn't been fool enough to jump into the street from a height like this."

"That's not very likely," said the serjeant; "for if that had been the case, there'd have been a crowd of gaping fools collected round the place. But hollo! what's that I see? There's two men getting into a boat from the yard next door, and as I live, one of 'em's Guy Harrowby! We're done, my boys, for the fellow's escaped us again, by G—!"

One of the men, however, shouted to some watermen below to follow in pursuit of the fugitives; but the parties addressed were not inclined to put themselves out of the way unless there was a certainty of being paid for their trouble; and after consulting together for a few moments, they came to an unanimous determination not to have anything to do with the business. Enraged at this disappointment, the serjeant and his men returned through the trap-door, and scampering down stairs, hastened to the waterside in order to take a boat and follow in pursuit.

In the meanwhile Guy Harrowby and his companion had not lost a single instant of time in making their way towards the opposite shore, and having reached about midway, they made themselves perfectly easy as to all danger being over for the present. Hitherto they had not spoken to each other, but now the silence was broken by Doublechalk, who, pointing towards the place they had just left, said:—

"Look on the house tops yonder, Guy, and you'll see the chaps that wanted to grab us just now. They twig us too, as sure as a gun! so pull away, my boy, and as we go along, I'll tell you what to do when you get ashore."

"There's no time to be lost," exclaimed Harrowby, "for they have left the roof, and in a minute or two they'll be following us in another boat. So you see all our trouble has been in vain; and they'll take me in spite of all that's been done,"

"No they won't, mate, if you keep up your pluck," answered Doublechalk; "we're too much ahead of 'em for that; and when once you're on land, I can direct you to a place where you may stay in safety till Dick Fordham, or some of 'em can follow and contrive some plan for getting you clear away."

"Where is the place you speak of?" asked Guy.

"About half a mile on the other side of Rotherhithe," answered the landlord; "you'll find a queer-looking, tumble-down cottage just a little off the road, and the man that keeps it, being an old friend of mine, will give you shelter for a short time if you mention my name to him."

" Is he to b depended on ?"

" As much so as any friend that you've got," replied Doublechalk ; " I once concealed him in the same loft that you've been in, and he has been grateful to me for it ever since."

" Was he never taken afterwards ?"

" Oh, yes ; but it was not for some months though, and that was not through any fault of mine. However, he got transported for seven years, and ever since his return to England, he has lived in the cottage you are going to."

" And has given up his old life, I suppose ?"

" Yes," replied Doublechalk, " he's given up thieving entirely, and now follows a business that's more profitable. He's a coiner, my boy, and makes plenty of money in more senses than one."

" Has he never been suspected ?" asked Guy.

" Bless your heart, he's too cunning to let anybody do that," exclaimed the other; " when he goes out he looks just for all the world like a beggar; and as he never interferes with any one, nobody ever interferes with him. Besides, he has very few visitors, and those are the parties that manage to get rid of the coin he makes."

" What is the name of this man ?"

" Peter Datchet."

" And you think there's no doubt of his giving me the shelter I require," said Guy Harrowby.

" I'm sure you'll find him a regular trump or I wouldn't send you to him at all," answered the landlord ; " it's not the first time I've sent a friend to him, and he's always given 'em a hearty welcome. You'll find him a rum sort of chap, but humour him a little, and he'll do anything to save a chap from getting into trouble ; so now, all you've got to do, is to make your way to his place without loss of time, and at night I'll send Dick Fordham to you."

The boat was now sharply propelled up to the landing-place at Rotherhithe, and Guy Harrowby sprang out, and walked quickly away without waiting for the ceremony of saying ' good bye ' to his companion. Doublechalk then left the boat in the care of a waterman, desiring him to answer no questions that might be asked, and then hurried away to be beyond the reach of the pursuers.

CHAPTER XX.

CHANCE NEWS.—AN INTRODUCTION.—THE COINER.

FEARFUL of being immediately pursued, Guy Harrowby took a more circuitous route than he had intended, and knowing perfectly well the direction of the cottage he was going to, he threaded his way through innumerable streets, hoping thus to baffle the police and prevent their obtaining any clue by which they might be able to trace him out. Upon further consideration he thought it would be better not to visit Peter Datchet till the darkness of night began to set in, and coming to a quiet looking public-house, near the outskirts of the town, he entered, and calling for such humble refreshment as he needed, he resolved to stay where he was till it was time for him to seek his place of destination. For nearly an hour he remained in undisturbed possession of the room, when two men came in and seated themselves at the same table from which he had been eating his bread and cheese. The man eyed him suspiciously, as people are sometimes wont to do when they fall into the company of strangers, and having apparently satisfied their curiosity, commenced smoking and talking over the affairs of the whole neighbourhood. At length, one of them addressing his companion, said—

" I say, Bill, did you see the lark there was a little time ago down by the water-side ?"

" No," replied the other, " what was it?"

" Why I did'nt hear all the rights about it," returned the first speaker, " but it seems, from what I can understand, that a chap escaped from the police over in Wapping ; and what did he do, but jumped into a boat and crosses over to this side."

" And did he give 'em the slip after all ?" asked Bill.

" I believe you ; he'd got somebody with him though, and both of 'em jumped on shore, and bolted away a good five minutes before the policemen in their boat came up."

" Lord !" exclaimed Bill, " what a rare bit of fun it must have been to see the Peelers when they found they were beat. Didn't they go back quite chapfallen ?"

" I should think so," replied the other, " for the watermen set up a grin at 'em, and while pretending to assist the chaps out of the boat, they managed, without seeming to mean it, to let two of 'em fall into the water."

" I should have died with laughing if I'd have been there to see it," exclaimed Bill, revelling in what he called the fun of the thing. " I'm a rare fellow to enjoy a joke, but somehow or another, I've generally the bad luck to be out of the way whenever there's any thing worth seeing. But I say, Harry, you haven't told me yet who the chap was that they wanted to lay hold of."

"There's a very good reason for that," answered the other, "for I don't happen to have heard his name."

"What had he been doing then?"

"Why I'm not quite cartain about that either," replied Harry, "some said, he'd been committing a murder; others that he'd returned from transportation before his time was up; and one chap told me that he was charged with having done both the things."

"Ah!" exclaimed Bill, "then it must be the fellow they've been advertising about the streets the last three or four days. They call him Guy Harrowby, and a reward of fifty pounds has been offered to any one that will apprehend and convey him to prison."

"Fifty pounds! no wonder then the police gave him such a chase across the river. However, the poor devil's got clear off it seems, for I'll be bound he hasn't wasted much time since he put his foot on the shore."

There was now a pause in the conversation between the two men, and Guy Harrowby, who had been listening to every word with breathless attention, drew himself as much as possible into the shade. In the course of a short time he got rid of the nervousness he had at first felt, and addressing himself to the man nearest to him, inquired if he knew what description had been published of the man who had escaped from the officers.

" Why, I cannot remember much of it now, though I read it on a wall where it was first put up," answered Bill ; " I know he's rather a young chap though, and has a downcast look with him, as might be expected when he knows what his fate would be if he happened to be caught."

" And caught he will be as sure as fate," observed Harry, " for the reward offered is a tempting one, and there'll be plenty of people trying to earn it, though I, for one, would rather starve than take any of their filthy blood-money."

" That's just my way of thinking," exclaimed his companion ; " I can always work for my living, thank goodness, and an honest penny is at all times better than an ill-gotten pound."

" Is it known which way the fugitive took after he came ashore ?" asked Guy Harrowby.

" No," answered one of the men ; " he was tracked down a few streets, I believe, but there all further trace of him was lost, and it's supposed he's made the best of his way to London, where he may bother his pursuers a long time."

" I don't know that," said Guy, " for no doubt plenty of people are looking for him there, and in my opinion he'd be sooner taken there than anywhere else."

" He must have been an infernal fool ever to have come to England at all," exclaimed Harry, " for he never could have expected to be safe in it."

" So we may think," observed Guy ; " but it's impossible for any one man to judge the motives of another. He may have come over through a sheer love of his country, or he may have a wife and family that are dearer to him than life itself, and if that should be the case, we ought not to judge his conduct too severely."

" May be that's it, Harry," exclaimed his companion ; " the poor fellow, I dare say, is to be pitied, and, at any rate, it aint for you nor I to say that he's done wrong in coming back to his own native country."

" But he'll have an awkward chance if they should happen to lay hold of him," said the other.

" You're right enough there ; and that reminds me how much I should have enjoyed the fun of seeing the two policemen soused into the water. Confound the fellows ! I never liked them since they locked me up one cold winter's night, because they chose to say I was drunk and disorderly."

" Nor I," said Bill, " since one of 'em broke my head with his truncheon, for no other crime than because I interfered to save a poor woman from his brutal violence. But they'll always be the same ferocious scoundrels, I suppose, for the magistrates never will hear a word that's said against 'em, under the excuse that the police must be protected in the performance of their duty ; so now the fellows know they can do as they like : and instead of being protectors of the peace, a great many of 'em are the first to break it."

" And for that very reason," exclaimed Harry, " I wouldn't lend a helping hand just now to those two fellows I saw fall into the water ; and I believe there was no one else that pitied 'em, for not a soul among the crowd offered to give any information as to which way the man had gone, and they had to make their way into the street, dripping with wet as they were, with a number of people yelling and laughing at their heels. It was rare amusement, I can tell you, and no one enjoyed it more than I did."

" And so should I if I'd had the good luck to have been there," returned his friend ; " but as I said just now, I'm always out of these good things, happen when or where they may."

" If you'd been there," said the other, " you'd have been as glad as I was to see how disappointed they looked when nobody would tell 'em which way the man had gone that they were looking after. I do believe in their rage they could have swallowed their own truncheons ; and at last they sneaked away to go and look after the chap that had given 'em so much trouble."

" Do you think they'll find him ?" asked Bill.

" I don't think they're very likely to do so," returned the other.

" The man, I should say, has lost no time in getting out of this neighbourhood, and if they really expect to find him, the best thing they can do is to make the best of their way up to London."

" Perhaps the man they're after hasn't gone there !"

" Very likely not," replied Harry ; " but be where he may, he's had lesson enough I should think to get clear out of this country as soon as he can. Not that I can take his part if there's any truth in what they say about his having committed a murder, but as that's a matter between him and his conscience, I shall not concern myself at all about it."

" I've heard something of this affair before," said Guy Harrowby, once more joining in the conversation ; " and in the opinion of many persons the charge of murder is never likely to be proved in a court of justice."

" How is it that he has been accused then ?" asked Harry.

" Of the particulars I have heard very little," answered Guy, as guardedly as he could ; " but I believe it was thought there was a better chance of his being taken if such a charge as that was spread abroad against him."

" Oh, if that's the case, I hope they'll never find him," said Bill. " Murder's one thing, and escaping from transportation another ; and for my own part I can't blame any man that cuts away from such slavery, if he has but one opportunity given him to regain his liberty. However, it's time for us to be off now, so good day to you, sir."

And laying down their pipes upon the table the two friends retired, leaving Guy Harrowby to reflect alone upon the conversation he had heard. That the officers who were in pursuit of him had been baffled he could not entertain a doubt, and feeling more easy upon that point than he had been before, he called for another pint of ale, resolving to stay where he was an hour longer; by which time it would be dusky enough for him to venture to the cottage of Peter Datchet, the coiner. During this time he had leisure to reflect upon the situation in which he found himself, and to think over various plans for the future, in the event of his succeeding at last in escaping from the many snares that had been laid for him by the numerous enemies who had risen up against him. Amongst other things that he had forgotten when he parted from Doublechalk, was to leave directions by which his wife might know the place of his retreat; but on the other hand, he expected to see Fordham before the night was over, and he had already experienced sufficient kindness from that person to feel assured that he would take immediate steps to relieve the anxiety she would naturally feel in his behalf. These and other cogitations occupied his mind till it began to grow dark, when several persons came into the room to spend their evening, and, wishing to avoid observation as much as possible, he rose and took his departure from the house.

And now, in order to escape the notice of those passengers whom he might meet, he took his way through the most obscure streets, till he reached the utmost limits of the town, when crossing over some fields he made his way towards the road, by the side of which he understood the cottage he wanted to find was situated. This task occupied more time than he had reckoned upon, so that when he reached his place of destination, darkness had completely set in, and the sky was studded with its countless thousands of stars. Passing through a gate, he crossed an ill-conditioned garden, and, as there was no other substitute, knocked gently at the door with his knuckles. He listened, but the silence of death reigned within, and having waited in vain for an answer to his summons; he repeated the knock, but on this occasion somewhat more loudly. This seemed to have the desired effect, for he could hear a chair move as if some one had risen from it, and then footsteps were heard cautiously approaching the door.

" Who's there ? " demanded a querulous voice from within.

" A friend !" was the brief reply.

" Your name ? "

" You would not know it if I was to tell you."

" Then how can you call yourself a friend ?"

" Because my purpose is not unfriendly."

" Who do you come from "

" One that you know well—Doublechalk, the landlord of the ' Seven Horse Shoes,' in Wapping."

" This announcement seemed to have the desired effect, for after the removal of several fastenings the door was opened, and a middle-aged man, having a candlestick in his hand, presented himself. He peered suspiciously into the face of his visitor, and being apparently satisfied with the examination, desired him to walk in. This was instantly obeyed by Guy Harrowby, and the door having been again carefully barred and bolted, Peter Datchet inquired what errand his visitor had come on from his old friend and companion, Tom Doublechalk.

" I'm on no errand of his at all," answered the fugitive. " To be brief with you, I'm pursued by some officers of justice, and he sent me here with a request that you will give me shelter for a few hours."

" What could Tom have been thinking of ?" exclaimed the coiner, his countenance towering with anger as he heard these words; " Does he want to get me into trouble that he sends to my house a man, who confesses that he has the hounds of the law dodging close at his heels ?"

" I didn't say they were anywhere near me," answered Guy Harrowby: " I only want to keep out of their sight, and in a few days I hope to be where they'll not be able to reach me."

" You've been committing a robbery, I suppose."

" No; but the offence is looked on as being quite as bad: I've returned from transportation before my time."

" Humph! Your name?"

" Guy Harrowby."

" Ah!" exclaimed Peter Datchet, " I heard of you, about an hour ago, from a man that was here on a little business. There's a murder charged against you, I believe, as well as that of being a returned convict."

" Some have accused me of it," answered Harrowby; " but it's a matter that you and I needn't enter upon just now. All I want to know is, whether you will give me the shelter that has been asked for by your friend Doublechalk."

" Why, as Tom has recommended you, I can hardly refuse," exclaimed the other. " He once assisted me in the same sort of way; but I think he might have been more cautious than to send a stranger to my house."

" He knows well enough that I'm to be depended on," replied Guy; and, as a proof of his confidence, he told me by what means you get your living here."

" The devil he did !" cried Peter, with alarm. " And, pray—what did he tell you was my business ? "

" A coiner."

"D——n! Then I may look upon myself as a ruined man; for, of course, you'll not consider yourself bound to keep my secret."

"I came here to ask a favour," replied Guy Harrowby, "and not to do you an injury. I have been driven from my last hiding-place by the officers of justice; and if you had refused me a shelter I must have been taken before many hours were over. Is it likely, then, that I should say or do anything to bring ruin upon the man that has served me?"

"Why, you'd be an infernal villain if you did," returned the other; "but there's no trusting to any one, now-a-days; and if it had not been for your using the name of Tom Doublechalk, you'd never have seen the inside of this place, I can tell you."

"But, as it is," said Guy, "I suppose I may consider this cottage my home for the short time I shall remain here?"

"Yes: but I hope I shan't have any more visitors."

"There'll be one more to-night, I believe."

"Who's he?" demanded Peter, sharply.

"A man that is doing all he can to get me out of this scrape," answered the fugitive. "I dare say you know a fellow named Dick Fordham."

"Yes, I know him well enough," replied Datchet. "When he's got nothing else to do, he sometimes tries a little in the way of smashing: and I only wish he'd keep at it more regularly; for, when he is at work he's one of the best customers I have. Ah! if it's Dick Fordham that's coming, he'll not find my door long shut against him. But you have not told me yet where you're going to, after you leave my place."

"That's because I don't know anything about it myself," replied Guy. "I leave the management of those things to my friends; and, as Dick has undertaken to get me out of England, I don't interfere at all, or even suggest any thoughts of my own, that I may have upon the subject."

"You're wise there, my boy," exclaimed the coiner. "Dick Fordham knows a move or two, whenever there's anything very difficult to be done; and, as sure as my name's Datchet, he'll get you clear out of this hobble. Let's see: I forget whether you told me where the last place was that you hid yourself from this confounded affair in."

"At Doublechalk's."

"Ah! up in the loft, eh? Cunning place that, aint it? I've been there myself before now; and all the time Doublechalk behaved like a brother to me. And it's a lucky thing that he did, too; for, if it hadn't been for that, he'd never have had the opportunity of sending you over here. But, d—n him, he needn't have told you that I was a coiner."

"I dare say, if the truth was known, he thought it the safest plan to trust to my honour."

"Honour!—that's a fine sounding word; but people like you and me have very little to do with it."

"At any rate," said Guy, "he knew I was to be trusted; and it was better to tell me the secret than to let me find it out of my own accord. I'm indebted to you for shelter, and I'll never return the favour with ingratitude."

"Perhaps not," exclaimed Peter Datchet; "and I'm the more inclined to believe you, because I know my old friend Tom would not have sent you here if he thought there was a chance of your doing anything wrong. Besides, you say Fordham will be here presently, and I know he wouldn't have taken so much trouble unless he thought you a decent sort of fellow."

"He has already done more for me than I had any right to expect," answered the fugitive; and, when you see him, he'll tell you that he'd do as much more if it was necessary. In short, I've found a friend in him when almost all the rest of the world were my enemies; and, all I can say about it is, that I'll go through as much for him if ever he should have the misfortune to need my services."

"I'm to understand, I suppose," said the coiner, "that you'll not want to stay here very long."

"Not many hours, I'm in hopes," returned Guy.

"Well, so much the better, not that I grudge you the shelter you've asked for, but your being here may bring danger to us both, and I don't see any use in two or three people getting into trouble because one happens to be wanted for some infernal thing or another."

"There's no chance of your getting into trouble on my account," returned Guy Harrowby; "for my pursuers have lost every clue to the way I've gone, and I took good care that no one should see which way I came. Besides, it was dark by the time I left the town, and after that I didn't meet a soul on my way to this place."

"But there's another difficulty that I didn't think of before," exclaimed Peter.

"What's that?"

"They may see Dick Fordham as he's coming here, and if so they'd be sure to follow him, for he's pretty well known, and then both you and I should be in a nice scrape."

"I might," said Guy, "but there's nothing about the place to show what you get your living by, so I don't see that there's much to be afraid of on your account."

"Don't you indeed," exclaimed the other, rising and throwing open the door of an adjoining room. "You now see, I dare say, all the implements and machinery used in coining, and if ever these things should come under the notice of the police officers, my career would come to a speedy conclusion."

"It seems strange, too," observed Harrowby, "that you should have been able to carry on your business all these years without having excited suspicion among your neighbours."

"Why," replied the coiner, "it's not to be so much wondered at when you consider how careful I have been to blind people as to who and what I really am. People here about can't make out what I am ; some think I am an eccentric, others that I get my living by occasional begging, and others again, that the people who come here support me by the contributions they bring me. Of course I never mix with any of the neighbours, so they can't worm out my secret ; and if any of them call, I never ask them into the house, but answer at the door any question they may have to put."

"I should think," observed Guy Harrowby, "that so much reserve would cause more curiosity than anything else."

"They may be as curious as they like," returned the other, "so that they don't want to pry any further into my concerns. I'm not bound to invite them into the house, for I never trouble any of them with a visit ; and there's not a person in the whole neighbourhood that can say I ever asked for a favour. That puts me beyond their reach, and whilst I give no offence, they cannot find an excuse for entering my doors without an invitation."

"I dare say they think you are a curious sort of fellow."

"I've no doubt they do," answered Peter Datchet, "but the thought of that never gives me much concern, since I care no more for them than they do for me. The only thing I'm afraid of is, that the officers may some fine morning or another pay me a visit, and whenever that happens it will be all over with me."

"But as you have escaped suspicion so long, I don't see why you should feel any fear about it now."

"Fear!" exclaimed the coiner, "I never knew what it was in the whole course of my life. I have strength left in my arms yet, and even if there should be six against me, I would let 'em se that they had a Tartar to deal with."

"What good would that be if they laid hold of you at last ?"

"They should never do that while I've the use of my arms," replied the coiner, and leading Guy into the next room, he showed him an immense hammer that he wielded with as much ease as if it had been a mere toy. He then pointed to a sword, and two brace of pistols, which were hanging on the wall, ready to be snatched down for immediate use."

"You see," he continued, "what sort of a reception I could give them if they were to come here to take me. I'm ready to give 'em battle at a moment's notice ; and, rather than be dragged to a prison, with the fear of transportation once more before my eyes, I'd fight as long as I could, and die at last upon my own hearth."

"At any rate, you are well prepared," said Guy ; "but, if overpowered by numbers, you would be obliged to yield like many as good men as yourself."

"I tell you that shall never be," exclaimed Peter Datchet ; "for you see, I have always one loaded pistol concealed in my bosom, and the moment I found myself in danger of being overpowered, I'd turn the muzzle against my own heart, and the only satisfaction they should have, would be to carry me out of my own house a corpse."

"Well," answered the fugitive, "I once made up my mind to the same sort of thing, but somehow they managed to surprise me when I was not aware of mischief being so near, and the consequence was, that they dragged me to prison, and shortly after that, I was tried and sentenced to be transported for seven years."

"And not liking your situation abroad, you took it into your head to escape at the first opportunity."

"I did."

"But what in the name of all that's most stupid made you think of returning to England, when you must have been sure there would be such a fuss made about it ?"

"Because I had a wife here, and from the situation in which I left her, I knew that by that time she must be a mother. Dearly I loved her, in spite of the thoughtless career I had led, and even the thought of the punishment that would follow the discovery of my return, was not enough to turn me from my purpose."

"Is there any truth in the story I have heard, that you murdered the man that was placed as a guard over you ?"

"A struggle took place between us," answered Guy, moodily, "and I left the man apparently in the agonies of death."

"It matters not how it happened," said the coiner, "for they'll call it murder, let it have been how it might.

"Well," replied Guy, "I have every reason to believe so ; and for that reason I am most anxious to avoid getting into the hands of my pursuers. I may have deserved the gallows, but were that to be my fate, it would bring sorrow and a broken heart to a fond and ever faithful wife."

"Does she know what has become of you ?"

"Dick Fordham will take care to let her know that, as soon as possible," answered the fugitive. "She has left a happy home in the country, that she may be near me, in case her assistance should be required ; and, no sooner has she arrived in London, than I am obliged to fly once more, though to what place it is impossible to say at present."

"It would have been better for you to be a single chap, as I am," observed the coiner. "Luckily, there's not a soul in the world to care for me, so that, happen what may, my death won't cause a moment's uneasiness to any one."

"True," exclaimed Guy Harrowby; "it would have saved me many a bitter pang, that I now suffer, when I think of the miseries I've brought upon her. Yet, who would thought on the day we married that all this mischief was brewing for us. It was impossible for me to foresee that I should ever be driven to poaching, and that in the end it would lead to the situation I'm now in?"

"Ah!" cried the other, "those that made those infernal game laws have much to answer for, though it's not an easy thing to make 'em think so. Your rich man believes that all the good things of this life were sent for his use only, and that the hard working man has a right to be content with the commonest fare, such as none of 'em would give the dogs they pamper and fondle as if they were so many Christian beings. And then they wonder if the poor man grumbles at the injustice that's done him, though the very game laws we're speaking of have led to more deaths than our rulers would like to think of."

"A low tapping was at this juncture heard at the window-shutter; and recognising the usual signal of those who came to him on business, the coiner opened the door without the slightest hesitation and gave admittance, as he had thought would be the case, to Dick Fordham.

"So I see you've got here safe and sound," he exclaimed to the fugitive; "but methinks you were talking rather loud just now, if you had any secrets that you didn't want to make public to the world."

"We were not talking of anything that we need care about being heard," answered the coiner; "the subject was poaching; and I was giving my opinion of the game laws to your friend here, that's all."

"And he, no doubt, agreed with you in condemning 'em," returned the last comer. "I know his opinion upon the matter, and it's not to be wondered at, seeing that he owes all the trouble he has gone through to the killing of a single hare, when he and his wife had no other means of getting a dinner. However we won't talk about that now, because we've something more important to attend to, and I suppose by this time you've been told what I allude to?"

"Yes," replied Peter Datchet, "I know he has got a lot of people after him that he don't want to see, and that my old friend at Wapping sent him here to ask for shelter till you could find a way to get him out of the country."

"That's it," answered the other; "but the mischief of it is that I don't see my way very clear just at present. The search after him has grown hotter than ever since he left Doublechalk's, and if he leaves the place now, he'll be sure to fall into the hands of those that are looking for him."

"What! if he takes the opportunity of going out on a dark night like this?"

"Pshaw!" retorted Dick Fordham; "what's the use of a dark night when we know it will be followed by a light morning? I haven't been able to think of any place where he can hide yet, though I've a notion he may find concealment in one of the deep gravel pits on Blackheath."

"That's a capital thought of yours, Dick," exclaimed the coiner; "for I remember seeing some of 'em that are completely overgrown with trees and bushes. No one will ever think of looking for your friend there; you can easily supply him with what he wants in the shape of eatables and drinkables."

"I see," retorted Fordham, "you don't care what becomes of the poor devil, so that you get rid of him."

"Consider the risk I run, my dear fellow."

"And consider the risk I have taken upon myself," answered Dick Fordham; "you've been glad to find a friend before now, and yet when it comes to the turn of some one else, you'd leave him to his fate, though you well know that the gibbet is staring him in the face all the while."

"Every man ought to look to himself first," exclaimed Peter Datchet; "not that I mean to refuse him a lodging for the night, because he has been sent by my friend Doublechalk; but all I mean to say is, that you must find some other place as soon as possible."

"There'll be no time lost about that you may depend on it," answered the other; "in the morning I'll go to Blackheath, and see which is the most likely place to hide in, and to-morrow, when it's dark and few people are about, I'll take him away, and relieve you of his company."

"I'm sorry for it too," exclaimed the coiner, "for he'll find but queer accommodation there I'm afraid."

"Accommodation is the last thing I shall think of," said Guy Harrowby, who had hitherto taken not part in the conversation. "Concealment from my enemies is all that I desire, and for the rest you may make your minds perfectly easy. I have had more hardships than this to encounter; and shall think myself lucky to owe my safety to the contrivance that has been mentioned by my friend Fordham."

"As for that," returned Dick, "I've made up my mind to get you out of this scrape, if possible, and when once I say a thing it isn't a trifle that will put me off it. Besides, I can make you more comfortable than you expect, for there's plenty of heath to be found about the place, and if I throw a lot of it down into the pit, you may make up a better bed than you have had for some time past."

"And as the spot aint very far from here," said the coiner, "you can call upon me, and I'll supply him, through you, with whatever food he wants. So you see I'm willing to lend a helping-hand,

Dick, though I don't want him to stay here at the risk of bringing after him a lot of my old enemies, the police."

"But they know well enough who you are."

"They do," he replied; "but they little suspect that so much of the bad money that's daily passing in London comes from my mint. It puzzles and amazes 'em to think where the storehouse can be, and I should be a fool to do anything that might serve to betray myself."

"There's no fear of anything wrong happening through giving this man a lodging for one night," exclaimed Dick Fordham; "he has given his pursuers the slip, and so completely are they at fault, that they don't know which way to look for him."

"How do you know that?"

"By making inquiries, to be sure; I aint such a coward as you are, and, before coming here, I asked everywhere that I thought information was to be got."

"And you learnt that the officers have lost all clue to the man they are looking after?"

"They're completely bothered," answered Fordham; "and a report has begun to go abroad that, after landing at Rotherhithe, he went on board a ship that was just then sailing for a foreign country, and that he was now, most likely, beyond their reach."

"Of course then, it won't be long before they convince themselves whether there's any truth in the rumour," observed Datchet; "they've only to go post-haste to Gravesend, where they can search every ship that is outward bound."

"True," answered Dick, "but that would be just giving us the time we want. I'm pretty quick at inventing a scheme, and while they're looking for Guy Harrowby in one direction I'll take him off somewhere else, and by the time they've found out their mistake, our friend here may be landed at some place where he'll have nothing more to fear."

"Capital!" exclaimed Peter; "your plan, my boy, is a famous one, and now I begin to see a chance of this man's escape that I couldn't perceive before. He shall have a lodging here to-night, Dick, and I'll do anything else for him as far as my own safety will allow."

"Give us your hand, old fellow," cried Fordham, at the same time extending his own; "I thought it was d——d strange if you had turned selfish all of a sudden, but it seemed so much like reality, that I had almost made up my mind never to speak to you any more."

"Did you ever know me turn my back upon an old friend?"

"I don't know that I can charge you with that, Peter," answered the other; "but I began to think it looked devilish like it just now, when you hummed and ha'd about letting him stop for the night, well-knowing, too, that he had been sent here by a man that once obliged you in the same way."

"Ah!" exclaimed the other; "Tom Doublechalk certainly did act towards me like a trump, and I've never forgot it from that time to the present. In fact, this man can tell you that I let him into my house the moment he mentioned the name of the person that sent him."

"Why, of course, you know that Doublechalk wouldn't send anybody that you need be afraid of."

"I was quite aware of all that," answered the other; "but I couldn't tell what sort of a chap it was that I let into my house. He might have mentioned Doublechalk's name without having any authority for it, and a very pretty situation I should have been in, if he had, after all, turned out to be an officer in disguise."

"And that," said Guy, laughing, "was, I dare say, the reason why you took so much pains to show me how well you are prepared in case of a sudden attack!"

"It must be confessed that was my reason," answered Peter Datchet; "I found, after a very little conversation, that you knew the sort of business I carry on here: and, in order to let you see that I was not to be taken unawares, I led you into the next room, and showed you the weapons that I keep always handy for immediate use."

"And yet," exclaimed Guy, "it seemed to me that you believed everything I had stated."

"Why, there was a little scheming in that," replied the coiner; "it was plain enough that I was more than a match for you in case of our coming to loggerheads, so I pretended to take in all you had been telling me. Besides, you had declared that Dick Fordham was coming here before the night was over, and I knew, if there was any truth in that, there was no danger to be feared from it."

"And now," exclaimed Dick, "I suppose you are quite satisfied that Harrowby did not come here as a spy?"

"I can't have much suspicion about that now that you have acknowledged him as a friend of yours," answered the coiner; "besides, haven't I promised that he shall have a lodging here to-night? and that don't look much as if I was afraid he'd afterwards do me a mischief. But you won't forget, Dick, that you are to find him some other place to-morrow?"

"Oh, I'll not forget that, depend on it!" replied the other. "In the morning early I'll go to Blackheath, and, I dare say, it won't take long to find a well-shaded pit where he may lay concealed till we can do something better for him."

"You may take your time about it," said Guy Harrowby, "for I have been so long buffeted about in the world that I can bear a good deal more without complaining."

"Yes: but your friends don't want you to bear more than can be helped," exclaimed Dick. "You've had a pretty good share of knocking about, according to my notion, and the sooner you begin to find yourself a little more comfortable the better ,should say."

"I should almost prefer being taken at once," said the fugitive, "than lead the life I have been doing lately. I am inclined to get my living in an honest way, if people would only let me; but instead of giving me a chance, I am hunted from place to place, like a wild beast."

"Then why don't you follow my example?" asked Peter Datchet. "I suffered the punishment they chose to give me; and, on my return, after serving out my full time, I took up my line of business; and, with all their cunning, I have not been found out yet. Besides, it is profitable; and, to tell you the truth, I have grown tolerably rich by it."

"What do you want with riches?" asked Dick Fordham, bluntly. "You have neither chick nor child to leave it to; and I should think you'd be glad to leave off work before they find out what sort of manufactory you keep here."

"Tell me why I should give it up," exclaimed the coiner. "Who can I harm except myself, even if a discovery should take place? and in what way else can I employ myself, after being employed in this line? There's no persons that I can mix with, because my character has been blasted; and I should be shunned like some venomous reptile, if I were to attempt to enter the society of my fellow-men."

"Have you ever tried it?" asked Guy Harrowby.

"No," he replied, "and what's more, I never mean to do so."

"Then it's impossible for you to say, that there may not be some men who would not encourage you if they saw any symptoms of an amendment in your life. Besides, by your own acknowledgment you have laid by money, and we all know that a man who has got money can always make friends, wherever he goes."

"If you were to talk to me from this time till doomsday, I should never think otherwise than I do at present," exclaimed Peter Datchet; "every man knows his own business best, and I shall stick to my opinion, let who will gainsay it."

"So do, old rough-and-tough," vociferated Fordham; "have your way, my boy, and then, I suppose, you'll be satisfied, even if they should some day or other catch you in the midst of your work. You've a right to be hanged if you like, and I can't see why the devil, Guy Harrowby, should take the trouble to turn you out of your own way."

"Aye,—laugh at me if you like," exclaimed the coiner; "pass your jeers upon me, Dick, because you know that out of old friendship I shall never harm you; perhaps, though, if anybody else had said as much, I might have taken the matter up a little more warmly."

"Oh, if you're beginning to get glumpy, I shall be off," rejoined Fordham; "so good night to you, and when we meet again to-morrow, I hope to find you in a little better humour."

The coiner was too much used to the rollicking ways of Dick Fordham to take any notice of what he said in this instance, and seeing he really meant to be off, he opened the door and bade him good night with as much heartiness as if nothing had happened to disturb the harmony of their meeting. This done, he made up the best bed he could, in one corner of the room, and telling Guy that that was all he could do for him on so sudden an emergency, recommended him to lie down at once, as his next night's lodging was likely to be even less comfortable. The fugitive at once acceded to this proposition, and in spite of the anxiety he felt was soon fast locked in the arms of sleep.

CHAPTER XXI.

AN EARLY VISIT.—THE MAGISTRATE.—LUCK'S EVERYTHING.

EARLY on the morning following the fugitive's last escape, the sergeant and his two men entered the "Seven Horse Shoes," and as Doublechalk had not yet made his appearance down stairs, they walked straight to his bed-room, and shaking him roughly by the shoulders, desired him to dress himself quickly, as he was ordered to appear before the magistrate, to answer certain charges that had been laid against him. The landlord rubbed his eyes, and appeared to be very much astonished at what he heard, but the demand was repeated, and on the second occasion it was accompanied with a threat, that if he did not very quickly obey, he would be carried by main force.

"Upon my word, gentlemen," he at length stammered out, "I haven't the least notion what you mean. I've done nothing that the magistrate can want to see me about, and, if you commit any violence, I shall do the best I can to trounce you, for daring to take into custody a respectable man like myself."

"Respectable!" sneered the sergeant; "you must be a mighty respectable man, truly, to help a felon to escape, when you knew the charges there were against him."

"Felon!" exclaimed Doublechalk; "who are you speaking of?"

"Why, Guy Harrowby, to be sure."

"What do I know about Guy Harrowby?"

"His worship will ask you that question by-and-by," returned the other. "My business is to take you before him, and if you won't go by fair means, you shall by foul, that's all I know about it."

"I suppose you won't object to my dressing myself first?"

"Of course you'll be allowed to do that," said the sergeant, "but we shan't lose sight of you at a moment though."

Doublechalk knew well enough that it would be useless for him to offer any resistance when there were three against one, and, jumping out of bed, he began to dress himself, though not by any means so expeditiously as he might have done under any other circumstances. He was, in fact, rather discomposed by this unexpected visit, and wished to gain as much time as possible, in order to collect his scattered thoughts together. At length, in a tone somewhat more submissive than he had hitherto maintained, he said :—

"Pray, Mr. Sergeant, will you have the kindness to tell me what his worship has got to say to a harmless man like myself?"

"It's not my business to answer questions," exclaimed the officer; "but, as I've mentioned it before, I may repeat that there are reports abroad of Guy Harrowby having been concealed in this house three or four days."

"Who says so?"

"I do."

"What reason have you for it?"

"Quite sufficient to ground an accusation on," answered the sergeant; "when we went into your loft yesterday, in search of the man I speak of, we found the trap-door open, plainly showing that he had been there, and had escaped when he heard us coming up the stairs."

"But you didn't find him there!"

"You needn't tell us that," returned the policeman; "the bird had flown, but he must have made his escape down the trap-door of the next house, for while we were still looking for him, we saw a boat push out into the river, and who should be in it but Guy Harrowby himself."

"The devil!" but what have I to do with that?"

"I rather think it will be proved that you had a great deal to do with it," replied the sergeant; "for I and these two men here are ready to swear that you were in the boat with him."

"Oh! you must have been mistaken," exclaimed Doublechalk, "for my neighbours all know I'm a respectable man, and that I wouldn't be guilty of conniving at the escape of a prisoner. So don't attempt to take me up on such a charge, or I shall bring an action against you for false imprisonment.

"I don't care what you bring an action against me for," said the other, "because I've got a regular warrant to apprehend you, and I'm not to be frightened from my duty by any threats of what you'll do to me afterwards. You must go with us, I tell you, Mr. Doublechalk, and if you don't choose to walk with us quietly, we shall get the stretcher and carry you to the police-office in state."

"Pshaw! what nonsense you are talking," exclaimed the landlord, not half liking this threat; "I've not said I would not go with you, have I?"

"You seemed to doubt our authority to take you."

"Very likely," he replied; and I still think it a great hardship that a respectable man should be roused out of his sleep in this way, because you happen to have taken it into your head that he has done something wrong. What will my neighbours think of me afterwards, when they hear that I've been taken up on a charge like this?"

"If nothing's proved, they'll not think a bit the worse of you for it," answered the sergeant; "but if you have assisted a criminal to escape from justice, you'll deserve all the hardship and exposure that you complain of."

"But you can't swear that I was the other person you saw in the boat," exclaimed Doublechalk.

"I can swear that you are uncommonly like the chap, though," returned the other; "and the two men that are with me are ready to take their oaths to the same effect."

"Ah!" groaned the landlord, "that's because there's a foul conspiracy entered into against me. I have enemies enough in the world, and now they think there's a fine opportunity to bring disgrace and ruin upon me."

"You had better tell the magistrate so when you're before him," returned the other. "It's what people always say when they get into trouble; but when put to the push, they can never prove their words. Besides, what reason can we be supposed to have for making this charge against you?"

"I can see how it is, clearly enough," exclaimed Doublechalk. "This affair mayn't be your doing, perhaps, but there's some one behind that has been trying to do me an injury."

"Who do you mean?"

"A chap named Heathingdon. Maybe, you'll tell me you don't know such a person?"

"I've seen him."

"And spoken to him of course?"

"Yes."

"I thought so; and between you and these other two men the conspiracy has been got up."

"There's no conspiracy at all about it," answered the sergeant.

"The gentleman came to our station-house last night, and had a long conversation with the inspector concerning the escape of Guy Harrowby. Of course, as I was one of the men that had been sent in search of him, they sent for me to ask what I had to say about the matter; and when I hinted my suspicion that you was in the boat with him, they ordered me to come here directly and take you into custody. When we came, however, you were not at home, so we paid you a visit, Doublechalk, at this early hour in the morning, for fear you should take it into your head to be out again when we came."

"An innocent man has no occasion to keep out of the way that I know of," returned the landlord.

"Very true, and if you can prove your innocence clearly, the magistrate will order your immediate discharge."

"Yes; but that won't satisfy people out of doors."

"What difference will that make?" asked the sergeant, "folks haven't a very high opinion of you as it is, for, as in duty bound, I've inquired your character in the neighbourhood, and from all I've heard, there's a pretty general opinion that your house is a receptacle for thieves and other bad characters."

"They'd better let me hear 'em say it, that's all," exclaimed Doublechalk, with well-dissembled anger, "I don't pretend to say that my customers are as respectable as you'd find 'em at the west end of the town, but considering that my house is in Wapping, I mean to say that you won't find a better conducted place in the whole neighbourhood."

"Have you any objection to tell me who those men were that we found sitting in your parlour yesterday?"

"How should I know who they are," demanded Doublechalk, "hundreds come into the house in the course of the day, and a very pretty thing it would be for me to ask 'em their names before I serve 'em with what they want."

"But the men I'm speaking of are very often here?"

"Ah! then they must be some of my regular parlour customers," exclaimed Doublechalk, "I've a good many of 'em; but who the men were that you're talking of, it's impossible for me to say, seeing that I happened to be out when you came."

"So they told us," answered the sergeant, "but that must be a lie, for there's good reason to believe that you were in the loft with Guy Harrowby, and that you showed him the way down some other trap-door to the boat, that afterwards carried you both over the river."

"If you'll take your oath to that, you wouldn't mind swearing anything," exclaimed Doublechalk, "as if a respectable housekeeper, like myself, would mix himself up in a business that was likely to bring him to ruin."

"Well," returned the other, "if you can get the magistrate to believe that it will be all right. But come, I say, Master Doublechalk, we can't be waiting all day; you're trying how long you can be dressing yourself, but it's no go I can tell you, for if you don't stir yourself a little more briskly we'll take you away just in the state you are."

The landlord had indeed been trying to delay the time as much as possible, but this hint was not thrown away upon him, and in two or three minutes afterwards he reluctantly announced that he was quite ready to go with them.

"I don't like going through the streets as a prisoner though," he said, "and I suppose you can so manage it that my neighbours sharn't see that I'm in your custody?"

"Yes, if you promise not to give us the slip."

"How can I do that when I can't leave my house and business?" demanded the landlord.

"Well," replied the sergeant, "upon that understanding you shall have all the favours shown you that's in our power to give. You may walk a little in front of us if you like and then no one will see that you are in custody; but, mind, there must be no attempt to run away, for the moment you do that we shall raise a cry of ' stop thief!' and then must follow all the exposure you are so much afraid of."

Doublechalk expressed his entire willingness to accede to this suggestion, and all now being in readiness, he, followed by the policemen, descended the stairs and passed by the bar without turning his eyes to the right or the left. On reaching the street he proceeded onwards at a moderate pace, and, as ill-luck would have it, met several of his acquaintances, with none of whom he could venture to stop and exchange a word or two, but who he was obliged to pass with a mere civil nod of recognition. All this mortified him exceedingly, and he was just beginning to step out with increased speed when the sergeant tapped him on the shoulder and reminded him of the agreement that had been entered into between them. Poor Doublechalk could only obey in silence; he slackened his pace and the others dropped into their former place, still keeping a close watch lest he should attempt to make his escape. In a little time afterwards they entered the police court, but as a case was just then going on, Doublechalk was placed a little on one side till the examination was concluded. In a few minutes it was over, and then the landlord was placed at the bar trembling for the result of an inquiry that threatened him with such disagreeable consequences.

"What charge have you to make against this man?" asked Mr. Thornley, the magistrate.

"Please your worship," answered the sergeant, "he is accused of having assisted a prisoner, under remand, named Guy Harrowby, to escape from our custody."

"When did this happen?"

"Yesterday, your worship."

"Have you any proof that he was aiding Harrowby to escape?"

"I think I can be positive that he was the man I saw crossing over the river in a boat with him."

"Can you swear that he is the person?"

"I—I—I believe I can," stammered the policeman.

"This evidence is of too loose a character to be admitted," exclaimed Mr. Thornley. "You must either swear that he was the man, or I shall be obliged to dismiss the case."

"These two men were with me at the time," returned the policeman, "and they saw him as well as I did."

"Can they swear to his identity?"

"Why, your worship," answered the sergeant, "we were so far off, that it would be impossible to take an oath about it."

"What was the distance, do you imagine?"

"As near as I can guess, the boat was about two hundred yards from the shore, and we, at the time, were standing on the top of this man's house."

"Was it light at the time?"

"Yes, your worship, as light as it is now."

"But, for all that," said Mr. Thornley, "you would be loth to swear to this being the person you saw in the boat with the man that has made his escape?"

"In my own mind, "I'm certain about its being the person," answered the sergeant.

"Witness," exclaimed the magistrate; "you must be as well aware as I am myself, that I cannot commit any one to trial upon such evidence as this. You are upon your oath, and unless you can state positively that he was the person you saw in the boat, I shall have no other alternative than to direct that he shall be immediately discharged out of custody."

"Will your worship be pleased to remand him till I can get further evidence?" inquired the sergeant.

"Certainly not," replied Mr. Thornley. "I have asked if you can swear that he is the person you saw, and your answer is that you merely believe such to be the fact. Now, whether you are right or wrong, it is impossible for me to decide; and I should myself be liable to dismissal were I to send to jail a man whose identity you are unwilling to swear."

"Your worship," exclaimed Doublechalk, venturing to put in a word now that he saw how favourably matters were going, "these men have dragged me from my home without the least excuse for doing so. I have a character to lose, and my appearance here to-day on such a charge as this, is likely to do me a great deal of mischief."

"What line of business does this man follow?" asked Mr. Thornley of the police sergeant.

"He is a publican, your worship."

"How is his house generally conducted?"

"Very badly, indeed."

"In what respect? Is he open late of nights?"

"Yes, your worship," replied the other, "and his house is always filled with bad characters."

"Humph!" ejaculated Mr. Thornley; "then it argues very little in favour of the police that have charge of that district. If the house is such as you have described, it is a nuisance and abomination to the whole neighbourhood; but, on the other hand, if proper steps were taken, such haunts as these would very soon be put down."

"He's been uttering nothing but falsehoods against me," exclaimed Doublechalk; "for I can assure you, your worship, that there aint a better conducted public-house in all Wapping than mine is. I can bring plenty of witnesses to prove that I never have any but respectable people in the place."

"Yes," said the sergeant, "but then your witnesses would be picked out from some of the thieves and vagabonds that are skulking about the house all night long."

"It's all very well for you to say these things against me," said Doublechalk, "but I know well enough why there's such a dead set made to ruin me. I don't choose to put up with extortion, and for that reason I'm a marked man."

"What is it you mean by not submitting to extortion?" demanded the magistrate. "The insinuation is a serious one, as far as regards the police, and I now ask you for an explanation."

"Well, then, your worship," replied Doublechalk, "the police generally look upon us publicans as so many victims that they've a right to fleece as much as they please; they expect to be supplied with what they want to drink without any charge being made for it, and two-thirds of the people in my line of business submit to it rather than run the risk of being summoned before the magistrates for every trifling thing. In short they're a complete pest, and the sooner their evil practices are put an end to the better."

"If this statement of yours is correct, it certainly ought to be put a stop to without delay," returned the magistrate. "I have heard such things hinted at before now, and it shall be my business to make immediate inquiries into it. However, this has nothing at all to do with the case before me; you are charged with having aided and assisted a criminal to escape, and if any evidence is brought forward to substantiate the accusation it will be my duty to commit you for trial."

A person at this moment forced his way through the crowd and entered the witness-box. It was Charles Heathingdon.

"If you will allow me, sir," he said, bowing to the magistrate, "I can give evidence in corroboration of what has just been stated by the police sergeant."

"Let this witness be sworn," exclaimed Mr. Thornley. And when the customary oath had been taken, he added, "If I mistake not, you were a witness in this court two or three days ago against a prisoner who has since escaped?"

"I was sir," replied Charles; "and I have to complain of the carelessness of the men from whom he was rescued."

"Really, sir," exclaimed Mr. Thornley, "I am not able to give my attention to two or three cases at the same time; the one we have in hand must be heard first, and then, if you have any complaint to make, I shall be most happy to give you every assistance in my power. I suppose, sir, you know that the prisoner on your left is charged with having aided at a subsequent escape of Guy Harrowby, the man against whom you appeared as witness a few days ago."

"I have heard part of the examination," replied Charles Heathingdon.

"Are you able to swear that the accused was the man who was seen crossing over in the boat with Guy Harrowby?"

"That I cannot do," he replied; "for the truth is, your worship, I was not near the place at the time."

"Well, then, I don't see what evidence you can have to give."

"I can confirm the testimony given by the last witness as to the character of the prisoner."

"What do you know of him?" asked Mr. Thornley.

"That he keeps a notoriously ill-managed house."

"Are you in the habit then of frequenting it?"

The blood mounted to the cheek of Charles Heathingdon as he heard the titter with which this question was received, but regaining what composure he could, he at length said—

"I am *not* in the habit, sir, of associating either with thieves or women of bad character."

"May be not," exclaimed Doublechalk, "but you have the credit of having destroyed the character of many a woman that was virtuous enough till she was acquainted with you."

Another suppressed laugh ran through the auditory, and the rage of the libertine could scarcely be kept within bounds at being made a subject for ridicule. The magistrate, however, immediately interposed his authority to put an end to this.

"I will not permit anything to be stated here that is irrelevant to the case," he exclaimed. It is our present object to inquire if there are fair grounds for committing the prisoner on the charge brought against him; but, at present, I must needs confess that the testimony given by the principal witness is anything but conclusive or satisfactory."

"At all events," said Charles, "it can easily be proved that the prisoner who has escaped has been seen to enter the house kept by the man now at the bar."

"Can it be proved," asked Mr. Thornley, "that he was there yesterday when the officers went in search of him?"

"There can't be any doubt of it, your worship," exclaimed the sergeant, "for we found a secret way that led into a loft on the top of the house."

"Well—and was the man there you were looking after?"

"No, your worship."

"Did you find any one else there?"

"Not a soul; but the trap-door was open, and there was every appearance of some one having just left the place."

"And, of course, you examined the roofs of all the houses that were adjoining?" exclaimed the magistrate.

"We did, your worship, but the man was not there; and, presently afterwards, we saw him in a boat, with the person that's now under examination."

"Well," exclaimed Mr Thornley, "I see we are now coming round to the old point; so, to save time, let me ask once more if you are prepared to swear that the prisoner before me is the man you saw with Guy Harrowby?"

"I shouldn't like to swear it, your worship, but ——"

"There's an end of the case then, and the prisoner must be immediately dismissed," exclaimed the magistrate; and, as the next unhappy wretch stepped to the bar, Doublechalk nimbly skipped down and shouldered his way through the crowd of persons that had assembled. On regaining the street, he hurried towards home, where he arrived just as Mike Rowley was coming out at the door.

"Hilloa, old fellow! where the devil have you been?" exclaimed the latter. How is it you've been out all the morning, without leaving word with your people where you was going to?"

"I was obliged to go," answered Doublechalk, with a knowing wink; "but come in, Mike, for I can't tell you what has happened, with all this crowd about us."

The worthy pair then entered the little parlour, and, the door having been closed, Mike Rowley exclaimed—

"What do you mean about being obliged to go? Had you any particular business that you didn't know of last night?"

"It was uncommon sudden," answered Doublechalk: "I was ordered away by three policemen, and nothing would suit 'em but I must go and make my appearance before the beak."

"The devil! What charge had they against you."

"Why, they wanted to make it appear that I had assisted Guy Harrowby to escape from the officers."

"Which, of course, they couldn't prove; or I shouldn't see you here at this moment," said the other.

"They couldn't swear to my being the man they saw in the boat along with Guy," answered the landlord; "and so his worship told 'em their case was broken down, and that I must be discharged out of custody. But they didn't like it, though; and especially Mr. Heathingdon, for I could see him looking as black as thunder, when he found that all he'd been saying was of no manner of use."

"How came he there?" asked Rowley.

"That's more than I can tell," replied the other, "for I didn't know that he was in the court till he all on a sudden stepped up into the witness-box. But there's no accounting for him, you know, Mike, for he's sure to poke his nose into every place when there's any mischief to be done."

"I should like to give him a good sousing in the river," exclaimed Rowley; "and I may do it, too, one of these fine days, if I have an opportunity."

"You'd better by half leave him alone," returned the landlord; "for he's just like a hedgehog—sure to hurt everybody that ventures to touch him. Besides, I gave him a character that he didn't like, and you should have seen his rage when he heard all the people tittering and laughing about him."

"What did you say?"

"Why, I told him that he had the credit of having destroyed the character of many a woman that was virtuous and respected enough before she became acquainted with him."

"And how came you to tell him that?"

"I could'nt help it," replied Doublechalk; "for the infernal scoundrel went and told the magistrate that my house was the resort of thieves and women of bad character."

"The devil he did," exclaimed Mike Rowley, "but what said the magistrate to that? Didn't he tell the police to watch your house more carefully in future?"

"He said something very like it," replied Doublechalk; "and then I up and told his worship what a set of leeches these policemen are to us publicans."

"Which, as a matter of course, he didn't pay any attention to?"

"Oh, yes, but he did though," answered the landlord; "he seemed surprised at what I told him, and said he'd make immediate inquiries; and if there was any truth in it, the practice should at once be put a stop to."

"Well," exclaimed Mike Rowley, "I've been waiting here some time; but little did I think the police had taken you to be examined before a magistrate. It's lucky for you though that they couldn't swear to your being the man that was in the boat along with Guy Harrowby; for, if they could have done that, it's likely enough you'd have been transported for assisting a prisoner to escape from the officers."

"Never mind what *might* have happened," returned the landlord. "I've luckily got off, man; and, what's better still, I'm now certain that there's no evidence to prove my having anything to do with getting Guy Harrowby out of the scrape. By-the-by, I forgot to ask you how it is Fordham ain't shown himself here yet?"

"Why, he's gone to look after another hiding-place for his friend," replied the other.

"Don't he think he'll be safe at Datchet's?"

"He may be safe enough there," answered the other; "but, somehow or another, Peter don't much fancy having him there."

"Why not?"

"Because he's afraid the officers may nose him out; and, if they do that, there'll be an end to the coining business."

"Has Peter Datchet grown such a coward, then?" exclaimed the landlord. "Has he forgot the service I did him, that he must refuse to shelter a poor devil that's in just the same sort of situation that he was?"

"I don't know much about it," answered Mike; "but Fordham called on me early this morning, and told me he was going to find a hiding-place in Blackheath for his friend, and that he should not be back again till he had left him comfortable."

"What place is there about Blackheath where he can hide?"

"I believe they've been thinking of some of the old gravel-pits thereabouts," replied the other. "Dick tells me some of 'em are overgrown with bushes and furze; and, by all accounts, it would puzzle a conjuror to find Harrowby there. So there, old chap, you know as much about the matter as I do; and, if you've no further questions to ask, I'll be off, for there's a little affair coming off to-night that will put me in ready money."

Mike Rowley did not, however, wait to hear whether there were any other questions; but, carelessly humming one of his favourite slang tunes, he left the house, and hurried off to keep an appointment that he had made with Sam Snatch.

CHAPTER XXII.

DICK'S MISSION.—AN ADVENTURE.—THE NEW LODGINGS.

FAITHFUL to his promise, Dick Fordham turned out at an early hour in the morning; and, after calling upon Rowley, took his way to Blackheath, where he had no doubt of finding the sort of place he had spoken of to Guy Harrowby. The task he had undertaken, however, was not to be performed heedlessly, for it was of the greatest importance that he should avoid observation as much as possible; and, in order to effect this object, he kept a sharp look-out to see when any one was approaching, and whenever he saw any one he gave up his search, and pretended to be sauntering about, as if with no particular object in view. In this way he passed three or four hours without finding a place that suited him; but at length, turning into a lane that seemed to be but little frequented, he saw an old pit, so completely overgrown with bushes that it would escape the observation of any person who was not absolutely in quest of such a place. Having satisfied himself that no one was near, he made a close examination, and found that it was about nine feet in depth, with an over-hanging ledge near the bottom that would afford excellent shelter in case of wet weather, and at the same time conceal him in case any one should be inquisitive enough to look down into the pit. Here a few arms-full of heath and broom would form a tolerable substitute for a bed; and, with a few books to read, he thought Guy Harrowby might make himself very comfortable till better lodgings could be procured for him, or an opportunity offered to get him safely out of England. Having thus far satisfied himself, he directed his way towards the cottage of the coiner, there to relate what he had done; and then, when the night was dark enough, to conduct the fugitive to his new hiding-place. Having no wish, however, to be there longer than was necessary, he went into a road-side public house, partly for rest and refreshment, and partly to pass away the time that he knew not otherwise how to dispose. Seating himself in the kitchen, which also served the purpose of a tap-room, he was soon afterwards joined by an old man and woman who appeared to be tramps, the former of whom, saluting Dick Fordham, inquired if he had not seen him two or three hours before on Blackheath.

" Very likely you might," he replied, " for I've been there the greatest part of the day, though I don't recollect seeing either you or the old woman."

" I don't know how you should," exclaimed the tramp, " for we were resting ourselves under some bushes, and I didn't want you to see me, because I'd taken it into my head that something was to be made out of you."

" Something to be made out of me!" returned Dick, startled by the strange tones in which the old man spoke; " did you suppose I had got money to give away to beggars?"

" The devil a bit of it!" he replied; " but I took you for a chap that a reward has been offered for."

" Who do you mean?"

" Why, Guy Harrowby, the convict that has returned from transportation before his time was up."

" And do you still believe that I am him?"

" I think it's very likely," answered the tramp; " and the more so, because you seemed to be looking about the heath to find some place where you might hide yourself."

" Then make up your mind not to receive the reward," exclaimed the other, " for I'm no more Guy Harrowby than you are. I know the chap you're looking for well enough, and, to save you the trouble of trying to get the poor fellow locked up, I can tell you that by this time he's far enough away from here."

" Bless your heart, man, I don't want to harm him," returned the other; " the reward that's been offered is a bit of a temptation, to be sure, and I thought I might as well have it as anybody else; but if he's got clear away I am glad of it, for they'd have put a rope round his neck, I dare say, if it had been his bad luck to fall into their hands."

" And serve him right, too," croaked the old woman, who seemed to be rather disappointed at what she had heard; " they say he's been guilty of murder, and if that's true, I should have thought the money honestly earnt that was received for giving him up to justice."

" Hold your tongue, you fool!" muttered her husband; " don't you hear the chap is far enough off by this time? and as we've no chance of getting the money ourselves, let's hope that he'll not fall into any other hands."

" I don't believe he's so far off as this man says he is," returned the woman, " it's only a trick to put us off our guard, and I wouldn't mind wagering all I've got in the world, that this chap is the very Guy Harrowby that people are making so much talk about just now."

" If you think that," exclaimed Dick, " you'd better give me into custody, and then you'd soon find out what a mistake you've made. I'm as honest as either of you are, I'll be bound, and perhaps you'd have more reasons to be afraid of appearing before a magistrate than I have."

" Pshaw! I don't suppose any of us are too honest, so the less we say about this matter the better," interposed the man; " at first I did fancy you were Guy Harrowby, and no wonder at it, for you seemed to be crawling about the heath as if afraid of being seen by anybody, and I couldn't help telling the old woman that I thought we were in a fair way to get the fifty pounds reward that has been offered."

" And supposing it had been so," asked Dick Fordham, " what good do you suppose the money would have done you?"

" Well, I don't know but what you're right there," exclaimed the man, " for I once knew a chap that received blood-money, and it brought him to the gallows after all."

" How was that?"

" Why, he was never sober while the cash lasted, and when it was gone he couldn't settle himself to do anything in an honest way, so first of all he took to thieving, which led him to commit a murder, and that murder cost the poor fellow his life."

" You say you knew the man?"

" Aye, too well; he was my own son."

" What occasion was there for you to tell him that?" demanded the old woman; " it's bad enough to know the poor fellow was hung, without opening your mouth, like a fool, to everyone, and telling 'em the trouble poor Tom brought on us."

"I'm very glad he told me of it, too," exclaimed Dick Fordham, "for I can now ask you both why you should be so hard upon Harrowby, when, after all, he has done no more than your own son did. You'd have thought it very hard, I dare say, if, when he had found a snug hiding-place, some one had gone and peached against him for the sake of a little money."

"I should have been guilty of murder myself if any one had done such a thing as that," exclaimed the old man; "aye, even if I had been sure of going to the gallows for it I'd have had my revenge if man, woman, or child, had sent the traps to the place where he was to be found."

"If that's your feeling," observed Dick, "I should think you'd rather pity Guy Harrowby, than help the people that like so many blood-hounds, are trying to hunt him to the gallows."

"I always feel more soft-hearted after I've been talking about my poor son," exclaimed the old man.

"And at such times, if you were to see him, I dare say you would not say a word to harm him."

"Not I," returned the other; "to be sure, I and the old woman want money badly enough, and that's what made us think just now of getting the reward."

"And suppose Harrowby, by means of his friends, could raise a small sum to put into your hands—would that induce you to lend your help towards getting him out of harm's way?"

"To be sure it would," exclaimed the woman; "we've no ill-feeling against him, and would rather do our best to get him out of trouble, if he or his friends can afford to pay for our services."

"Do you know of a good place where a man might be concealed for a few days?" asked Dick Fordham."

"Yes," answered the tramp; "and I suppose, by your asking that question, you want it for the man Harrowby."

"I do," whispered the other, looking cautiously round, to see if anybody was listening to them; "so tell me where the place is that you are thinking of."

"My own hovel, where the old woman and I live."

"Whereabouts is it?"

"Oh, a good bit from here," replied the other. "It's in the marshes, about half way down Sea Reach, and there isn't another human dwelling-place within five miles of it. No one ever thinks of landing there either, for it's a cheerless-looking desert, and we've never seen a soul there since the smugglers have been driven away by the revenue officers. We used to have plenty of company when they run there goods there, but now we never see anything, either of them or the coast guard."

"And at that time," said Dick Fordham, "I suppose you were assisting in landing their cargoes?"

"You are right there," answered the other; "it was a rare busy time with us, and we could make plenty of money, as well as spend it. Now, however, we can do nothing more than act the part of a go-between, by taking the news of the arrival of a cargo to the person in London that generally buys it."

"Have you never been suspected?"

"I suppose not, for we've never got into any trouble about it. People don't take us for either more or less than tramps, that travel about for a living in the summer, and dwell nobody knows where in the winter."

"Then you think a man might find concealment for a short time at your place?" asked Dick Fordham.

"I'm sure of it," replied the other, "for as I said before, we're never annoyed by the calls of visitors."

"You seem to be settling this matter very nicely between yourselves," exclaimed the old woman; "but I'd have you know that I must have a voice in it, so before you go any further, I must have some understanding as to what money we are to receive for the trouble and risk we shall have to run."

"That I can hardly tell you, till I've seen some other persons on the subject," replied Dick. "You may depend on it, however, that we shall give as much as we can afford."

"When shall you want him to go to our place?" asked the tramp.

"Directly."

"It can't be for two or three days anyhow," replied the other; "for we're now on our way to London, and it will be that time, at least, before we return home."

"Well then, say the third day from hence," exclaimed Dick Fordham. "If you like, I'll meet you at this house with the chap you'll have to take care of, and if you travel by night there'll not be much chance of his being seen. At the same time, I'll bring you a couple of sovereigns by way of earnest, and you shall have as much more afterwards, as I can manage to get together."

"It mustn't be less than ten pounds in all,'' interrupted the old woman, "or I for one won't answer for his staying long at our place."

"You shall have it, old lady," exclaimed Dick. "I can promise you as much as that, from one or another of his friends, and we must trust to Harrowby paying it back, as soon as he's able. But mind, there must be no false play about it, or you'll bring a nest of hornets about your ears, I can tell you."

"Ah, you need not be afraid of us, if you keep your own part of the promise," said the old woman. "We don't want to see the poor fellow sent to the gallows ; only if we run a risk for him, we expect to be paid for it."

"And suppose, he should be traced there," asked Dick, "would there be any chance of his escaping, think you?"

"Yes," replied the man, "and a very capital one, I can tell you. Our place is close to the river-side, and we've always a boat ready for immediate use, so all he'd have to do, would be to jump into it, and half-an-hour would land him over on the Essex side, where he'd find plenty of places among the marshes to hide himself for at least a month or two."

"That's capital," exclaimed Dick Fordham; "by Jove! it was a lucky thing I fell in with you, for we were hard put to it to find a place for the poor fellow to hide in."

"You couldn't have suited yourself better, anyhow," said the old man, "for although we can't make him very comfortable, he'll have the consolation of knowing he's safe, and that, I take it, is all he wants just at present."

"I'm in hopes you'll not be burdened with his company more than three or four days," returned Dick, "for we only want to keep him snug till we can get a birth for him on board a ship, and then he goes abroad to spend the rest of his days in a foreign land, where it's to be hoped he'll find more peace and quiet than he has in his own country."

"That can be managed easily enough, I dare say," observed the tramp, as he and his wife rose to take their departure. "So remember, three nights hence we shall expect to meet you here, and then your friend can go with us, and we'll give you a direction where to find him afterwards."

Upon this understanding, the old man and woman left the house, and as it now seemed late enough for his purpose, Dick Fordham soon afterwards followed their example, and, having first satisfied himself that no one was watching him, he again resumed his way towards the cottage of Peter Datchet, the coiner. On arriving there, the usual caution was observed by the inmate before he ventured to open the door, and no sooner had Fordham entered, than he anxiously inquired if he was come to take his friend away with him, as he was afraid he could not remain there long without being followed by the people he was trying to avoid.

"Oh, yes, old chap," returned the other, "you may make yourself quite easy about that, I've found a place where he may hide himself without any thanks to you, but mind you, it may come to your turn to want a friend some of these days, and then you'll not find any of your old pals quite so ready to serve you, as they were on a former occasion."

"What more would you have of me?" demanded Peter. "Haven't I given your friend a lodging at the risk of getting myself into trouble?"

"Yes, but d——d unwillingly though."

"That's because I feel inclined to take care of myself rather than of any one else," answered the coiner. "You know what a devil of a thing it would be for me, if it was known what sort of business I'm carrying on here, and I don't want to be sent over the herring-pond again, any more than this other chap does."

"Perhaps not," said the other, "but what have you done with him? How is it I don't see him?"

"He's in the next room," answered Peter Datchet; "there's no saying who may call here, so I thought he had better be where he would not be seen."

Upon hearing this, Fordham opened the door that had been pointed out, and the fugitive immediately came forward.

"You see, old friend, I haven't been worse than my word," exclaimed Dick, "Iv'e had rare trouble to find a place where you may be snug for a little while, and after all, the one I've chosen aint so comfortable as I should have liked."

"Any place will do in my present wretched plight," answered Guy Harrowby; "I feel that my presence here is anything but agreeable to your friend, and I had determined, if you didn't come by ten o'clock to-night, to take my leave of him and chance what might follow."

"What's he been growling at you then?"

"No," answered the fugitive; "he has made me as comfortable as he could, I dare say; but it was easy enough to see that he was afraid of my being followed here, and I'd rather risk myself, than he should get into any trouble on my account."

"Why, there wasn't any fear of his getting into trouble," returned Dick, "no one can guess that you are in this neighbourhood, and what's more than that, I've heard a good many people talking about your escape, and the general opinion seems to be that directly after landing at Rotherhithe, you made the best of your way back to London. That's the place where they'll be looking for you, Guy, and not in this tumble-down old cottage of Peter Datchet."

"That's more than you can answer for," exclaimed the coiner. "It may be all very well for you, Dick, to think there's no danger, but I've a right to look to myself, and to take care not to get into a dilemma that it wouldn't be so very easy to get out of."

"Well, then, make your mind easy, old chap," continued the other; "for I'm going to take him away with me as soon as it is dark enough. I know of a place where he may find a lodging that will do for him just for two or three days; but I shall keep you to the old bargain about supplying him with what food he may require while he stays in this neighbourhood."

"Aye, aye, I'll do that," replied Datchet, "but you must come and fetch what's wanted, you know."

"To be sure I will; my visits will be paid here after nightfall, because it will be dangerous for me to go to him while there's people about."

"And how long do you suppose this is to last?"

"Only till the third night from this," replied Dick Fordham; "he's then to go to a place where he'll be more comfortable."

"Where's that?"

"You mustn't ask any questions," returned the other, "because I only mean to let two or three, besides myself, know that secret. It's a long way off though, and from what I've heard, Guy Harrowby may remain there safe enough till we can find some place or another for getting him out of the country."

"How did you happen to find it?" asked the fugitive; "for it's clear you can't have been any great distance off since you were here last night."

"I don't mind telling you that part of the business," replied Dick, "because there can't be a great deal of harm come of it. The truth is, I met a couple of tramps as I was coming here, and as I found, after being with 'em a little while, that there was no danger of their blabbing a secret like this, I told 'em I wanted a snug place for a friend to hide in till we could do something better or him."

" Then it's all up with me," exclaimed Guy; " for when it's known who I am, they'll be sure to hand me over to justice for the sake of the reward that has been offered for my apprehension."

" You don't suppose I was fool enough to go preaching about the affair till I knew they were to be depended upon?" exclaimed Fordham. " I found that a son of their own had been hanged, and when they heard that you was trying to escape the gallows, they promised to give you shelter till I go down to take you away to some other place."

" Are you sure they'll keep their promise?"

" I don't think there's much fear about it after the bargain we've made," returned Dick. " They're to be paid for what they do, my boy, and if they should play any of their scurvy tricks, I can easily be revenged, by just saying a few things that I happen to know about 'em."

" Oh, if you've got 'em at all under your thumb, that's quite enough," exclaimed Peter Datchet. " That will keep their tongues quiet if anything will, so your friend may trust himself with them, and all I hope is, that he will manage to get out of this awkward business as well as you expect."

" Not many thanks will be due to you for it though," retorted Dick Fordham. " He might have stayed here a few days as well as not; but you must needs take it into your fool's head that he'd be found out, and so the poor fellow must be driven from pillar to post to find a shelter just where he can. But never mind, Doublechalk shall know all about it, and he'll be in a fine passion when he hears that you wou'dn't accommodate his friend after he has done all he could to get you out of the same kind of hobble."

" Tell him what you like about me," said the coiner; " and when all's done, he can't blame me for taking care of myself; besides, I've had him here a whole night and a day, and if that don't look like a wish to serve Tom Doubledot, I don't know what the devil he'd have of me."

" Well, it's no use talking about that, now," exclaimed Dick; " there's a place looked out for my friend just a little way off Blackheath, and for want of a better lodging he must put up with the inconvenience of the one I've found for him. He'll be dull enough though, I'll be bound, all day; so if you happen to have got such a thing in your possession you must lend him a book or two to amuse him."

Peter Datchet hereupon went to a cupboard, and took therefrom three or four tattered volumes that, from their dusty appearance, seemed not to have been used for many a long day. Having knocked them together to beat out the accumulated dirt, he threw them upon the table before Guy Harrowby.

" There's all I've got," he said, " and if you leave 'em behind when they're done with it won't much matter, for as you may see by the dust they've gathered, I don't very often bother my head with reading; they're interesting enough though I dare say, and will both improve and employ the mind of your friend till he comes out of his hiding-place."

" What's this?" exclaimed Fordham, taking up the nearest that came to hand, " humph! the Newgate Calendar, a capital book this, certainly, for a man that's got the fear of the gibbet constantly before his eyes. Couldn't you find him anything better than this to pass away his dreary hours?"

" There's another close by you," replied Peter, " perhaps that may suit him better."

" The Life of Jerry Abbershaw!" exclaimed Fordham, opening it at the title-page. " Your collection of books, old fellow, seems to run all upon one subject; but, I suppose, it's the sort of thing that pleases you better than anything else."

" Such as they are, your friend can take 'em if he likes," said Peter Datchet, " I never look into a book myself, for when my day's work's over I can always find more amusement in a pipe than in anything else."

" Do you go to the public-house to smoke your pipe?"

" Yes, and there's good policy in it too. If I was to stay at home too much the people hereabouts would be making their remarks, and ask all sorts of questions as to who I am and what makes me live here by myself. Besides, if anything should happen to be up it would come to my ears all the sooner, and then I should be the better prepared to guard myself against danger. So now you see, Dick, why it is that I go out sometimes on an evening to mix among my neighbours."

" And I dare say a rum sort of a chap they think you?"

" I don't care what may be thought about me," exclaimed Datchet, " as long as they don't guess the sort of business I'm carrying on here."

" But I should think they must have a notion that things aint exactly as they should be," observed Dick Fordham.

" If there had ever been a thought of that kind," returned the coiner, " they wouldn't have let me remain quite so quiet. The truth of it is, no one troubles his head about me, and that's why I didn't want your friend to be here, when I knew the hue and cry was out against him, and it was more likely than not he would be traced to my house."

" How could that have been if he hadn't shown himself?" asked Dick," " but, never mind, we shall be able to manage this business without your help, and I'm only sorry now that we ever asked a favour of you."

" You talk as if I hadn't good reason for what I've done," exclaimed the other, " don't I know what would be the end of it if once it were known what sort of a game I'm carrying on here

Would there be any mercy shown, think you, and is a man to be blamed for keeping himself snug and quiet when he knows the consequence of a discovery?"

"You have done quite right," said Guy Harrowby, "and so far am I for not blaming you for it, that I am thankful for the shelter you have given me when I was in need of it."

"There now," exclaimed Peter, "you hear how reasonably he can talk about this matter. He seems to be a decent sort of chap enough, and I'm only sorry I can't do anything more for him, but the truth is, I'm afraid; so you may call me coward, or anything else you like, after that."

"And a coward you certainly are, though I little thought ever to call you one," answered Fordham.

"I care nothing for what you say of me," retorted the coiner, "and as for Doublechalk, I can well enough excuse myself to him when next we meet ; if anybody's to blame, it's him, for he'd no business to send here a person that he knew has been searched after in every hole and corner."

"It was more my fault than his," said Guy, "because I had no business to come here to save myself at the risk of bringing you into trouble. However, I'm glad to find that no harm has come of it, and I feel grateful to you for the short time you've let me stop here."

"You've more need to be grateful to Doublechalk," exclaimed Dick Fordham," for if it hadn't been for making use of his name, you might have asked long enough before you would have been suffered even so much as to pass the threshold. But that's neither here nor there now, so tuck the books under your arm, Guy, for it's quite dark enough to set off now, and by the time we get to your new quarters there won't be anybody about to watch our motions."

Harrowby had no objection to offer to this ; and having been provided with a sufficient supply of food to last till the next night, they left the coiner's hovel, and took a narrow lane, where few persons were likely to be met, and which led by rather a round-about way towards Blackheath. As they walked along, they spoke but little, for fear of attracting attention towards themselves ; and on two or three occasions, when they heard people coming along the lane, they crossed to the other side of the hedge, and threw themselves flat on their faces till the strangers had passed on their way. All this served to delay them a good deal : but, at length, they came out into the Deptford-road, when they assumed a bearing of greater indifference, conversing freely as they went along, and acting in every way so as to excite as little as possible the attention of any policeman that they might happen to meet. A short time served to bring them on Blackheath, where they paused to look round them, in order to see if any one was watching ; and having satisfied themselves that all was right, Dick Fordham led the way towards the spot that he had pitched upon as a safe hiding-place for his fugitive friend. About a quarter of an hour served to bring them there ; and Dick, leading Harrowby to the edge of the pit, desired him to look into it.

"I don't know whether you can see quite to the bottom of it," he said ; "but it was quite dry when I was here this morning, and, in my opinion, you may make a very good shift with this lodging till we can get you to a better."

"Is it deep ?" asked Guy.

"About nine feet, I should think."

"But, in case of a heavy rain coming on, I should have no shelter to cover me."

"You'll find a better shelter than you expect when you get down," answered Fordham. "At the bottom a place quite long enough for your body has been scooped out, for some purpose or another ; and that you can make your bed-room at night and a place of shelter in case it should come on to rain heavy. When you are safely landed, I'll throw you down some heath to make up a bed with ; and, as the night's warm enough, I'm much mistaken if you don't get a more comfortable night's rest than you looked for."

"How am I to get down." asked Guy, trying in vain to penetrate the darksome abyss, upon the verge of which he was standing.

"Oh! that's to be done easily enough," replied the other. "You've only to catch hold of some of these shrubs that are growing at the edge of the pit, and then let your body gradually down. You won't have much more than three feet to drop after you leave your hold."

"At any rate," said Guy, "the greater the difficulty the less likely am I to be discovered. So, good-night to you, Dick ; and, when you've thrown down the heath you spoke of, I'll make up my bed under the ledge, and I dare say, my night will be passed quite as comfortable as the last was."

Harrowby then threw his hat and books down into the pit ; and, having shaken hands with his warm-hearted friend, he descended precisely in the manner that had been recommended. Dick then proceeded some little distance to gather a sufficient quantity of heath ; and throwing this down, he inquired of his friend how he liked his new lodgings.

"As far as I can judge," replied Harrowby, "it seems to be dry and comfortable enough for my purpose ; but I shall be glad to change it for a better as soon as possible."

"Have you found the place where I recommended you to make up the bed?" inquired Dick Fordham.

"Yes, and a snug berth enough it seems to be," answered the other.

"How far does it go underground?"

"About five or six feet," replied Guy Harrowby.

"That'll do famously for a hiding-place in case any one should have the curiosity to look down," exclaimed his friend. "There'll be very little chance of your being seen there; so keep yourself out of sight as much as you can, and to-morrow, about this time, I'll come here to see how you're getting on, and to bring you something to eat and drink."

He then withdrew, and Guy Harrowby immediately employed himself in making his dormitory as comfortable as circumstances would permit. This occupied some little time; and, having at length completed his arrangements, he crept into his narrow chamber, well pleased at the prospect of having a good night's rest.

CHAPTER XXIII.

A REPROOF.—FRIENDSHIP IN ADVERSITY.—THE DEFEAT.

NOTHING could exceed the rage and disappointment [of Charles Heathingdon as hour after hour passed away, and yet no tidings could be heard of the man he had sworn to destroy, let the trouble to himself be what it might. Money to a considerable amount he had given in various directions to procure the assistance of those who were most likely to further his object; but still he seemed as far as ever from the accomplishment of his design, and every moment that passed away served to increase his fear that Guy Harrowby would find means to leave England before any clue could be found. Be that as it might, however, he was determined never to relax his efforts whilst the slightest chance remained; and he was just about leaving his hotel to pay another visit to Jane Harrowby, when one of the waiters came to inform him that a gentleman had called who wished to see him. Thinking he might have some information to give respecting the person he was in search of, he desired the visitor to be shown in; and, to his surprise, his father's friend, Major Corfield, entered the room.

"Egad, Charles, I'm glad to have found you at last," exclaimed the officer, as soon as the first salutations were over. "I've searched London pretty well through, and was just going to give up in despair, when, quite by an accident, I heard that you were lodging in this hotel."

"Has anything particular occurred at home, that you've taken so much trouble to find me?" asked Charles.

"No: but Colonel Heathingdon is naturally uneasy at your long absence, and the care you have taken to conceal yourself."

"I have not had a thought of concealing myself," answered Charles; "indeed, so far have I been from wishing to do so, I have been constantly walking about the streets, and visiting all the most public places in the metropolis."

"And all, I dare say, for no other purpose than that you may have your spite against the unfortunate husband of Jane Harrowby."

"You have guessed it, Major Corfield," returned the young man, haughtily; "but I have yet to learn by what authority you take me to task for what I am doing?"

"I assume no authority, young gentleman," exclaimed the major; "but, as a friend of your father's, I take the liberty of saying that the task you have undertaken belongs more properly to a thief-taker, than to the son of a man so honourable and so justly esteemed as Colonel Heathingdon."

"The reproach, if deserved at all," retorted Charles, "would have come much better from my father than from yourself. I know Guy Harrowby to be a returned convict, and have good grounds for suspecting that he has been guilty of a murder, so that I have done nothing more than my duty in assisting as much as lies in my power to cause him to be apprehended."

"That may be all very well as far as it goes," exclaimed the major, "but I happen to know there is another motive, which nothing you can say will palliate. The man's wife happens, most unfortunately, to have attracted your notice, and because she has had virtue enough to resist your dishonourable advances, both she and her husband are to be hunted and persecuted till your revenge has been gratified."

"Did my father send you here to admonish me," asked Charles Heathingdon, "or am I to understand that you have voluntarily taken the task upon yourself?"

"Your father would have come instead of me," answered Major Corfield, "but I saw how angry he was, and fearing lest a quarrel should take place, I came to see if a little gentle remonstrance would turn you from your purpose."

"Really, major," exclaimed the other, impatiently, "your advice might have been spared till I asked you for it; I feel no inclination to listen to your lectures, and shall, therefore, be obliged by your changing the subject of our conversation.

"My dear sir, I have not come here to offend you by giving my advice, but to recommend some other course that will be more honourable to you. And now we are upon this subject, I would be permitted to ask if you are aware that Jane Harrowby has suddenly left her home?"

"I know she is now in London."

"Was it through any persuasion of yours that she came?"

"I have had no more to do with it than you or anybody else," replied Charles. "She has come,

I believe, to seek her husband, and I have strong reasons for believing that she knows where he has concealed himself."

"Suppose she does know it," exclaimed the major; "would you have the woman betray her husband, when she is so well aware of the fate it would lead him to?"

"The law would make her do so, if I was only certain that she possesses the knowledge that would lead to his discovery. She would not be allowed to defeat the ends of justice, even though it may go against the grain to say where he is."

"All that may be true enough," exclaimed the major; "but if the woman has any love for her husband she will not be frightened into an admission that she is aware of his hiding-place. Indeed, from what I have heard of the female, she has sufficient strength of mind to resist every attempt that may be made to intimidate her into assisting to send her unfortunate husband to the gibbet."

"Upon my word, Major Corfield," retorted the young man, "you appear to feel a great deal of interest in behalf of this most notorious malefactor! That he is a murderer there can be no doubt, and yet I verily believe you would rather see him get off without punishment than assist to give him up to those who have the administering the laws."

"You are right enough there, Charles," replied the other, laughing, "for I have no ambition to become an amateur officer of justice, when there are so many more honourable ways of employing myself. If the laws are outraged, there are people enough whose business it is to look after the offenders without my interfering in matters that don't concern me."

"Then you think I am wrong for having exerted myself to procure the punishment of this man?"

"I think you have taken a great deal of unnecessary trouble, considering you have nothing to do with the matter," replied Major Corfield; "nor am I singular in that opinion, for your father is much annoyed at your conduct, and he desired me to say that he wishes you to return home immediately."

"Two or three days hence I will obey him," answered Charles, "by that time, I dare say, Guy Harrowby will be safely lodged in a prison, and, my task being ended, I shall have no further desire to remain in London."

"Have you any grounds, then, for supposing that you are likely to obtain a clue to Harrowby's hiding-place?"

"Most certainly," returned Charles; "I have told you that I suspect the secret is known to his wife, and I am resolved, if there is no other way left, to intimidate her into confessing where he may be found."

"You know where she is to be found then?"

"Yes: I followed her the other night to her lodging, and have since had an interview with her."

"What, upon this subject?"

"I have no other reason for seeing her now," replied Charles Heathingdon, "she has treated my attentions with scorn, and whatever love I may once have felt is now turned into scorn and indifference. Had she acted otherwise, Major Corfield, she would not have had to rank me amongst the most inveterate of her husband's enemies."

"That, young man, is a confession that reflects little credit on you," exclaimed the major; "you have been guilty of great immorality in paying your addresses to a married woman, and the offence is rendered even more serious by the feelings of revenge her rejection has given rise to. Have you thought of the disgrace an exposure must bring upon you?"

"From whom can the exposure come?"

"From the woman herself," answered Major Corfield; "she may, perhaps, be quiet about the matter, at present, but if once her husband is shut up in a prison, all motives for secrecy will be at an end, and she will then expose the reasons that have induced you to become her inveterate and untiring persecutor."

"She can prate whatever she pleases," exclaimed Charles Heathingdon, "for the world will scarcely heed what she says against one who has never yet been the subject of calumny. My character, Major Corfield, whatever you may think about it, is not to be destroyed by anything this woman may say against me."

"For the sake of your father I am rejoiced to hear you say so," replied the officer, "he, I know, would take it much to heart were you to disgrace the name you bear, for he is jealous of his honour, and nothing would cause him deeper affliction than to hear that you have done aught to bring down upon yourself the disapprobation of the world."

"He has no reason to be alarmed on that account," said Charles, "for I am as careful of my honour as he can be of his own. As for this affair, I consider it my duty to assist all in my power to apprehend a criminal, and nothing that you have yet said will alter either my opinion or the determination I have formed."

"You are a younger man than myself, Mr. Heathingdon," exclaimed the major, "and your small stock of experience will not enable you to judge properly in an affair of this kind; however, my advice does not seem to be received in the same kindly spirit that it is given, and for the present, therefore, I will say nothing more about it. If I understood rightly, you are going on a visit to Mrs. Harrowby?"

"I am."

"Will you permit me to accompany you?"

"I have no objection in your doing so," replied Charles, "for the only motive I have in view is to discover whether she has any knowledge of her husband's hiding-place."

"Why persist in demanding that of her," asked Major Corfield, "when she has already declared that she is entirely ignorant upon that subject?"

"Because I am unwilling to throw away any chance," said the other; "I have made up my mind to pursue this matter till my object has been gained, and I do not think Jane Harrowby will stand out much longer, when she knows that her obstinate silence will not have the effect of preventing the punishment her husband so justly deserves."

"I shall myself hear what she says," returned the major; "and perhaps, hen you have received her answer, you will be guided by my advice?"

"That will depend upon whether it accords with my own opinion," exclaimed Charles; "your interference may be well intended, Major Corfield, but, to tell you the truth, I would much rather have been without it."

"Perhaps you would, also, rather that I did not accompany you to her house to-day?" returned the other.

"I should have been glad if you had not made the proposition," answered Charles Heathingdon, "but, as you have done so, I shall not think it worth my while to offer any opposition to it."

"Under those circumstances," exclaimed the major, "I shall not think of going with you. In the evening I will call here again, and then, perhaps, you will have no objection to acquaint me with the result of your interview?"

This proposition was gladly acceded to by the young man, and as soon as the major had taken his leave, Charles Heathingdon snatched up his hat and left the hotel to pay his unwelcome visit to the convict's wife.

We must now return to Jane Harrowby, who, after waiting in the greatest anxiety and doubt, was agreeably surprised by a visit from Dick Fordham, who, to save her suspense as much as possible, announced at once that her husband was in a place of safety, and with every prospect of getting clear away from his pursuers. This intelligence was most consolatory to Jane, and, having first opened the door, to see if Mrs. Toddy was listening, she inquired where her husband was concealed, and whether there was any possibility of her seeing him.

"I sha'nt tell you where he is," exclaimed Dick; "because if anybody should ask about him, you can tell 'em with a good conscience, that you don't know. And as for seeing him, you must'nt think of doing that till we've got him all right and safe out of this country."

"Is he far from here?"

"No, not above four or five miles; but he'll be a good bit further off before long. We're obliged to shift him about you know, Mrs. Harrowby, for fear any one should happen to find out where we've taken him."

"Is he safe, think you, among the people he is with?"

"He aint in a place with any one," replied Fordham, "so of course there can't be anything to fear on that account."

"When did you see him?" inquired Jane.

"Last night," he replied; "and I'm going to him again as soon as it's dark enough. Luckily, there's no moon just now, so I can go to him without any fear of being seen."

"You have indeed been a kind and faithful friend to him," exclaimed Jane, wiping away the tears, that she found it impossible to restrain.

"Why, as for that, ma'am," returned the other, "it would have been hard indeed, if I'd turned my back on him when he was in the midst of his troubles. It's bad enough for him to be hunted about as he is, and if one pal won't help another when he's in need of assistance, he don't deserve to find a friend if he should ever happen to want one."

"And there are others, I believe, besides youself, who have assisted in keeping him out of harm's way."

"Yes," replied Dick, "and jolly good trumps they've proved themselves, too, for though a large reward has been offered for the discovery of your husband, there isn't one of 'em that's been rogue enough to turn against him. The other day, too, when they were taking him back to the police-office, we managed among us to rescue him, and from that time to the present neither Mr. Heathingdon nor any one else has been able to discover him. To be sure, they pretty nearly had hold of him the day before yesterday, but we got him into a boat, and he was over on the other side of the river before the infernal police could come within reach of him."

"You spoke of Mr. Heathingdon," said Jane; "are you aware whether he is still in pursuit of him?"

"Aye, he's as hotly after him as ever he was," replied Dick, "but he may as well give up the chase, for there's plenty of us to lend a helping hand against him; and, if things should come to the worst, I'd no more mind shooting the scoundrel than I would a dog."

"For Heaven's sake, let there be no bloodshed," exclaimed Jane, earnestly. "Save my husband, if possible, but let not a life be lost in your efforts to do it."

"Why, surely you can't feel any pity for such a scoundrel as this Charles Heathingdon seems to be?"

"I have little reason to regard him with kindness," answered Jane; "but, ruthless as he has ever proved himself to be, I would not for the world have his life sacrificed."

"What!" exclaimed Fordham, "not if there was no other way to save him from the clutches of his enemies?"

"It may be avoided by keeping him out of sight till the search begins to flag," answered Jane Harrowby. "You say there is no fear of his being discovered at present, and it may happen that in a short time we shall have an opportunity of getting him abroad."

"I hope so," returned Dick; "for the poor fellow can't be very comfortable as it is, and the sooner we get him out of England, the sooner will he begin to find the comfort of a little rest and quietness."

"What part do you think of taking him to?"

"That's quite uncertain at present," answered Fordham; "because, it will depend upon what vessel we can get to take him over the water. For my own part, I should prefer Holland, for the simple reason, that the government wouldn't suffer him to be taken away, if at any time our English officers were to follow him there."

"Wouldn't they afford him the same protection in France?"

"Yes: but he wouldn't be able to find any work there, I'm afraid," answered Dick. In Holland he'd be sure to get employment; and then you might join him there, with the young 'un, and things would have a chance of going on more comfortably than they've done for some time."

"It matters not to me where he goes to, so that we can but find peace and safety," she exclaimed. "It is so long since I have known what happiness is, that I could now be content with any secure home, even though it was in a wilderness."

"Aye," answered the other, "a wilderness might do, as far as that goes; but you know, Mrs. Harrowby, you'll want something to keep the pot boiling. Now, Guy is as well able to work as ever he was in his life; and, as he means to turn out a steady and industrious chap, the best thing he can do will be to go where he may pick up a decent livelihood."

"Your words afford me more consolation than I have felt for some time," exclaimed Jane; "and most anxiously shall I look forward to the time when I may rejoin my husband, no matter where it may be. The labour that supports us, however, shall not be all his: for I will assist him in his work; and, whilst my mind is so employed, I may perhaps forget the troubles that have so severely afflicted me."

"Well, it's a long lane that has no turning," observed Fordham; "so I dare say you'll find your reward for the worry and anxiety you've gone through. As for Guy, he'll be quite in spirits when he hears that you are happier than when I last saw him; and, as I shall see him to-night, I'll let him know that you're looking forward to better days."

Mrs. Toddy at this moment came bustling into the room, and, in great alarm, informed her lodger that she had just seen Mr. Heathingdon walking up and down in front of the house.

"He seems as if he was going to knock at the door," she continued; "and I ran down to tell you, that I might know whether to send him away or not."

"Tell him I am not at home," exclaimed Jane, in alarm. "He comes but to threaten me, and at this moment, I feel but ill prepared to endure his violence."

"If you'll let me be present," interposed Dick Fordham, "I can promise you there shall be no danger from him. I'll hide myself in this cupboard," he added, opening the door as he spoke, "and then, if he should come any of his nonsense, I'll make my appearance, and send him to the right-about."

"That's a capital thought of yours any how," exclaimed Mrs. Toddy, delighted at this suggestion, "and I think when he finds that this poor creature aint without friends to take her part, he'll not hunt her up quite as much as he's been doing lately."

"He'd better not, I can tell him," returned Dick Fordham, "for I owe him something already, and if he don't mind what he's about, I shall pay him off before he goes away from this house."

"Let there be no violence offered to him, I entreat you," cried Jane Harrowby, earnestly.

"That'll depend upon whether he deserves it or not," returned the other; "for if once he puts my blood up, he must take the consequences, that's all I know about it. I shall hear all that passes, and it will be his own fault if I happen to deal with him more roughly than he likes."

"Be calm with him, I implore you," said Jane, "or I shall be sorry that you were in the place when he came."

"I hope there'll be no occasion for you to be sorry, ma'am," returned Fordham; "but if he drives me to it, he must put up with whatever happens. If he don't come to frighten and bully you, I sha'n't make my appearance at all; but if I hear anything like threats, he had better look out for squalls, because I shall never be able to keep my temper when I hear him blustering and railing against a poor unprotected woman."

"If I may judge from what he has done before, I don't think he'll come for anything else," exclaimed Mrs. Toddy. "I was present the other day part of the time that he was here, and if I'd been a man, he should have been shown the other side of the door in less than no time."

"Why didn't you send out for a policeman?" asked Dick.

"Because I saw this good woman didn't wish me to do so," replied the landlady. "Of course,

I didn't know what reason she might have for it, as he had it all his own way, and when he got tired of railing at her, he marched himself off."

"Well," exclaimed Dick, "he'd better not give her any of the rough side of his tongue to-day, I can tell him, for if he does, there'll be such a storm about his ears that he wont be likely to forget in a hurry, I can tell him."

"Again I repeat my request that you will not get into any quarrel on my account," cried Jane Harrowby; "as it is, I have found him a cruel and relentless enemy, and he will be still more so

should you do or say anything that may give rise to his anger. This I unfortunately know from experience, and I dread to think of the mischief he may do if he should take it into his head that he has been insulted through me."

"As for that," returned Fordham, "I don't see that he can do anything more than he has already. The scoundrel swears that he'll never rest till he's brought your husband to the scaffold, and if we may judge from what he's done already, we may believe that he means to be as good as his word."

A loud double-knock was now heard at the door, and Mrs. Toddy opening the cupboard door, begged of Dick Fordham to hide himself at once, and by no means to come out till the visitor was gone, unless he found that there was any occasion to do so. This he promised to attend to; and no sooner had he concealed himself than the landlady hastened to let in the newly-arrived visitor. As Charles Heathingdon entered the room, she followed him; but with an impatient gesture he desired her to retire, though not without muttering at the impudence of some people, who ordered *other* people about as if they considered them mere nobodies. Charles saw the terror which his presence had inspired in the unfortunate woman he had come to visit, and seating himself opposite to her, he said, sternly—

"I suppose, Mrs. Harrowby, there's no occasion for me to explain the motive that has brought me here to-day?"

"I can guess your object," she replied, "but my mind remains unaltered since I last saw you."

"You are determined then not to reveal the place where your husband is hiding himself from those that seek him?"

"Really, Mr. Heathingdon," she replied, "you are mistaken in supposing that I know where he is; I am as ignorant of that fact as yourself; and it is my wish to remain so, since it places me beyond the reach of your threats."

"'Tis false!" he exclaimed furiously; "you must surely know where he is, and to certain am I of it, that I am now resolved not to leave this house till you have told me."

"Won't you, indeed!" cried Mrs. Toddy, opening the door a little way, and just popping in her head; "you are rather bounceable, sir, it seems to-day; and, can tell you the young woman has friends about her that you don't expect."

"I have desired you to leave the room."

"Very well, and haven't I done so?" asked Mrs. Toddy; "I know you told me to leave the room, but I shall listen outside the door if I like, and you shan't hinder me."

And with this, the old lady retired, but it was only to resume her former situation, where she could overhear all that took place.

"I would not advise you to place any reliance upon the assistance that person may have promised you," said Charles, in a lower tone than he had yet used; "the object I have in view is perfectly justifiable, and it may be as well to remind you, Mrs. Harrowby, that there are means within my reach to compel you to reveal the secret of your husband's hiding-place."

"You have heard me declare before," she exclaimed, "that I know not where he is, and even if I did, it would not be my duty to turn informer against my husband."

"Were it your own child," returned the libertine, "the law would compel you to assist in his apprehension. If you still refuse to say where Harrowby is, you will be taken before a magistrate, and there charged with aiding to conceal a criminal from the justice he has too long evaded."

"Your threats cannot move me, sir," she replied, "because even if I could be base enough to betray my husband, it is luckily out of my power to say where he is."

"Do you mean to tell me, then, that you have not seen him since your arrival in London?" asked Charles.

"As Heaven is my witness! I have not."

"Neither have you had the curiosity, I suppose, to inquire where he has secreted himself?" demanded the other.

"I certainly have asked that question," she replied, "but those that could have told me, refused to do so in order that I might swear with a safe conscience that the affair is as great a mystery to me as it is to yourself, or anybody else."

"Who are the persons that have refused to tell you?"

"That is a question that I shall not answer," replied Jane.

"Remember, you may be made to do so."

"I know of no power that can compel me," she answered.

"Why are you so obstinate?" asked Charles Heathingdon, "when you must be well aware that your silence cannot retard the discovery of your husband more than a few hours. It may be natural enough for you to wish to screen him from the consequences he has brought upon himself; but you owe obedience to the laws of your country, and, if you break them, the consequences will be heavier than you perhaps imagine."

"Your words will not frighten me into compliance," replied Jane; "for the duty a wife owes to her husband is, in my opinion, quite equal to that which she owes to the laws. You appear to believe, sir, that I may be forced into a confession; but the last few days have served to convince me that I am not without friends, as well as enemies, in this dark hour of trouble and adversity."

"Friends you may have," exclaimed the libertine, "but they are not such as can render you a service, if once I am compelled to take you before a magistrate."

"If you desire that I should appear in a police-office I will accompany you of my own free will," she replied. "I have done nothing to be afraid of, though you have yourself cause to shrink, if I explain the base motives that have induced you to persecute and annoy me."

"Such a charge would not be listened to," returned Charles; "for it would at once be imagined that it was only done in spite for the course I have adopted. My own word would be sufficient to convince the magistrate of the groundlessness of such an accusation; and my next step would be to press for your remand, if I could produce further evidence to prove that you have connived at concealing an escaped convict from the punishment of his crimes."

Dick Fordham could hardly restrain himself three or four times from rushing out of his hiding-place; but he wished to hear still more of the libertine's villany, and he, therefore, remained where he was—vowing, within himself, to punish Charles on the very first occasion that might offer itself. As for Jane Harrowby, the threats that were uttered had very little effect upon her; and, assuming an appearance of as much courage as she could command, she said—

"I suppose, Mr. Heathingdon, you will now leave me? I have answered you: and neither threats of danger, nor promises of favour will ever alter my determination."

"This obstinacy will but bring upon you misery that might be avoided," exclaimed Charles. "Hitherto I have tried to prevail upon you by fair means; but now, unless you give the information we want, I shall charge you with aiding and assisting the escape of a felon; and, when once that step is taken, there will be no way left for me but to proceed to extremities."

"For myself, I care not what you do," she cried; "but for my child I do most earnestly implore you to pause, ere you send him, as well as his mother, to prison."

Overcome by her terror, Jane Harrowby snatched up her sleeping infant, and fell upon her knees before the heartless libertine, who had thus worked upon her most tender feelings. This was too much for the patience of Dick Fordham; and, bursting out from his hiding-place, he raised Jane from the lowly attitude she had assumed, and, casting a threatening glance toward her persecutor, exclaimed—

"You may think this all very fine," Mr. Heathingdon, "but you've carried on this game long enough; and, if you don't take yourself off in double quick time, I'll give you such a mauling that your own mother should'nt know you."

"Who are you that dares threaten me?" demanded Charles, hardly able to restrain an impulse he felt to strike the person against whom he was so unexpectedly confronted.

"It matters very little who I am," retorted the other: "I'm here to protect this woman; and, if you don't leave this house directly, I shall do something more than merely threaten."

"Scoundrel!" vociferated the libertine, "you shall be made to repent this insolence, if there's any law or justice in the land."

"I'm no more a scoundrel than you are," answered Dick; "so, don't come to calling names, or I shall lose my temper, and you'll have good reason to repent it."

"The repenting will rather be on your side than mine," exclaimed the libertine; "for I suspect you are one of those that rescued Guy Harrowby; and, if I am right in my conjecture, you will have a chance of paying a visit to the inside of Newgate."

"And, if all people had their deserts, it would not be very long before you found yourself in the same place," cried Mrs. Toddy, who had entered the room as soon as she heard Dick Fordham leave his hiding-place. "You thought to have it all your own way, I'll be bound; but this poor creature aint quite so friendless as you thought, and you'll have to leave my house no better than you came."

"Your triumph will not be a very long one," exclaimed Charles; "though! I may have been thwarted by the presence of this meddling fool. However, I shall now apply to the magistrate for a warrant, and Mrs. Harrowby may expect in a few hours to make her appearance in a police-office."

Having uttered this threat, Charles Heathingdon turned away, with a look of mingled scorn and hatred; and, with inexpressible satisfaction, Mrs. Toddy closed the door upon the unwelcome visitor.

"Thank goodness, he's gone at last," she said, on returning to the room, "but he seems in a terrible passion though, and if he does what he threatened, I don't know what'll become of my poor lodger and her helpless babe."

"Don't be afraid about them, old lady," said Fordham; "because there is no fear of his going for a warrant: and, even if he did, no magistrate would grant one, unless he could give good reasons for accusing Mrs. Harrowby of aiding to conceal her husband. Not but what he'd be glad to do her a mischief, if he only knew how to go to work."

"Do you think she had better move away to other lodgings?" asked the landlady.

"It would be about the worst thing she could do; for then people would be sure to say, 'she knew her guilt, else she wouldn't so easily take the alarm.' No, no, Mrs. What's-your-name, she must stay where she is, for the present, and I'll keep a good look-out to see that no harm befal her."

"I fear you will take upon yourself more than you can perform," said Jane Harrowby. "You have already undertaken to assist my husband in making his escape, and all your attention will be required to save him from his enemies."

"Well," he replied, "if I can't look after you myself, I can find plenty of people that'll gladly lend a helping hand to assist the wife of Guy Harrowby, when she's in danger of being run down by a piratical scoundrel, like this Mr. Heathingdon. So be of good heart, Mrs. Harrowby, and by-and-by things will look more smilingly than they do at present. You shan't be lost for the want of friends, anyhow; and as this old lady seems to have a kind heart towards you, I think we may fairly expect to come off with flying colours at last.   But I must be off now; for I've some distance to walk, and Guy will begin to fancy I've forgot the promise I made to see him to-night."

Jumping from his seat Dick Fordham bade the two females good bye, and was out of the house in a moment.

CHAPTER XXIV.

THE SOLITARY.—A FRIENDLY VISIT.—FUTURE ARRANGEMENTS.

WHEN Guy Harrowby awoke in the morning, he found himself stiff from his long exposure to the air, and he could not but confess to himself, that his bed had been a far more uncomfortable one than he had expected.   Still, the recess in which he had rested himself would afford an excellent retreat in case strangers should happen to pass by the pit; and he had, besides, the consolation of knowing, that his sojourn there would not be of any very long duration.   Yet, he knew, alas! that he would have many other dangers to encounter, before he could entirely free himself from the pursuit of those who were in search of him ; and, though every reliance was to be placed upon his friends, there were so many chances against him, that at times he almost resolved to surrender himself up, rather than prolong the misery to which he had been reduced.

When he had eaten some of the food that he had brought from the cottage of Peter Datchet, his next resource was to read one of the volumes lent to him by the same worthy.   But the Newgate Calendar offered little amusement to a man in his situation, and when he passed from that to the life of Jerry Abershaw, he found that it was but a repetition of the same crimes, and hair-breadth escapes.   Then the day was a miserably tedious one to him, and as it drew towards a close he looked forward with some satisfaction to the promised visit of Dick Fordham, from whom he hoped to hear news of his wife.   But the day was not destined to pass over without alarm, for on a sudden, he was startled at hearing the voices of two men talking together, near the edge of the pit, and from the conversation that passed between them, he learnt that they were a couple of cricketers who had been playing near the place, and who were looking for a ball that had been struck beyond the bounds.

"Are you sure it came as far as this, Jackson?" asked one of the men of his companion.

"Oh, yes," replied the other, " I am sure it came plain enough through that hedge, but where it went to afterwards I don't know, unless it bounded into this old gravel pit."

" What say you to one of us going down, to see if it's there ?"

" You can do as you like about it, Collins," replied the other, " but I am not going to risk my neck just for the sake of a rubbishing cricket ball, that's hardly worth a shilling when we find it."

This latter declaration was heard with no little satisfaction by Guy Harrowby, who, as soon as he was aware of his danger, had crept for concealment into the recess, where he had slept. The men, however, continued their search, till one of them exclaimed impatiently—

" What's the use of wasting our time any longer, when the game's waiting for us?   For my own part, I shall go back and see if any of our chaps have brought another ball."

" There isn't another, and that's why I want to find this one," answered Jackson.   " It can't be very far off, that's certain, so let's have another look, for I dare say it's run into some of the bushes that grow round this pit."

" More likely it's gone into the pit itself," returned the other ; " so just hold my hat, will you, while I lay myself down and look to see if it's at the bottom."

Guy Harrowby drew himself to the very furthest extremity of the recess, to avoid being seen. Every moment he expected that the prying eyes of the man would detect him, and it was with no little satisfaction that he at length heard him declare, that he could scarcely see the bottom for the shade that was thrown down by the trees and bushes that overhung the pit.

" And if it is there," said Jackson, " we may consider it as good as lost, for neither of us are inclined to go down, so we must go back and tell our companions that the game must be finished another time."

" I say," exclaimed Collins, who was still peering into the depth below, " what a famous place this would be for a man who wanted to hide himself.   Anybody might be here for a twelvemonth without a chance of being found out."

" And nice quarters he'd find there I should think, from the look of the hole," returned his companion.   " A fellow must be hard put to it, if he went down there for the sake of hiding himself."

" Yet, for all that, I shouldn't wonder if some one has been there," said Collins.   " You may laugh at my fancying it, but 'any port in a storm,' you know, and people don't expect to find a palace when they want to conceal themselves."

" Why, you're looking down there as if you really saw somebody," exclaimed Jackson,

half in

joke, and half in earnest. "What makes you keep staring into the place so? Is there any one there, old fellow?"

"Not that I know of," replied the other; "but there's a queer-looking place hollowed out at the bottom, and if you wouldn't mind going down as well, I should uncommonly like to go and have a peep, just to satisfy my curiosity."

"Catch me at it, that's all!" exclaimed Jackson; "I've no fancy for going into such dark, dreary-looking places, or, if you mean to have a search down there, you must go by yourself, for the deuce a bit will I accompany you."

"Then there's an end of it for the present," returned Collins, rising from his recumbent position, "but I don't mean to say that I shant go down to-morrow or next day, if I can find any one with more pluck than you have."

What answer was made to this Guy Harrowby did not hear, for the two men moved away, and when all was perfectly quiet again he crawled out from his hiding-place, glad once more to breathe a somewhat purer atmosphere than he had found in the narrow recess in which he had crept for concealment. Looking upwards, he saw that the shades of evening were rapidly drawing on, and as no other strangers were likely to intrude upon his privacy at that hour, he seated himself on a stone, anxiously waiting the moment when Dick Fordham was to make his promised appearance. His mind, however, was far more uneasy than ever it had been before, for the last words of one of the speakers announced to him the probability of a visit, and in that case, only two alternatives would remain for him, as he must either submit to be captured without offering resistance, or, in a desperate struggle, run the chance of sacrificing another life.

Thus now, in this retired spot, did he find himself in as much danger as ever he had been, and as weary did he feel of plunging from one difficulty into another, that he was almost tempted to clamber out of the pit and surrender himself at once into the hands of justice. Upon further reflection, however, he thought it would be better to wait till he saw Fordham, whose advice was generally worth taking, and to act upon whatever opinion he might give upon the subject. Whilst these and other uneasy thoughts were passing through his mind, the darkness of night closed in, and after waiting nearly another hour in the most restless anxiety he began to think that something had occurred to prevent the promised visit of his friend. His thoughts were then directed to all sorts of reasons, probable and improbable, that might have given occasion to the delay, and just when his fears had become most excited he heard the well known voice of Dick Fordham hailing him from the pit's mouth. The heart of the fugitive leaped within him as this sound reached his ear, and scarcely had he replied to the hail, than the latter let himself down from the top, and placed himself by his side.

"Well, old fellow, here you are all safe and sound, I see," he exclaimed, taking Guy's hand; "you've passed one day and night without discovery, as there's no reason why you shouldn't get yourself comfortably out of this scrape."

"There's more reason to be afraid than you fancy," answered the other; "for not long ago two men were standing just upon the brink of the pit, and if one hadn't been an arrant coward, his companion would have come down."

"The devil he would! Do you happen to know whether he suspected anyone was concealed here?"

"He said it was just the place where a man might hide himself," answered Harrowby, and from what he said, I at one time thought he was sure to come down; however, good luck was once more on my side, and they went away, but I'm not quite sure whether I may not have a visit from them again before long."

"If they do come you must quiet 'em, that's all I can say about it," exclaimed Dick Fordham; "self-defence, you know, will justify a man in almost everything, and of course you won't suffer yourself to be easily taken, when you know what will be the consequence of your capture. But what the deuce, Guy, brought the chaps so near to your quarters?"

"From what I could overhear," replied the fugitive, "they were a couple of cricketers, who having lost their ball, came here to look after it, and while doing so they came to the edge of the pit, and then they took it into their heads that it must have fallen down here."

"I wonder they didn't come to look for it."

"So they would," answered Guy; "but one of 'em didn't half fancy the dismal appearance of the place, and all the other could say didn't have the effect of convincing him that there was nothing to be afraid of."

"And what did you do with yourself all the while?"

"I crept into my dog-hole and lay there, expecting every minute to be dragged forth," replied Guy.

"Did they stay very long?"

"Not more than a quarter of an hour, perhaps, but to me it seemed to be an age."

"It's well for 'em I didn't come while they were here," said Dick, "for if I had I should have made some excuse for a quarrel with them, and then I know how it would have ended."

"And so do I," observed Harrowby, "for it would either have led to my apprehension, or I must have fled from here before any other hiding-place was provided."

"Well, never mind, my boy," exclaimed his friend, "you've had an awkward chance it seems. but as its ended much better than it might have done, I give you joy of your happy deliverance from danger. So now let's talk of others a bit; and in the first place, Guy, I must tell you, I have seen your wife and the young 'un."

"Ah! and are they both safe and well?"

"Yes; but the old 'oman has been terribly frightened though."

"By whom?"

"Why by Charles Heathingdon to be sure."

"The villain!" exclaimed Guy Harrowby, "I hoped, Dick, that I should have been saved the shedding of his blood, but he does all he can to drive me on to desperation. If he confines himself to hunting me about like a wild beast I can forgive him; but if he turns his spite against my wife, alas! he must take the consequences of his own evil deeds."

"You may trust all that to my management," answered Dick, "for, rough spun as I am, hang me if I'll see a woman ill-used without taking her part."

"Where did he meet with her?"

"At her own lodgings, where I happened to be at the time, to tell her that you were safe."

"And did he threaten her in your presence?"

"Yes," answered Dick Fordham, "but he didn't know I was so near to him though. The truth of it is, we had notice of his coming from the landlady, so, by her advice, I hid myself in a closet, where I listened to all that passed, and where at length she threw herself upon her knees to him to ask for mercy to her child; I rushed out of my hiding-place, and its lucky for him that there were females present, or he might, perhaps, never have gone out of the house alive."

"And the scoundrel, I suppose, sneaked off as soon as he found that she was not unprotected?"

"He didn't stay very long afterwards I can tell you," replied Dick Fordham; but before going away he swore vengeance, and amongst other things threatened to go before a magistrate and take out a warrant to have her apprehended."

"For what?" asked Guy, quickly.

"Why for nothing more than that he suspects she knows where you are hiding yourself."

"And does she know it?" inquired Harrowby.

"She knows no more than the police themselves do," answered his friend. "All I told was that you were safe and well, but I wouldn't say a word about where you were hiding yourself, because I thought it best that she should be able to swear with a safe conscience that she knew nothing more of you than might be convenient for her to state."

"Yet for all that, exclaimed Guy, "the magistrate will have the power to remand her if he thinks there is reasonable ground to believe that she is assisting to aid my escape."

"You are wrong altogether there, my dear fellow," returned Fordham; "a magistrate has not quite so much power as you fancy, for unless this Mr. Heathingdon can swear that she keeps back information that may be of importance, the case must be dismissed, and then my gentleman will look rather more contemptible than he'll like. For that reason it was that I refused to tell your wife where you are, and, as she understood my motive, she wisely let me have my own way in the matter."

"Your intention was, no doubt, kindly meant," said Guy, "but was she not most anxious to hear of my safety?"

"Why, of course she was, and I could hardly help letting out the secret, only I knew it would be better for all parties to keep it quiet till we see how matters are likely to take. As things are, at present, we must be cautious you know, Guy; but when once you are safely landed on the other side of the water I may tell her where you are, because it won't be long before she'll follow you, and then there'll be nothing more to fear from those that bear you an ill-will in this country."

"Does she know that I am waiting an opportunity to get away from England?" asked Guy Harrowby."

"Oh yes, I took good care to tell her that," replied the other.

"And what does she say to leaving her native land, perhaps for ever?" inquired the fugitive, eagerly.

"Why she acted as every other good and dutiful wife ought to do," replied Fordham. "She may not like the idea of leaving old England, but as her husband's safety depends upon his getting clear away, she forgot her own feelings upon the matter, and said she should be glad to follow him even if it should be to the furthest ends of the earth."

"Her's has been a sad and heavy trial, though she deserves not the hardship she has met with," exclaimed Guy Harrowby. "When she married me it was with the expectation that peace and happiness would be her future lot. Yet, what has been the consequence? Almost from the commencement she has had nothing but misery to endure; and now, added to her other suffering, she has to bear the insolence of a scoundrel, who would take advantage of the helpless situation in which my own conduct has placed her."

"If you are talking about Mr. Heathingdon," returned the other, "I can only say you have no reason to be afraid of him, for I have undertaken to protect her from insult, and d——n me, but I'll keep my word, whatever may come of it."

"Dick Fordham," exclaimed the fugitive, as he took his hand," you have been a true friend after all, and I believe you have honour enough to be trusted with the guardianship of my wife and child. See that no harm befall either of them while I am away, and above all things, keep a watchful eye upon Charles Heathingdon, who, as he failed to destroy me, will, I am afraid, turn all his vengeance against those that he knows are dearest to me."

"You may depend on it I shall not give him a chance of playing off any of his dirty tricks," answered the other ; "and as for your wife, I think she's pretty safe where she is, for the landlady seems to have taken a liking to her, and if we may take the old woman's word for it, Mr. Heathingdon won't be allowed to enter her house again."

"How can she help it if he goes there with a warrant?" demanded Guy Harrowby. "It will not do to resist the law, so its my opinion the best thing my wife can do, will be to leave her present lodging with as little delay as possible."

"It will be no use for her to do that," returned Dick Fordham, "because the chap will be sure to hunt her out, go where she may. Besides, its quite enough for you to be hunted about from place to place, without her having to find a fresh abode every two or three days."

"Then it would be better for her to return to the country, where she has friends enough to take part with her, in case her persecutor should follow her there."

"I differ from you about that," exclaimed Dick."

"And why?"

"Simply, because I think for every reason, it will be better for her to stay in London," he replied. "The poor creature is in terrible suspense about you, and the only thing that seems to afford her satisfaction is the hope of hearing of you through me or any other person that will take the trouble to let her know how matters are going on. And more than that, her going away won't hinder any mischief that Charles Heathingdon may mean to do her, for he can get a warrant in the country as well as in London, and it, perhaps, wouldn't be so easy for her to get off there as she might do here. Then there is another thing to be considered, you'll have to make a move of it yourself before long ; and if the place should happen to prove a tolerably safe one, I don't see why she shouldn't follow you there after a little while, and then she'd be safe from the persecution of this Mr. Heathingdon."

"That would, indeed, be a happiness to me," exclaimed Guy ; "but i'm afraid, Dick, your kind wishes in that respect will never come to pass. It is more than I expect; more, perhaps, than I deserve, considering what I have done in the last few years."

"Nonsense, man!" returned the other; "what's the use of making yourself miserable about the past. Wouldn't any convict escape if he had but a chance given him? and, as for the death of the man that was placed as guard over you, it may have been an accident, and if so, there was no help for it."

"It wouldn't be looked at in that light though, if they happen to lay hold of me," exclaimed Guy Harrowby,

"Were there any witnesses by when the thing took place?"

"Not a soul was there."

"Then how can they prove the charge?"

"By what they call circumstantial evidence," replied Guy Harrowby." The keeper was found dead in my cell, and as I had made my escape, it would at once be judged that I had murdered him for the sake of getting away. In short, there's people that have got into disgrace, through my giving 'em the slip, and they'll take good care to make up a case against me if once I should fall into their clutches."

"But you shan't fall into their clutches, old fellow, while your friends can help it," exclaimed Dick. "We've managed so far to baffle 'em, and in my opinion we shall be able to do so still if you'll only follow our advice."

"Hitherto I have done so," replied the fugitive ; "and having found the benefit of it, I shall continue to place all my dependence on you and my other friends."

"Then you'll not object to stay in this place till we can get you to the other one, that I told you of?"

"Yes," he replied ; "I'll stay here, though I've a notion its not quite as safe as you fancy. The men I told you of may come again to-morrow, and if they do, you may make up your mind that its all over with you."

"Then, I'll tell you what I'll do," exclaimed Dick Fordham, as a new thought struck him. "Nobody hereabouts knows me, so to-morrow I'll station myself within view of this place from morning till night, and if these chaps should come, I'll find some means or another to introduce myself to 'em, and fish out what they're up to."

"And what then?"

"Why, then, if they tell me they're going to examine this place, I'll tell 'em a yarn that shall frighten 'em out of the notion. I can say that I've been down into it myself, and that I found such horrible imps and fiends there, that I was glad to make my escape as soon as possible."

"And, suppose your report should rather serve to excite their curiosity than their fear?" exclaimed Guy. "The men may not be alarmed at what you say, but persist in their determination to come and satisfy themselves."

"In that case you must lend a helping hand towards frightening 'em away," returned Dick Fordham. "I should offer to go with 'em, and the moment you here us at the edge of the pit, you can raise a hideous noise, and they'll be sure to believe it comes from some of the imps and fiends I shall tell 'em about."

"It might answer the purpose for a short time," exclaimed Harrowby; "but the men would spread the news all over the neighbourhood, and then the chances are that some three or four sturdy fellows would come to satisfy themselves whether there was any truth or not in the report."

"I've thought all about that, and am prepared for it," said Dick Fordham. "Its pretty sure they would come, but they would find you here though, for I should get you out of this pit directly, and take you back to the cottage of Peter Datchet, where you'd remain till the return of the old man and woman, that you are to go and live with next."

"Datchet has already objected to give me shelter."

"He had better not stick to that, though," returned Dick; "for, if he does, he may expect that it won't be long before he finds himself in a scrape."

"Would you inform against him for being a coiner?"

"If I don't, somebody else will," replied Fordham. "The fellow knows well enough that he is in our power; and, if he'd shut his door against any of us when we want a shelter, he must take the consequences of it."

"That would do no good, after the mischief was done."

"Perhaps not; but there's some consolation, you know, Master Harrowby, in having one's revenge."

"A very poor one, though," exclaimed the fugitive; "and for my own part, I should like to go anywhere else, rather than to the house of a man that wouldn't receive me with a welcome."

"Where would you go to?"

"That I must leave to your own judgment; but, may be, it might be as well to remain where I am for a day or two longer."

"What! when there's a chance of those chaps coming in the morning to satisfy their curiosity?"

"If they do, I must take my chance about it; that's all I know," replied Guy Harrowby. "It seems likely enough that I shall be grabbed after all the trouble we've been at to prevent it; and if so, I shall not have much to grieve about, for anything's better than being hunted about from place to place, with a certainty of being caught at last."

"D—n it, man, but they'll send you to the gallows, as sure as ever you fall into their hands."

"I know all about that, as well as you can tell me," exclaimed Guy. "They would hang me; and so much the better—for I'm heartily tired of life, and the sooner I'm out of this world, the sooner shall I be out of my troubles."

His friend was about to remonstrate against the absurdity of this notion, but before he could do so, they were startled by hearing a voice calling to them from above, and looking up, they saw that their visitor was no other than Peter Datchet.

CHAPTER XXV.

CONCLUSION.

FOLLOWING the directions given by those who were below, the coiner let himself down into the pit, and no sooner had he landed himself in safety, than he informed them that officers were in close pursuit, and that there was every reason to believe they would before long trace the fugitive to his hiding-place. This news was almost as alarming to Dick Fordham as it was to his companion, and having expressed his opinion that they must change their quarters as soon as possible, he inquired of Datchet how he happened to know there was so much danger as he spoke of.

"Why," he replied, "the truth of it is, I was at Greenwich just now, and whilst taking a pint of beer in a public-house, four men came in and began to make inquiries about a man that they were in search of. By what they said, I soon found out that it was Guy Harrowby they were looking after, and just as I was coming away to give notice of the danger, two other chaps came in and told the officers about a pit that they had seen on Blackheath, and the likelihood there was of any one hiding himself in it."

"They were the two cricketers I've been telling you about, I'll be bound," exclaimed Guy Harrowby.

"That's true enough," said the coiner, for I heard 'em say something about losing a ball, and while they were looking for it, they found a pit that would just do for any one that might happen to be in want of a hiding-place."

"And what said the officers to that?"

"Why, there was one chap, that didn't seem to be an officer at all," replied Datchet, "and he asked a great many questions, besides promising the men a reward, if they would act as guides to the place they had been speaking about."

"Do you know the name of the person you were speaking of?"

"Yes, they called him Mr. Heathingdon."

"'Tis, then, as I suspected," exclaimed Guy Harrowby; "he was determined never to give up the chase till I was captured; and now, I suppose, there's no chance of my escaping him."

"Aint there, though?" exclaimed Fordham. "He's got people as deep as himself to deal with, and we shall give him the slip now, if we look sharp."

"What use can there be in escaping from him, since it can only be for a few days?" asked Guy.

"If we can manage to do it for a few days, I don't see why we can't get you away altogether," returned his friend; "but at any rate it's worth a trial, so put yourself under my care, old fellow, and I'll soon take you to some place or another where they'll not be able to find you."

"Where would you take me next,?"

"To Peter Datchet's to be sure."

"That I'm sure you won't," exclaimed the coiner, bluntly, "They'd be sure to trace him there, and though I'd do almost anything to serve a friend when he's in trouble, I'll be hanged if I risk having a search made over my house."

"Nor do I wish that you should suffer on my account," said Guy Harrowby. "They'll be sure to find me now, go where I may, so the best thing I can do will be to give myself up without further delay."

"If you do, I'm a Dutchman!" exclaimed Fordham. "No, no, I've had trouble enough to help you out of this scrape, and I must now have my own way, unless you want to offend me.

"But where am I to go?"

"To Peter Datchet's," I tell you; I don't care what he says against it, as he'd better give in with a good grace, or there'll be something happen to him before long that he won't like."

"What, you'd split against me, I suppose?"

"Very likely I might, so there's no mistake about it," answered Dick Fordham; "its not the sort of thing I altogether like, but I've made up my mind that Guy shall go back to your cottage, so you'd better give in without any further nonsense. or you'll be sorry for it afterwards."

"If it is only for a day or two I don't mind," returned the coiner, "but it must not be for any longer time you know, or they'll be sure to come and look after him there."

"And if they do, you've got arms in your house, and you and Guy must defend yourselves as anybody else would do when hunted into a corner."

"Would you have us commit murder?" asked Datchet.

"Not if it can be anyhow helped," replied the other; "but men won't suffer themselves to be taken quietly, you know, and if anything should happen to Mr. Heathingdon it will serve him right, because he had no business to make himself so busy in this affair."

"There shall be no chance of blood being shed on my account," said Guy Harrowby, "for if they should fall in with me, its my intention to surrender myself quietly."

"You'll get no good by it if you do."

"Very likely not, but at any rate I don't feel inclined either to commit any more crime myself, or to let other people do it in my behalf."

"They'll hang you whether you do or not," observed Fordham.

"I know it, and am prepared to meet the worst, let it happen when it may."

"Then you are a greater fool than I took you for," exclaimed the other, "and all the trouble I've been taking to get you out of this scrape has been thrown away."

"Don't think me ungrateful," answered Guy; "because I know you have exerted yourself in my behalf, and I am truly thankful for it; but fate can't be prevented, so as it seems I am not to escape after all, the only way is to give myself up quietly when the time comes."

"If that's what you mean to do," said Dick Fordham, "you may as well go and surrender yourself to 'em at once."

"Perhaps if young Heathingdon was not with the officers I should do as you say," answered the fugitive.

"And so you don't like the notion of giving yourself up to him?"

"I know he'd exult in my downfall," exclaimed Guy Harrowby, "and the thoughts of seeing his grin of exultation is more than I can bear; I should be likely to fell him to the earth in my rage, and it is even possible I might take his life, in revenge for the injuries he has done me."

"And serve him right too," observed Peter Datchet, "for the fellow seems to have done you all the mischief he could, and if he had me to deal with he'd have reason to repent what he'd done before I'd finished with him."

"What good should I get by killing him?"

"Why you'd have the satisfaction of being revenged."

"And a very poor satisfaction too, seeing that my own death would quickly follow it," returned Guy. "The scoundrel has, somehow or another, always managed to get the best of me, and if I was to meet him I should not be able to contain my rage, and the last act of my unhappy life would be to take away the life of another fellow-creature."

"Very well," exclaimed Fordham, "and are you weak enough to think there'd be any harm in ridding the world of such a fellow as that? Hasn't he all along been seeking your life, and isn't it fair that you should return the compliment?"

"You and I wouldn't agree upon this subject if we were to talk about it for a month," returned Guy Harrowby. "We should only be likely to get into a quarrel, and that's what I don't want to do with a person that has been so good a friend to me, when there were few others that I could depend upon."

"At any rate," said the other, "I suppose you mean to try and escape from 'em to-night?"

"I do most certainly," answered the fugitive, "though I believe it won't be of any use, if the officers are as near to us as Datchet says they are. It's clear they are now on the right scent; and even if we should happen to get away from this place, it's most likely they'd meet us before we got far off."

"Then all we've got to do is, to take care we don't fall in with 'em," exclaimed Dick Fordham. "We know there's a chance of coming full butt against these chaps, so we'll take a round about way, and then I think we may get to Datchet's place, without any fear of being seen by 'em."

"I wish you could think of some other hiding place for him," said Peter Datchet.

"I dare say you do," answered Fordham; "but as it happens that I can't think of any other just at present, you must make up your mind to let him be your guest for a little while. There'll be no danger of anybody going there to look for him, and even if they should, Mr. Heathingdon will be too well pleased at finding him to do you any harm for having him in your company. And as for searching your house, there's no fear of their doing that, if once they get hold of the person they're looking after."

"When so many difficulties are thrown in the way, I'd rather not ask the favour of even a night's shelter," exclaimed Harrowby. "It was only for my wife's sake that I wished to avoid being taken, and had I been given a shelter for the short time it was wanted, I had made up my mind to surrender myself as soon as the officers went there to look for me."

"Peter Datchet knows best how to act in this case," said Fordham, "but I can only tell him, that if he refuses it will be the worst day's work he ever did in his life."

"Haven't I said he shall go with me, and what can a man say or do more than that?" demanded Datchet, sullenly.

"Aye, but it's only force that's made you do it," exclaimed Dick, "and your unwillingness takes away all the merit of the act; however, as I see no other way just at present, he must go with you I suppose, and to-morrow night he shall go somewhere else, a long way from here, and there I hope he may remain in quiet till we can get him out of the country all together."

"That I'm afraid is a harder job than you fancy," said Guy.

"What makes you think so?"

"I've many reasons for it," answered Harrowby; "one of 'em is, that the officers and young Heathingdon are close upon my heels, and besides that, I've a sort of notion, that I shall this night either be in a jail or lose my life in an affray with those that come to take me."

"Do you often give way to these sort of whims?"

"I never did before that I know of," exclaimed Guy; "but the more peril a man is in, the more likely is he to be superstitious. There may be nothing in it after all, but I certainly do think, that before to-night is over, I shall be dragged off to a prison."

"If you think that I won't leave you till the morning," said Dick Fordham.

"And why not? you could do me no good by staying."

"Couldn't I though!" exclaimed the other. "You think, then, I suppose, that I would not stand up, back and edge, to save a friend from falling into the hands of his enemies."

"I know you too well to doubt that," replied Guy Harrowby; "but we've heard that there's four of 'em against us, and it would be of little use to resist such odds as that, when we know that they will come well armed to secure their prisoner."

"Yes, but we shan't be without arms any more than they are," replied Fordham. "Our friend here keeps pistols in his house always ready for immediate use, and if there should be any occasion for it, the police would get such a peppering that they'd be glad to run off without troubling themselves to make you their prisoner."

"What good should we get by that?" demanded Guy. "We might, to be sure, make 'em retreat, but it would only be to return in greater numbers; and then our friend here would stand a chance of being captured as well as myself."

"Yes," groaned Peter Datchet, "and then it would be all up with me, for they'd discover the coining apparatus, and I should be sent out of the country for life by way of keeping me from doing any further mischief. However, I've given my word that Guy Harrowby shall have a lodging in my house for to-night, so let's be going at once, or we mayn't have quite so good a chance presently."

This suggestion was immediately acted upon; and after listening for a minute or two to ascertain if all was quiet, Dick Fordham crept out of the hiding-place, and was quickly followed by the other two. They then took a survey round them as well as the darkness of the night would permit, and having pretty well satisfied themselves that no one was near, they proceeded across the heath, all of them keeping the most profound silence. At length, as they were passing by a spot that was thickly overgrown with bushes, their progress was suddenly arrested by four or five men rushing out. One of them, by his voice, was immediately recognized as Charles Heathingdon, who, singling out Guy Harrowby from the rest, seized upon him, and shouting loudly to his companions, commanded them to assist in capturing the prisoner; but this was disregarded by the officers, who went in pursuit of the other men, and the two were, therefore, left to struggle with each other for the mastery: and fierce was the contest that now ensued between them, for each was resolved never to give in whilst a chance of victory remained, and when both of them at length fell on the ground they still kept a firm hold of each other, till panting and overcome with exertion they had used, it seemed uncertain on which side victory would declare itself. At that moment, however, the officers returned from their unsuccessful pursuit of Fordham and his companion, and flying to the assistance of Charles Heathingdon, they in a few moments separated the antagonists, and were in in the act of handcuffing the fugitive, when he, with a last desperate effort, dashed away from them, and snatching from the libertine a pistol, which he carried for his protection, he turned the muzzle towards his own breast, and discharging the contents into his body fell bleeding to the earth.

"D—n him, he's done us after all," exclaimed one of the policemen, as he hastened to raise the wounded man to see in what part of the body the wound had been inflicted. "The ball," he added, "hasn't gone very far from his heart, I see, and I don't much fancy he'll live till we get him to the nearest surgeons."

"A few minutes, and it will be all over with me," said Guy Harrowby faintly. "Yonder miscreant thought to send me to the gallows, but fortune has so far favoured me, that I shall not leave this world by a death of shame."

"Convey him with all speed to a surgeon's," exclaimed Heathingdon, furious at the frustration of his plans. "The wound may not be mortal, and I may yet have the satisfaction of witnessing the full accomplishment of my vow."

"It is in vain to look forward to your revenge now," said Guy, "for life is passing rapidly away, and in a few minutes I shall be beyond the malice of my enemies. You have pursued your game with a keen scent, Mr. Heathingdon; but after all, you will be disappointed in the chief object you had in view. I die by my own hand, and the only regret I now feel is, that my wife will be left the more completely in your power."

"Come, I say, old fellow," exclaimed one of the policemen, "if you're really going to die, you may as well tell us first of all who the men were that bolted off just now as soon as they caught sight of us?"

"That's a secret that I shall carry out of the world with me," answered Guy Harrowby. "They are friends that have stood by me in the midst of my misfortunes, and mine shall not be the lips to betray 'em to their enemies."

"Oh, very well," returned the other, "if you won't tell us, we must find it out the best way we can, that's all I know about it."

"Why are you wasting all this time?" exclaimed Charles Heathingdon, "when every moment is of consequence towards saving his life?"

"What would you have us do, sir?"

"Raise him gently in your arms, and then convey him with all the speed you can to the first surgeon's that happens to be in your way. His wound may not be so dangerous as he imagines, and if we can recover him, he will still have to suffer for the heinous crimes he has been guilty of."

Having no alternative, the men proceeded to obey the directions that had been given them, but no sooner did they attempt to raise the wounded man, than a marked and fatal change was observable in his countenance; this was succeeded by a gurgling in the throat, and then, after a few convulsive gasps, the spirit of the wretched man fled for ever.

"He's dead sure enough, sir," said the policeman, "and the worst part of the business is, that the fifty pounds reward has gone with him. However, it's no use grumbling now; so, if you like to leave us, these chaps can stay here, while I run to the station-house to give information of what has taken place, and then, I suppose, they'll send a stretcher to take away the body."

This suggestion was silently acquiesced in by Charles Heathingdon, who, disappointed in his revenge, returned home, to meditate in silence upon the defeat he had sustained. Whilst in the pursuit of his object he never once reflected upon the odium his conduct would bring upon him; but now, he foresaw nothing but the world's scorn in future; and, to avoid that, he resolved to go abroad, where, in fresh society, he might hope to find some few that would not shun his acquaintance. On applying to his father for money to defray the expenses of travel, his request was promptly complied with, and in the course of a few days he reached Paris, where he soon became a confirmed gamester. But his career was not doomed to last any long time: for, one night, having lost a considerable sum of money, he became involved in a quarrel with one of the parties by whom he had been victimized, and who, being a practised swordsman, challenged him to meet him on the following morning. Charles Heathingdon had too proud a spirit to decline the challenge, and, at the appointed time, the meeting took place between them. The Englishman, however, was no match for his opponent, and, after a few passes, he received a wound that proved mortal in the course of three or four days afterwards.

The grief of Jane Harrowby, when she heard of her husband's death, was uncontrollable. For some time she she was deaf to the voice of consolation; but at length the perseverance and kindness of Mrs. Toddy began to have a beneficial effect, and she was even induced to acknowledge, that, great as the bereavement was, the death of Guy had saved him from a fate that she, as well as himself, had looked forward to as being almost certain. Having no further motive for remaining in

London, she and her child returned to her cottage in the country, as soon as possible after the funeral of her husband. On her arrival there, she found that kindness from her neighbours that was so much needed to soften her afflictions; and, being visited shortly afterwards by Colonel Heathingdon, she received from him a purse containing twenty pounds, with a promise that the gift should be renewed every six months, as some recompence for the injuries she had received from his son. It was not without reluctance that Jane consented to receive it; but the offer was pressed with so much kindness that she at length consented to become the pensoner of a man whose character for stainless honour was the subject of general admiration. In time, news reached her of the death of Charles Heathingdon; and though she rejoiced not at hearing it, she from that moment felt that all fear of persecution was at an end.

As for Dick Fordham and his associates, we have never heard what became of them; but, as their names do not figure in the pages of the Newgate Calendar, we may fairly presume that they were turned from their evil courses, or were lucky enough to escape the fate that generally overtakes the guilty.

THE END.

PRINTED AND PUBLISHED BY E. LLOYD, 12, SALISBURY-SQUARE, FLEET-STREET.